Melisa Melling

RAKESH SATYAL is the author of the novel *Blue Boy*, which won the 2010 Lambda Literary Award for Gay Debut Fiction and the 2010 Prose/Poetry Award from the Association of Asian American Studies. Satyal was a recipient of a 2010 Fellowship in Fiction from the New York Foundation for the Arts and two fellowships from the Norman Mailer Writers Colony. His writing has appeared in *New York* magazine, *Vulture*, *Out* magazine, and The Awl. A graduate of Princeton University, he has taught in the publishing program at New York University and has been on the advisory committee for the annual PEN World Voices Festival. He lives in Brooklyn.

ALSO BY RAKESH SATYAL

Blue Boy

Additional Praise for *No One Can Pronounce My Name*

"This is not a tableau of exotic spices and brilliant saris, of flashbacks to fables told in a village back in the old country. This is a brave portrait that sheds light on the parts of Indian culture that are seldom seen by those outside it."

—*The New York Times Book Review*

"It says something about both the reach of Satyal's story and his wry skill as a storyteller, that, while I was reading, I kept thinking of Barbara Pym."   —Maureen Corrigan, NPR's *Fresh Air*

"A smart, delightful book full of intricately drawn characters that makes an unforgettable statement about what it means to find the place where you belong."   —*Town & Country*

"An extraordinarily compassionate work of fiction . . . Through a successful blend of pathos and humor, Satyal bravely explores themes of intimacy, identity, and sexuality, asking his characters—and his readers—to closely examine the inalienable qualities that make us all human. With emotionally charged prose, he masterfully depicts the modern-day immigrant experience in a manner that is both deeply personal and universally relatable, transforming the foreign into the familiar."   —*BookPage*

"Gentle, funny, and utterly charming."   —*The Seattle Times*

"A funny, compassionate portrayal of the immigrant and second-generation immigrant experience."

—*Chicago Review of Books*

"[A] well-crafted and heartwarming story chock full of characters you can't help but root for . . . Compulsively readable."

—Lambda Literary

"Satyal captures his characters' experiences within a close-knit Indian community, rounded out with excellent supporting characters . . . who have their own stories to tell, resulting in a vivid, complex tale."   —*Publishers Weekly*

"Insightful . . . An enjoyable read with an East Indian flair."

—*Library Journal*

"A funny, uplifting novel that delivers emotionally complex characters."   —*Kirkus Reviews*

"Satyal expertly describes the everyday struggles that define his characters, and he elevates the extraordinary moments of normal life in this skilled and thought-provoking novel."

—*Booklist* (starred review)

"A bighearted, hopeful, and often very funny novel about the unpredictability of love . . . as well as a celebration of how, in America, it's never too late to rethink who you are—or who you might become. Satyal has created a set of characters you'll cheer for."

—Hanya Yanagihara, *New York Times* bestselling
author of *The People in the Trees* and *A Little Life*

"Affecting, kindhearted, and infectiously readable, *No One Can Pronounce My Name* is full of memorable characters joined by their yearning to belong. Rakesh Satyal spins a funny and unpredictable multigenerational tale that glitters with warmth and wisdom."

—Maria Semple, *New York Times* bestselling
author of *Where'd You Go, Bernadette* and
Today Will Be Different

"This humane, moving, and very funny book offers something precious and rare: a novel devoted to the life-giving bond of friendship. Through a quintessentially American tale of misfits and dreamers, Rakesh Satyal has given us a fresh vision of America: a country of strangers seeking connection, of households lit with contrary desires, held together by resourceful and enduring love."   —Garth Greenwell, author of *What Belongs to You*

"Rakesh Satyal writes with both tender empathy and sly wit, and his characters are vulnerable, admirable, and idiosyncratic. *No One Can Pronounce My Name* beautifully explores the challenges of asserting individuality in the face of societal and cultural proscriptions. Movingly and believably, Ranjana and Harit find each other, and then, thanks to their lovely friendship, themselves."

—Kate Christensen, author of
The Great Man and *The Astral*

NO ONE CAN PRONOUNCE MY NAME

NO ONE CAN PRONOUNCE MY NAME

A Novel

RAKESH SATYAL

PICADOR

NEW YORK

NO ONE CAN PRONOUNCE MY NAME. Copyright © 2017 by Rakesh Satyal. All rights reserved. Printed in the United States of America. For information, address Picador, 175 Fifth Avenue, New York, N.Y. 10010.

picadorusa.com • instagram.com/picador
twitter.com/picadorusa • facebook.com/picadorusa

Picador® is a U.S. registered trademark and is used by Macmillan Publishing Group, LLC, under license from Pan Books Limited.

For book club information, please visit facebook.com/picadorbookclub or email marketing@picadorusa.com.

Designed by Steven Seighman

The Library of Congress has cataloged the hardcover edition as follows:

Names: Satyal, Rakesh, author.
Title: No one can pronounce my name : a novel / Rakesh Satyal.
Description: First edition. | New York : Picador, 2017.
Identifiers: LCCN 2016058277 (print) | LCCN 2017004550 (ebook) | ISBN 9781250112118 (hardcover) | ISBN 9781250112132 (ebook)
Subjects: LCSH: East Indian Americans—Ohio—Fiction. | Domestic fiction. | BISAC: FICTION / Literary. | FICTION / Family Life.
Classification: LCC PS3619.A8228 N63 2017 (print) | LCC PS3619.A8228 (ebook) | DDC 813'.6—dc23
LC record available at https://lccn.loc.gov/2016058277

Picador Paperback ISBN 978-1-250-11212-5

B+T 18.00 8/20

Our books may be purchased in bulk for promotional, educational, or business use. Please contact your local bookseller or the Macmillan Corporate and Premium Sales Department at 1-800-221-7945, extension 5442, or by e-mail at MacmillanSpecialMarkets@macmillan.com.

First published by Picador USA

First Picador Paperback Edition: May 2018

D   10 9 8 7 6 5 4 3

For John Maas

What are you but a drum and a tube and a wire, black heart?
A fire in the dark?
—OWEN PALLETT, "IN CONFLICT"

You just came over here and shot my foot!
—MY FATHER, TRYING TO ARGUE WITH MY MOTHER

I

HARIT DESCENDED THE RUBBER-COATED STAIRS of the bus and tripped as he jumped to the sidewalk below. He turned around to see if anyone had noticed, but the bus was already pulling away, leaving a dispersing cloud of smoke and people. It was a short walk from the bus stop to his house, but within ten paces he began to sweat. The heat seemed so hot here because the surroundings didn't look as if they could stand it any more than the residents. The thick roofs (many-shingled and arched), the roads (bracketed in deep curbs), and the trees (branches bursting and then shivering in leaves) were all suited to a cold landscape. Harit had seen this theory proven during his first winter in Cleveland, when snow piled on top of those shingles, nestled into those curbs, and spackled the leaves in ice. But in the summer, the neighborhood seemed like a tired, old man who could not endure such exertion.

The house in which Harit lived stood opposite a large baseball field. The field was surrounded by a sextet of light posts so large that they could have constituted a new Seven Wonders of the World had another counterpart been shoved into the ground. It seemed that a different group of boys appeared on the field every night, clad in uniforms of red, yellow, and gray polyester, or—during practice games—an assortment of sweats and mesh. Their hollers would last until 9:00 P.M., when the lights would shut off with an ear-splitting pucker. The field's diamond was on the opposite side of where the bus stopped and Harit's house stood, so he didn't have to interact with the kids very often. But there were those afternoons when a ball would find its way to Harit's side of the field, and some fragile little kid would run over to get the ball and look terrified that Harit was going to do something awful to him. There was that quick shake of the head, a short *No*, and Harit, who should have learned to look in front of himself and not at others by now, would move away.

Today, thankfully, he had an uneventful walk home, and when he slid his key into the back door of his house, he had one second of peace. But as soon as he turned that key, it was time to get into costume.

He wasn't sure why he put on the rose oil anymore. It had seeped into his skin by now; Teddy had already sniffed him and asked why he had started to smell like someone named "The Dowager Countess," whom Harit didn't know but who, according to the tinny voice that Teddy used to say her name, sounded like a very small woman. Harit cursed himself when he remembered that he had run out of lipstick yesterday. Luckily, he had a bit of raspberry Chapstick left, and a few heavy circles around his mouth pretty much did the trick. The sari that he had been using for the past week was beautiful, a peacock blue, but he had started to smell in its folds a stale version of his own pungent body odor. He tipped the bottle of rose oil against his index finger and, trying not to stain the fabric, flicked small droplets onto it. He then whipped the sari into the air the way he did with his blanket when making up his bed in the morning. He sniffed the sari again. There was still the unmistakable sourness, but the rose oil now clouded it enough that his mother's old nostrils would not detect the smell.

She was in her armchair in the living room, and the stereo was going. Gital Didi had brought a new batch of cassettes for her, and the latest one was a Mohammad Rafi best-of collection. That voice, normally lively, was so muffled by the old stereo's speakers that it sounded as if poor Mohammad himself were trapped inside the machine. Harit—for all the sadness of the situation—had to stifle a laugh as he looked at his mother, this sentinel of a caged megastar singer. She had taken to wearing a pair of gigantic, purple-rimmed sunglasses—also a gift from Gital Didi—which made Harit's job both easier and harder. Easier because they filtered out such mistakes as his Chapsticked lips; harder because they made his mother even more inhuman and unapproachable. Her eyes, even under the gossamer of burgeoning cataracts, were a pair of darting, glimmering circles that were abnormally large for her face and that had often made people mistake her for a South Indian instead of a Punjabi. But now, with her new eyewear, she had become a wax figure of herself, an effigy upon which some child had played a prank. Still, something in her defied total weakness. The way that her mottled hands rested on the chair's armrests, the way that her white sari, though jaundiced with time and overuse, flowed like the raiment of Saraswati, the way that her hair, ghastly white, held its bun save for a few defiant wisps—it all emphasized her determination to mourn forever.

"Is that you?" his mother asked in Hindi. It was always the first thing that she said. She didn't speak English anymore, and she used the informal *you* in a childlike manner.

Harit gave his usual response: "Yes, Mother. It is Swati."

He wasn't exactly sure how the dress-up game had started. It had just seemed like the logical thing to do. He had found himself holding one of Swati's lipsticks to his mouth and knew that it would be a routine. He had never thought of putting on women's clothing before and had certainly never thought of putting on makeup, but in the midst of his suffering, or the catatonic nothing that turned out to be suffering, he had done both of those things so easily that he wondered if perhaps he had once dreamed about doing them, if they had been occupying the same part of his mind that a childhood phobia of snakes or an affinity for *lassi* had occupied. Perhaps it was because, at the beginning, it wasn't just his mother who needed Swati to be alive but Harit himself. That was it: he did not question his actions because part of him believed that Swati was the one performing them.

His mother's eyesight had turned blurry by then, and there had been times when she had confused Harit with Swati. The brother and sister could not have looked any different—Harit with his large eyeglasses, mustache, and messy, long hair sprouting from a receding hairline; Swati with her beautiful face, dark hair pulled back in a ponytail, and that smile. Her teeth were not terribly white or straight, but her smile brightened up her entire appearance, and that was something that no amount of dissembling could give Harit, who hardly ever smiled and, maybe worse, did not understand why smiling was such a big deal. He practiced Swati's smile in his bathroom mirror before offering it to his mother. He looked as if he had indigestion. But it was a sign of just how far his mother's eyesight had dimmed that she took this horrible version as the real thing.

He first approached her three days after the funeral, after they took Swati's body to the entirely un-Indian local crematorium, after the people there burned her off with a lack of ceremony that stunned not just Harit but all of the families gathered. At the end of it, the owner handed Harit his sister's ashes in an urn that seemed too plain—*What did an ideal urn look like, though?*—and Harit was surprised at how light it was. Since Swati's passing, their mother had not spoken—or wept, for that matter—and generally stayed clear of Harit, so it wasn't very difficult to hide the urn from her. She was folded into the backseat of a car by three aunties who stood by like ladies-in-waiting, while Harit was driven home in a separate car by the pandit's wife. For the next three days, his mother sat in her armchair, not moving, not speaking, not even getting up to use the bathroom.

At the end of the third day, soon after the lights from the baseball field had gone out and left them in the gray dust of a nighttime house, Harit entered the room dressed in his costume. He was almost as dazed as his mother and, later, would remember the experience as if it were something he had seen years ago in a strange movie.

"Is that you?" his mother asked when she saw him, and it startled him to hear her voice, not just because she was speaking but because she said this sentence as matter-of-factly as if Swati had come in with a cup of chai. He had expected her first words after this long silence to be torn, exhausted, hollow.

"Yes, Mother. It is Swati."

He didn't have time to worry if she believed his impression because his mother broke down. Her outburst lasted only a few seconds, but Harit would never forget the way that his mother's body unfurled, as if she were a ball of *paneer* expanding after being freed from a cheesecloth.

"*Arré, beti*, you scared me so much. I was so scared! I was— Don't ever leave me like that again. I would—I don't know what I would do. My child is home. My child, my child . . ." She was weeping horribly, hitting her eyes with her hands. Harit had seen her cry only once before, when he was seven and her cousin Jyoti had died of tetanus. Instantly upon hearing her cry now, he felt just as he had then, vulnerable and terrified, a weak child with a weak mother. He backed away from the living room and ran to his bed, rocking himself to sleep in his sister's sari and wishing that Swati were there to pat him to sleep, as she had done for so many years.

"You know, in French, the word *sale* means dirty," Teddy said. "So you can imagine what French people think when they come here."

Teddy was always dropping French into conversation. He once tried to teach Harit how to speak the language, but Harit's "*merci*" kept coming out like "mercy," and that is exactly what Teddy gave him after the fourth, and final, lesson. The funniest thing was that Teddy didn't seem to know that much French, either.

"Did you hear what I said?"

Harit heard the short sound of metal on glass—the tip of a hanger flopping onto the counter as Teddy looked at him in anticipation. Harit was fixing a round table of ties. Red was the color of choice that summer, so the assortment before him contained varying shades of it, each tie shooting its color outward, as if mimicking the tongue of Kali.

"Uh, yes, I heard," Harit said. He nudged one of the ties back into place and then looked up. Teddy was holding a blue blazer with gold corduroy lapels.

Teddy snorted. "Someone's in a *mood* today," he said, taking the blazer and walking it over to where its colorful clones were hanging. Harit watched him saunter, feeling, as he often did, that every interaction with Teddy, regardless of how brief, had to Mean Something.

Harriman's was a department store that had undergone several evolutions of decor since its birth forty years before. Harit often thought of what he must have been doing while the store was being built. He would have been four then. The faux-wood walls were hoisted against real-wood planks while he had his first taste of sweet *halwa*. The original tan carpet—tufts of which Harit could still see popping up between layers of the newer, navy blue carpet—was rolled into place while he sat in his open-air classroom, seeing the skeletal script of words he had, until then, known only by sound. The marble staircases were given a final polish as Harit's equally pristine soles bounded up the red stone steps of his temple. As Harriman's opening day came to a close, coiffed housewives shuttled out of the glass front doors, milk shakes from the second-floor parlor in their bellies; Harit sat on his house's front step, licking the cool dribble off a mango Popsicle.

He found the job through Gital Didi's friend Sameet, who had worked briefly in the storeroom. Sameet had been charged with the task of moving gigantic boxes of women's shoes from one end of that musty concrete bunker to the other. Harit, on the other hand, parlayed his interview into the more important position of working in the Men's Furnishings department. Not the Men's department, which included dress shirts and slacks and sweaters. The Men's *Furnishings* department, which involved "*accoutrements*" (another Teddyism): ties, cuff links, suspenders, wallets, clips, hats, pocket squares, scarves, and—partly because the space devoted to it was adjacent to the Men's Furnishings section, but more because it didn't fit into any of the store's other categories—luggage. The department was the also-ran of the store, but working in it still beat the storeroom, even if Harit came to realize that twiddling one's thumbs was only slightly better than sweating.

Although Harit's English was far from ideal, it was augmented by a certain attention to pronunciation and vocabulary that set it apart from that of most Indian people. This made him the best Indian presented to the people at Harriman's in quite some time. For his interview, he showed up dressed in his nicest outfit—a tailored herringbone jacket, brown corduroy slacks, cream dress shirt, and maroon silk tie. He waited for Mr. Harriman, the general manager, in a poorly lit office on the top floor. The office was very plain. Given the grand appearance of the store, Harit had envisioned a lavishly furnished room that resembled a professor's study—not this, which brought to mind a hospital without the cleanliness, a DMV without the people. Mr. Harriman's secretary, Stella, brunette with a pointy nose and small face, carried the unmistakable expression of someone who didn't have *a damn clue* as to how she had ended up in a job like this. Why was she assisting the general manger of a department store when working *in* the store, graceful behind a perfume counter, seemed so much more attractive? Harit could only assume that the pay was better in her current position.

"Mr. Harriman will see you now." She said every word as if it were new not only to him but also to her. Harit nodded politely and walked up to her desk. She flinched slightly, and he realized that she had not intended to walk him to Mr. Harriman's door. To put her at ease, he pointed in the direction of the office, indicating that he was headed that way.

Mr. Harriman—whose first name Harit never learned—was in his late sixties and was a smart dresser, contrary to the dour and unbecoming photograph of him that Harit would eventually see in the employee break room (E. H. HARRIMAN—no first name—engraved on a placard under it). Harit would soon learn that when Mr. Harriman got particularly stressed, his skin became red and he looked like a bell pepper. His voice was by turns mellifluous and grating, and he had an unexplained southern accent.

"So, Mr. Singha, what brings you to Harriman's today?" Harit's last name was Sinha, but Mr. Harriman added a *g* to it, as if it were a Thai beer.

Harit did not understand the question. Why else would he be here? "I have come to see if I might find employment."

Mr. Harriman threw his head back and laughed. His teeth sparkled. "Right to the point. I like that in a salesman."

"Oh, I did not come for a salesman position," Harit said. Mr. Harriman's mouth fell into a frown, and Harit panicked. "Uh, I would love to be considered for a salesman position, but I was informed that you need men for your storage room."

"Ah, yes, yes, we have had many helpful boys from India, but I like the look of you, Mr. Singha. Do you have any sales experience?"

Harit wished that Mr. Harriman had looked at his résumé. It clearly indicated that he had done his schooling in Commerce and that he had worked for several years back in India as the operator of the projector in a movie theater, before coming to the States and working as a janitor at a medical supplies company. None of this made him an ideal candidate for a salesman job.

"No, sir. No sales experience."

"Do you like Harriman's?"

"It is a nice store, sir." This was the first time that he had ever set foot in it.

"Well, Harriman's is the crown jewel of this community,

Mr. Singha. I opened decades ago with an aim to make it the premier shopping experience in Greater Cleveland, and it is my belief that it has remained such since that time. We've survived the supermall, the cybermall, and about a million apps that turn your phone *into a mall*." Harit could tell that Mr. Harriman had given this speech several times. "Throughout the years, we have employed a wide variety of employees. A former assistant manager of ours was African American!" Mr. Harriman raised his eyebrows, as if Harit were supposed to be very impressed. Harit realized in this moment that Mr. Harriman was offering him a salesman job because of his ethnicity.

After the interview, Mr. Harriman walked Harit out of the office and said to Stella, "This is Mr. Singha. He is going to be working in Men's Furnishings. Can you get his paperwork started, sweetheart?"

Stella looked up at them as if Mr. Harriman had just said that Harit were making a trip to the moon.

On a Thursday afternoon, Teddy asked Harit if he wanted to go for a drink after work. "Fancy a drink?" was the way that Teddy phrased it, and it struck Harit's ear strangely, for the Anglo-bred English he had learned gave "fancy" a sexual connotation—a mundane question made illicit in Teddy's mouth.

Harit offered up a quiet "I must tend to my mother at home," but no sooner were the words out of his mouth than Teddy was pulling him by the shirtsleeve and saying, "No ifs, ands, or buts, mister." They left the Thursday night quietude of the store—Thursdays were generally calm before the weekend rush on Friday—and soon they found themselves in a TGI Friday's in a nearby mall that Harit had passed on his way to work but had never examined up close.

"Table for *deux*, please," Teddy told the pimple-faced hostess.

Her eyes flicked from Teddy to Harit and back. "Two of you?" she asked, already plucking two menus from a stack and turning on her heel.

"Yes, darling," Teddy said as they walked down the middle of the restaurant. "Honey, you need to get yourself some nicer pumps." He pointed to the girl's old shoes even though her back was turned. She ignored him.

Their booth was in the far corner of the restaurant, under an oblong window that looked out on the mall instead of the parking lot. Through the window, Harit could see a girl standing attentively in a hat and apron at the cookie shop in the food court—waiting for anyone at all to bite.

"It's about time we did this," Teddy said, opening his menu and scanning its contents with one outstretched finger, the way one might do to a tax form. It struck Harit how out of place Teddy was. Harit had only ever seen him in the store and, once, briefly in the parking lot, but now, against the red and orange swells of the bar and grill, Teddy looked like a paper doll that had been plucked from a book. "What are you gonna have?"

Harit had never had a drink with another person in his life. He'd never had a drink, period, until after Swati's death. A week after the tragedy, Gital Didi came by with a few groceries for his mother, and in the middle of pulling bundles of coriander, tubs of yogurt, and flour from the brown paper bags, she pulled out a six-pack of Bud Light and set it on the counter, as if it were the most natural thing to give him. Harit froze in the middle of the kitchen, eyeing the beer as if it were a squirrel that had bounded in through an open window. Gital Didi said, "Perhaps that will help," and turned away to put a gallon of milk in the refrigerator. Later, after his Swati act, while reaching for that milk to make a nighttime *lassi*, Harit saw the beer, large and prominent on the small shelf. He lifted the whole six-pack up, the cans thumping against each other, and eyed the cold metal carefully. Then, as he had done at ten years old when extracting an orange Fanta from his parents' icebox, he set the package back on the shelf and pulled off one can. He took it to his room, sat on his bed, opened it—the *psst* of the can making a much louder sound than he had expected—and had to shove it into his mouth to stop the foam from hitting the floor. He sucked at it, the bubbles burning his throat and the taste acrid and so bitter compared to soda. By the time he finished the can, he was already drunk. He spent the rest of the evening moaning with heartburn into his pillow, but the next night, he drank two more cans, finally realizing why people got drunk—to forget things.

By now, he was used to the scratch of the alcohol at the back of his throat, but he also had no idea what it was like to drink in front of someone—or, more precisely, what it was like to be drunk in front of someone. It was this worry that made him order a Coke.

"A *Coke*?" Teddy said. "I didn't take you out so that you could order a Coke, sweetheart. Time for a big boy's drink. I'll have a vodka soda, and make his a rum and Coke," he said to the waiter, a butch young man with spiked hair, huge arms, and orange-tanned skin.

"Sir, please, a Coke," Harit said, stroking his hair nervously with his right hand.

"Absolutely not!" Teddy laughed. "Rum and Coke. Rum and Coke." He pounded on the table with his fists and chortled. The waiter gave an exasperated sigh and walked away. "Well, what's *her* problem," Teddy said. His face transformed from gleeful mockery to discomfort as his fleshy cheeks and thick neck erupted in a hectic blush. Harit was confused, assuming that Teddy was referring to the hostess, who was not even in sight.

A minute later, the waiter reappeared with a glass of clear liquid over ice for Teddy and a Coke for Harit. Teddy sat quietly as the waiter set the drinks down and walked away.

"Well, cheers, dear," he said, raising his glass into the air. Harit picked his drink up, clinked it against Teddy's glass, and took a sip. He gagged. The burning sweetness in his mouth must have been rum, and the rum must have been half-piss. Teddy burst out in laughter again.

Harit had always thought the jolly dry heave of Teddy's laugh to be comical, but here, in this crowded restaurant where the people in the booth next to theirs peered over the partition to give a stern eye, he hated it.

"Honey, don't tell me you've never had rum before."

"No."

"Have you ever had a *drink* before?"

Harit looked at Teddy angrily and said, "Yes. I have had several."

"Oh, really?" Teddy was chortling again. "When?"

"After my sister died."

Harit hadn't expected to be so mean-spirited, but the words came out of his mouth quickly. He didn't regret speaking them. If anything, he felt empowered, especially when he saw Teddy's face fall and his blush darken to purple.

"Oh, my God, I am so sorry," Teddy said. "How did it happen?"

Instead of responding, Harit took his glass and tipped the rest of its contents down his throat. He closed his nose as he had done years ago when taking his mother's sore throat remedy of honey, black pepper, and masala. Then he said, "Where did the waiter go?"

The inaugural outing ended as Teddy gave Harit a ride home in his beige Camry, Harit fumbling to find his house key because he was tipsy and because it was ten after nine and the baseball field lights had gone off. He had just enough presence of mind to make his costume look presentable and carry on the usual level of conversation as Swati with his mother (which wasn't much). Contrary to what he thought would happen after the initial rush of rum at the restaurant, he did not get sick but fell into a pleasant sleep the moment he lay down. He woke up two hours late the next morning. He sat up in bed and was greeted with a pain that reminded him immediately of how he had felt upon spotting Swati's crumpled body at the foot of the stairs—a punch to the forehead. He managed to get dressed and take a few sips of water from the kitchen tap, and then he realized that he had not given his mother her usual cup of tea that morning. Her grief and fading vision had confined her, and she relied upon him to do little things like these when Gital Didi wasn't around.

He looked into the living room. His mother's head was drooping, and there was no music playing. He started forward but then noticed over the rim of her sunglasses that she was looking at her hands. He realized, his brain like a rusty machine sputtering into action after neglect, that she had been in this exact same position last night. She had not met his eyes but had been looking at her hands, and he had been so worried that she would not believe his clumsy disguise that he had not thought about why she had been doing so. Now, he saw that she was holding a teacup, and he realized that he had no idea how long it had been there. It could have been since yesterday morning, although he normally remembered to take it out of her hands before leaving for work. He had no recollection if he had. The pain in his forehead was making him forget.

"Ma, are you all right?"

She looked up at him and shook her head.

Harit wanted to ask her if she needed another cup of chai, but for some reason he felt that the room had become menacing, that another word would make his mother crumble or disappear. He heard a car whiz past outside, then another car's engine start. He heard the drip of the kitchen faucet, which never stopped making noise however hard he twisted its knobs shut. And there was the swish of his mother's breath as it exited and entered her nostrils. He could not remember the last time that he had looked at his mother like this, without speaking. Perhaps more notable, he could not remember the last time that his mother had observed him. Despite her failing vision and her oppressive eyewear, she seemed to be seeing right into him.

Now was the moment when he should come clean. He could stop this charade and tell his mother the truth. No more nights twisted into a sari, no more makeup, no more tiptoeing.

As he looked at her, he thought of a story that his mother had told him when he was a child: a crow, weary from flying, chanced upon a jug of water in the forest. He perched on the rim of the jug, his ribbed black claws clutching the clay, and put his head down to drink. However, his beak was far too small to reach the water. He tried several times, and every time, he found himself even wearier than when he had begun. Eventually, he had no choice but to fly away, cursing the fact that he had ever stopped.

"But you see," his mother said those many years ago, "another crow came along, and after seeing that his beak was far too short to reach the water, he thought of a plan."

Harit could see his childhood bedroom now—its yellowed walls veined with cracks, the blue stripes of his bedsheet, the honey-like spill of a lamp lighting his mother's lively eyes, and Swati's hair, spread like a dark wooden fan on her bed, which sat opposite his.

"This clever crow grabbed a nearby pebble in his claws and plopped it into the jug. He found another pebble, and another, and another, until the level of the water came to the rim of the jug. He then dipped his beak in and drank to his heart's delight."

Harit remembered how joyous the story had made him. Like every child, he thought his mother had made the story up herself—a sentiment echoed by the look in Swati's own eyes and, of course, in the grin that bloomed on her face.

It was not until a few years later that he heard from a schoolyard acquaintance, Ranga, that not only was the story an Aesop's fable, but that his mother also had changed it in an odd way.

"There are not two crows in the story," Ranga said, raising his hands in the air, palms up, as if each one were a crow. "There is only one crow, and he figures out the puzzle for himself." He brought his palms together, bowed as if he were a servant, then erupted in laughter.

Harit was hurt that his mother had changed the story, especially because he couldn't understand why she had made the change at all. Why put another crow in the tale, especially when its story was so tragic?

By the time Harit got to work that morning, it was ten o'clock. He had never been late to work before, and he didn't know what to do. Most mornings, he arrived at five minutes before eight, clocked in at his register, then waited in the break room for his coworkers to show up. It was a drab space, with a quartet of buzzing appliances—a vending machine of candy bars, a watercooler, an off-white refrigerator, and a tea-and-coffee machine that spat liquid into fragile paper cups. A collection of plastic chairs and round tables, scattered by day's end, was always set right by the janitor come morning, and Harit loved having this order to himself. (Having once been a janitor, he appreciated this dearly.) Since he hated the tea that the machine in the break room made, he brought Taj Mahal tea bags and simply pressed the HOT WATER button to make his own brew. He toasted Mr. Harriman's portrait—his sole companion—and drank up the tea and silence.

By eight-thirty, the fifteen or so salespeople of the morning shift would gather and loiter with their coffees, bagels, stinky fast-food breakfasts, and gossip. Since the store was such a beloved establishment, the majority of the employees had been working there for years. Most of them were women who smelled sweet and wore dresses as puffy as their hair. It wasn't that they were mean to Harit, but except for a smile in passing or an odd question about his ethnicity ("When do you plan to move back?" "In India, do you drink eight glasses of tea a day instead of water?"), they rarely engaged him directly in conversation. One of them, Ruby, was in her seventies, and Harit originally attributed her reticence to old age; but one afternoon, when he asked her if the store was closed on New Year's Day, she looked up from folding a blouse and said, "I'm busy." Her voice, which had always been warbly, was resolute in its judgment of foreign people.

For the most part, they left the socializing to Teddy. His status as Harit's companion in Men's Furnishings made him the obvious stand-in for a conversation partner, and there was an unspoken relief that no one else had to handle Harit. With Teddy around, a greeting, a question, a discussion involving Harit was replaced with a head nod. That was good enough for his coworkers, and truthfully, that was good enough for Harit.

On Monday mornings, Mr. Harriman came into the break room and gave them a short speech—which things on sale were particularly desirable, or whose morale was highest and therefore most exemplary. Then he would say good-bye and give the floor to Stella, who would read off a list of employees who had sold "instant credit cards"—Harriman's charge cards that gave preferred customers discounts on merchandise. Every time you rang someone up, you had to ask the customer if he or she wanted to "open an instant credit"—a carefully monitored Harriman stipulation. People had been fired for failing to pop the question within earshot of Mr. Harriman—or so the word went. Marla Palmer, a woman in her fifties who was the acknowledged star of cosmetics, held the record for the most instant credits ever opened—well over a hundred—and hers was always the first name called. Every week—every single week—she turned on one heel when her name rang out, then bent in a curtsy and screwed her heavily rouged face into a "surprised" grin. Harit rarely hated people, but he absolutely loathed her. He preferred Ruby's type of obvious dislike to this put-on humility.

Or maybe it was the fact that he had never opened an instant credit. Not one. After two months at the store, Mr. Harriman pulled him aside and said that he no longer had to ask people to open them. "Teddy has done such a stand-up job opening ICs"—a handy store abbreviation—"that it would be overkill to have both of you asking." Harit wanted to point out how only one of them ever helped a customer at a time, so how could Teddy ask one of Harit's customers to open an IC? But Harit picked up on the motive behind Mr. Harriman's leniency and knew that he was being given a break.

Today was a Friday, though, and there was no meeting on Fridays. These mornings were usually boisterous, since everyone had to discuss their plans for the weekend, and Teddy often brought in doughnuts for everyone. This morning, by habit, Harit went to the register to clock in, then realized that he probably should not be seen until he knew how upset Mr. Harriman was at his tardiness. He took a look around to see if he could spot Teddy. Sure enough, he was busy helping a woman pull a red canvas suitcase from a high shelf. In the midst of tilting the suitcase to show the customer an extra pocket, Teddy caught Harit's eye and nodded, as if to say, "I'll be right there." Harit went into the storeroom to flick through stacks of shirts and shake shiny boxes of dress shoes. Even though he and Teddy didn't get to sell these objects—seeing as shirts and shoes belonged to Men's and not Men's Furnishings—they were still tasked with taking inventory of them.

"Well, well, if it ain't Mr. Fashionably Late—literally!" Teddy said.

"I am so sorry, Teddy. I have never been late before. Is Mr. Harriman angry?"

"Dear, calm down. Calm down. Harriman is just fine. I told him that your power was out this morning and that you were waiting for the electric company. I could have also told him that you don't have a cell phone, but I figured that he could do without that piece of information, honey." Teddy called Harit "honey" so much that Harit had started to wonder if Teddy simply couldn't pronounce his name. "He just said that he would dock you one emergency day."

They had five emergency days in a year without monetary punishment. After five days, you had to pay fifty dollars for each day missed. Harit was not particularly happy to have lost one of his days, but he had taken only two days off work since beginning at Harriman's, and those had been because of Swati.

"Why the sad face, honey? You're totally fine. I'm going to go man the station. Go ahead and just do inventory today. I'll take care of the register."

Harit was relieved to have an easy task. His headache had subsided even though he had drunk only one cup of tea this morning and not his usual second cup in the break room. In fact, he felt strangely peaceful amidst the nice-smelling leather of the shoes. Instead of bending over with his clipboard and examining the shelves and stacks, he decided to plop the boxes on the floor, lie down with his back against the wall, and comfortably take notes about how many pairs of each design remained in stock. It felt comfortable because it felt like something he would have done as a child. He was one step away from emptying the contents of these boxes on the floor and lying in a bed of shoes just to be wrapped in their leathery smell while he dozed off.

He couldn't remember the last time that he had thought of something so frivolous. And why was he, a Hindu, enjoying the smell of *leather*? That was blasphemy. His body felt braided with energy. He could feel himself shaking.

Then Harit wondered how Mr. Harriman had believed Teddy's story. If Harit's power had been out and he had no cell phone, how would Harit have called *Teddy* to let him know this in the first place? It didn't make sense.

Perhaps Teddy was right and Harit was paranoid. Mr. Harriman had better things to do than worry about him.

FOR TEN MONTHS, A LARGE, GREEN SIGN HAD been flashing beside the highway: COMING SOON: PARADISE ISLAND—*BEYOND YOUR DREAMS*. That was all it read, not a single hint as to what Paradise Island was. The effect of this was thrilling. Traffic slowed as people drove past, and Ranjana took some comfort in thinking that others shared her curious fascination with the sign. All the same, she felt that it had been placed there for her benefit or her entertainment or, very possibly, her unraveling. She felt a particular communion with the concept of "Paradise"; it was a word that so many Americans used to euphemize India when they were being polite, when the truth was that, to them, India was a whole host of other things before it was Paradise (dirty, crowded, impoverished). To Ranjana, India did often represent Paradise; she missed parts of it as an angel would miss Eden; and to see the word *Paradise* every day to and from work was like passing her childhood temple or a favorite movie house. As a writer, that was how she saw things—not as what they were but as what they represented.

Paradise Island. It sounded like one of those horrid reality shows that her coworker Cheryl was always talking about: bright-haired twentysomethings dumped on an island for sex, fluorescent drinks, and black-and-white video clips in which their teeth, hair, and bathing suits gleamed in the same grainy hue. Yet Paradise Island's intrigue had to do with elusiveness, not visibility.

The tension of not knowing what it was invaded her thoughts. Its meaning to her life was magnified by her need to know exactly what it was meant to be. She did not understand what kind of marketing tactic this was, this forced mystery. It was one thing to whet a public's appetite, but to prolong the process had the adverse effect on people. They became annoyed, obsessed with something that had never even existed.

One day Ranjana took the exit and drove to where the sign indicated Paradise Island would be. She could not drive all the way up to the sign. Instead, she was stopped by a chain-link fence, behind which sat various piles of earth and debris indicating a work in progress. Afterward, she stopped at a nearby Starbucks to have some tea.

"Excuse me," she said to a blank-eyed employee who was collecting used cups, discarded lids, and trampled napkins with a broom and dustpan. The boy barely looked up when Ranjana spoke. "Do you know what this 'Paradise Island' is?"

He snorted. "The hell if I know. You're, like, the tenth person to ask me that today."

"But what *is* it? They've been building it for months."

"Look, I wish I knew, ma'am. My manager is pissed. He thought it would get us more customers. But that thing's just been sitting there for months, and we have no effing clue."

Ranjana went home and, enjoying the silence of an empty house, fixed herself a *mooli paratha.* If she wasn't going to find out what that bloody Island was, she was going to gorge on something that she didn't have to share with her husband. She stood at the kitchen counter, dunking hot pieces of the *paratha* into a pot of yogurt. She loved the contrast of the cool and hot on her fingers. In the pot, the yogurt looked like glaciers giving off a soft radiance.

Nothing taunted Ranjana more than a blinking cursor. Her eyes were beginning to cross as her computer screen burned into a hot indigo.

There had to be something besides the premise of the story itself; that was easy enough. Ranjana had devoured all of the series, knew all of the tricks. She had read about southern vampires—she often replaced the word *southern* with *Madrasi* in her mind—and she had read about Yankee vampires (she labeled these "Punjabi"). She had read about vampires that loved men and women alike. She had read about teenage vampires, nineteenth-century vampires, vampires with roots in Egypt, vampires with roots in India. Aztec vampires. Vampires with hearts of gold, vampires with fangs of steel. What was there to *do* with a vampire that hadn't already been done?

So, tonight, she settled on the idea of an arranged marriage involving a vampire. She was capable enough as a writer to understand that she was drawing a deliberate parallel between her life and the lives of her characters. Ranjana had had an arranged marriage, and recently she saw something cold and almost menacing in Mohan. But instead of being drawn to the vampire-husband in question, she was repelled by him. What if vampires were not creatures of icily inviting mystery but, rather, creatures as threatening as our human instinct would have us believe? Sex would not be alluring, then. Romance would be as dead as a vampire's body.

Ranjana put her head in her hands and tried to massage the purple flashes out of her eyes. She knew why she was seizing upon this idea right now, but she wasn't sure how she could turn it into a viable story about vampires. The flashes dissipated from her eyes and were soon replaced by vulgar words in block letters across the computer screen, as if from some tabloid news story. But instead of MURDER or DRUGS, they were awful words used to describe the female anatomy.

How could Mohan be so reckless? If he was going to search such things online, why would he not cover his tracks and delete them from the search history? But he hadn't, and Ranjana, before writing, had clicked on the search history and come across site after site about—she could barely bring herself to think of this term when it referred to her husband—"oral sex." Page after page showed a white woman with pink skin, her legs opened to the face of a tan man with curly hair. Page after page gave explicit tips on how to perform this act—an act that Mohan had never performed on Ranjana.

Ranjana pulled her head out of her hands and looked at the blinking cursor again. Of course: if Mohan was looking up this stuff, it wasn't in service of her. He was learning these things for someone else. He had a pink girl somewhere. It was this realization that propelled her fingers forward and made her start typing so furiously that the cursor didn't even have a chance to blink again.

She never thought she would obsess over vampires and witches and werewolves and ghosts, but *this* was the way in which Ranjana could permeate the wall that separated her Indian life from the omnipresent glitz of American pop culture. She read Anne Rice first, in 1995, once she had been in this country for four years. Elaine

Bush, a nosy neighbor, recommended *Interview with the Vampire* because the movie was coming out at that time. Ranjana bought a paperback from the grocery store and tore off its cover and title page so that Mohan would not judge her. She stayed up reading it late into the night, on the couch, her nightgown soaking up the cold of the early morning and making her shiver all the more as the story progressed.

The thing that surprised her most about the book was that, in terms of plot, it did not surprise her that much. She had expected to be scandalized—had *wanted* to be scandalized—but the more she read, the more the story seemed like a hidden affirmation of herself. It was like discovering that she had a second spine. Contrary to what she had expected, there were things in India that had prepared her for white-skinned corpses and young damsels in the brambled backwoods of Louisiana. The grandeur of white houses with shapely verandas called to mind temples that she had seen at six years old on a family trip to Kerala. The vampires themselves seemed like countless depictions of demons pierced by Krishna's or Rama's sword, blood gushing forth. Except in these Western vampiric fantasies, it was the evil demon winning the battle, not the dew-skinned gods. As she read *Dracula*, then Charlaine Harris, then Laurell K. Hamilton, then Sherrilyn Kenyon, then joined the ageless hordes devouring Stephenie Meyer, she found no true scandal in what she read. She worried that the books would be full of sex—and they were—but she had prepared herself for this fact beforehand, so its impact proved less injurious. Or so she convinced herself. Now that she had stumbled across Mohan's online secrets, she could not help but feel that she had brought this upon herself. She had carved out her secret world and relished its seduction, but it was an entirely different thing to watch your own life become corrupted by such seduction. Real-life stories often found their way into fiction, but the opposite could be true: fiction could, cruelly, become real life.

"I tell you, I never laugh as much as I laugh in yoga class," Seema said. "These skinny white people, all twisted up, trying to copy us. Yesterday, instead of wearing pants, a woman came in wearing the bottom of a *salwar kameez*. She's one of these girls with a nose ring, you know, so many of them have them. And she thinks she is so Indian. She came up to me and started talking to me about all of these poses we'd done, as if she were the Indian woman and not I—and her Sanskrit pronunciation was terrible! Absolutely terrible."

"Yes, but you don't speak Sanskrit, either," Ranjana interrupted, straining the tea and watching the beige-colored beard that clung to the bottom of the strainer as the milky liquid fell through it.

"Yes, but I do not go around pretending that I do. I barely know how to speak Hindi anymore!"

They had known each other for years, had spent countless weekend *pujas* and parties sitting next to each other and discussing children and films, but for a long time, there had never been any occasion to speak about their own lives with any sense of consequence. They knew that their relationship to each other was the result of communal responsibility; they were like chunks of pineapple and honeydew in a fruit salad—tart and plump but there merely for the collective purpose of volume. Motherhood solidified their friendship further. Seema had one child, like Ranjana. All of the other women in their circle had at least two kids, but Ranjana and Seema were the odd women out—Ranjana because of her own physical limitations, Seema because of her own choice. Seema's insistence on having one child and one child only had made her anathema to the other Indian women for years. What sort of woman stopped at one child, of her own accord? And Seema had a daughter, not a son; at least a son, a sturdy heir, would have made sense. But a daughter—and a daughter like Gori, so sour and uninspired. Like Prashant, Ranjana's son, Gori had just left for college—barely, it seemed. And what was she going to study? God only knew.

Seema did not seem particularly concerned. She went to her yoga classes and cooked fancy meals at her monthly dinner parties—for white friends—and generally seemed to love her life now. She had given birth to Gori at twenty-one, and now that Gori was off at school, even though it was only an hour away, Seema was a free woman. Her husband, Satish, did not pose much of a problem. He came home at seven o'clock every day and, according to Seema, seemed to be content with his life. He played tennis and tended his garden and watched Zee TV until he fell into a gurgly slumber. True, he did behave like an old man, not like a man in his early forties, but Seema seemed genuinely entertained by him.

"What else are we supposed to do? The first eighteen years of our parenting are over," Seema argued. "Gori is gone, and there is nothing to be done until she graduates."

This was Seema's take. But in this, she was also different from the other Indian mothers. Most of them found a way to insert themselves into the lives of their children while they were at college. At least once a week, Shilpa Jindal took a foil-wrapped casserole dish to Neil's dorm; Ranjana once saw her place it in the passenger seat of her BMW so lovingly that it could have been an infant. Everyone knew that Anita Aggarwal's son, Alok, had changed his cell phone number to prevent her from getting through to him at all times of the day. Some of the mothers had changed their own telephone habits, lest they meet this same hurtful fate, but within a week, they were all back to their old ways. Ever the anomaly, Seema seemed unconcerned, even though it was generally assumed by the other parents that Gori smoked pot all of the time. Perhaps that was why Seema let Gori do these things—she was probably smoking pot herself. That would explain so much, especially why she went to these sad little yoga classes with white women who pierced their noses and had tattoos wrapped around their upper arms like snakes.

"Ranjana, the tea is going to be like melted ice by the time you get it over here, *yaar.*" Seema slapped the table and giggled.

Ranjana was being distant. The truth was that she was wondering just how strong her friendship was—if she could safely divulge what she had learned about Mohan to Seema. Yes, Seema was an entertaining and dedicated friend—if Ranjana had an emergency at three in the morning, she would dial Seema immediately—but this was the kind of information that felt horribly explicit in their community. The fact that it was so salacious made it harder for Seema to use it as gossip with the other women, but at the same time, they all complained about their marriages constantly, so Seema wouldn't feel *that* out of line bringing it up. Ranjana lifted the cups carefully and turned; in her rumination, she had not only strained the tea three times but had also poured it so absentmindedly that it threatened to spill. In all her years making tea, she had never spilled a drop. But then something odd happened: as she set the cups on the table, she glanced at their shiny porcelain and saw it transformed into gleaming fangs. Startled, she pulled her right hand back, and the cup in that hand, which she had intended for Seema, shot forth a stream of hot tea.

"*Arré!*" Seema screamed, rising from her chair and clutching her wrist like she was Spider-Man about to shoot a sticky web at a rooftop. The tea couldn't have been that hot, but that was Seema for you—angling for the dramatic. "*Yaar*, what is the matter with you? Ho, it burns!"

"I am so sorry, *ji*," Ranjana said, turning around, tearing a paper towel from its roll, and rushing to the fridge. She pushed one of the two shiny pedals on the front of the fridge and felt the cold jostle of ice cubes as they hit the towel. She returned to Seema and placed the ice on her wrist. "I have never spilled a drop of tea in my life."

"This is going to leave a mark," Seema said, looking at her newly red wrist. It was an unspoken understanding between them that Seema was not worried about her skin but about how this burn might affect her yoga poses.

"No, it won't," Ranjana said. "It will be better before you know it."

Still, Ranjana felt that this momentary lapse in her behavior was the start of something bigger, a result of the secret that she had uncovered.

Ranjana knew that she didn't know all that much about sex, but she knew enough to know that she had never had an orgasm. Clearly, the discomfort that she had felt years before, when they were still having sex, the relentlessness of it all, the way in which she could count the huffs and puffs that Mohan made into her ear—she knew that none of it constituted what people described as that great release. She read about it all of the time—Anne Rice had as many orgasms in her books as commas—and she wondered if the precarious feeling that she experienced during sex could be equated with the tense lust found in vampire stories. Was a fumbling, uncomfortable lovemaking session with Mohan the equivalent of being gripped at the neck with some undead's teeth against her skin-hooded vein? They were both situations of physical discomfort laced with a foreboding sense of danger.

She looked for opportunities in which she could transform Mohan into someone enticingly threatening. Sometimes—and she hated herself for this when she thought of it—she wished that she were like Mona Gupta or Sushil Patel, women whose husbands, everyone knew, beat them regularly. Maybe if Mohan were violent, she would at least feel something legitimately passionate in her marriage. Instead, the firmest slap that Mohan could deliver would be flipping a puri onto his plate.

But no—she did not really believe or want this. Nobody wanted to be in an abusive relationship, and although she could never be sure how people were defining feminism these days, she was rather certain that this was a decidedly antifeminist mind-set.

It seemed like an American myth that people ate to replace the lack of romance in their lives; Ranjana thought that this was too easy an explanation for so complicated a problem. Yet now, for example, she was leaning against the kitchen counter, eating *bondas* and dipping them in a thick *raita* that she had made early this morning before work. As her tongue sang with flavor, she realized that just last night, she had been lamenting the sour hub of Mohan's body in her bed. She had been thinking about how little desire she felt for him, or, rather, how she felt none at all, and she had gotten up today with a craving for *bondas* and *raita*. She had replaced her husband with a feast. The soft contours of her body, made softer every day, were due to her sexual frustration. To be fair, the spare tire around Mohan's torso was due to her own reticence toward him. They were getting fatter in their sexual sadness.

Ranjana was still in her scrubs. The doctor's office had her wear scrubs even though she was not an RN, just a receptionist, but the office claimed that patients would feel more trusting if they believed a legitimate nurse was attending to them. This made her feel disingenuous, but the scrubs were as comfortable as wearing a *salwar kameez*. Nevertheless, all she wanted to do was change into a nightgown and take a nap.

Alas, here was Mohan, bustling into the house, back from his own office, settling into his recliner with the newspaper.

"There is some leftover okra, and I can make roti," she proffered. This was a low point: proposing what they should eat for dinner *while she was already eating.*

Mohan sighed and shifted his newspaper, then said, "I don't want leftovers. . . ."

Ranjana echoed his sigh and said, "I can make *chole*"—and she *could* make it because she had picked up some chickpeas on the way home, having known all along that Mohan would not eat the okra. Later, Ranjana would eat the okra herself, after she had eaten the *chole*, after she had made roti, rice, and some impromptu *lassi* that had Mohan farting into his armchair postdinner. They watched Zee TV and caught up on the news, the anchorwoman's cloud-like hair and lilting voice a stark contrast to the weight of Mohan's gas. Then Ranjana got up and said that she was going to work on her recipes.

"Working on recipes" was Ranjana's cover-up for her writing. She told Mohan that she wanted to create a cookbook for Prashant so that he could make Indian food for himself at the dorm. Both Ranjana and Mohan knew that Prashant would never do such a thing and would therefore never need the cookbook, but Mohan evidently took some comfort in Ranjana's efforts to keep their son more Indian and more "self-sufficient."

"Self-sufficient" in Mohan's mind translated to "frugal," and frugality was the thing that Mohan valued most. When Ranjana was pregnant with Prashant, an American woman had asked

Mohan if the baby was going to be a boy or a girl, and Mohan had replied, "I don't care, as long as it's healthy and smart with money." The woman had laughed nervously and joked, "And a boy, right?" Mohan's answer, unironic: "Well, yes."

So off to the spare bedroom Ranjana went, closing the door tight behind her. She sat at the tiny desk to pick up where she had left off the day before. No egg curry and *biryani* recipes for Prashant. Vampires and damsels for Ranjana.

It was easily her favorite time of day: work barely a memory, dinner accomplished, her husband appeased, a story her only world for an hour or two. It was at once fun and disorienting. She had traveled across the world not so that she could live in a different country, one of promise and prepackaged foods, but so that she could live in an imaginary country of her mind. She looked out the window and saw the Turners' house next door, their pit bull barking into its bowl of water and the kids upstairs playing video games, and she felt incredibly lonely. Then she directed her eyes to the computer screen and went to the only place where she could comfort herself. That was what writing really was—an excuse to gild your loneliness until it resembled the companionship of others. It was entertaining yourself when you had no other entertainment. It was the way out.

Not even daring to open the Web browser—lest she dwell too much on Mohan's deviance—she wrote until the pit bull tired itself out and curled into a ball in its paint-chipped doghouse, until the Turners' kids turned off their infernal machine and shut their TV-ravaged eyes for the night, until the world outside became a dimmer, quieter version of itself. Then she tended her hair with a comb she kept by the desk, opened the door, tiptoed into the master bedroom, where Mohan, now in his pajamas, was still reading the newspaper, and she inserted herself into the stale sheets and imagined her characters whispering her to sleep. Her reverie was interrupted occasionally by the click of Mohan's saliva as he chewed on a mint-dipped toothpick, the newspaper unfolding and refolding every few minutes, the sound like a bucket of water being poured on a big rock.

Ranjana's late-night writing sessions were not the only artistic secret that she kept from Mohan. After seeing a flyer on a bulletin board at the grocery store, she had joined a writers' group that met once every two weeks at the YMCA. They gathered in a multipurpose room that housed a massive collection of rainbow-colored plastic toys. The organizer, Roberta Shuster, was a mild woman in her midfifties who lived alone in a condo near the building.

The participants in this group were not unlike the ones in Seema's yoga class—aiming for the ethereal, but with frequently hilarious results. The most vocal member, Stefanie, was in her late thirties and wore at least three layers of dark clothing, the top layer normally shiny. She had a storm of hair, a collection of titian dyes, that made it seem as if she were wearing a mud-covered fox on her head. She wore a silver necklace with a pendant of a snake curled around a dagger, and when she got particularly excited, she would tug at the pendant until Ranjana thought the necklace would snap and send the dagger flying into someone's eye. Stefanie had presented three works in the past few months—a novella about mermaids living in a sea-bound hostel off the coast of Normandy, a collection of poems inspired by Elizabeth Taylor, and her "magnum opus," a manuscript that now exceeded a thousand pages and that she had been writing, she claimed, for the past fifteen years.

The plot of Stefanie's novel, even given its copious length, was still somewhat elusive to the group. The main premise was that women had become so dominated by the awfulness of men that once a woman had been wronged significantly by three men in her life, she acquired lupine powers and became immortal, hungry for their blood, and, as a result of these first two circumstances, sexier than ever. The main character, Stasy, was obviously Stefanie. Stefanie changed the character's hair color to blond, but she did not change the fact that Stasy loved to dye her hair practically every other week. Furthermore, Stasy wore a necklace just like the one that Stefanie wore, with the notable difference that Stasy's snake was curled around an arrow instead of a dagger.

The foil in the group to Stefanie's grand presence was Cassie, a soft-spoken woman in her midtwenties who normally dressed in jeans and a baggy sweater and who was, undoubtedly, the best writer of the lot. Unlike Stefanie, Cassie had presented only one work, a lavishly written story about a teenage girl who had the ability to move people's hearts from one body to another, thereby changing whom her victims loved but without changing the knowledge they had of their pasts. It was a strange pitch—or "log line," Roberta would have said, referring to how an editor at a publishing house might log in a submission—but the writing itself was so gorgeous that very few people in the group could offer legitimate criticism. Naturally, they were all jealous of Cassie's ability, even Ranjana, especially because Cassie was considerably younger than the rest of them. She showed up in her dumpy clothes and no makeup—presumably straight from a nap, given her overall sleepy appearance—and bested them all.

Perhaps more revealing was when Cassie offered her criticism of other people's work. In this, she was both reverent and utterly cutthroat. She knew that she was the best of all of them, and she milked her commentary, saying, "Well, hm," biting her lip, looking down at the floor for a moment, then offering something candid like "I don't think that your story is going anywhere. And how many times can you use the word *rippling* in one paragraph?"

This particular comment had been directed at Wendy, a woman in her early forties whom Ranjana had overheard tell at least five people she was "Yes, named after Wendy from *Peter Pan*, and did you know that J. M. Barrie made up the name Wendy? So, like, compared to most other names, which have been around for centuries, even millenniums, my name is like a rare breed of creature, like evolution or something." Wendy would giggle after she said this and lick her teeth, which were about as sharp as Stefanie's dagger and which had a smudge of lipstick on them at least 70 percent of the time. Other than this blemish, however, Wendy was undeniably attractive, with green eyes and luscious blond hair. She worked as a private massage therapist and had once held a free session for the entire group after one of their meetings. Her hands had jiggled Ranjana's back as if it were a door that she had been trying to unlock, but Ranjana had felt very refreshed afterward.

If only Wendy were equally adept at writing. It was true that Wendy overwrote; Cassie wasn't exaggerating when she accused her of using the same decadent words over and over again, and everyone in the group seemed to wonder how Wendy could be so passionately invested in her work when it seemed, from these repetitions, that she never revised it. But Wendy was so nice that Ranjana felt herself empathizing with her, if only because Ranjana knew that she would never have the courage to withstand Cassie's provocations.

Colin, the lone man of the group, owned as many *Star Wars* T-shirts as there were *Star Wars* movies and had thick glasses and ponytailed hair that made him seem like a nearsighted painter whose eyesight had worsened over time. None of his characters was ever fully human; the closest one of them had gotten to being so was a half-wombat woman who ate only bark and grass. Thankfully, Colin didn't overly sexualize his characters; on the contrary, he erred on the side of romance, writing more about the sharpness of their intellect than the curvaceousness of their bodies. Still, whenever a sex scene did occur, it was so overly studied that it was as if Colin were wearing a sign that read I'M A VIRGIN.

Today was Ranjana's day to present. She had stopped home momentarily to print out her pages, which she now held rolled up, the paper crinkled and worn, as if it had been printed centuries before. She berated herself for this nervous habit; everything always became rolled up when in her hands. As she sat in the classroom now, she wondered if she had been trying to erase the work she'd done, ashamed of its mediocrity.

The first time that she had read in this class, it was a very short story, about a young Indian woman pining for a young neighbor on her small farm. It was an exercise, a trifle, a raffle ticket for admission to this group of writers. They smiled sweetly at her, all of them too absorbed in their own work to care what Ranjana had to give them. The second time she had read, she had stopped herself midway and apologized, saying that she had to revise more. Again, they were sympathetic, Stefanie twirling her necklace, Cassie exhaling softly and looking elderly in her judgment, Wendy placing a hand on her heart and tugging gently, as if ready to pull it out and present it to Ranjana as a condolence, Colin adjusting his thick glasses while nodding his head. The next two classes belonged solely to Stefanie and Cassie, and then Roberta had broken the rhythm the next week with her own book, which was a romance novel in the Jude Deveraux vein, all sloping hills and horses and bodices torn like wrapping paper. The listeners all shifted uncomfortably, the tight bun of Roberta's hair so much at odds with the salaciousness of her story.

Now, Roberta was looking expectantly at Ranjana, and the other writers all perked up in their chairs. Ranjana smoothed out her pages, cleared her throat, and began to read. She could feel Cassie's wry stare burrowing invisibly into her cheek. The section she was reading wasn't from her manuscript; it was a tepid story based on a recent ceremony at her temple. As she read, her voice quavered, as if made of liquid. She had rarely felt so judged by other people, had not experienced anything quite like it since her adolescence, when other Indian mothers constantly seemed to be judging everyone's children. As she finished the last sentence of her five-page excerpt, her throat tiring, she wondered if it were even necessary to have villains in her stories. There were enough enemies sitting right here.

IT WAS THE FIRST TIME THAT PRASHANT had ever had a crush on an Indian girl.

As with most other areas in his life up until now, he had directed his attention to all things American. He fixated upon the thin, almost weblike skin and candy-scented hair of the white girls around him. The girl whom he had treasured in high school above everyone else, Amber Ferguson, had no Indian foil, nothing in common with any of the *desi* girls in his class. Her long legs, the blue of her eyes, her skin so fair it matched her teeth, her hair so fine it moved together because not to do so would have seemed criminal, transfixed him as only an exotic creature could. She didn't want anything to do with any of the Indian boys, which made her even more elusive and therefore desirable. She cringed whenever one of them let his gaze linger even a split second on her, and there was her boyfriend, Chase, who looked like Bradley Cooper.

So it was fitting that, in his first week at Princeton, Prashant should fall for Kavita, a fully formed ABCD—an American-Born Confused Desi. In many ways, Kavita was just as American as Amber, but she held on to the two Indian aspects that were always the most compelling—religion and language. She was a self-professed "proud Hindu." Apparently this had been the crux of her admissions essay, the paragraphs of which, it was rumored, she had structured according to the layout of the Upanishads. This drove Prashant totally crazy with desire because his own Hinduism was shoddy at best. His parents had always been relatively lazy when it came to practicing their religion, and, well, we all wanted what we didn't have.

He had just written a paper about this for his introductory literature course. In Plato's *Symposium*, Aristophanes maintained that men and women were amorphous, dual-gendered beings that had been split into the two sexes, forever yearning for each other to make themselves whole. (Prashant's professor, a recent transplant from Vanderbilt with a lilting southern accent, played the class a song from *Hedwig and the Angry Inch* that told this very story.) In the same course, they had been reading Ovid's *Metamorphoses*, in which the story of Narcissus appears. Prashant argued in his paper that Narcissus was doomed to fail because he lusted after something exactly like himself: himself. To follow Aristophanes' line of thought, this was antithetical to human nature; we wanted not ourselves but the unattainable other. Prashant had obviously been thinking of Kavita, had infused the essence of her into the paper and felt the prose flowing easily from his fingertips onto the keyboard because the slant of her eyes, the bounce of her ass, willed it so. She was Indian but still unattainable, representing some part of his culture but still eluding his grasp, and if he was going to tumble headfirst into a cesspool of his own making, at least he wouldn't be like Narcissus, chasing after someone like himself.

The teacher gave him a B+, commending his connection between the two texts but questioning where homosexuality would come into play; was Prashant intimating that Plato, of all people, allowed nothing for same-sex longing? It was at this point, while Prashant held his paper in his hands and contemplated the vermilion scribbles covering it, that he realized his instructor was not simply genteel but most likely gay. Any man who could not properly contemplate something as perfect as Kavita Bansal's ass had to be.

It became evident to Prashant that he had chosen the wrong major. Given his father's profession, he had always felt rather acutely that he had a predisposition for the scientific. He was one of those kids who didn't feel particularly threatened by his father's line of work. He didn't see his own tendency toward chemistry as something strictly dictated by his father's background. It was merely logical to Prashant that he should find interesting a subject that made up his father's vocation. He was an even-keeled kid, a good student, and as someone who didn't feel a penchant for the dramatic or overly emotive, he found that science was very much in keeping with his demeanor.

He had been assigned the usual books in his high school English classes—*The Great Gatsby*, *1984*, *Brave New World*; later, the heftiness of *Moby-Dick*, a book whose more staid passages on whaling he found enthralling (he kept this to himself). Then there was the hilarity of being assigned *A Passage to India*, a book that he was forced, along with his other Indian classmates, to analyze as if he had nothing in common with the characters in it. In many senses, he didn't. It wasn't like he could relate to being an Indian man accused of rape in the hills. ("Not yet," his friend Vipul quipped moronically.) He realized that he approached a book, regardless of its emotional dealings, from a somewhat disassociated perspective. He applied a scientist's cool assessment to the otherwise shifting, swirling cosmos of literature. Oddly, his teacher loved this. The comment "Very cogent" appeared with alarming consistency on his papers.

Something had shifted recently, and even though he attempted to deny it, he knew that Kavita was the reason why. Although she had gotten a 2400 on her SATs (a common achievement at their school), although she had won some huge science fair by examining how she could save wildlife during oil spills, and although her own parents were both doctors, Kavita had chosen English as her major. Prashant began to see, as he "bumped into" her on campus, that she almost always had a book in hand. She read as she walked, and accessorized her books with a complicated series of sticky notes, something that Prashant noticed even from afar. This kind of system seemed unnecessary, since many people claimed that she had a photographic memory. It was generally acknowledged that she would have been the most hated person on Earth if she were not the most beloved. Teachers fell under her spell as soon as everyone else did, if not earlier.

Prashant wished with a painful fierceness that he could be in one of her classes, but he wasn't in her classes because his major was chemistry, not English. That one intro-to-lit course was all he could manage because the rest of his schedule was overtaken by science. His major was not just chemistry; it was a laboratory's worth of chemical studies. (One of his classes, an accelerated amalgam of two separate courses, had the nickname "Turbo-Chem," which sounded like a lame superhero.) Still, he didn't find his coursework all that crippling because he was good at it—really good at it. As Dr. Moore, one of his professors, put it, he was "preternaturally inclined to the study of chemistry."

He should have found his teachers' collective encouragement comforting, but it had the opposite effect in him. He didn't want to be another stereotypical South Asian kid who was "good at math." He didn't want to be easily inclined to something; he wanted to be challenged. It took no great rumination on his part to draw a connection between this and Kavita. She challenged who he was as a man more than anyone he'd ever met. Ha—"a man." He couldn't refer to himself as a man without snickering. He was short, with a slight belt of fat at his waist and thick, intractable hair that he had clearly inherited from his mother. He often wore clothes a size or two too big. This was true of a lot of his Indian friends, as if, subconsciously, their parents had dictated that they buy clothes into which they could grow eventually, even though their mothers did not want them to put on weight. For every "Eat something, *beta*," he got an equal and sometimes stronger reaction of "Really—another samosa?" It was no surprise that his emotions were equally conflicted. The more confusion that people lobbed your way, the more you overanalyzed everything; the more that you were challenged, the more being challenged became a kind of comfort.

He had reached a point when all of those SAT vocab cards he'd studied were infusing themselves into his daily speech. The truth was that he did not find chemistry the most compelling forum for this newfound mental capacity. Inspired by Kavita, he now wanted to apply his verbally inspired skills to something that lay outside the realm of equations. He wanted to move people with his words. This made him feel less Indian than ever—a state in which he luxuriated.

They appeared like magic: flyers indicating Kavita Bansal's candidacy for freshman class president. A third of the flyers simply disappeared, tucked under mattresses (and held in left hands) all over campus.

Prashant stole one, of course, but the shame he felt over this dissipated when he realized, in the dining hall one night, that he was far from alone. He had made a couple of reliable guy friends, both from his chemistry study group: Doug, an African-American, fellow chem major from Connecticut who was on the ultimate Frisbee team; and Charlie, a mechanical engineering student who was the only one of the three of them who might be considered cool. Charlie had gone to Exeter but was from California. His father was the long-retired head of a large bank, and his mother was a former Miss California. Girls seemed to find Charlie irresistible, something Prashant attributed in part to his name. Girls often imparted a singsong tone to it—"*Char*-leee"—and Prashant sighed internally at the thought that no one would ever be able to do such a thing with his name. Instead of pronouncing his name correctly—"Pruh-*shahnth*"—people pronounced the first syllable of his name as if it rhymed with a lamb's "baa," and the second syllable became something you stuck into a wound—"Praaa-*shunt*."

Charlie addressed this:

"Dude, we need to find you a nickname. A good one."

Prashant bristled but knew his friend was right. "But this is my name. I shouldn't have to leave my name behind just because of other people's ignorance."

"It's not ignorance, man. People just can't do it. Why do you think I dropped my Italian class? I can't roll my *r*'s. That doesn't mean I hate the Italian language. It's just a fact. So I'm taking Japanese instead."

Of course. Charlie was the type of maddening individual who would see studying Japanese as tantamount to studying Italian.

"I'm not sure that's an altogether relevant analogy, but whatever," Prashant said.

"What Chaz means," Doug tried to clarify, "is that you're not going to get any ass until girls don't feel retarded saying your name."

"Yo, don't call me Chaz, dude," Charlie said.

Slack-jawed, Prashant looked at Charlie. "You don't want to be called Chaz, but I can't be called by my real name?"

"Shut up, Ass-shunt," Charlie said. "Or I'll make *that* your nickname."

Later that evening, as Prashant unscrolled Kavita's flyer from under his mattress and viewed it against the glare of his bedside lamp, he thought of what he might use as a moniker (he also thought of how lucky he was to have a single room). Did he go with a slightly embarrassing spinoff of his own name? How about just "P"? Did he dare take up "Pras," who had been a member of the Fugees? He wasn't exactly the most perceptive social animal, but he did know that trying to copy a rapper's coolness was a sure route to embarrassment. When he was in sixth grade, an eighth-grader had given him the name "P-Dawg," and at the time, it had felt good to feel at least slightly gangsta. But that would not hold water now. He needed a man's name.

It killed him that people pronounced Kavita's name just fine. There were some people who couldn't put the soft *t* into her name, making it rhyme with *margarita*, but most people had learned the proper way of delivering the right sound. For the first time, he resented her. How dare she hijack his college experience? How dare she show up with her perfect smile and heaven-made hair and hell-made ass and make him question his own name?

He ran into her at the student center, a utilitarian mass of gray concrete, mauve-painted brick, and wood-varnished tables among striped couches. Unlike many of the other students, who opted for sprawling on those couches, Kavita was perched with great poise at a table, her shoulders hunched and one hand stroking the black magic of her ponytail. Her bearing was unmistakable even when her face wasn't visible. The feeling he had seeing her, alone at this table in the busiest of places on campus, was likely the same feeling he would have had seeing a celebrity at a coffee shop. It was actually not that bad a comparison, for she often had a gaggle of people surrounding her, especially after the announcement of her campaign.

This opportunity in the student center was unique. It provided unobstructed access to her. He felt a slight panic when he realized that, at any given second, someone may approach her and ruin his chance. No worry—he deserved to approach her. If his professors were to be believed, he was a chemical genius. He was going to change the face of chemistry, and he would need a woman with disparate interests to complement his brilliance. He was going to graduate from one of the best schools in the country and get some wildly high-paying job for some enormously grand company and make more money than his parents had ever dreamed of. Why shouldn't he feel compelled to speak to the prettiest girl on campus? He was Bill Gates and Steve Jobs before jowls and unruly facial hair. This was his chance.

She greeted him first. "Prashant! How are you?"

"Good, good," he said, trying to sound calm.

"Can you believe we have only a week till fall break? Everyone always said how fast our time would go here, but this is crazy, man." She was the type of chick who said "man" unironically. He might explode.

"Yeah, it's crazy how fast our time is going here." He sounded like a kid who had been taught to repeat a question when providing its answer.

"You doing anything fun for it?"

"I'm just going to be back at my parents' house. Might see some of my friends from high school. How 'bout you? You doing anything fun?" He was impressed with himself for asking a question.

"Actually, my *masi* in Chicago is very ill, so I'm going to go out there to help her."

Are you fucking kidding me? he thought. Could she be any more perfect? He imagined her in Mother Teresa's blue and white sari, and something stirred below. Great. Blasphemous nun-lust. He was one sick fuck.

"I'm so sorry to hear she's ill. What is the prognosis?"

PROGNOSIS. FOR THE LOVE OF GOD.

"She's not expected to make it, sadly."

"Oh. I'm—I'm so sorry."

"That is so sweet of you, Prashant. I really appreciate it. Would you like to sit down?"

"Um, sure," he said, taking a seat. He had come to the student center for a quick slice of pizza at the food court, but his hunger had vanished. He felt particularly meager next to her, with no backpack while she had an arsenal of books and papers in front of her. "What are you working on?" he asked.

"I have a biology midterm coming up."

"Biology? I thought you were an English major."

The slight widening of her eyes showed him his mistake: How did he know her major?

"Yeah, I'm an English major, but I'm actually thinking of doing a double-major in mol bio." Mol bio = molecular biology. She was double-majoring in English and *biology*? OK, this was just getting cruel. To his surprise, he found himself saying as much:

"OK, now you're just being cruel."

She laughed loudly. Prashant could feel the envy of everyone within a hundred-foot radius, as if it were a collection of poisoned darts shot into his skin.

"Really? A double English and biology major?" he said. "I've never heard of such a thing."

"What can I say? I'm a closet science dork. Don't tell anyone." She whispered this last part jokingly. The tone of her voice alone made him want to confess his undying love for her. She was wearing a white blouse and black sweatpants, and he understood what Shakespeare meant about being a glove against Juliet's cheek. *Oh, that I were a stitch in that blouse, that I might touch Kavita Bansal's boob.*

"Have you gone to any of the SASA meetings?" she asked.

Here it was: the moment of cultural reckoning. SASA stood for the South Asian Student Association, and he knew that Kavita—being the proud Hindu she was—had become an active member in the association. She probably held an office in it already. The truth was, even though many of his best friends in high school had been Indian, he had made the acquaintance of very few Indian kids on campus. Since he was a chemistry major, there were enough South Asian students from which he could choose, but college afforded him the opportunity to wash away his high school life and be socially reborn, so he wanted to choose his cohorts carefully. There were two other students from his high school who had come here, a girl and a guy, but they were both nonstarters. The former was socially mobile in a way that put him off entirely, and the latter was so introverted as to be invisible. That's why the convenience of making friends with his chemistry study group had been welcome. It had taken care of his social structure for him.

"I haven't been to a SASA meeting yet, unfortunately," he said. Then, unbidden, another moment of candor: "Honestly, I'm not sure how excited I am about it."

"Oh?" It was obvious that she found this answer disappointing. He could see the movements of her thoughts, the carefully stitched-together pattern of her compassion. She composed her response and reaction carefully, aware of the need to seem charming and understanding. To Prashant, this moment of being asked about SASA seemed like the few times when he'd been asked by a Christian acquaintance if he had ever considered taking Jesus as his savior.

"I'm not sure if I see the point in joining an Indian group. I've spent plenty of time around Indians."

She laughed again, and the air seemed to refract the vibrancy of her laugh. "Point taken, but I don't know. There's something fulfilling about contributing to the Indian presence here. It adds diversity to the campus in a visible way."

"Yeah, I guess so." He could feel the noncommittal tone of his voice. Although he wasn't lying about his skepticism, he did not like the image that it created. He beheld the mess of books in front of her, the general atmosphere of action and enthusiasm that she represented, and he wanted to be that committed. She would want a guy who was like that.

"Listen to me," she said. "I just said 'Indian presence.' I sound like a complete asshole."

If she said one more charming thing . . .

"Maybe I should stop judging and actually go to a meeting," Prashant replied.

"That would be great. We're having a samosa study break Wednesday night, actually. Who doesn't like free samosas?"

"My mom makes samosas from scratch," he said. "She thinks the frozen ones are cheating."

"So does my mom. I bet my mom's are better." Was she flirting with him? This was exactly the thought that he wasn't supposed to have. If he let himself think that she was flirting with him, then he was assuming that he stood a chance, which he obviously didn't. It was unwise for guys like him to think out of their league. It was inevitable that their tête-à-tête should be interrupted by someone. Sure enough, the interested party here was Juliana Hanson, a long-legged field hockey player whose own face approximated Kavita's in terms of symmetry but who wasn't nice like Kavita. Prashant decided to avoid her snottiness by getting up preemptively and saying that he had to grab a quick bite before finishing a problem set. The words "problem set" seemed to dangle in front of Juliana like a pile of wet garbage, but there was Kavita's trademark charm again, a tilt of the head and a look of mock-hurt in saying good-bye. Prashant gave her a pointed "See you at Samosa Night," and as he headed down the steps toward the food court, he thought of how an otherwise mundane event could contain such possibility.

His mother called him that night. She had been calling more than he'd anticipated. It seemed odd to him that she was the parent who projected an air of neediness. While Prashant was growing up, his father had been undoubtedly the more uptight of the two. Then again, Prashant had begun to notice an increasingly resigned nature to all of the Indian fathers he knew. They seemed to acknowledge that their wives increased in anxiety as they aged, leaving the men to settle into Good Cop mode. He saw the change in his father's personality as if it had taken physical form; even his good-bye as he had left Prashant's dorm room had pricked at Prashant like a needle, an immediate sense that his father's nourishment had come to an end. Prashant was going to study science at this hallowed university, and regardless of the admonitions and odd attempts at wisdom that his father had dispensed through the years, it now seemed that he would leave Prashant to his own devices. (Those attempts at wisdom, by the way, included such gems as "If you get a girl pregnant, your life is kaput" and "Unlike women, mathematics has never broken a man's heart.") In one sense, this was flattering; his father trusted Prashant to make the right decisions. On the other hand, there was something disorienting about being, for the first time, free of his father's intense surveillance.

Now his mother had stepped in to take up the mantle, which surprised him. She had a desire to be eternally, undeniably cool—something that he saw in himself. She had a tendency to hold on to his youth as if it were hers. She was certainly one of the more Americanized aunties in her set of friends, and he had been told numerous times by the other Indian kids, especially girls, how much they liked his mother for this very fact. Her habit of reading mystery novels and keeping up with Anderson Cooper and Bill Maher; the day she had come to pick him up from school and was sucking a Starbucks Frappuccino; her occasional trips to Banana Republic. He wasn't actually sure if these attempts to be cool had to do with (a) the inherent habits of women, (b) the inherent habits of Indian women, or (c) the inherent habits of his mother, but it was clear that she was having some sort of midlife crisis.

At this juncture in his life, it was important to do away with worrying about his parents and what they wanted from him; instead, he would focus on his own worries. Not just his studies but, well, someone like Kavita Bansal. He had told his parents that he wanted distance—and he was, indeed, physically distant from them, hours away from where they lived—and now, feeling the acute pain of what it meant to be totally into someone, he was glad that he had set boundaries ahead of time. He worried that telling his mother about his feelings for Kavita would exacerbate her precarious emotional state.

As of late, his thoughts of Kavita had put him on such high alert that his motor skills were not his own. So when his cell phone rang now, his hand shot out to answer it as if he were under a spell. Before he knew it, his mom's voice was ripe in his ear.

"Hello, *beta*. How is everything?" There was an edginess to her voice on the phone that startled him.

"Good, good. Kind of busy working on a problem set."

"Oh, OK. I just wanted to see how things were going. Your dad is staying late at the office for some faculty gathering."

See: most Indian mothers would have said "faculty function"; "function" was their catchall term for any social event. His mother's use of "gathering," therefore, felt as anomalous as her drinking a Frappuccino.

"Classes are going OK?" she asked. She was doing something while she talked; there was the clattering of a pan and the snap of some taut vegetable. This comforted him. It wasn't like she was sitting in the recliner in the living room with the lights dimmed and some sad Hindi music playing while she dabbed at her eyes.

"Yeah, everything's fine. Just a lot of work." Did he sound as rude as he felt? Guilt had begun to seep into his phone conversations with her, and he felt at once resentful and justified in this. "How's the office?"

He hadn't been upset about his mother's decision to take the job working in that doctor's office, but he did hate having to ask about it. The job seemed, to put it in a snobby way, *beneath* her. A few years ago, he had come upon Manju Auntie, his friend Parul's mother, working the drive-through at Burger King after her husband's death, and the sight of her in that askew visor, to say nothing of her huffing the words "BK Broiler" into a headset, was the most depressing thing that he'd ever seen.

"Oh, the office is the same," she said. "I'm sorry to bother you, *beta*. Just your sad old mother hen checking in." She laughed, but there was an unmistakable sadness to it. God, this was awful. "I'll let you go."

I'll let you go was the most damning of sentences, passive-aggressive and wounded at the same time.

"Sorry that I'm so preoccupied. This homework is just really hard."

"No problem, *beta*. Good luck. Love you."

"Love you, too."

As he hung up and bent back over his work, he wondered if he *could* confide in his mother about Kavita. He had never done such a thing—he had never even dated anyone—so he wasn't sure how his mother would take this. But if she were so invested in seeming hip, she would probably welcome the discussion.

No—he would be a total mama's boy if he did that. He was certain that his friends from high school would do no such thing, and not just because they hadn't really dated anyone, either. Anyway, his mother had no concept of dating. Indians, on the whole, were ignorant of this process. Of course, Americans wrongly assumed that all Indians were the "victims" of arranged marriage—and his parents' marriage had certainly been arranged—but marriages these days weren't so much arranged as urged, like marriages out of F. Scott Fitzgerald or Henry James: a series of social conveniences that capitalized on people's proximity to each other.

He really *was* beginning to think in literary terms; he'd have to file this thought away as a possible topic of conversation with Kavita. After all, it was his duty now to catalog impressive thoughts in order to convince her of his attractiveness.

IT BECAME A RITUAL: Harit and Teddy went to have drinks on Thursday after work, always at TGI Friday's, always in the booth at the back of the restaurant, always with the same hostess and waiter. The waiter was not particularly thrilled with this arrangement, and he had given up speaking to them altogether. He delivered their drinks "as if they were *on flombay*"—another Teddyism—which meant that he spilled a part of the drinks on the table with every visit, and it was a rare evening when Teddy didn't have to take a napkin and sweep up the swirls of liquid before they trickled off the edges. Teddy brought to this action the same sort of flair he had for de-linting suit jackets and wrapping a scarf in tissue, and Harit had to admit in spite of himself that he loved the way Teddy's agile fingers pulled at the napkin and brought it fluttering onto the tabletop like a light bird.

When he drank, Harit began to notice things about Teddy that he had never noticed before. This ran counter to what he had always thought happened to people when they drank; he had always assumed that drinking dulled one's brain and made important details go flying past. But the sugary tartness of the rum heightened his senses, and he saw in Teddy a mixture of pathos and humor. Harit had never been one to laugh easily, but there was so much to laugh about when it came to Teddy. Not laugh at, but about.

Teddy's nose was like a tiny, pink egg on his face. The color of his hair resembled *barfi*—white laced with yellow. His wardrobe was composed entirely of garments from Harriman's, and those garments usually came with piping. More than anything, the funniest thing about Teddy was his shape. With his sizable paunch, he looked exactly like the cash register in the Men's Furnishings department—an old-fashioned register, with a sloped interface and a stout money barrel. In fact, with his full jawline and pudgy chin, Teddy had a head like a miniregister atop the register of his torso. Whenever Harit drank, he imagined Teddy's mouth opening and a tray of bills shooting out.

Their chat in the store was usually a series of fey observations by Teddy about customers, clothes, and coworkers. However, Harit learned a great deal about Teddy during their second outing. Teddy was from somewhere in Ohio but had moved to New York after high school. He had "tried to make it" in the city, the meaning of which Harit didn't fully understand, but from Teddy's mention of "auditions," Harit assumed that it had to do with singing. "Honey, I've lived a million lives. I'm like a cat. But a really feisty cat. I'm Cleocatra." Teddy looked at Harit questioningly. Harit stared in return. "You totally didn't get that joke, did you?"

Harit threw back his head and laughed. He was surprised to realize that it was not the rum making him do this but the fact that he found Teddy's comment genuinely funny.

Humor aside, he found something very strange about Teddy's viewpoint. From the way Teddy talked about his past, it sounded like he should have been a very old man, in his seventies. He reminded Harit of some of the ancestrally English gentlemen in Delhi who had visited the movie theater: just as the carriage of their bodies conveyed something elegant, something pearled in appreciation of the Raj, Teddy moved and spoke as if he came from an older time. Harit tried to imagine Teddy as a boy, but he found it difficult. All Harit could picture was a little American boy in piped clothing and a little cash register paunch, and now it really was the rum that was making him laugh so hard.

"Honey, you are blotto," Teddy said. He supplemented this strange word with a shake of his now-empty glass. He had learned to use gestures so that Harit could understand his slang.

"No, I am not. I know when I am drunk, Teddy. I am fine."

"It's OK if you are, you know. I'm really happy that you're finally living a little."

"This is 'living'?" Harit motioned to the restaurant, its candy-striped tablecloths, baskets of sauce-slathered foods, and the four monstrous flat-screen TVs that sat above the bar.

"You know, you have a point there," Teddy said. "Do you want to go to a bar?"

"There's a bar here. This is a bar."

"No, I mean a proper bar. A good gentlemen's establishment."

"Yes," Harit said. Then he realized that he had actually just said, "No, I can't." Even the rum was not letting him stray.

Though in her sixties, Gital Didi was not, in fact, a *didi*—older sister—but a friend that Harit's mother had made only weeks before Swati's death. They had met at a temple gathering for the holiday of Karva Chauth. Gital Didi lived four blocks away, in a small condo into which she had moved after her husband's death from cancer. She had a son, Kaushal, a medical student in California who rarely came back east to visit. What she was, then, was a woman with plenty of time on her hands, and since the same could be said of Harit's mother—and be the understatement of the year—the two of them were often together. After Swati's death, Gital Didi came to their house at least once a day, and although Harit's mother offered little in the way of conversation—a soft "Yes" here, the occasional thirty-second anecdote about Swati there—Gital Didi did not flag in her commitment.

It was still more conversation than Harit got from his mother.

Gital Didi bathed his mother and fed her, and although Harit had told her that it was his responsibility and that she shouldn't burden herself, she insisted.

"It is not right for a man to do such things," she said, time and again.

"But I am her *son*," Harit would reply.

"*Idli sambar* or *rajma chawal*? I can make either one."

She insisted on cooking at their house. Harit suggested that she make the food at her condo and bring it over, since their kitchen was so meager, but she refused, saying that the aroma of cooking was "essential to the well-being of a Hindustani home." Her comment caused Harit some offense, since *he* cooked in the house, for himself. He knew that the real reason for her persistence was because she wanted to be in their house as much as possible.

Harit was jealous of her. Not because he wanted to do those things for his mother but because he didn't. He wished that he wanted to, so that he could be a good son. He could rationalize his behavior all he wanted—*I am not a very good cook anyway; It is good for Ma to have a friend; I dress in a sari to keep her alive*—but Gital Didi did the things that a son was supposed to do for his mother. American children disrespected their mothers all the time. He saw it every day at Harriman's—young girls contradicting their mothers and scolding them and emphasizing, again and again, how their senses of style were different. Haughty admonitions, annoyed harrumphs, deceptive entreaties—this was what passed for familial devotion in this country. Harit wanted no part of those children's selfish disrespect. Yet every time Gital Didi ignored his request to do chores for his mother, he joined the ranks of those selfish Americans by feeling relieved.

Perhaps he felt indignant because his mother had changed irreversibly and he did not feel that he really knew this woman, this artifact in an armchair. He realized that he would never taste her cooking again, would never know what it was like to see her laughing with abandon or intent. He would never know again what it felt like to have his mother comfort him. All of that was lost, except to his memory, which was beginning to be washed away by alcohol like a steppe by the swishing waters of a river.

He envied Gital Didi this more than anything—that she seemed to understand the woman in the chair. Since she had known Harit's mother for only the past year, Gital Didi could enjoy her company without the barrier of previous memories, like having eaten her *kadhi* in their Delhi kitchen—which always smelled like smoke and coriander—or feeling the roughness of her palms as they washed the back of his neck with milk. Gital Didi did not see in Harit's mother the aborted joy that Harit saw; she saw a friend who would listen to her talk all day. If only things could have been so easy for him.

"Dear, where did you put the register tape?"

Teddy was slapping red markdown stickers onto a stack of waterproof wallets. He was in even higher spirits than usual, which was driving Harit a little crazy. The Harriman's Halloween Sale was approaching, and this was not the time for unflagging optimism. During big sales, Mr. Harriman did away with all pleasantries and transformed his melodious voice to a bark.

Harit was tagging a batch of gingham Van Heusen dress shirts. He was entranced by gingham patterns because they were something that he had seen rarely in India, these pastel blues and pinks and yellows. He could not remember any time he had worn such bold colors there, aside from when everyone would celebrate Holi and douse each other in magenta dye.

The look of approbation in Mr. Harriman's eyes as he approached now made it seem as if he had seen right into Harit's gingham-patterned thoughts.

"Singha, what are you doing?"

"I am tagging these shirts, sir." The answer sounded so basic that Harit struggled to elaborate. "For the sale, sir."

"No, noooo," Mr. Harriman said, rubbing his forehead with one hand. "Those are not the shirts that we need tagged! The Geoffrey Beene shirts are the ones on sale. How many of them have you tagged?"

Harit felt like vomiting. He had already tagged five cases' worth. "I am so sorry, sir. I will fix the problem."

"How many cases, Singha?"

"Sir, I will stay late tonight and make sure they are all fixed."

"Have you gone fucking deaf, Singha? How. Many. Cases?"

Harit would have been paralyzed with fear if he hadn't been so tremblingly nervous. "Five, sir."

"Jesus Fucking Christ. And I bet you still haven't started on the suit markdowns."

Mr. Harriman was right.

"You know, Singha, this is a real disappointment. If I don't see all of these shirts tagged right—and *displayed*—by the end of the shift . . . you'll see what's what."

Harit did not know what this phrase was supposed to mean—"what's what"—but it sounded to him like being fired. He felt the blood pumping in his ears. He looked down at the case of shirts that he was tagging and wanted to burst into tears. Then Teddy came to his side.

"Well, well, someone's in trouble!" Teddy gave Harit's shoulder an encouraging rub. Harit wanted to punch him. But Teddy offered to help fix Harit's mess, and Harit felt guilty for his initial anger. Soon enough, Teddy was plucking an expensive fedora off a rack, placing it on his head, and exclaiming, "I'm an old hat!"

Harit actually knew this phrase, and it was one of those coincidences that seemed divinely orchestrated, a random comment with a memory so firmly attached to it that he could have been living in a film. Old Hat was the name of a hat shop in his neighborhood in Delhi; its owners were a white couple from America. The woman had a face that must have once been pretty but that had been crinkled with time and then sunburned in the Indian climate. She wore hats all of the time, and it was unclear if she did this because it promoted her store or if the store had sprung forth from her penchant for headgear. The hat that she wore most often was wide-brimmed with a sunflower on it, and it stuck out unmistakably amidst the dusty heat of the Karol Bagh district. Her husband was an equally grand individual who sported kurtas but had hair long and braided like his wife's. The couple befriended the shopkeepers to their right and left, both of them tailors. When Harit would pass the shop on his way to work, he would nod at the owners, but they were often preoccupied, chatting with their neighbors. They had moved to India to enjoy their retirement, it was said, but they never seemed to spend their spare time with Indian people. Since they lived above their shop, a string of other white couples would often enter the storefront, with corresponding silhouettes appearing in the second-floor windows moments later. Harit imagined Teddy having two such parents—free spirits with a flair for the dramatic. Harit then imagined what Teddy's attempts at Indian fashion would look like.

It was the image of Teddy in a kurta, leaning on the doorway of Old Hat, that made Harit feel angry. The distinction between Harit, the Indian immigrant, and Teddy, the exaggerated American, was important to maintain, and to conflate the two images was bizarre. Thinking of that doorway made Harit think of the doorway to his house here in America, and thinking of his house here in America made him realize something: aside from repairmen, an American had never set foot in it.

As he continued to set up for the sale, Harit could not stop thinking about this—what an isolated life he led! He had always thought of Teddy as being his only American friend, but now, as he examined his life further, he came to the sad realization that Teddy was his only friend of any kind. The Indians who formed the core of his social interaction—the people he saw at temple, the handful of Indian men who came in when heavier shipments needed unloading—were merely accessories to his life. He was lonelier than the white couple in Delhi, who, though they had a limited circle, had still found people to entertain. How had Harit, in this socially voracious new land, managed to end up more isolated than those two?

That night, Harit tossed in bed, as was his routine now. There were times when he felt that he had forgotten what his body was for. The human body, after all, was made to be useful, to perform. Humans had hands for crafting and, yes, caressing. Private parts for pro-creation, private parts to pleasure and be pleasured. But none of Harit's body parts seemed to play such roles in his life. His hands tagged ties and aligned belts. His mouth muttered single-syllable words, words so slight that they barely qualified as another language. His legs—his legs carried him to the bus that proceeded to do the real carrying.

And his private parts. Even as a very small child, he was aware of the stirring between his legs, the undeniable hardness whenever he came into contact with the firm plane of a floor or a wall. His first wet dream came at the age of thirteen, and he thought at first that he was simply wetting the bed again. A year before, he had eaten beets for the first time and screamed when using the bathroom afterward, thinking that he was bleeding from the inside. His mother, in what was meant to be a helpful tone but which sounded like anger, explained that it had been the vegetables themselves, their red color like that dye squirting from a *pichkari* during Holi. So Harit's first reaction, upon seeing the sticky white liquid on his sheets, was that he had eaten something similarly surprising. Only a year or so later, during a perfunctory lesson on sex education in school, would he learn what had happened to him.

The truth of the matter was that the little he knew about sex was due to—*arré, this was so embarrassing*—due to Kama Sutra images he had seen in books and on dirty playing cards. He hadn't even begun to allow himself to enter the dangerous world of porn—he'd never had a computer, anyway—so his induction into the world of Sexual Being had been a shoddy thing, comprised of masturbatory fumbles during which he envisioned the breasts of Kama Sutra drawings. And to avoid that pathetic fact, he had begun to focus less on what he thought sex was and more on what kind of pleasure his hand against his—*arré, here it was again—lingam* could give him. Sex for him was not defined by what body parts in general were capable of but rather what Harit's right hand could do to Harit's *lingam*. (Also, he assumed that his *lingam* was big but, devoid of real-life experience, he couldn't quite be sure.) He had assumed that he could not be in the brotherhood of man, that he could not be part of something larger than himself. It was too hard to situate himself within that vast throng, so he pared himself down to the act of touching himself. And inevitably, after he was finished focusing on what Harit could do to Harit, he was left with the shame of having done something debased, which seemed all the worse not because he understood it but because he didn't understand it. And it was so much harder to justify doing something if he didn't understand it.

Tossing again in bed, he moved beyond the thought of his loneliness to the thought of love. Had he ever really envisioned a life in which he could find love? He wasn't sure that he was capable of being intimate with anyone. It was one thing to espouse a feeling, an idea of companionship. But it was another thing entirely to imagine a life that was informed by the presence of another person and that person's affection. Had he ever imagined calling his wife to see if she could stop at the grocery store on the way home? Had he ever imagined holding the eyelid-soft crook of her arm as they discussed having children? The horrible conclusion was that he had never thought of what it would be like to negotiate one's physicality to that of another human because he had not thought it possible. Every look in the mirror confirmed this line of thinking for him.

Perhaps this was why pretending to be Swati felt cathartic to him; he could be someone else, someone whole. Of this, his mother could be proud.

FOR THE PAST YEAR, RANJANA had worked as one of two re-
ceptionists in the office of a proctologist. Technically, the term was
"colorectal surgeon," but nobody seemed to say this. The doctor,
being from north India, had a very common last name for that part
of the country, but Ranjana wondered why, oh, why he couldn't
have opted for the less offensive spelling of *Bhatt.* True, the spelling that he had chosen was closer to the actual Indian pronunciation, but how had he come to this country knowing what his
profession would be and *still* chosen to spell it *Butt*?

Dr. Butt was a slight, easily excitable man with a head of tight
curls and almost no chin. He had the type of nasally whine that
seemed to strike Indian men who adopted the timbre of their own
mother's voice. He bore a striking resemblance to the title character of *Fantastic Mr. Fox,* one of the first books that Ranjana had ever
purchased for Prashant. She hadn't noticed this until one day when
her car was in the shop and Prashant had come to pick her up.
Prashant had pointed out the resemblance right away, and it was

something that Ranjana always remembered fondly—a time when she and her son had burst out in laughter together.

Ranjana had found the job through Seema, who had seen it posted in the lobby of her yoga studio. It wasn't financial necessity that had spurred Ranjana to pursue the opportunity. The truth was that she was bored and wanted something to occupy her, especially as Prashant's college years approached. At first, Ranjana applied for the job secretly, without telling Mohan; she knew that he didn't want his wife working, even if they needed the extra money. He was of the firm belief that a working wife indicated weakness and financial instability on the part of her husband, even if that wife were a neurosurgeon like their friend Sateja Datta.

"Poor Raneshwar," Mohan said one evening while slurping his tea. "It is so humiliating that Sateja has to work all of those hours. And she missed Avnish's Ganesh puja the other night— humiliating." Avnish Doshi was one of Mohan's tennis buddies, and Ranjana was friendly with his wife, Manjeet.

"Sateja was operating on an eleven-year-old's brain," Ranjana said. "And she was *successful*." Ranjana didn't mention how it had technically been Manjeet's Ganesh puja, not Avnish's, since Manjeet had done all of the work.

"And what of her own children? They spent Ganesh puja without their ma. What about *their* brains?"

For her interview with Dr. Butt, Ranjana spoke for about five minutes with the other receptionist, Cheryl, who asked whether Ranjana had ever stolen from an employer. Then Dr. Butt gave a short head nod to indicate that she would suffice.

Afterward, Ranjana found herself flipping roti on the stove and wondering how to tell Mohan about her new job. In the adjoining sitting room, Mohan was eating from a TV tray and watching Wimbledon on their flatscreen. Then Ranjana remembered:

Dr. Butt had a gold membership to the racquet club. Gold members could bring a friend to the club whenever they wanted to, free of charge. Only a handful of the Indians, even the wealthier ones, held this distinction, and Mohan would be very interested in joining Dr. Butt's ranks.

"I have some very good news for you, *ji*," Ranjana said.

Mohan didn't say anything but looked up. Ranjana had made *idli sambar*, and Mohan's fingertips were stained brownish green. An uneaten *idli* rested in his right hand.

"I have been offered a receptionist position in Suneel Butt's office."

Mohan had the ability to turn his entire face into a frown. His bushy eyebrows furrowed, threatening to eclipse his eyes. His cheeks dropped; even his nose seemed to elongate. It was some cruel trick of nature that he looked handsomer like this, a thinness restored to his face from years ago.

"Why were you offered this?" he asked.

"Because I applied for it. Seema's friend recommended me."

Already he was sputtering. The *idli* fell back onto his stainless steel plate. He did not care for Seema, obviously. She was too wanton for him, and the only reason why he hadn't threatened to put an end to Ranjana's friendship with her was because he was too lazy. "I do not care what Seema—"

He stopped. Oh, how simple it was to see his face contort into revelation. Ranjana could see the exact workings of his mind: he was making the connection between Seema and Dr. Butt, then making the connection between Dr. Butt and the racket club, then making the connection between the racket club and himself. "Hm. Well."

"And you know this will help with the expenses for Prashant's books," Ranjana said. "The cost for this semester alone was eight hundred dollars. We cannot ignore that." She sighed. She saw that she was going to have to broach the tennis subject directly, to solidify it in his mind. "And you know what? Dr. Butt has a gold membership to the club. I am sure he would welcome the opportunity to treat his receptionist's husband to a match or two from time to time."

The frown was back, the nose stretching. Ranjana understood the inner tennis match of her husband's mind: on the north end of the court, Allowing His Wife to Work and Therefore Signaling Financial Distress to Their Friends; on the south end of the court, Mohan Chaudhury, Suited and Booted, a Truly Golden Boy in the Club. Would his nose keep stretching, a toucan husband? Or would it retract?

"How many hours would you be working?" he asked, his nose shrinking.

Cheryl, Ranjana's coworker, was not very organized. She was a sweet woman, a fact reinforced by how well stocked she kept the candy dish, but she was also that rare, most dangerous thing: a receptionist with a faulty sense of alphabetical order. *J*, *K*, *L*, and *M* were particularly perilous, and she could never figure out if *Mc-* preceded *Mac*. Her disposition was perfect for the job (in a proctologist's office, it was especially necessary to put patients at ease), but even though Cheryl was always ready with a comforting or amusing comment, she made innumerable mistakes that Ranjana always had to correct.

At first, Ranjana wondered why Dr. Butt had even hired Cheryl in the first place. Ranjana found out during lunch one day.

"He got me cheap," Cheryl said at Wendy's. In front of Cheryl sat a Spicy Chicken sandwich, a bloom of rectangular fries, and a

"Biggie" Diet Coke the size of a water tower. With only a modicum of embarrassment, Ranjana loved Wendy's (though she drew the line at a Frosty, which she found creepy in its beige ooziness). Wendy's wasn't as greasy as McDonald's, and Ranjana found their fries to be perfection, as crisp and delicious as food from a cart in Delhi. "Charlie had just lost the job at Chase, and there was no more time for me to keep looking, so I didn't even negotiate." Charlie was Cheryl's husband; he now worked as an assistant manager at Whole Foods.

"Why don't you ask for a raise?" Ranjana said, spearing one of the mandarin oranges in her Asian Salad. She couldn't imagine any instance in which Cheryl could be justified in receiving a raise.

"Can you imagine asking that man for more money? I want to make at least a little more, but instead, here I am." She motioned to the Wendy's, as if it were where they worked.

Despite Cheryl's flightiness, Ranjana was glad not to have a crabby coworker. More important, Ranjana enjoyed the job. In fact, it shocked her sometimes how much she liked being confined in the small square of their cubicle, behind a ledge and sliding window. She never tired of seeing the inquisitive, concerned faces of the patients as they came into her view. She saw them as individual pieces of theater, each with its own story, although it didn't strike her until a few months after working in the office that she was something of a theater piece to the patients, too. Everything in the office was either white or a muted earth tone—beige carpet, beige cabinets, dull silver medical implements, the white puffs of cotton swabs—but Ranjana was deep brown, her black hair streaked with gray.

Today, Ranjana watched as Cheryl put down the wrong date for a patient's hemorrhoid operation. Dr. Butt's directions could not have been clearer: he had come up with the woman's chart and said in his high whine, "Cheryl, please note that Mrs. Wilson will be coming in next Friday for her operation." Ranjana, already on the lookout for errors, saw Cheryl enter the operation into the computer for the following Saturday. Ranjana was all the more incredulous of this mistake because they didn't even do surgeries on Saturdays. Cheryl, oblivious, clicked her bubble gum and went back to filling out her Sudoku.

It was a Wednesday, and the office was in its last appointments of the afternoon. Ranjana was in a depressed mood, still smarting from her writing group the day before. The women hadn't been that critical, but Ranjana knew this about herself: she had a tendency to scrub away anything good in the interest of self-critique. It was like a disinfectant that burned as it cleaned.

Her melancholy vaporized when she looked up to see a very attractive Indian man standing in front of her. He had sweeping black hair and a striking face, with a trace of red in his cheeks and a pink bloom for a mouth. He was wearing a simple black hooded sweatshirt and jeans, but his looks transformed these ordinary garments into high fashion. He was gay, Ranjana could tell. Dr. Butt had a lot of gay patients.

"Morning," he said.

"Good morning, sir," Ranjana said.

"I have a four P.M. appointment with Dr. Butt." He laughed, his shoulders fluttering and his hair moving with them. "Ohmigod, that never gets old."

"You bet your butt it does," said Cheryl from the back of the cubicle. The muffle of her voice meant that she was still nose-down in her Sudoku book.

The patient laughed as he signed in. He sauntered away and plopped himself down next to the magazines. Ranjana waited for it—the disappointment as he flipped through the available selections: *Time*, *Popular Science*, *The Journal of the American Medical Association*, and *Redbook*, the last of which Cheryl had chosen. He tossed them aside and pulled out his phone.

His name was Achyut Bakshi. As Ranjana pulled up his chart, she was shocked to see that he was twenty-two. He looked so much older. Some of the gay men who came to see Dr. Butt seemed to be way beyond their ages. Some of them were HIV-positive, and Ranjana, in spite of herself, still didn't feel entirely comfortable around them. Lately, she had heard Dr. Butt talk of HIV's prevalence in India and how it was spreading wildly there, so Ranjana felt that she was being confronted by it in more ways than one. She didn't worry that she would catch the virus simply by interacting with someone, but it unsettled her that Prashant was close in age to some of the young, positive men who came in. Ranjana tensed slightly as she glanced at Achyut Bakshi's chart and checked his status. He was negative, and she felt awful for having pried—she was supposed to look only at patients' basic information and not their medical details.

Mindy, one of the nurses, came for Achyut's file and called him into an examination room. He hopped up excitedly and went with her. How could he be so happy? It seemed like such a difficult life, full of so many potential problems and fears and cruelties. As a Hindu, she could only assume that Achyut had done something divinely reproachable in his past life. Perhaps he had been straight, an adulterer, and here was his corresponding curse: gay life and a visit to the proctologist's office.

Ranjana wasn't sure if Achyut's fate was better or worse than *working* in a proctologist's office. If it were better, then in her own past life, she may have been the spurned wife of that very adulterer, due for a step up in this life. If it were worse, then perhaps she had been the hussy who had seduced Achyut long ago. From some silky underpinning of her soul, some fantastical longing that she could not position, she felt herself wishing it were the latter. She wanted to be one of the characters in the stories she read and wrote.

Dr. Butt was getting ready to leave the office. Wednesday was the day of the week when he and Mohan played tennis together. Yes, it had happened: faster than Ranjana could have predicted, Mohan had wiggled his way into Dr. Butt's good graces and made himself a regular tennis partner at the racket club. Mohan had the odd distinction of being somewhat lazy off the court but very determined while on it, and Dr. Butt commented frequently on how his own game was improving under Mohan's athletic auspices.

Dr. Butt rushed out the door with his duffel bag and bid Ranjana and Cheryl a quick good-bye.

"I gotta run, too," Cheryl said. She was tucking her Sudoku notebook into her bag, from which sprouted countless gum wrappers and her own copy of *Redbook*. "Do you mind locking up tonight?"

"Sure." Ranjana was debating whether or not to get some quick writing done before she headed home. The end of the workday was peaceful, free of the loud noises that Cheryl made all day—her gabbing, her typing, during which she hit the keys so hard that the noise sounded like hail, her gum chewing, her Sudoku scribbling, the general noises of an oblivious person.

But seeing what a beautiful day it was outside, Ranjana decided that she might as well take advantage of the nice weather and go for a little drive before heading home and doing her writing there.

After making sure that her workstation was powered down, she pulled out her set of keys, stepped outside, and snapped the front door shut. Locking it with a click, she realized that someone was standing right next to her. She flinched.

It was Achyut Bakshi. He was grinning, a newly smoked cigarette still fresh on his breath. In the daylight, he looked even older.

"Mr. Bakshi," Ranjana said, putting a hand to her chest. "Did you forget something?" Even though his demeanor was far from threatening, Ranjana could not shake the general unease of being surprised by a man.

"No, auntie." Ranjana was taken aback that he would call her this. He had skipped professionalism entirely and was on a decidedly friendly basis. "I was wondering if you might want to get a coffee."

Ranjana's voice caught in her throat.

"Or a chai," he said. "Would you like to get a chai?"

She laughed at this, and Achyut chuckled nervously. His nerves made her wonder if she had been mistaken. Perhaps he was not gay. Perhaps he was making a pass at her. She had seen his chart, though; he had checked a box indicating that he had sex with men. Just to be safe, she said, "I'm married, Mr. Bakshi."

"I'm not trying to seduce you, auntie. I just don't have many Indian people in my life right now, and I could use someone to talk to."

Ranjana almost said yes. She looked at this young man and remembered his age: he must be just out of college. She thought of Prashant, and she softened. Then her mind darted to Mohan; she imagined him in his ridiculously high tube socks and too-tight tennis shorts and the determination in his eyes when he lunged for a ball, his tummy jiggling. If he could have his fun afternoon, couldn't she have hers?

No, she couldn't. She could write about doing something daring, but it was much harder to do daring things in real life. "Thank you, Mr. Bakshi," she said, "but I must be getting home." She hurried to her car and drove away as if he had been yelling after her, but in her rearview mirror, he was silent and motionless.

"You don't get out enough, *yaar*," Seema said, placing some pastel-colored sweets on a plate and setting them in front of Ranjana. Seema was growing in health, a fact made evident by her bare arms, which seemed to have been dipped in a fountain of youth: her elbows were like ripe walnuts, the folds of her armpits as smooth as a baby's mouth. "When was the last time you did something for yourself?"

Ranjana wanted to tell her about the encounter with Achyut Bakshi but wasn't sure how to explain it. She worried that Seema would turn it into something vulgar, would suck out all dignity or grace that it might have contained.

"I do my writing," Ranjana said. "What could be more personal than that? I still don't share that with Mohan."

"That's not all you don't share with Mohan, *yaar*," Seema said. She grinned as she broke up a pink, powdery chunk of *barfi* and placed the crumbs on her tongue as if counting them. "When was the last time you had sex?"

"Seema!" Given what she had recently discovered about Mohan, Ranjana did not find this question even remotely funny, even as Seema continued to grin and put more sweet crumbs on her tongue. Ranjana wanted to stand up and storm out, but she knew that Seema would see this only as entertainment and learn nothing from it. "You go too far."

"No one else is home, Ranjana," Seema said. "You can tell me. Don't pretend like you don't think of these things."

" 'These things.' This is one thing, and it would be nice if you respected the privacy of such matters."

"*Arré*, don't act like you visit me to 'respect such matters,' Ranjana. This is what girlfriends do. This is how we keep each other sane." Seema switched into Hindi for this last sentence, an obvious effort to make the conversation respectful, at least linguistically.

"Seema, this is not your yoga class," Ranjana replied back in Hindi. "I am not like those women. You should learn to understand the difference."

"I think you should learn to let out your frustration, Ranjana. I'll tell you what: Satish and I have sex once a week."

"Seema!"

"And not just some preplanned day of the week, like Monday mornings or Wednesdays at midnight or something. We keep track of each other."

Ranjana put her face in her hands.

"Fine, *yaar*, we don't have to go into 'such things' now. But I am simply trying to help."

"How?" Ranjana slurped through her hands. "By reminding me that it's been years since Mohan and I did that?"

"*Years?*"

"Oh, don't act like you didn't know that, Seema," Ranjana said, switching the conversation back into English and dropping her hands back into her lap. "Years. I couldn't tell you the last time we did . . . that."

"It wasn't when Prashant was conceived, was it?"

"Oh, Seema." Ranjana smashed up her own piece of *barfi* and dropped the carnage into her mouth as if downing a fistful of pills.

No, Prashant's conception had not been the last time. But Ranjana was not lying; she did not know the last time that she and Mohan had made love. Ha—*made love*. As if it had ever had that tinge to it. She found the expression horrible and cruel anyway. Making love could not be confined to a bed. You could be reminded by any number of things that you weren't making love, that love wasn't being made. When Mohan grabbed a roti off a plate, a plate that contained rotis of decreasing heat as one went farther down the stack, the stiffness with which he performed this act made no love at all, just carelessness or annoyance. The way in which he slumped in a series of maneuvers, like a beached seal, while turning in his recliner—what sort of love did that make? The bony grip of his fingers on the steering wheel when he was driving, Ranjana's own hands clasped in her lap or massaging her temples—what sort of love did any of this make? They were making excuses— that's what they were making. A marriage was a series of excuses made with your bodies in tragic, taxing collusion.

The thing was, he wasn't a bad man. If he were a bad man, if he made belittling her his primary hobby, she probably would have left years ago. He was still capable of romance, though. It hadn't fled entirely. Sometimes he cooked for her. She'd come home to find him sitting at the kitchen table, a couple of dishes steaming up their glass lids. He didn't make many things, but what he made was good—*aloo gobi*, or egg curry, or even *dosa* (which he made from a mix, and which he filled with his *aloo gobi*, but he got an A for effort). As with most men, there was a get-out-of-jail-free card attached to these offerings. If Mohan cooked for her one month, he was exempted from repeating such a task for the next three months. At one point, Ranjana had sat down with a calendar and tried to figure out if Mohan's advances were cyclical, but she stopped herself, realizing that such an act was both debasing and mean.

To his credit, he did work hard. He got up very early in the morning—which, yes, most Indians did—but his regimen was sound. He would do a series of exacting yoga exercises for about twenty minutes (another reason why he disliked Seema was her willingness to pay an American person to lead her in Indian exercise).

Then he would have his breakfast—two hard-boiled eggs, a cup of tea, a grapefruit, and a handful of cashews. He would spend the rest of his day at the university, teaching and advising, pouring his energy into the minds of inquisitive young chemists.

Fleeing from Seema's invasive questioning, Ranjana decided to do something that she had never done: she drove to the university to sit in on one of Mohan's classes. She had never attempted this because Mohan always said that he wasn't comfortable with her entering his professional arena. Ranjana often humored herself by thinking that the real reason why he said this was because he felt anxious about impressing her. Now, in light of what she knew, she wanted to see if his behavior at school was appropriate. For all she knew, he was flirting horribly with a number of students in his class.

Once she was in the dim auditorium, she saw the main reason why he had advised her against attending: the students were rude, lazy, and defiant. Defiant laziness really was the mark of so many of these American children, and Ranjana prided herself on the fact that Prashant did not exude such disrespect. During Mohan's lecture, as she sat in the dark anonymity of the last row, she witnessed the following acts: at least four students sleeping, one of them snoring; a boy texting frantically on his gigantic phone, which resembled one of Prashant's childhood Transformers; a boy and a girl passing notes to each other incessantly, the occasional kiss sealing their collaboration; a girl knitting a scarf in pink wool, although she took notes every few minutes; and one Indian boy who kept drawing concentric circles in his notebook until Ranjana thought he'd drill a hole through the page, the desk, the wooden floor, and Earth itself. This last culprit was the most heartbreaking: not even an Indian kid was paying attention to her husband's chemistry lecture. What if this kid failed the course? That would be the end of India as an emerging global superpower.

This experience might have instilled ire in many a wife—the public embarrassment of her husband—but Ranjana felt pity for Mohan. Even though she did not understand the particulars of what he was teaching, the chalk equations on the blackboard like scattered rice, she did know that there was an order and intelligence to them. Even though he had been teaching for more than twenty-five years, he seemed to be engrossed in what he was describing. Ranjana had rarely seen him so excited. This both saddened and heartened her. He had his equivalent of her writing: his teaching. She could not begrudge him the satisfaction he felt in exercising this part of himself, yet she couldn't help but feel a sense of loss on her part. Why couldn't Mohan get so excited about her?

She diluted her anger with logic: she couldn't reproach Mohan because she wasn't excited about him, either. Who had started this? Had Mohan's coldness triggered hers? Or was it her unattractiveness that had begun all of this? After all, it was her looks that had fled first, not Mohan's. Mohan had still been attractive before Prashant's birth; he had that thick head of hair, the long, smooth face, and he still smiled. Ranjana had never felt particularly attractive, but then again, such things had not been huge concerns for her before marriage.

Marriage, however, brought out the self-scrutiny. All along, she had thought that having a child would mitigate the tension of being a spouse; you had a child and then focused on giving everything to the child. But as her hips widened, as her hair became courser and started to thread with gray, as her complexion changed with each of Prashant's childhood milestones, she knew that not caring about beauty had been foolish. All that time, she should have been as narcissistic as those girls she had always mocked, the ones who thought themselves important and enjoyed being fawned over, stars like Rekha or Madhuri Dixit or Nargis. She should have been treating her hair and skin as carefully as if they were children. Now, here she was, a grown woman without the experience of beauty. She had not cultivated beauty, so now she lived without it. To Mohan, a man enthralled by science, how could uncultivated beauty—*never* cultivated beauty—ever be as beautiful as a blackboard full of equations?

Achyut Bakshi didn't have another appointment for two weeks, and Ranjana, already guilty that she had looked at his HIV status, forbade herself from checking why he had come to see Dr. Butt in the first place. She didn't tell Cheryl about Achyut, for fear that she would become emotional. Clearly, she didn't have feelings for him; that would have been trite and downright impossible, given their limited interaction. Yet his youth had invigorated her simply by way of its proximity. She could not help but think that his presence might present the opportunity to succeed where she continually failed with Prashant.

After all, her conversations with Prashant were the same, again and again. Yesterday, he had called her on his cell phone as he was walking to the dining hall, and their words to each other were almost exactly what they had been the week before:

"Hi, *beta*."

"Hi, Mom. What's up?"

"Not much. Your dad is taking a nap. How are you?"

"Fine. Just walking to dinner. Had a quiz today in math. Went OK."

"It went OK?"

"Yes. I just said it did." He had adopted a tone of resigned annoyance with her. He sounded like a jaded criminal—answering her questions without conviction or passion.

"How is everything else, *beta*?"

"Fine. Work is good?"

"Never a dull moment," she said. He snickered, either because he found her comment amusing or he pitied the boredom of her job. What did he tell his friends about her work? Did he brush it off, or did he make fun of it? Was Prashant proud of his mother?

"OK, well, I'm at the dining hall, so I'd better go. Tell Dad I said hi."

"I will. Eat well, *beta*."

"Yup. Love you, bye."

At least he always said that he loved her, even if it was always followed with a "bye" in one swift breath. That was not something that she could expect from Mohan, and it was certainly not something that she needed from someone like Achyut. She simply wanted to feel like a woman worthy of attention from someone in the prime of youth. Then she wouldn't feel so detached from everyone, including herself.

Although she hadn't looked at Achyut's chart, she had looked up the date of his next appointment in the computer. Consequently, in spite of herself, she had been looking forward to today for the past two weeks. Like the last time they had met, she lamented the fact that she had to wear scrubs. It wasn't like she had that many fancy outfits, but it would have been nice to wear a blouse and some nice pants, just in case Achyut apologized and asked her to chai, just in case their conversation left the confines of her glassed-in cubicle again. She had spent ten minutes fixing her hair this morning, using an emerald-encrusted butterfly clasp that she had unearthed from an old jewelry box in her closet. She had pulled the

messy poof of her hair in one hand and secured it with the butterfly, anchoring it at the nape of her neck.

Cheryl commented on it as soon as she saw her, of course, calling it "purty." Ranjana hoped that Cheryl would let it drop, lest
Achyut become aware of her efforts when he came in for his appointment. True to character, though, the butterfly grew in intrigue
to Cheryl as the day passed.

"Hey, Dr. B," she said when he surfaced after a particularly long
consult. "Check out this one's hair." She used a vernacular with
Dr. Butt that Ranjana could never have pulled off. Dr. Butt, usually so buttoned up, somehow seemed to find Cheryl amusing, perhaps because her cheerfulness put the patients at ease and made
them fond of coming to his office. "Don't you think it looks nice?
Like a princess."

Ranjana wheeled around and gave Cheryl a death stare.

"Do you have princesses over there in India?" Cheryl asked.

"It looks nice," Dr. Butt said, uncomfortable and clearly eager
to change the subject. "Cheryl, please schedule a follow-up for
Mr. Docker."

Achyut's appointment was at three in the afternoon, which
seemed like an eternity the more that Ranjana waited for it. She
had brought a lunch of two *aloo parathas*, and before noon even arrived, she was unzipping the Ziploc bag and tearing off little bites
that left a thin film of grease on her fingers and spice on her breath.
Aware that she was a mess, she deigned to ask Cheryl if she could
have a piece of gum to get rid of the odor.

Three o'clock came, then ten after three, and Ranjana worried
that Achyut was not going to come at all. He was merely late,
sauntering in just before three fifteen in the same clothes that he
had been wearing last time. If he was as nervous to see Ranjana
as she was to see him, he didn't show it. He was even handsomer

than Ranjana had remembered. She felt ashamed again, mainly because this was a man only a few years older than her own son.

He walked up to her and signed in, his head bent, as if he were actively ignoring her.

Cheryl spoke. "Hey, hon, welcome back." She had been crunching peppermint candies all morning, and Ranjana could smell the sweetness of her breath as it wafted forth. "Did you see what Black Beauty did to her mane?"

Mortifying.

At least the comment made Achyut look up. He examined Ranjana's hair, and his features softened. "Well, look at you," he said.

Ranjana shouldn't have been associating with a patient, but whatever. Without having to ask Achyut, she assumed that they would meet as they had last time—outside after work hours. It was Wednesday again, another evening when Mohan and Dr. Butt had their tennis match, and it was as easy as pie to get Cheryl out the door early. "I'll close up," Ranjana said. Cheryl protested unconvincingly, already picking up her bag to leave as she demurred. As Ranjana turned off the lights—the fluorescent bulbs flickering out as if sighing themselves to sleep—she felt as if their energy were flowing into her body.

They went to Buzzed, a new coffee shop located a couple of blocks from Dr. Butt's office. Ranjana figured that it would be the kind of place that Achyut liked—metallic and full of students and twentysomethings like himself. She hadn't thought enough about how incongruous she would be in such a venue, not until she looked around and saw countless pairs of mascara-ridged eyes staring at her. The wind had somehow picked up during their short walk over, and Ranjana could feel the wispy mass of her hair expanding like the smoke from a volcano. Worse—she was still in her office scrubs, which made her look even wider and less kempt than usual. Achyut shuffled forward, his hands deep in the pockets of his hooded sweatshirt.

"What can I get you?" he asked.

"Tea, of course."

"English Breakfast?"

"What an imperialist!" Ranjana quipped.

Achyut smiled, getting or not getting the joke. "Maybe. No, really—what do you want?"

"Earl Grey. But please go find a seat. This is on me. What do *you* want?"

He made a short sound of disapproval, and Ranjana put up one hand in protest as she dug in her bag for her pocketbook. "Just a regular coffee, black," he said.

As she paid the cashier, she wondered how on earth she had agreed to this. She didn't know this person at all, and he was a patient. She looked around again, then understood the looks that she was seeing on people's faces: they assumed that she was Achyut's mother.

She found him in the one corner that was not near a window, with his hood up and his face even more striking under it.

"So, Mr. Bakshi, what do you want to tell me?"

"Are you really going to keep calling me 'Mr. Bakshi'?"

"Achyut." Simply saying his name made her hot with nervousness. She never addressed Mohan by his name.

He sighed and took a sip of his coffee. Ranjana noticed the flick of heads as people snuck surreptitious glances at him. Even under his hoodie, he commanded attention.

"So, are you a student, Achyut? Recently graduated?"

"Just graduated, yeah. From the University of Pittsburgh."

"What did you—?"

"English. That's always the next question that people ask. And yes, an English degree is just as useless as it ever was."

"You were born here, I take it?" she asked.

"Yes."

"Have you been to India?"

"No."

"Are you interested in going?"

"Of course. I wish I could just fly there and tool around. A buddy of mine did that, but he's rich."

"And what do you do now, Achyut? For work."

"I'm a bartender."

"That must pay well." *Did this sound condescending?*

"It does, actually. So much for my English degree, right?"

"I am sure that people appreciate an educated bartender. You can dispense advice from the works of great writers." She could feel an edge to her voice, something steely yet playful: flirtation. Her knees were together, her feet apart. It was wrong to be here.

"What do you do for fun, auntie?"

"What do you mean?"

"For fun. You don't seem to be having too much fun at work, so you must look for it elsewhere."

"I beg your pardon," she said sarcastically. "Working as a receptionist is *tons* of fun." Achyut laughed, again. She was entertaining him consistently, and it fortified her. "I'll tell you what I do for fun: I try to figure out what Paradise Island is."

Achyut's eyes widened. "Ohmigod, right? What the eff is that place? It's driving my friends crazy."

"Not just your friends, Achyut. It's driving me mad, too. I don't understand what they are attempting to do to us."

"My buddy Eric says they ran out of money, that it was

supposed to be done by now, but they just abandoned it. There's supposed to be all of this development in Cleveland now because New York and L.A. and all of those cities are becoming too expensive. But maybe there isn't as much demand as they're saying."

"What was it supposed to be in the first place? No one seems to know."

"Seriously. Ohmigod, I can't believe you just mentioned that. You're, like, totally awesome, auntie. My friends would effing love you."

Ohmigod. Ranjana had heard Indians using this term all the time, even young immigrants she met at temple or at parties, though the Indians pronounced it with a *t* sound at the end: *Ohmigot*.

"Paradise Island...," Achyut said ruminatively. "Paradise wasn't even an island, was it? Wasn't it a garden? But that's Christianity. I'm a bad Hindu: I don't even know what the version of Paradise is in Hinduism. All I know is that you probably need good karma to get in, and I don't exactly have that."

Achyut's muddled interpretation of these two religions confused Ranjana almost as much as Paradise Island itself. In truth, she wasn't sure what his karma would be. On the one hand, he had to see a proctologist. This meant that he wasn't doing particularly pious things with his body. But as little as Ranjana knew him, she didn't feel that he was ill-intentioned. His attentions to her, though suspect at first, did not feel predatory. If anything, it had been her own prejudices that had transformed his actions into something sinister. She was hardly justified in passing judgment on him anyway, given the books that she read in private and the stories that she attempted to craft. She saw him now as a young man in need of guidance. He needed someone to confirm that his cheery outlook on life was justified, that he could continue to enjoy himself, even if he was dealing with weighty matters. He needed a distraction.

"I'm sure that your karma is just fine," Ranjana offered, not because she knew it for certain but because she felt that this was a time to be affirmative, not judgmental.

"Yeah, but I think that our culture has made it pretty clear that being gay is not all that good for it."

So he had been thinking what she had been thinking. It made her feel all the more guilty for having thought it in the first place.

"Most religions want gays to roast in Hell." He said this matter-of-factly. He leaned forward and blew on his coffee, then slurped up a sip by leaning over it, as a little kid would do. He had the beginnings of a beard, and a couple wayward droplets of coffee shone in it like tiny, amber beads. He was tall, well over six feet, and he resembled one of those plastic birds that Ranjana had bought Prashant years ago, one that flipped forward on the axis of its long legs, its beak sucking up a bit of water. "Don't you think most Hindus want gays to roast in Hell?"

"I wouldn't say that," she said, shuddering at the bluntness of his words. "Our Paradise, so to speak, is not like Christianity's, you know. It's more of a spiritual plane than an actual end point. And just as our Paradise is different, we don't really have what Americans think of as Hell. There is a Hell, but it is more like a judgment in court. People must perform tasks related to the sins that they committed and can earn back their karma. I like to think that no one burns in Hell forever."

"I'm pretty sure my punishment for being gay is going to see Dr. Butt. I love him, but that is one dude that I don't want up there."

Ranjana couldn't help but giggle. She couldn't believe that she was sitting in a café talking about a rectal exam.

"My friends and I were really upset when the Section 377

decision was overturned," Achyut said, referring to the law that had recriminalized gay sex in India. "I think that we all thought that things in India would keep getting better little by little, that all of the changes here in the U.S. would have a positive effect, but I dunno. That also seems like a really naïve way of thinking because we can't just assume that change over here will lead to change over there. We actually have to acknowledge that India doesn't always see the progress over here as a good thing."

Ranjana had heard only vague details about 377 and the ramifications it had for the community that Achyut was talking about. "In all honesty, Achyut, I do not know much about this subject."

"I'm not surprised to hear that," Achyut said, leaning back with his coffee cup in his hand and looking more serious. "It's hard to know how much to care about something like that if you're not gay or know someone who's gay. I'm assuming that you don't have a good gay friend?"

"I have you," Ranjana ventured.

"Yeah, look at us—already discussing Hell. We're fast friends already."

Ranjana laughed again. She could feel herself creating the sound, since she was simultaneously fending off a sense of embarrassment. This shocked and annoyed her. She wanted to be comfortable with befriending a young gay man, in front of other people, in a state of quasi-flirtation, with a hot cup of tea in her hands and adrenaline surging through her body. She was here, after all, and could start enjoying her life more, as Seema had encouraged. The truth was that, like Achyut's karma, her self-doubt had accumulated over many years.

When she was no more than eleven years old, she had told her next-door neighbor Sandeep that she loved him. He was fourteen at the time, already handsome, eyebrows like storm clouds on his burgeoning brow. He had plucked her hand off his shoulder and told her that she was crazy. It was a tiny scar on a knee, the memory of a childhood fall, this sight of Sandeep walking away from her. It was, in truth, the solitary spoil of her love life. As she walked around the fire with Mohan on their wedding day, she still remembered Sandeep, his abandonment. *Abandonment!* So scant was her experience with actual romance that she had seen this tiny infraction as the most damaging of rejections. There was no such thing as a little heartbreak, a tiny loss. Not to a person like her, not to a woman who took desperate pride in clipping a butterfly to her aging hair. Sandeep had moved away a year after his refusal, and she had never seen or heard from him again. Sitting at a coffee table now with Achyut, she saw so little separating that damaging moment and her current anxiety. An attempt to transcend one's physical station in life, she thought, was a futile thing. Perhaps her own karma, too, was volatile.

Achyut must have seen how lost in her thoughts she was because he broke her silence with an exclamation:

"Ohmigod, you know what we should do? Ohmigod."

"What should we do?" Ranjana asked.

"Why talk about Hell when we can go to Paradise?"

With the exception of Prashant, Ranjana had never been the driver while a male companion was in the passenger seat. They parked next to a chain-link fence, beyond which lay the object of their disappointment. It was as unfinished as ever. Ranjana had hoped they'd at least see a tractor, something that hinted at a project in progress, but no, it was the same old piles of rubble and coarse earth. The back of the large wooden sign, its insidious message facing the highway, looked like an instrument of torture.

On the drive over, Ranjana confessed to Achyut that she was in a writing group (he was the only person who knew besides Seema now). The more she talked about her work, the better she felt, but she still couldn't shake the overall feeling of negativity that she associated with it. As she turned off the ignition, Ranjana told Achyut about Cassie's frequent criticisms of everyone's work. Achyut waved this away with one hand like it was the stench of skunk on the highway.

"Please. She sounds like a loser. Look at you: you couldn't possibly be more fabulous, auntie."

"You can call me Ranjana Auntie, Achyut."

"Ranjana Auntie," he said. "What does 'Ranjana' mean, by the way?"

"I don't know."

"You don't know? How can you not know what your name means?"

"What does Achyut mean?"

"'Imperishable.'"

"Well, well. That almost sounds like 'Paradise Island.'"

"I always like to think about how it contains 'Paris.' I really want to go there."

"You've never been?"

"Nope. But I feel like I would just love it there."

"Usually, when I travel to India, my layovers are in Frankfurt or Amsterdam, but I did have a layover in Paris once. I didn't get to leave the airport. I sat in a French McDonald's and had a tea. But sometimes I lie and say I've been there."

"I'd do the same thing. People who've been to France are just cooler."

Ranjana was silent for a moment as she scanned the mess in front of them. "You know, in a way, this is very Indian. I've never really thought of it before, but Delhi is littered with buildings like this—unfinished buildings. Things shoot up there so quickly now. If you walk around the city, you'll see dozens of structures like this, being built, abandoned. Or they're crumbling."

Achyut sighed and pulled down the sun visor in front of him. His face was brightened by twin strips of light. Ranjana could see narrow wrinkles already emphasizing his eyes.

She could feel a confession coming from him; his eyes were still with it.

"I got kicked out of my house. My parents found out."

"That you're . . . gay?" She'd rarely ever said this word aloud, and she felt the *g* catch in her throat before it came out.

"Yeah. 'Gay.' Gay, gay, gay. What a crock of shit."

She was startled by his curse word, even though she'd heard him say others. She had never cursed in this car, and any time that Prashant did so, she pinched his cheek.

"Yeah, so, they kicked me out," Achyut said. "Well, I guess 'kicked out' isn't the right phrase. They told me that I had to change my lifestyle or take it elsewhere. So I'm staying with my friend Amber. She actually doesn't have too bad a place. She works downtown and makes good money. I don't see her all that much because I'm at the bar by the time she comes home from work."

A terrifying thought came to Ranjana: Achyut was going to ask to stay with her. That's what this was all about. He needed a place to stay, and that was why he was befriending her. Legally, it would be a nightmare. She couldn't take in this man without inviting a darker reaction from his family. Not to mention Mohan's reaction at such a thing.

Once again, Achyut read the expression on her face. "Auntie? Ohmigod, no. Ha-ha—no. I am not asking to stay with you."

Until her shoulders melted back into their usual place, Ranjana hadn't noticed that they had been hunched up to her ears. "Oh."

"No—I'm just telling you this. I'm not gonna lie—it's great to have a mother to talk to about this, even if it's someone else's mother. I mean, even though I didn't grow up around you, I might have, in some other world. And even if that doesn't sound like anything . . . it's something. If I'm being honest, that's why I approached you in the first place."

He went on talking about his family and how they had found out about his sexual orientation. His mother had gone through his cell phone while he was asleep, snatching it up while it was not six inches from his head. Worse, it was not a boyfriend whose messages she had read but an older man he had slept with only once. His mother had woken Achyut up, then screamed for his father to join her in questioning him.

His parents ran an insurance company. His younger sister, Vandana—who listened to hard rock music, had pink hair, and seemed generally laid-back—still found his lifestyle abhorrent.

"That was the hardest part. I once lied for her when she was spending the night with her boyfriend, giving up her virginity. I mean, she smokes weed all the time, and she still ratted me out. She knew I was too good a guy to tell on her. I wish I had. Well, I also don't wish that I had because I'm not that type of person."

Ranjana had never thought about the possibility of Prashant's being gay. He was such a typical boy. Would she have turned him out of the house if he were gay? Absolutely not. Your child was your child. Nevertheless, most Indian parents, she knew, would be very upset to have a gay child.

"I am flattered that you told me all of this, Achyut," Ranjana said. "I have to go, though." It was an abrupt response, perhaps, but they had spent over an hour together and the sun had just set.

By the time she drove him back to the coffee shop—where he had left his bike—and drove home, she would have just enough time to put dinner on the stove before Mohan pushed into the house, smelling of fishy sweat and his clothes stuck to his body as if he'd been doused in water.

"No worries," Achyut said. "I'm just glad that we got to have this talk. I know that it's out of the blue and kind of weird, but you don't know how hard it is not to . . ." His voice trailed off, and she saw that he was biting his lip. He looked at her and shrugged. "Just—thank you."

When they got back to the parking lot outside Dr. Butt's office, Achyut hopped out of the car and turned to her. "Can I get your number, auntie?" She stiffened. "No need to worry. I'm not going to call you at some crazy time. I don't even have a phone right now, after my mom took it. I just—can I have it?"

She pulled a pen and tiny notebook out of the glove compartment and wrote her cell number on it. Achyut took it from her and then snickered.

"What?" Ranjana said.

"Nothing. It's just that I think this is the first time that I've ever asked a woman for her number." He shut the door and was gone.

THE SAMOSA STUDY BREAK OCCURRED in the lobby of Whig Hall, a white, classical-looking structure that had an exact twin, Clio Hall, opposite a walkway. Together, Whig-Clio constituted the home of the debate teams and larger political discussions on Princeton's campus. Prashant, generally not interested in political matters, had not set foot in these places, so he was surprised to see that their interiors were rather plain. The presence of the small South Asian student body did not help this effect of shabbiness, and Kavita was made all the more impressive in this setting. In some chameleonic trick, the darkness of her hair and eyes deepened when placed amidst a group of Indian girls. Although she fit seamlessly into the WASP-y hordes around campus—her beauty leveling any racial discrepancy—she could still pass as a proud *desi* woman.

She came up to him almost immediately. At last, a vulnerability: a tiny dab of mint chutney was smeared under her mouth. Prashant felt a small glimmer of power as he pointed it out to her. She grinned and licked gently at her lip, swiping the dab away and laughing the moment off.

"I'm so glad you actually came," she said. "And look—you didn't even have to wear a turban."

"Mine's at the cleaner's," he said.

"Is there an apostrophe in 'cleaner's' in that sentence?" she asked.

"There most certainly is," he said. "You should know that as an English major."

"Ahem," she said.

"Oh, right—an English and *mol bio* major. Par-doe-nay-mwah," he said in mock-French.

"Oh, no, I'm only getting a French certificate, not majoring in it," she said. He hoped that she was kidding but was pretty certain that she wasn't. "Do you know they're offering a Hindi course now?"

He shuddered internally. She was going to ask him about his own proficiency in Hindi, and he would have to admit that he was terrible at it. Sure, he had some conversational basics, but he couldn't watch a Hindi movie with a great level of understanding, and anytime that an Indian person had ever asked him for directions, he had always botched his response.

He decided to head her off at the pass.

"My Hindi isn't exactly great. I did get a five on my AP Spanish exam, though."

One of the girls standing near them heard this sentence and decided to butt in. "You should take the class! Hi, I'm Rashmi." She put out her hand. He shook it and was impressed at the firmness of her handshake. Prashant could see that she was exactly the type of person he wanted to avoid, the overenthusiastic participant who would want him to join a mailing list and a dance group and a community service project. "We had to fight hard to get it recognized by the university, but we now have the class. It's superinformal and easy, so you should come. One hour on Thursday nights."

Any self-respecting student already knew that Thursday night was one of the biggest party nights of the week, since very few upperclassmen had classes on Fridays.

Luckily, Kavita intervened. "Prashant is a chemistry major, so that's a lot of work right there."

Rashmi had the audacity to roll her eyes.

"Let's get you a snack," Kavita said, diffusing the tension. She took Prashant to the large but rickety table that held three tubs of samosas and a mess of spilled chutneys that resembled a Jackson Pollock painting. It was funny to see the few American students eating samosas; instead of pecking at them with their hands and getting their fingers coated in ghostlike potato, they bit into them as if they were exotic fruits. They weren't prepared for how hot they were inside, which caused them to fan their mouths, as if someone had put jalapeños on their tongues.

Prashant loaded up a plate with two fat samosas and a careful but generous serving of the three chutneys—mint, tamarind, and coconut. He thought of his mom's cooking, how she pureed her own chutney, poured it into Tupperware containers, and tucked them into the freezer to be used at odd times of the year. He felt another pang of guilt for his tone with her on the phone the other night.

"So," he said, tucking a piece of samosa into his mouth and trying to seem nonchalant. "How handily do you think you'll win the election?"

She clicked her tongue and swiped the air. "Oh, come on. It's a fair race. Odette's got a great chance, and Richard has a bit of the jock vote." Odette Kim was an extremely affable actress who had been in a few commercials when younger. Richard Bender was a high school basketball hero who was now pursuing a degree in electrical engineering. Odette's flyers featured her face placed onto the Quaker Oats logo—her most high-profile commercial gig—with the phrase "How 'Bout Dem Oats?" Richard's flyers featured a drawing of a basketball with a lightning bolt through it with the phrase "Best of Bolt Worlds." Neither flyer really made any sense.

"It's a totally unfair race," Prashant said. "Face it: everyone loves you."

"Ha," she said, and looked away with an expression that bordered on bitterness. It was shocking to him to see her make such a face. She usually seemed unflappable, incapable of being wounded.

He pressed on, not sure how he had just offended her. "I'm just saying, you are so smart and funny and . . . charming. I'd want a person like that to be my president."

This was embarrassingly earnest, and she reacted accordingly. She made a caring frown, then touched his forearm reassuringly in a way that had become like a lifesaving elixir. "You are so sweet. I appreciate it. I guess I'm just nervous, is all. The thing is," and she leaned in, somewhat comically but also seriously, "I want to win *really badly*."

They both laughed, but he could see that she had an undeniable wish to win. It was the thing that most students at this school had in common. Even though he considered himself more reserved than most guys here, he knew that he still possessed a constant desire to succeed, to be the best in his class, to justify his presence here by collecting impressive accomplishments. It wasn't enough to get into a great school; you had to continually and handily prove that you belonged there more than everyone else. As with most things in his life, he found something very Indian about all of this, but the other students, regardless of background, seemed to believe it just as firmly. Were Indians really more successful than other people, or had that been a lie, a cultural red herring that his parents had used to make him get good grades growing up? He looked now at Kavita Bansal and didn't quite know the answer. She was the ultimate Indian American, but perhaps her success had nothing to do with her ethnicity and everything to do with her unique intelligence.

"The only thing I've ever won are chemistry awards," he said. "And those weren't national or anything. They were just at my high school. Though I did make National Honor Society, of course."

"You know, I didn't," she said. His jaw fell open in genuine shock. "No, really, I didn't. I'm sometimes not the best test-taker. I get nervous."

"You must have done well on your SATs and ACTs and all that," he said.

"Well, yeah."

"You got a perfect score, didn't you?"

"No!" She was obviously lying.

"Swear on this bite of samosa that you didn't get a perfect score on your SATs." He held out his last bit of pastry.

"Fine," she said, rolling her eyes.

Then, the awkward moment that was bound to mar their otherwise great interaction occurred: via the many Indian weddings he had attended, in which newly anointed husbands smeared an inaugural bite of cake on their brides' faces, he assumed that he would feed her this bite. Meanwhile, she thought she would pluck it from his hand and pop it in her mouth. What ensued was their hands colliding, the samosa somersaulting in the air and landing on the ground. Prashant could have sworn that it had made an actual THUD, but that would have been impossible. He bent down to pick the piece off the floor, then stood up with it. For a split second, he thought that she would eat it anyway, which was mental. He placed it back on his plate, then tried to resume the conversation.

It was the type of awkward encounter that not even Kavita Bansal's affability could erase, and the rest of their conversation was stilted. The Hindi class was raised again, he remembered, though there didn't seem to be any firm commentary on it one way or the other. Soon enough, Kavita was off to socialize with others. *To make her rounds.* Prashant lingered by the now-emptied table for a bit, thinking that she may circle back to him or at least give him reassuring nods from her various posts around the room, but it became clear after a certain point that this was not going to happen. He deposited his paper plate in the large gray trash can, a mess of roof-like trays and sewage-like dashes of chutney. He turned and scanned for her once more. He locked eyes with her, but her wave good-bye was perfunctory. When he got back to his room, he buried his face in his pillow.

At least he had gotten some quality time in with her, but he replayed the samosa moment in his mind and kept cringing. The one good thing was that the study break had made him tired, and he fell asleep fully clothed, abstaining from self-flagellation for one night.

He had to give them credit: his parents had more or less heeded his directions not to smother him, so their impending visit was justified. (Less justified: the fact that his parents insisted on driving the seven hours to see him only so that they could have dinner for an evening, then spend another seven hours driving home.) Aside from those awkward phone calls from his mother, Prashant had been relatively free from their inspection. Like some futuristic robot putting up a force field, he had enabled every possible Facebook firewall to prevent his mother from seeing his pictures, even though they weren't particularly damning. There were various snippets of pastel shirts and red Solo cups of beer and the occasional appearance of cleavage and tan legs. Of course, there was also Prashant teetering with drink and the occasional drag or toke. However, the university seemed to transform its bacchanalia into something acceptable and almost bolstering. Prashant had come to see it as a place where people simply got shit done. The difference between students at Princeton and students at party schools, he thought, was that students here got in their partying, doing damage to their brain cells and campus shrubbery in equal part, but the next morning there they were, sprawled over their library books—clean-shaven or ponytails neat—glistening and peppery. This was how he wished to present himself to his parents: glinting and clean and sanitized.

He thanked the Lord yet again that he had no roommate, especially when he saw his parents come bustling in. They examined his room as if they were auditing him, and his mother was, yet again, trying to dress half her age. She had on a loose-fitting pink blouse, tight white slacks, and sandals. Immediately, he noticed that there was something different about her. She had trouble concealing her thoughts—something that he had always seen in her "group of aunties." They assessed each other as if they had a superpower that rendered their faces unreadable, but you couldn't have read their judgments more clearly if they were scribbled across their foreheads with a Sharpie. He remembered seeing Seema Auntie examine his mother's hair across the room, and from the way that Seema Auntie's jaw tugged downward, it was as if someone had actually put the hair in her mouth. Here, in his room, his mother's face bore a smirk, but there was a lightness around her eyes. She seemed content, and for a moment, Prashant was hurt. He had taken some solace in his mother's addled state, the thought that his absence may have caused her pain. Instead, she seemed to be doing just fine. Better than fine. He wondered what was up.

His father sat on his bed while his mother leaned against his desk.

"So, you are keeping up with your studies?" his father asked.

"Yes," Prashant said. "More than keeping up. I'm leading my thermodynamics class."

"Very good, *beta*," his father said, putting both hands in the air, as if in surrender. "I was always very good at that subject."

"Yes, I know, Dad. That's why you told me you would 'hold your head in shame' if I got anything less than an A."

"Well, it's true," his mother said. His father shot her a grumpy look. They had clearly fought about something in the car, but her sunny disposition persisted.

"Have you made some fun friends?" she asked. "Can we meet them?"

"It's a busy time of day, actually. People are usually leaving class right now and studying before dinner." It was five thirty, and he wanted to get them to a restaurant for a quick meal before stuffing them back into the car. He didn't want them to meet any of his fledgling friends—and he certainly wanted as little opportunity as possible for them to come across Kavita Bansal. He could imagine how much his mother would dote on her.

He took them to Zorba's Brother, a Greek diner that was cheap and reliable. He was obsessed with their falafel sandwich, a warm and mushy flavor-bomb that acted as everything from a study snack to a dinner feast. His whole family was vegetarian, so this was a great option: a gathering of slightly spiced vegetables and chickpeas and bread.

"So, Mom, what's new?" he ventured. "You look great."

She brightened at this, pulled a strand of hair behind her ear. "Why, thank you, *beta*. Everything is fine. Work is the same. Been going to temple more often. Are you going to temple here?"

"There's an Indian group that I visit from time to time," he lied. It wasn't like his family was all that religious, but he felt a sudden urge to profess duty to the gods and to his parents.

"What do you discuss?" his father asked. He had taken on that demeanor he usually had when he was enjoying his food: quietude tempered with dipping sauces. *Tzatziki*, baba ganoush, hummus, and hot sauce gleamed joyfully on his plate.

"Oh, just various passages from Gita and all that." Could they tell he was lying? His father's insistent chewing and his mother's small sips of Diet Coke betrayed nothing.

"How is work with you, Dad?" he asked. Perhaps they could connect on some science-related topic, though his father didn't intercede in his studies all that much. People probably assumed that he had been instructed expertly by his father through the years, but he had just been a smart guy who understood math and science easily. The connection between him and his father was osmotic.

"I tell you, some of these students are so lazy," his father said. "All they want is partial credit. No one wants to get everything right. They just want to do the bare minimum and get out." The way his father pronounced "bare minimum"—*beer meeneemoom*—made him sound like some small bird. God, his parents were so weird. Maybe it was seeing them after this short but intense stretch of preppy living that made them seem so peculiar. He felt a quick and delicious sense of having become a full snob. He had been biding his time, waiting to be clear of high school, before he could assert his own snobby tendencies. He was Indian, after all. Although his parents were decidedly more reserved and, frankly, less rich than their friends (a college professor and a receptionist were not, say, an engineer and a doctor), they had been in the company of many wealthy families, and this had taught Prashant what to revere when it came to social superiority. Looking out the window of this restaurant, he saw the Gothic structures and sturdy gates of the university and felt a distance growing between himself and his parents. This riveted him.

To his surprise, they didn't seem all that upset when he told them that he needed to get back to his dorm and start on his homework. His mother still bore that bemused look on her face; his father was already in his PTSD-like post-meal state, quasi-catatonic and rubbing his paunch as if he were keeping a bag of rubies in it. They hugged him good-bye. His father rolled down both front windows as they pulled away, waving one hand out of his window as his mother waved both of hers out of the passenger side. After their departure, he found himself walking past his dorm and in the direction of the Student Center. He really did need to get back to work, but he felt restless and thought that a coffee might do the trick. What he was denying, at least till he was halfway to the building, was that he was inventing tasks around campus in the hope that he would come across Kavita. It was a compact campus, and with the trees lifting themselves regally over his head, the sun now descending and the light in the sky purple and important, he felt the likelihood of running into her was high because there were only so many places she could go. She could be in the library or finishing up food in the dining hall, but the Student Center seemed like the most logical place.

He wasn't sure what he would do once he found her. They still hadn't spoken since the samosa study break, and he had avoided liking any of her posts on Facebook or Instagram because the thought of overstepping his bounds even further was bloodcurdling. He should just turn around now and wait to run into her naturally, but then again, didn't college students stock up on coffee all the time? What was so bad about stopping to get a cup post-dinner? He had to stop second-guessing everything. Girls wanted a guy who was assertive, who made decisions and stuck to them and didn't question his own intentions.

The café in the student center was a dim, oak affair. A row of booths ran across one wall, while an assortment of tables and chairs and a couple of plush couches finished the space. Innocuous pop music played over the stereo, peppered with the occasional R & B song that seemed to restore people's energy. Prashant got in line behind two other students, both in baggy sweats and flip-flops—odd, since it was autumn and therefore chilly outside—and he scanned the room as subtly as he could, finding no trace of Kavita.

He ordered his coffee, then sauntered out of the café. He could feel himself trying to copy the gait of the preppy jock. Those guys felt at ease because they were stars on the field or the court, but he felt that his own proficiency in science should be regarded as equally valuable. He walked around the two main floors of the student center, then took the elevator up to the third floor, which contained another small library and a smattering of tables where people sat hunched over books, with half-eaten granola bars and Nalgene water bottles scattered among them. He had given himself over to the insanity of his hunt now, and he sipped in a leisurely manner as his sneakers plodded over the carpet. People's heads bumped up as he passed—a delinquent in their midst—but he responded with curt head nods and a further scanning of the room. No sight of her. He pictured his parents, small-talking on their car ride home, and he wondered what they would make of this somewhat crazed mission.

Only when he caught his own reflection in one of the long windows did he understand how foolish he was being. He really did have a difficult problem set to finish, and he was probably going to go over it late-night with Charlie. He couldn't let himself get distracted from his studies. If anything, Kavita's accomplishments would demand more studying from him. He tossed his half-full coffee into a trash can, then walked back home through the evening, under lamppost after lamppost, feeling with each step that he was contributing to his own success. He didn't want to be his mother and father eating a rudimentary Mediterranean dinner. He wanted back on the train to status and success, if only so it could deliver him to the girl of his dreams. These dreams may have been recently formed, but he felt committed to them with a newfound sense of adulthood. There was no question that this place was making him feel more adult all-around, and it was not an issue of studies and chemical equations and grades and moving up the social ladder that befit this sentiment. It was more that he felt romantically engaged for the first time in his life. His worries that he would be a loser, a virgin, a sexually frustrated guy forever—they were scattering like leaves off a tree.

HER PARENTS NAMED HER PARVATI not because of the goddess but because it sounded like *parivartana*, the word meaning "change." They needed a change. Her father was a farmer on a flat plane of land with a dozen sullen cows. All of the cows had died the summer of her birth, when the sun was so hot that it looked larger than the face of the person right next to you. A dozen dead cows was the gravest luck—was actually no luck at all. "Bad luck" was a term for something that didn't exist; you either had good fortune or you had none.

They named her Parvati, and everyone imagined Shiva's consort, beautiful and supine on a lotus. But they wanted her to be Shiva himself. Strong and determined, no slave to a field of dead cows.

A neighbor boy, Ashwin, who lived a long field and a mountainous ridge away, gave her a pair of overalls. He took them off himself and was naked. Neither of them thought anything of it, though Parvati had never seen anything like the lazy flop at his waist. She took the cross of cloth onto her body, wore it until it stank of dirt. Her room—small, wooden, a third of her home—was both spacious and oppressive. Sitting on her cot, she painted her toenails red and wanted another girl to admire the job. She practiced kisses against her arm and imagined that her arm looked like her but with long hair.

She led the new cows into their pen while pushing her short hair behind her ears.

At dinner, at their table of five wooden planks, a kerosene lamp quivering on one of its joints, she touched herself in her overalls, in front of her parents, and didn't realize until she was back in her room, when her center shivered, that what she had just experienced was not to be discussed with others yet. She turned on her side and nuzzled her arm.

"What are we going to do to have Parvati meet someone?" her mother said, resting her forehead on her hands. She had given birth to Parvati at fifty, and since she had grown up in Delhi, she knew how strange this was. She had escaped to this farm because of it.

"There's the boy over there," said her father, sipping a frothy cup of milk while nodding to the ridge far away. Her mother kept rubbing her forehead into her hands, and Parvati pulled up the overall straps at her shoulders, ran her tongue under her lower lip, and walked into the field.

Over the ridge, there were other people who would know more, who wouldn't put their heads in their hands but who would put a hand on her shoulder and point to something on a blackboard. She'd seen this in the newspaper. She knew that all of this was temporary. She would be here for a time and then go somewhere else for a time and would end up in America. All she had to do was sip her milk and study the wooden walls of her room and wait for it to happen.

Soon she left the farm and took a job as a seamstress so that she could pay for her schooling. She understood that not everyone behaved the way that she did. They gave her weird looks as they shuffled the *sabji* on their plates and yelled at each other under frenzied ceiling fans. She wore overalls as a matter of course, and men, more so than they did with most women, picked at the cloth on her legs and ran their hands over her stomach. She kept her hair short, and she became so accustomed to the feeling of men's spit against her neck that she couldn't tell it apart from the landing of mosquitoes. When she spoke with other women, she stood with a hand on one hip and a snack in the other and wiped her hands on the front of her clothes when she was finished. They found this distasteful, clicking their tongues and dispersing, but she had seen South Indians who dipped their entire forearms into their plates of food and licked the length of food off with their tongues, so she didn't understand why her behavior was so off-putting.

One day when she was feeling particularly alert during her literature class, she raised her hand six times and answered six different questions assuredly. After class, the teacher sat on her desk and looked at her over the glasses on his nose. His manner was generally mild, but he could be wry and had an annoying habit of overusing the word *perhaps*.

"How is your English so good? Are you a diplomat's daughter, perhaps?"

People wondered this about her often. Her casual appearance read as the arrogance of snobbery.

"No," she replied.

"Then how did you learn?"

She was genuinely surprised by this question, in light of where it was being asked. She held an open palm toward *Ivanhoe*, which they were reading in class. "Through literature."

Her professor sighed through his nose, a grumble crawling up his throat. "That is a very rare thing, you know. For someone, especially a woman, to learn English in such a fashion. And so well."

She had nothing to say to this, not because of shyness but because of spite. She hated this type of attitude. Already, in the scant time that she had been in Delhi, she had seen how little women could become in men's eyes—smaller than men's eyes, smaller than their reflections in men's eyes.

The professor, dyspeptic by her silence, rubbed his stomach. "I think that perhaps you are too advanced for this course. Perhaps you should think of taking one of the graduate courses."

"Perhaps I should," she said, getting up. She heard him stifle a burp as she walked out of the room. Down the hallway she went, to the registrar's office, and demanded to be switched into a graduate course on rhetoric in the work of Kant. She was sitting in it and raising her hand the next day.

She had few friends. She was disconcerted to find that women could be as abrasive to her as men. They poked her in the back and picked at her hair; they often fled a room when she entered it, though she couldn't tell if they did so in jest or out of actual fear. From time to time, she tried to switch her behavior: she would stay silent in class and try to engage others in conversation in the hallways. But group criticism could be startling, its fluctuations as smoothly guided and controlled as a school of fish making a turn. She had never felt trapped. She had always had the mountains over there and the field over there and the sky, big and friendly, but she found it enormously unfair that a place that was intended to expand the mind could become its cage.

As it was, the person to befriend her was a man. He was a teaching assistant in a course on fairy tales—a course that focused on Western tales and made no mention of their frequent basis in

Indian folklore. She wanted to write about this, wanted to give credit to the centuries of countryside storytelling that had traveled continents to reconstitute themselves in the European parlors of *les précieuses* and Charles Perrault. Parvati took an interest in this teaching assistant, who was named Jaideep, though her interest did not feel romantic, only intellectual.

"You have short hair, and I have long hair," he said right after she introduced herself. His hair was straight and shiny like the hair of an East Asian woman, and he wore it in a ponytail. What he did not say, and what was more important, was that he looked almost girlish, while she had the stern countenance of a man. (Not just any man—a taciturn uncle, some guardian of an orphaned ward out of a Dickens novel.)

"You have on a brighter shirt than mine." He did. It was fire orange under a navy blazer.

"One must always be ready to make a colorful impression."

She thought, briefly, that he was going to be one of those people, one of those men, who told her how good her English was. Instead, he said, "Have you chosen your dissertation topic yet?"

She had to inform him that she was, in fact, still an undergraduate. His lips parted at this, the closest he would come, she could see, to showing astonishment.

"Well, then, perhaps I can advise you?" he asked. This time, the word *perhaps* felt earned and natural.

They began to meet in his small office, the darkness of which he tried to mitigate by keeping all of his papers and books in tight order. She would hand her typed pages to him and watch as he read—his ponytail remained still against his back, like some sleeping animal—and she would note that he took her own work much more seriously than he took his own. As his eyes flicked over the pages, she could see that he had decided to make her work his work, that the two of them would find academic solace together. He would finish reading and immediately begin talking, bringing forth a sharpened pencil and drawing out his revisions as if they were a complicated cricket strategy. What stuck with her during these sessions was how her body, the rumblings and pressures of which she felt constantly, disappeared. In its place, her mind became her dominant feature. After a short lifetime of feeling judged physically, this felt like liberation.

Despite the grand differences in their looks, they were still different from everyone else, so they were seen as a couple. This was scandalous, but it was a covert scandal, judged silently and without direct commitment from their usual critics. They didn't quite savor this détente—its very existence was disturbing—but they did take advantage of it, laying claim to study rooms and classrooms and picnic tables when they needed to do work.

Their physicality with each other was effortless. They didn't go so far as to lie down. She did not tuck his hair behind his ear with her thin fingers. Instead, they leaned into books together and touched shoulders. Parvati continued not to feel sexual about him, but she also knew that he was handsome and that, underneath his carefully beautiful presentation, there was a sensual person who knew how to give pleasure.

She spotted him on campus with a younger woman—one of the very women who had subjected her to taunt after taunt. The woman, Prabha, was growing prettier, a stack of books pressed against her breasts like a loved child. Unlike Parvati, she touched his hair, her sari lifting to reveal the smooth beckon of her bare stomach. Finally, Parvati felt a surge of attraction, but toward this woman. Afterward, when she studied with Jaideep, Parvati could smell the change in his body. His overall behavior didn't change with Parvati in any meaningful way, but she found it hard to keep her calm with him. Something about the way he was with Prabha smacked of brutishness, and it reinforced Parvati's own confusion about Prabha's beauty while making her feel jealous of both of them.

"You saw that I am with Prabha, didn't you?" he asked, looking at her intensely in his office, the way that he looked at her writing.

Parvati felt how exaggerated her shrug was. "Yes. She is very pretty."

"You do not seem very happy about this."

"You are very perceptive," she said. They both heard the electric crackle of her tone, and they started giggling. Soon, they were crying against the table, their shoulders shaking against the wood. They were aware more than ever that their great emotional connection was with each other, not with other people. It was a connection of mind-set and demeanor, which seemed more important than one of the body.

They decided that they couldn't explore their lives outside of the college without each other, a wedding of friendship. They got married in her village. Her parents watched, still and wordless, but they prepared what was, for them, a sumptuous feast of *paneer* and roti. Only the four of them were there to eat it. (Although she was not the child of a diplomat, he was, and his parents were in China.) They both got better jobs teaching at Allahabad University, and they lived in an apartment that was hardly bigger than Jaideep's first office had been.

Toward the end of Parvati's dissertation—she was such a fast study that she ended up finishing hers a month before Jaideep finished his—she told him how she had coveted Prabha's curves while still finding Prabha's personality distasteful. Meanwhile, she expected Jaideep to reveal his own desire for men, but he said nothing. Instead, he taught her the word meaning "lesbian." Still, she suspected that there were students of his—eager, expectant—with whom he had occasional dalliances. She did not have a problem with this. Her problem was fulfilling her own desire.

When they eventually had sex, hoping for a child, there was something endearing in having his hair hang into her face like an air-swayed tree. When she became pregnant, she felt her body become something out of the fairy tales that she had studied. Her stomach grew away from her as if striving for a journey. She soldiered into the changes, glad that her body was finally accomplishing something. "Dreams," or "nightmares," would not have been accurate to describe the episodes she had at night. She thought of them as "winds": a wind of the child emerging as a tiger; a wind of its legs pedaling the air; a wind of leaving it in the field behind her parents' house; a wind of the baby looking exactly like her, a grown woman, so she could study her body's angles. She had grown up touching herself and not knowing what it meant, but now she knew what it meant: she loved her body. This was a solution. She didn't need to look outside of herself for ways to fulfill her desire. This baby, what it was doing to her body, was an answer.

She had known a girl named Swati at school who had been part of the teasing throng, so Parvati named her daughter Swati because she wanted to transform the story: she would raise a girl who would not stand aside as others attacked.

She was thrilled when Swati emerged—not a tiger, nor a foundling, nor a mirror of Parvati but a bustling, happy baby.

Swati would not be normal because both of her parents were abnormal. Parvati became obsessed by this; the ecstasy of her pregnancy had given way to the fever of motherhood. She could not situate herself in the fairy tale now: was she the kind mother who saw the kids off to the forest path or the witch who trapped them on it? Within the next year or two, before Harit was born, she realized that not only would she quit her teaching but that she would erase all memory of it. She was terrified that if Swati read her academic writings about fairy tales, Swati would be daunted and fail to cultivate her own personality. Surprisingly, Jaideep did not discourage this. He welcomed it, supporting Parvati and releasing her from her academic studies as easily as he had once engaged her in debate.

As Swati grew, Parvati feared once again that something horrible would befall her daughter. She kept these thoughts private, sewing her terror inside herself. Every crawl of Swati's, every amble, every cheery dance and discovery was an opportunity for Parvati to envision horrible things—a broken arm, a severed foot, a sickeningly thrilling moment in which Swati was consumed in flames until she was nothing but a smoking heap of cooling cinders. Parvati could not share such things with Jaideep, and something between them began to harden. But no matter. Once Harit arrived, she managed to hide her frenzy; in its place was a smooth, even hardness that she was convinced would make her a better parent. Each night, instead of coddling her children, she would lie straight in her bed, which sat next to Jaideep's, and think of how dearly she loved Swati. Harit she loved, but it was her first child, whom she saw as the continuation of her willful youth, that she saw as the effort of her sacrifice. She had vanished her earlier life so that Swati could thrive.

Swati would not know about the small village and the mountains and the field, its rolling sameness, and the snooty professor and the quick leap that Parvati had taken to the higher edges of study, the man with the ponytail and his commanding sensuality. She would not know about what her mother had done to make her life richer, and this would increase Swati's sense of isolation as she grew up.

It was not until Swati was gone that Parvati realized her folly: in trying to allow her daughter the space to become extraordinary, she had given her an entirely ordinary mother. She could not have expected that she would be the one to remain. Her parents had named her after *change*, but she could not have expected that cruelest of all changes, death.

Now she had Harit. Harit, who had always been quiet, who, if he was curious about the world, never told her as much. If she had sewn her grief into herself before, it now grew and filled her up, and she found it impossible to pull herself up and speak to him; a paralysis of sorts had set in. Harit, dear Harit, whom she had named after the color green because that is what she remembered of her field. She heard him coming home late, stumbling, the snacks she could hear him making—flour dumped into a pan of oil, wrappers split open to spill out a clatter of candies or chips. She suspected that he had picked up something of his father, a bend in the wrist and a sway to his walk, and when he first began that startling game of dressing up for her, she could not muster the strength to speak to him, playing along to satisfy the urges that he clearly needed to engage. If he would only come to her with a direct explanation of his feelings, she could explain herself, tell him the many things that she had withheld from him and Swati and even Jaideep, tell him that she had visited the doctor, with Gital, and found that cataracts were not that detrimental and could be treated, that "macular degeneration" was the ailment to truly fear—that she could still see relatively well. But unless he came to her as himself instead of in a disguise, she could not make the effort to speak with him. Her grief needed an equal force to shock it out of its cage.

Meanwhile, Gital had insinuated herself into their home, and Parvati was well aware that Gital had become obsessed with her. One quiet night, Gital lowered herself before Parvati's chair and kissed her cheeks, then her mouth, and a few days later, Parvati lay with her on the couch, Gital touching Parvati's lips with her own soft, lightly wrinkled lips. Gital twisted herself along Parvati's length until she gave a tough but meaningful cry. Parvati then did the same with Gital, though no cry escaped her. No cry *would* escape her. She had given herself up to create something extraordinary, and then that extraordinary thing had died, and she could not muster up more strength after having mourned so thoroughly.

So, she waited.

RANJANA DIDN'T KNOW WHAT SHE was doing with Achyut. She had never behaved like this, her comportment with strangers a longtime matter of tiptoeing and averting her gaze, often from her own image. Interacting with strangers was very much like being a bride: just because it was an occasion for something out of the ordinary didn't mean that it was a time for self-indulgence. There was a larger purpose to it, which was to endure.

Take, for instance, the process of immigration years ago: flying all the way from India to Frankfurt to New York. Mohan's arm wrapped around her back, not her waist, protecting her but moving her along. The weather cold, as she had expected for the winter, but so much rain, a type of rain that she had never felt, which seeped into her sari and coat and deepened their already dark colors. It all felt like an extension of the wedding itself, and Ranjana kept her head down and her center knotted up. She simply had to tolerate getting from one end of the world to the other without losing the unmistakable, ephemeral foundation of her status-as-bride.

When they finally arrived at their family friends' house in Edison, New Jersey, Ranjana had to use three towels to dry herself off, including one of the enormous beach variety. Naked in a cramped child's bedroom, she caught her reflection in a long mirror, stickers clustered at its bottom. The abbreviated wings of her shoulders, her breasts small, as if hung on her frame with a sling, the slim columns of her legs intersecting in a dark cloud. The *mehndi* on her hands and feet had lost none of its scarlet polish. There you had it: she had made it to America. She was a wife, if her hands and feet were any indication. As she pulled on a nightgown that her host had given her, a fluffy white bag with small, pink ribbons festooning its front, she could feel Mohan's arm still fastened around her.

After they moved to the Cleveland area, where Mohan had gotten a job at Case Western, and slowly negotiated their way into an American life, Ranjana learned to reemphasize her shyness when dealing with her white counterparts. Mohan did all of the talking anyway, moving them into their campus housing with little fanfare, everything as he had envisioned it, he claimed. Ranjana became obsessed with the number of reflective surfaces in their home: the toaster, the microwave, even the pearly block of their refrigerator. The bathroom mirror, sectioned trifold in its vanity, the silver disc of a mirror affixed to the shower's tile so that Mohan could see himself shaving. One room, where Ranjana kept her sewing machine and Mohan kept his books, even had a wall covered entirely with mirrors. A mural of a flock of geese, in a yellow-brown hue, was spackled across it, although Ranjana could still catch slivers of her face and her limbs around it. She had never been vain— and she wasn't now, either—but the prevalence of mirrors gave her the chance to examine her appearance. Perhaps she was not as unimpressive as she had always assumed; the only mirror on which she had relied all her life was the collective reflection of her family's gaze. She had one sister and one brother, both older, both now in California, and they had borne the dark eyes and long faces and shiny smiles of her parents. She had dark eyes, but set too widely apart, and her face followed suit, broad and uneven. A smile could not thrive under these circumstances, especially not under the unruly mantle of her hair. All of these deficiencies had been pointed out by the suite of aunties who had taken up roost in her childhood home. They had pecked at her hair and eyebrows, pinched the vulnerable skin at her hips, taken her face in their hands and turned it side to side. Successful in their examinations, they had built Ranjana's self-criticism step by step.

Since they were absent from Ranjana's new American life, she sought the unbiased approval of this mirror-flecked apartment, hopeful yet aware of her naïveté. She did not make a grand discovery; she was every bit as unimpressive as they had indicated. Free of the tribunal of aunties, she began to take grim pleasure in seeing her homeliness anew. Mohan found her one afternoon as she stared at one of her eyes in a teaspoon, holding it to her face as if looking through a monocle. She brought it to the table in a quick thud. She sensed his assessment of her across the table as if it were an aroma; he dipped a dry biscuit into his tea. He must have found her vulnerability much more flavorful than his snack, and he voiced as much to her later in bed.

"I go through all of those papers in that tiny office all day, and I know that I am grading these idiots' homework so that I can come take care of you." Her back was turned to him, the warm silhouette of his body aligned with hers. Through her nightgown, she could feel his arousal and wondered how dissatisfied he would be with the whimpering carnal assembly that she had examined in that mirror. Mohan breathed into her ear, his breath hot, but he fell asleep before she could be expected to do anything. She watched the numbers on the digital clock of their bedside table as they rearranged themselves in glowing red stick figures. If she strained hard enough in the dark, she could make out her reflection in the face of the clock, lined in spare moonlight, the snoring mountain of Mohan's body behind her.

If Mohan hadn't been so lax in observing his wife, if he hadn't settled into his comfortable routine, if he hadn't mistaken the increasing richness of her food as the sign of a spouse's affection, if he hadn't been so busy watching stories about agriculture and cinema on his TV, if he hadn't spent more time scratching partial credit onto his students' papers than he spent focusing his gaze on his wife's nervous tics, if he hadn't been, in a word, *happy* with the way his life flicked from day to day, then perhaps he would have seen his wife transforming. He would have noticed how she spent her free money and time not just on getting her eyebrows waxed, as Indian women had to do, but also on getting her nails done in a nice salon, a task that most Indian women accomplished in the perfumed station of their master bathrooms. Maybe he would have noticed how his wife always seemed to work latest on the nights when he played tennis; maybe he would have noticed how she got up early to make *atta* and *masala* instead of preparing them the night before. Same went for packing his lunch. When he got ready in the morning, Mohan would find Ranjana sitting in front of the TV with her cup of tea, her hair newly washed, and all of her chores already done for the day.

This change occurred over the course of a month. It could not have been more concentrated in its ascent. But Mohan didn't notice such things. If anything, he just assumed that Ranjana had finally put aside the little death that had been Prashant's departure. Now she could behave like herself again. Now he could have the wife he had known when they first came here, one who had no friends and no job and only her husband to eat her food with approval. Perhaps he could cradle her body in bed again.

To be sure, the more that Ranjana recalled their early years in America, the more she saw that Mohan's ideal situation was one of monotony, the status quo when they'd first arrived here. *Everything was just as he had envisioned it.* She had always assumed that he meant that he had prepared himself for the logistical feat of their immigration, sight by sight, signed paper after signed paper. Now she understood. He had envisioned his ideal American life ahead of time and would see to its realization as best he could: mainly sedentary, comfortable with the objects that built its ordinariness— stainless steel dishes of fennel seeds and spices, salt and pepper shakers, oven mitts burned at the tip from handling one hot dish after another. An American life that was as reliable, present, and reinforcing as his recliner. And there in his recliner he sat as Ranjana crafted their meals over the heat of the stove. And felt, by virtue of her after-work Paradise Island forays with Achyut, as lucky and incipient as Prashant, off on the adventure of his college life. She had heard about second acts in life but had never believed in them. Although it was not like Achyut was already a best friend or, certainly not, a lover, it was an exquisite surprise to Ranjana, the idea of youth's desire to engage her, and youth's being entertained in turn.

It felt altogether uncharted to her, for example, to find out if she had a sense of humor. She didn't know if she could be funny; she had never been given the opportunity, not even with her child, who did not seem particularly adept at such things himself. As much as it terrified her to find out that she might have neither wit nor guile, the simple act of exploring this was thrilling. If Mohan hadn't been so rigidly methodical, then perhaps he would have laughed at a joke, just one, and precluded all of this from happening.

It was like one of the stories her cohorts in writing class would have crafted: Mohan going away on a business trip and leaving Ranjana by herself. He had a lecture to give in Minneapolis, a town where they had a few Indian friends who were more than happy to take him in. It was out of the question for Ranjana to accompany him, as the university would pay only for Mohan's travel.

So on a Thursday evening, Mohan drove them to the airport, relinquishing the wheel only when he was properly in possession of his suitcase, his carry-on bag, a crooked fedora, and a light jacket. He waved good-bye to Ranjana while giving a quick admonition about keeping the car in good condition.

As she drove away, moving through the red and white cascade of lights clogging the airport roadways, she felt as if she had, until now, been covered in feathers and was finally molting off their fluffy weight. Dropping Prashant off at college had been heartbreaking because, in reducing her household to just herself and Mohan again, it had represented an entrenchment of her wifely duties. Prashant had hugged her, put his lips to her ear and whispered, "Good luck." This was not meant as a general well-wishing but as a sympathetic gesture. Prashant and Mohan, like any Indian father-son duo, had engaged in many spiteful fights over the years—Mohan's exactitude clashing with Prashant's passivity—and Prashant knew that he was leaving his mother with a more potent version of the behavior he had found so maddening. Ranjana now understood Prashant's relief fully because it was exactly what she felt in this moment. She wanted to go home, brew a pot of tea, put on some old Anup Jalota *bhajans,* and sit at her computer.

Which is almost exactly what she did, except when she reached for the *bhajans,* she espied an old Mukesh tape covered in a compact rectangle of dust. She popped it into their years-old stereo, which Mohan never let her touch—he always asked her what she planned to listen to and then put the cassette in for her, so protective was he of his electronic things, which seemed to have spirits and souls to him—and the music came wafting out in violins, sliding chords falling like sheets onto a bed, then the steady pulse of tabla and flutes, then Mukesh's voice, singing about a young woman and the man she had yet to meet. Ranjana danced a dance that she had learned twenty years ago. She did not know how she remembered the steps, but her body repeated them now. Her feet, soled in the hoarfrost of age, moved in patterns that had last been inscribed into the floor of her childhood home. The world was telling her to go back to that time, before marriage, before motherhood, when anything was possible. She took the bobby pins from her hair, then resumed her dancing, pulling her fingers through that thick mess and imagining that her hair was much longer, straighter, and shinier. When she closed her eyes, she could be every bit the earth-tickling siren she wanted to be, especially with the right soundtrack.

Achyut knew about Mohan's trip, and reliable as ever, he e-mailed Ranjana Friday morning to invite her out for the evening. That is, he invited her to come to the bar where he worked. A group of his friends was getting together that night at a nearby diner and then planned to head to the bar at around 10:00 P.M. Even though Ranjana had now hung out with Achyut several times—more trips to

Paradise Island, random cups of tea at different cafés, even a trip to Panera for cinnamon rolls—Ranjana had never made plans for that late in the evening.

She replied that dinner was out of the question. She could not, in good faith, join a group of his friends in a brightly lit public place and pretend that she belonged among them. No, she would dress up for the evening and meet Achyut at the bar, simply because she wouldn't run the risk of bumping into anyone that she knew. "Don't expect me to drink alcohol," she wrote. "I don't drink and will not make an exception for you." This wasn't entirely true; she had been known to take a sip of wine in rare cases, but she did not have any interest in making this one of those rare cases, especially because she was going to be driving.

If the Indian women in her set had known what she was planning, she would never have been allowed into their confidence again. Even Seema, so progressive, would find a way to spin it into some lurid tale. Like any good bevy of Indians, they passed judgment on everything, from the way in which a woman wrapped her sari to the type of napkins that she provided at dinner parties. They were all subjected to the sort of intense scrutiny that defined murder trials, purchasing a home, or sizing up jewelry. The most talked-about social occurrence in all their years had been when Sonya Mehta, a former model whose likeness had been used as the logo for a film company in Bombay, had told them about one of her dreams.

"In my dream, I was on a bicycle," she said, stroking her sari where it was draped off her shoulder. She was wearing a dozen gold bangles on each arm, and the wide plane of her forehead seemed to glimmer. "I was in Delhi passing through a market and saw a tomato stand. There was a shopkeeper placing the final tomato on top of a stack, but when he saw me, he fell forward and knocked over the whole stand. It was only then that I realized I was naked! I was naked and riding a bicycle through town!" She was giggling, pressing one hand to her mouth, as if stifling a sin, her nails spackled in magenta. No one in the circle echoed her laughter. The subject changed immediately to the amount of homework that all of their children had. Sonya stayed and sipped her tea quietly, giggling periodically so as to bring the story back into discussion, but the group had already erected a wall of disapproval around her. Fifteen minutes later, she was getting up to use the restroom, leaving behind, with a model's uncanny grace, an air of being above her companions and worthy of their biting criticism. Naturally, it was all anyone could discuss for weeks afterward; Sonya's "naked story" was recapitulated in countless phone conversations and e-mails. Seema, who had been in the kitchen during that particular conversation, was obsessed with hearing an account of the incident. Soon, she was cracking jokes about it to the other women as if she had been there all along.

Ranjana shuddered to think what would happen if someone caught her going to a *bar*, and at ten o'clock at night. If she thought about it, she wasn't sure she had ever been in a bar. She had been in restaurants that had bars in them, but she had never gone to a separate space, certainly not with the intent of imbibing. None of the women in her circle drank, not even Seema. Prashant drank, she knew, but it had never impaired his judgment or, more important, his grades. Mohan had a couple of drinks when he and the other men met at their Saturday parties, but if he were ever drunk, he didn't show it. Although many of the men nursed their Johnnie Walker throughout the evening, Mohan opted for Budweiser, drinking it out of a tall can on which America's red, white, and blue were repurposed into a florid design. Mohan's breath, exiting his nostrils in the quiet car ride home, would waft over to Ranjana, the smell steely and yeasty, like stale chapatis.

Fretting over her Indian group would just ruin the night, so Ranjana tried to push it out of her mind. She had enough to worry about just getting ready for the evening and socializing with Achyut in a group setting. Speaking to him at a bar, while he flitted from customer to customer, was the exact opposite of whispering to him across a car, next to Paradise Island, as it lay slumbering in yet-to-be-ruined ruins.

To manage her stress, she cleaned her closet for the first time in two years. (Before beginning this process, she broke down and flipped frantically through Mohan's shirts, sniffing them to see if they smelled of someone else's perfume and shaking their fabric to see if any stowaway hairs fell off of them. Only after finding nothing objectionable or actionable did she begin her closet-cleaning in earnest.) She took everything out and laid it on the carpeted floor of the master bedroom, then put it all back in relatively neat order after paring her choices down to four outfits. None of them was Indian; she knew that she could never get away with wearing a sari or even a *salwar kameez* in a bar. Any depiction of a bar that she had seen always involved a crowd of men and women swaddled in tight clothing and a variety of hats—baseball and cowboy. Prashant had given her a pair of blue jeans last year during Christmas (at his behest, they celebrated the holiday every year with a plastic tree that they assembled out of a kit), but she had never worn them, not just because she found jeans crude but also because she didn't think she could fit her thighs into them. If she wore the jeans, she could wear a blouse on top, as well as some nice earrings, her wedding ring, and some bangles. She pulled the jeans off the bed and spread them across the front of her body, the denim barely wider than her hips.

Achyut worked at a bar called FB, which Ranjana understood to be an abbreviation of Facebook. The bar was located much closer to Ranjana's house than she had imagined. Her sense of propriety had placed it on the other side of town, but in reality, it was only four miles from her house, on a harelip road just off the exit that she took every day. She arrived ten minutes early and waited in her car, glad that the bar was tucked away behind a batch of trees and a high metal shoulder that shielded it from the highway. The parking lot was not brightly lit, and the bar itself was covered in small, red lightbulbs, like a demonic Christmas tree. A burly white man, a stool next to him, stood guard at the door. Ranjana had never shown her ID to anyone other than the bank or an airline. To kill some time, she pulled out her pocketbook and extracted her driver's license from one of its dank plastic windows. Part of the print came off on the plastic as she pulled, and she was worried at first that this had rendered it illegible. Thankfully, most of the ink remained, and anyway, it wasn't as if the man at the door would be looking at anything besides her hideous picture. She had opted to keep the same one throughout the years, and she didn't know if the distortion of the photograph made her look better or worse. The obvious mess of hair, the separation of her eyes exaggerated by a slight ripple in the picture's surface, the maroon background making the flash-brightened pallor of her skin all the starker—this photo was either a reinforcement of her appearance or a mockery of it.

Ten minutes later, when she walked up to the man and presented her license to him, he looked at the picture and Ranjana in quick succession, then let her through without a blink. To Ranjana, this meant that the picture was, sadly, a likeness.

She couldn't have been more ill-prepared if she had walked into a spaceship. That was exactly what the place resembled with its slab of a bar, behind which hovered an intricate chandelier of glasses, bottles of alcohol, and vases. It was as shiny as chrome, an evenly spaced collection of red-cushioned stools huddled next to it. On the ceiling, light fixtures with rainbow-colored bulbs rotated frantically. The brilliant offal of their lights moved in healthy riot on the floor, then crawled up the rippling bodies of people in the bar. In a booth above and beyond the crowd, a DJ held one hand to his ear and moved the other in a seductive beckon to the crowd. Ranjana was bumped to the side by a man who was being supported by two young companions; the cologned grit of their bodies filled her nose. She spotted a woman with bouffant hair, then realized that the person was too big to be a woman. She reexamined the men who had just passed her and knew that she would find similar clusters throughout the bar. Achyut had neglected to tell her what sort of place this was, and she vowed to have one cup of soda before making her exit.

Achyut's outfit of a hooded sweatshirt and jeans had become as expected to Ranjana as his thick black hair and the thin slice of his grin. So to find him bare-armed, his hair alive with product, was as surprising to her as the bar itself. His arms looked like Ranveer Singh's in a Bollywood movie. Her reservations about befriending him skyrocketed. She had never been in the presence of someone who had the universal allure he had; men leaned on the bar invitingly, Achyut the nexus of a carousel and they his painted horses. A black light hung over the bar, and when Achyut smiled—as he did at every guest—his mouth erupted in neon purple. Ranjana waited for two men in front of her to finish ordering so that she could lean over the bar and catch his attention. Both of the men were wearing tank tops, their arms as chiseled as Achyut's. As they ordered, she noticed that their arms brushed against each other incessantly, and neither man made an effort to stop this from happening. Then the man on the right reached around and placed his hand in the waistband of his companion's pants. Ranjana looked away, saw two men kissing, and decided that the waistband marauders were the more desirable sight.

The men in front of her finally walked away, and Ranjana charged to the bar, determined to catch Achyut's attention, to bid adieu, and to leave straightaway. He didn't notice her for at first; he was busy crafting a bundle of drinks in tiny glasses, hooking a tiny lime wedge in each. A lithe gentleman gathered them all in his hands, clasping his chin over them and grinning at Achyut. A companion of his swirled a twenty-dollar bill down to the bar for Achyut, and Achyut brought his hands together in a *Namaste*. Looking up, Achyut finally spotted her, his mouth gleaming once more.

"I'm so glad you came!" he said, leaning over and hugging her, which he'd never done before. "Did you meet the gang?"

"I didn't realize there was a gang. But Achyut—"

"They're right here. Oh, wait—just let me help this guy and then I'll introduce you."

Ranjana wanted to leave without waiting for him to come back, but her curiosity about his friends was too strong. Within five minutes, Achyut was back in front of her, pointing to the end of the bar, where a motley group was standing.

One of Achyut's friends was named Jesse, and he was as tall as Achyut, just as good-looking, with chocolate brown hair, dressed almost the same. Another was Tyler, baby-faced and wearing a navy blue T-shirt so tight that it seemed of a piece with his large arm tattoos. Sean was a short yet burly man from Ireland, about

Ranjana's height, which made his proximity to her all the more awkward.

Then there was the pair of girls with them. Amber, Achyut's roommate, had a dried cactus of dreadlocks atop her head and a generously exposed bosom that Ranjana could hardly ignore. Charity was the other girl, a platinum blonde and wearing a black turtleneck, paisley skirt, and an assortment of silver rings.

Ranjana hoped that the collective personality of these friends was an assortment of wit and intelligence that would redeem this visual madness. She thought of her own acquaintances. Even though Achyut was Indian, would her friends have put him off the way that Amber's fungus-like hairstyle repelled Ranjana?

An encounter like this was proof: this experiment in culture, this gesture in the direction of assimilation, was doomed. You could not reconcile these two spheres of being. In the past few decades, this country had tried to instill a feeling of progress in not just Indian people but also in people of all colors. We were supposed to feel united, all of our children starting from the same place, where cultures melted into each other, yet the divide between Eastern ethnicity and this American setting was greater than ever.

Example: The wide, hairy expanse of Mohan's chest and his round belly, so unlike Achyut's broad, hairless torso and his sculpted arms.

Example: A stainless steel pot filling up with milky tea in the linoleum haven of your kitchen while, next door, someone was making a kale smoothie.

Example: Seema telling a traffic cop once that she didn't understand how the speed limit worked, feigning ignorance until he ripped up the ticket and sent her on her way.

Example: Prashant's third-grade teacher, convinced that he had cheated on a math test because he had gotten a perfect score.

Like the lime-skinned ghosts of sci-fi movies, Indian people existed outside the normal landscape of America. Ranjana thought of all of this as Amber approached her.

"It is so good to meet you!" Amber said, pressing Ranjana against her bosom. Charity placed one hand on Ranjana's shoulder and squeezed. Jesse deepened his hands into his pockets, just like Achyut always did; Ranjana wondered if this was a sign that they were boyfriends. Tyler shook Ranjana's hand, his paw rough and meaty. Sean was easily excitable, and he began a long monologue on how many Indian people were in Dublin now.

"There are a lot of Eastern Europeans, too, lots of Czechs, but I love the Indians the best. They're so polite, and the food is so good." His accent had a way of scattering his voice in many directions at once.

"Ugh, I've never cared for Indian food all that much. Curry is gross," Amber said, oblivious to how offensive this sounded.

"Nice purse, Amber," Charity said. Ranjana looked but didn't see any purse on Amber's shoulder. "I meant 'personality,'" Charity pointed out, noticing Ranjana's expression. "We abbreviate everything."

"Ah, yes," Ranjana said. "My son does that a lot. Everything is an abbreviation. Like this bar—'FB.' He uses that phrase all the time."

Jesse laughed, an extended hiccup. Amber threw her head back and cackled, like a potted plant come to horrifying life. Charity put her hand out and squeezed Ranjana's shoulder again; if Charity didn't watch it, Ranjana would scratch her hand off with her newly manicured nails. Tyler shook his head and took a sip of his clear, condensation-pimpled drink.

"Um, I don't think that means what you think it means," Sean said.

"It means Facebook, no?"

"No, no, not Facebook."

"Then what?"

"FUCK BUDDY," Amber shouted through her giggles.

Ranjana's head throbbed with shock.

Achyut chose this moment to interrupt. "Hey, what can I get you, Ranjana?" He had dropped "Auntie" from her name.

"I actually have to get going. I'm not feeling that well."

"Oh, Ranjana, I know a lie when I hear one. Do you have a problem with the bar? I didn't mention it was a gay bar, did I?"

"No, you didn't."

"Do you have a problem with gay bars?" Amber asked, and now Ranjana saw why she was being so aggressive: in some crazy way, she saw Ranjana as competition. Why on earth a woman of her stature and outlook and general spirit would feel threatened by Ranjana, who was so out of her element among these tank-topped musclemen, was an enigma.

"No—I. I've just never been in one. And—well, just look at this place. Look at me. Some of the men in here are wearing more jewelry than I am." She paused. "But mine's nicer."

Everyone laughed, and Ranjana softened a bit.

"Stay, Ranjana," Achyut said. "Please. This is the least threatening place for women. Nobody's going to hit on you."

It hadn't even occurred to Ranjana that someone might try to hit on her. She had never been hit on before; the closest she had come to flirtation had been with Achyut, and that hadn't been flirtation.

So Ranjana stayed, and ordered a Sprite, sniffing it first to make sure that it didn't contain alcohol, and stayed as quiet as she could, and grew truly antagonistic toward Amber's chest, which she would have burned with a torch if one were within reach, and held her drink on whichever side Charity was standing so that she didn't have to endure the shoulder squeeze again, and grew to pity Jesse for his reticence, and felt the beat of the music through her soles, as if the floor were dancing on her feet instead of the other way around, and saw a connection between the spastic moves of these dancing gay men and the ways in which *desi* teenagers threw up their hands and scalloped their bodies during bhangra, and wondered what her behavior might have been if she were drinking alcohol because now she was on the dance floor, trying to bob to the music and not look like a total lunatic.

Jesse had fluid feet that accented the length of his body. Sean and Charity danced close enough to be a straight couple. Tyler stood against the wall. Amber danced with complete abandon alongside two handsome strangers. This wasn't exactly fun, but it wasn't a chore, either. In fact, maybe this was fun. Ranjana hadn't defined humor until now, so perhaps her concept of fun needed similar renovation.

All the while, Achyut was back behind the bar. Every time she looked at him, a customer had an arm around his neck or trending that way. He looked truly happy. His parents had thrown him out of the house, but he had been reclaimed by the men in this room. The bar, in essence, was a loving foster home, and she understood why he wanted her here—to cement that metaphor. She had been so busy thinking about why this was not a place for her that she had forgotten the true purpose of this friendship, which was to mother and mend him.

After an hour of nonstop movement, she managed to extricate herself from the group and make her way to the bar. By this point, sweat was an outfit. Her hair probably looked as big as Amber's now. Another Sprite was in order. She hoped for a moment of peace while she waited for Achyut, but this was not to be. A tall, amply round gentleman, whose age she could not guess in the dim, sidled up to her and took one of her hands in his.

"I do believe you're the most darling thing I've seen," he said.

Oh, god, she was defying the odds and getting hit on after all. Then she noticed how smooth his hands were, smoother than hers, and surmised correctly that she had nothing to fear.

"Thank you," she said, averting her gaze and trying to catch Achyut's attention. As strange as the situation was, the smoothness of his hands was certainly out of the ordinary, and she began to stretch her eyes back to him, giving in to the inevitable conversation.

"How did a lovely Indian woman like yourself end up in a place like this?" She could smell a sweetness on his breath that was more like candy than alcohol. The wrinkles around his eyes were kind, and it occurred to her that his age was much closer to hers than it was to that of the other people in this bar. He was, then, a possible confidant.

"I—came to visit the bartender," she said. A better explanation didn't come to her, and she felt in this moment the pathos of her evening, the tenuous correlation between herself and the glistening man who had invited her.

The gentleman sucked in through his teeth, as if impressed, but his pudgy face contorted at the same time into a look of exasperation. "Atch-yoot. How did you come to know that genteel Om?"

She smiled at this baffling phrase and didn't know how to respond. Shrugging, she looked back in Achyut's direction. The man's grip on her hands tightened.

"I'm Teddy," he said, with meaning. His eyes flashed with some hidden agenda. "I know someone that I'd really like you to meet."

And this is how Ranjana came to know Harit.

IN THE MIDST OF HIS COLLEGE LIFE, Prashant could not help but recall the fumbling of his high school years: a succession of forming crushes and being crushed, then finding new crushes. He came to understand that a guy like him—most guys, in fact—lived in a world of soiled sheets, soiled tissues, and damaged egos. The ones that didn't were obvious winners, guys who excelled at sports or who had been blessed with heads of hair that belonged in J.Crew catalogs and who could attract real girls to fulfill their desires. Eventually, he and his Indian friends had to admit that if they were going to make it with anybody in high school, they were going to have to aim for a one-off encounter with an Indian girl.

This girl could not be one of their district but someone removed, an interloper whose school system didn't intersect with theirs. If the girl's family appeared only rarely at their regular gatherings, then the threat of retribution (should the situation prove a failure) was not as much of a danger. Therefore, blasphemously enough, he began to think that a "function" during Diwali or Holi would make the best opportunity. Typically, these took place at a nearby community college, bringing together different Indian families from various parts of the state. These functions featured an assortment of "performances"—mostly dances by girls decked out in saris and *dupattas* and lots of makeup. For a situation that was far from ideal, this was as ideal as it got.

A few of the performances included boys. Prashant had been blessedly freed from the responsibility of performing a long time ago, but a couple of his friends—chiefly, Sanjay and Gaurav—still got badgered by their mothers into joining a dance number. Prashant always took pleasure in seeing his friends flinch as one auntie or another applied makeup or an extra sash to his costume. At the same time, it was perhaps more of a punishment to be in the audience, sandwiched between his parents and forced to watch every act. They were excruciating, the countless dances, the same moves—and often the same songs—used again and again. If insanity were truly doing the same thing over and over again and expecting a different result, then en masse Indians represented the most dangerous of psychotics.

A Holi function held during his sophomore year of high school: after about four hours of pounding feet, slapping hands, clacking sticks, feeble applause, and the audience's constant talking, Prashant emerged from the auditorium with almost his whole body asleep. The one part that wasn't asleep—never, in fact, seemed to rest— was looking forward to this after-performance respite, when it might actually find some release. Prashant found an inconspicuous bathroom on the other end of the building and rubbed one out in a stall.

Afterward, he went to the lobby, where a huge buffet had been erected. Gaggles of Indians cut each other in line just to get a plateful of food, after which they would go off to some corner to gossip with people they saw only twice a year. Prashant found his crew easily enough. Sanjay and Gaurav had already doffed their head-dresses and sashes but still wore kurtas and half-erased eyeliner. None of the guys had the energy to chide them for their girly attire today; the river of punch lines seemed to have run dry.

"I'm so not in the mood for this shitty food today," Sanjay said. "Who wants to make a Chipotle run?"

There was never a time when they didn't want to make a Chipotle run, so fifteen minutes later, they were huddled around a stainless steel table at that establishment, their mouths gnashing at dripping, lettuce-laced burritos that took Sanjay's and Gaurav's lipstick off better than any napkin or tissue. They knew that their mothers would be furious if they found out that they'd ditched the *prasad* for this place, but there was something about the camaraderie of fast food that fused them together way more than any shoddy religious get-together.

"See anyone promising?" Vipul asked. His family was strictly vegetarian, but in recent months, he had introduced meat into his diet, like a *desi* version of taking up smoking. A string of pulled pork dangled from his burrito like crushed sinew from a giant's mouth.

"Did you see that girl Sandhya?" Sanjay asked.

"Totally," said Gaurav. "She is ridiculous. She doesn't even look Indian."

"I know—that's hot," said Vipul.

"Do we know anyone who knows her?" Prashant asked. He had definitely noticed her. She was a passable dancer onstage, but it was actually her indifference toward dancing that made her so attractive. She seemed like the kind of pretty girl who impressed parents but who probably lit up a joint from time to time and could hang just fine with the guys.

Vipul confirmed this. "I heard that she parties with some of those douche bags—Nikhil, Avinash, Roshan. I think she sticks around for the weed."

"Who's got some, by the way?" Gaurav asked. He was still wearing his kurta, as was Sanjay, and Prashant felt embarrassed sitting with them. There were now so many Indians in their area that kurtas and *salwars* were pretty standard sights, but Prashant still felt odd sitting with two guys whose pajama bottoms were so tight that their junk was visible.

"I'm out," Vipul said. "Smoked the last bit I had two nights ago. I could call Chalaak." Chalaak, whose name meant "cunning" in Hindi, was their dealer, a rare Indian high school dropout who dated white girls exclusively even though he insisted on blasting bhangra music. He worked part-time at an Indian video store to put on a convincing front, but he made thousands of dollars by supplying people like Vipul with steady fixes. Thankfully, Prashant knew another one of Chalaak's customers: Gori, Seema Auntie and Satish Uncle's daughter.

"Gori's always packing," Prashant said. "I saw her sitting by herself in the auditorium, totally baked out of her mind. She'll probably cough it up for us easily enough."

This all seemed perfectly logical to them: exhorting the drug services of one girl at a religious function so that they could impress another drug-inclined girl in attendance. They found Gori soon thereafter, seated in the same place where Prashant had seen her. She was a chill girl, barely interested in anything but pot, and there was a laid-back inflection to everything she said. Most of the guys suspected that she was a lesbian, but Prashant somehow knew that this wasn't the case. His friends just couldn't accept the fact that a girl like this didn't find them attractive. Prashant assumed that she had some good-looking guy of indeterminate ethnic background whom she hung out with when she wasn't at home.

"Yo, Gori," Prashant said as he slid next to her in the auditorium. There was a tabla-and-harmonium duo performing for the lunchtime crowd. "You packing?"

Gori snickered. "I'm doing just fine, thanks. How are you?"

"Sorry," Prashant said. "Sorry. How are you doing?"

"I'm just fucking with you," Gori said. Her voice was deep, gravelly, and she was twisting a tangle of her hair between two fingers. She was clad almost exclusively in sweats; her parents had clearly given up the idea of getting her into traditional garb for events like this. "Here you go," she said, producing a long cylinder in which religious incense was normally kept.

"Really?" Prashant said, mocking her choice of transport.

"Hey, this is as religious as I get. You want it or not?"

And so that afternoon found Prashant and the gang loitering against the wide brick wall of the community college with a joint. Naturally, once they were high, all they could wonder was what would horrify their parents more—getting high or attending community college. Then the conversation turned to where they wanted to go to college—even though they were only sophomores—and then, finally, they seemed to remember, as if it were a ribbon tied around their fingers, that Sandya, the hot girl, was the project of the day. Since Prashant had scored the weed from Gori, he claimed the conquest of Sandya as his own. Because the others were so stoned, they relented.

"Should I just invite her out here to join us?" Prashant asked. "She was just sitting with her parents, watching the shows."

"She probably realized what assholes those other dudes were." None of them could think of anything in particular that those guys had done, but they were the rare Indian guys who were tall and good-looking and as popular with white girls as they were with Indian girls, so they were easily worthy of hatred.

"Then I'm going to go find her," Prashant said, heading back toward the school's entrance.

"No," Vipul said. The so-called whites of his eyes looked as if they were made of cotton candy. "I'll get her."

"Why?" Prashant asked. "I called dibs."

Vipul laughed, which looked like someone was shaking him by the shoulders. "Right. You called dibs. Whatever. You can't just go and ask her to come and smoke weed. You'll look like a douche. And you're too high."

"*I'm* too high?" Prashant said, now giggling through his purple haze. "What about you?"

They were all laughing now, complete idiots. How they thought they could score with someone like Sandya was totally mental.

A few hours later, all the rest of the guys had gone inside and Prashant was by himself, looking at the sun as it moped into the horizon. It was Holi, springtime, and the world was getting warm and dusted off. Soon, it would be summer and he'd be smoking even more and still trying to get laid. Materializing as if from some fantasy, Gori appeared, probably not as baked as he was but not entirely sober, either, and Prashant found himself making out with her and feeling her up. They had known each other practically all of their lives, but not even that kind of connection could have prepared Prashant for the taste of her mouth, its alternate sweetness and toughness. Due to her baggy clothes and demeanor, he'd never been able to see that she was stacked, which made her personality instantly more interesting. They made out for maybe ten minutes, hardly a word exchanged between them, and then Gori pushed herself away, took the tube of incense out of his hands, and playfully smacked him on the nose with it.

They would continue to see each other at all of the usual gatherings, but Prashant would find no instance in which to rekindle this nascent romance. For the rest of high school, the closest he would come would be a peck on some homecoming date's cheek or, in one rare moment of confounding luck, a chance to touch Shalini Patel's bared right breast on their prom date. Luckily, he was coming of age during the Golden Times of Internet smut, and a tanned barrage of porn stars would constitute not just the bulk but the entirety of his dating life.

Then he went off to college, to succeed in all the ways in which he had failed. But college had brought him to Kavita Bansal, and now he felt more unprepared and lost than ever.

TO HARIT, WHO WENT TO TEMPLE regularly, though unobtrusively, it seemed quite shocking that he had never seen Ranjana before. He had a rather impeccable knack for remembering those in attendance, and it seemed odd to him that someone like Ranjana—someone so, in a word, peculiar—would escape his notice. He had often thought of his own face as being striking in its uniqueness—and not of the good kind—but Ranjana's was its own kind of oddity. He had to admit, with the physical affinity that exists in shivers instead of words, that he found her eyes alluring, even though they were uneven founts of exhaustion. It dawned on him that he was seeing in her a reflection of his own body—in essence, a female Harit, this one in slacks and a sweater instead of Swati's sari.

They convened at a French restaurant, of course—La Ronde. It was a dim, many-tabled affair with tablecloths that Teddy called burgundy instead of red. Teddy had insisted that he treat them to dinner, and he wore an outfit that, even for him, was comical in its sophistication. His blazer had lapels like a tux jacket, and the dress shirt he wore was so crisp that it could have been made of meringue. He had some strange pomade in his hair, and even his skin seemed cheerier.

Harit and Teddy came together in Teddy's car, and Ranjana showed up ten minutes later. Harit knew that she had purposefully arrived late, so as not to be a married woman waiting eagerly for two men, neither of whom was her husband. Harit and Ranjana made weak if well-intentioned *Namastes* at each other while Teddy grinned like a child. Then he strode forth and announced that they were the Porter party. The difference between Teddy's reception at TGI Friday's and this restaurant was incredible. The maître d' at La Ronde was a charming man around Teddy's age who gave a little bow when Teddy spoke to him, and he led them to their table with a bounce in his step. They had arguably the best spot in the restaurant, a small plush booth on a raised dais with an assortment of plants overhanging it.

Harit decided to bury himself in his menu for the first few moments so as to buy himself some time. His embarrassment at Teddy's insistence to pay dissipated when he got a look at the prices. Not that he ate steak, but he couldn't believe that it cost close to $30. He made a note to order a vegetable quiche. (Harit's mother had never eaten in a French restaurant; in truth, neither had Harit. Neither of them ate eggs all that often, either, so the entire notion of quiche existed far from their world.) Ranjana seemed to see in the menu the same refuge as Harit; if her nose had been buried any deeper into it, she would have been asleep.

Naturally, Teddy took the lead in conversation.

"So, I couldn't just let a lovely little thing like this get away from me," he said, flicking one hand at Ranjana. "I gotta tell you, I've been going to FB for years, and I have yet to see anything so darling as this one shaking what her mama gave her like she done owned the place." This statement contained so many turns of phrase that it made Harit reexamine his entire comprehension of the English language.

Ranjana tittered and said, "Oh, Teddy." In that moment, one might have mistaken them for lifelong friends. Harit felt lonely, and he wondered what his mother had thought earlier tonight, when he told her that he was going "out to dinner with friends." He had never attempted such a social experiment under her watch. Regardless, she had consumed his Swati act—as well as a couple of samosas that he held in front of her mouth as she chewed gingerly—and Harit even thought he saw a smile on her face when he said the word *friends*. But then Teddy had pulled up in front of the house, so Harit had rushed back to his bedroom, changed, come back down, and given her a quick peck on the forehead before darting out the door.

Their waiter was a friendly young man in his midtwenties who had wonderful posture. If he was confused by the clumsy trio they made, he didn't show it. He rattled the specials off in a raft of words that seemed to stun Ranjana and turn Teddy into a firework. Ignoring the concept of "ladies first," Teddy responded by immediately ordering the French onion soup and something with a very long name that he said was a wonderful veal dish. He also ordered a bottle of wine, a pinot noir, while Harit and Ranjana shifted uncomfortably. Harit knew better than to go against Teddy when it came to spirits, and in any case, perhaps the wine, like their drinks at TGI Friday's, would make conversation easier.

At Teddy's insistence, Ranjana ordered a salad with many ingredients and the French onion soup (making sure that it was a version with vegetable broth instead of meat broth). Then it was over to Harit, who was so confounded by the entire process that he blurted out that he'd have exactly what Ranjana was having. This elicited a chuckle from Teddy, who let him have his soup but changed Harit's entrée to a different salad with many ingredients. (Evidently, ordering the exact same courses was poor form.) Just before the waiter left, Harit remembered that he had originally wanted the vegetable quiche and switched his order. His waffling indicated a nervousness to please Ranjana—and he did want to please her, but his actions made him seem more nervous than he actually was. It was a heightening of feelings that weren't quite there.

"Now, honey, when did you immigrate, again?" Teddy said. Ranjana, taking a sip of water, clearly thought that this was addressed to her before seeing that Teddy had, in fact, turned to Harit. Thank God—Harit was not the only one thrown off by the use of the word *honey*.

"In 1999," Harit said, intentionally not mentioning his mother and sister, how all three of them had come here after his father's death in India. He had always thought of 1999 as being relatively recent—and it was, by most standards—but as he said it now, he realized that it carried within it many years of interactions, none of which approached this evening in terms of oddity.

"And you, sweetheart?" Teddy asked Ranjana. Harit took some comfort in noticing that Teddy had veered away from trying to pronounce Ranjana's name, as well.

"My husband and I immigrated in 1991," Ranjana said, and Harit noticed a stiffening when she said "husband." He felt sorry for her; this was no situation for a woman. The other people in the restaurant probably thought the same. He chanced a look around the room, and there did seem to be a few others casting bemused looks in their direction. What a sight they must have beheld: Harit in his herringbone sports coat, his frazzled hair a perfect complement to Ranjana's own poofy version, and then this jolly, over-the-top host between them.

Where *was* Ranjana's husband, after all?

As if reading Harit's mind, Teddy said, "And where is your man tonight?"

This also seemed to unsettle her. Good. She was not some reckless woman with no regard for family or rules. "He is playing tennis. He does it every Wednesday night."

"Do you ever play with him?" Teddy prodded.

The question was evidently so original to Ranjana that she turned a quarter ways toward Teddy. She was contemplating it earnestly. In that moment, there seemed to be a calm in her face that was directly opposed to the weirdness of the question, to the weirdness of the situation, to the weirdness of the evening.

"No, I never have," she said. "I think my presence would make too much of . . . a racket."

Teddy laughed and flicked his hand at her again. Harit, on the contrary, was not sure what to make of this quick reveal of humor. Was tonight an occasion for laughter? He thought once again of his mother. The glimmer of his dinner plate was so much brighter than the turned-off TV that she faced now, its surface the dull gray of a pencil scribble.

Wine was to Indians what garlic was to vampires. That's what Ranjana thought before Teddy even ordered it. She knew that he would order a pinot noir even though she didn't drink much wine. Ever since that movie *Sideways* had come out, people blindly followed the wisdom of the main character, who extolled the savory benefits of the stubborn pinot grape. Conversely, merlot, for which the character had razor-sharp contempt, had become an unwanted stepchild.

She had to stop herself—she was already looking for reasons to find Teddy annoying. This was unfair—counterproductive and mean-spirited. If anything, he had saved her from the situation of staying at FB with Achyut and his ragtag friends. Teddy's appearance had given her the opportunity to strike up a conversation in which she could look truly engaged before announcing her fatigue convincingly to the others. They had waved to her as if she were going on a long journey instead of merely driving home. Teddy had kept her outside the club for another fifteen minutes, telling her everything he could about Harit in a meandering way.

"Darling, you just have to meet Harit." He said the name as most others would have—*Huh-REET*—but he mispronounced it with such conviction that one would think he were in the right. "He is the sweetest, but he's so lost. I think he needs someone to bring him out of his shell. He really is a frightened turtle. And we need you to be the turtle whisperer."

Perhaps Ranjana was getting cocky—now that she had ignited her obsession with humor and the having of it—but that comment wasn't funny. It was probably what made her tell Teddy that she would be delighted to meet up with them. Pity, not wine, was really the ultimate social lubricant.

Her pity continued into this evening. She really did feel for Harit. He was entirely out of his element here, and it was surely his first time in a restaurant like this. The look on his face when he opened the menu and saw its cursive innards was the present version of her immigrant past. How many menus had confounded her over the years? She tried to remember the first time that she had been to a French restaurant. She couldn't remember it, but she did remember *a* time, with Mohan: a professors' dinner, during which an arsenal of shiny *salades niçoises* and slimy chicken paillards was deployed among the non-Indian people while she and Mohan munched on confounding piles of ratatouille. Ranjana had learned something from that experience, which was that there was something to be gained in every social interaction. You could take the various experiences and store them inside yourself like you were a curio cabinet, and later, after you had gone through a succession of situations, you could stand back and marvel at the cohesive collection they made. That was what a person was—a curio cabinet of experiences.

She ventured to speak to Harit directly, in Hindi.

"Do you have other relatives here, Haritji?"

This was clearly an uncomfortable subject. Harit shook his head and said, in English, "Just my mother and I. And you?"

Teddy was holding his wineglass by his lips as if it were a mouthpiece through which he was giving clues to 007.

"My brothers and my sister live in California," Ranjana persisted in Hindi. "It is my husband, my son, and I here."

He, again, in English: "It is my bad memory, I am sure, but I do not believe that I have seen you at temple. Do you go on Sundays?"

It was an inevitable question, and there was no way to answer it properly. If she lied and said yes, he would try to see which friends they had in common (though she suspected that he had few social connections). And if she said no—which she decided was the best choice simply because it was the truth—she was casting herself as a blasphemer who didn't attend temple regularly.

"Sadly, it has been quite some time since we went. We do *puja* at home." This was partly true; it occurred once every, oh, century. "The complications of raising a teenager in this country . . ."

As she had anticipated, this seemed to cause him no small amount of concern, but she decided that this wasn't entirely her fault. It was, rather, the fault of his small social circle. Temple was not just a religious place for him but a sanctuary—the sanctuary that it was truly supposed to be. She knew the type, the Indian who needed the reliability of a religious space. To be sure, there was no end of companionship that one could derive from a temple's smiling gods.

So she didn't go to temple regularly, but what had he expected, exactly? It was true that families had a tendency to dissipate when their children grew into adolescence. Or, well, some families. Many were fierce in their dedication, their attendance rising. But even Harit himself had seen his own dedication waver in light of his association with Teddy; he now went once or twice a week instead of his usual three times. He normally sat in the corner where the elderly men alternately gurgled prayers and dozed. He stayed away from the chirping aunties in the kitchen and the kids who ran rings-around-the-rosie in the lobby. He found solace in the prayers, and he listened attentively to the words of wisdom that the pandit added in between them. Harriman's presented numerous chances for him to feel alien, but a temple, even though fragile compared to its counterparts in India, surrounded him in familiar moments that knew nothing of long-gone sisters and distant mothers.

To be fair, Ranjana had not been through his family's tragedy, so what did she need of temple? Her family was her temple. Yet Harit also sensed that there was something fragile about her home, as well. Her stiff reaction to any mention of her husband indicated this.

Their soups arrived. Harit had never wanted to mutter an expletive so much. He liked onions. He liked soup. But what was this invincible sealing of goo on top? He punctured it with the spoon that lay alongside the bowl; then he pulled a wand of cheese toward himself, brown dewdrops of broth sliding down it.

He looked across the table and met Ranjana's eyes. At long last, they had the first genuine, shared laugh of the evening. Teddy, bending over his bowl and looking up through a mouthful of soup, practically spat it out.

"*Ji*, do not worry," Ranjana said, now twirling a turban of cheese around her spoon. "I have never been able to figure out how to eat this." She tugged her spoon and snapped the stuff free. A string of cheese flopped over the rim of the bowl and onto the saucer beneath it—messy, unseemly, but not to be helped. Then she ate the bite daintily. It was a merciful gesture. It hinted at sympathy.

What sort of person was he? What was it that mattered most to him now—now that his sister, his role model and inspiration, was gone? He found mockery in the word *relation*, because it was so easy to live your life in relation to family. To think of your life as defined by the lives of the ones around you simply because they bore your name. Swati had been a loveable force by which he had crafted his own life. This evening, he needed her approval; he needed to know how she ate soup, how she sat in a booth, and how she managed to do these things while fluent in conversation. Her accent had been comparable to his, but her manner of speaking would have eventually, outside of death, reached Teddy-like levels of good humor. Could he now ever achieve a similar level of conversation without Swati to guide him?

Ranjana seemed to be equally proficient in becoming American. The way she pulled the cheese, the way she managed a small sip of wine without its looking overly studied, it was clear that she had honed her social skills to something beyond culture. As Harit watched her eat, he wanted to seek out things that he did routinely here in the States that would never have been part of his days in India. He had an image of ties, of his ability to straighten them and make them into a fan of cloth, and that simple image sustained him throughout the rest of the dinner, even when his large quiche arrived, even when he saw the facility with which Teddy chewed his veal and Ranjana parceled her salad into frizzy, compact turns of a fork. He would find small gestures and moments like these that he could master, and these would move him out of his sheltered existence and into an assured, confident life. Life was digestion, then sustenance.

Naturally, Teddy insisted on dessert when they finished their entrées. He held the dessert menu toward the waiter, pointed to one item, and held up three fingers in the European way, with his thumb extended. As they had eaten soup together, they would eat sweets together. By now, Ranjana was looking at her cell phone every few minutes. She was mindful of the time, and Harit again felt supportive of this, the distinct attention to her husband. How reliable Indian women were! The reliability of Ranjana's dedication as wife, the reliability of Swati's smile, the reliability of his mother's silent mourning. The last of these was particularly persistent. Harit had heard Jewish coworkers at the store speak of "sitting shiva" when a family member died, and he had originally thought that it was an homage to Shiva, the god of destruction. If ever a phrase had been appropriate for his mother, it was that one. She had been sitting shiva so thoroughly as to destroy most identifiable elements of herself. But in Ranjana, in this moment, Harit saw the opposite, the Brahma to his mother's Shiva—newness, and creation.

Teddy was getting tipsy now, having had custody of the wine bottle all this time. His cheeks were flushed, and he had now unbuttoned the top button of his meringue shirt. "I've never been to

India, you know," he was saying. "Always wanted to go. A friend of mine is a flight attendant and gets to travel all over the world. Said India's one of his favorite destinations. People there are so friendly—obviously—and he said the food is amazing as long as you know where to eat."

"How did he find the proper places to eat?" Ranjana asked.

Teddy brought his wineglass back to his mouth, and his eyes glazed over in thought—a look that Harit now understood as an expression he often made himself, during their mall outings. He decided to avoid doing so in the future; it was incredibly off-putting.

"Well, that's a good question, now isn't it." Teddy took a sip. "I suspect it was from the other flight attendants, but who even knows with that lot." He chuckled, a sound as bitter as the wine, and Ranjana met Harit's eyes. It was a complicit moment; it was clearly the two of them against Teddy, and although Harit felt guilty for being "against" the man who was trying to help him make a new friend, he realized that in any group of three, there were always two people against a third. Better to be part of the winning two.

Their desserts arrived. "*Crème brûlée*," Ranjana said helpfully to Harit, and then Teddy spelled it. When he said the first *e*, he slanted his right hand one way; when he said the *u*, he brought his fingertips together, his palms facing downward to form a flesh roof. Harit remembered this from his aborted French lessons with Teddy— the occasional marks above letters that he found much less interesting than the ones in Hindi.

"Where do you have your hands manicured?" Ranjana asked Teddy, who flicked his hand at her again.

"I just want to take you home and wrap a big bow around you. I do them myself. I don't trust other people to touch these babies. How about you?"

"I do them myself most of the time, too, but I treat myself every once in a while. Now that my son's off at college, I think I should go more often."

"Her son's a freshman at Princeton," Teddy said to Harit. Ranjana had blurted this out that night outside of FB.

"Yes. He is quite bright. He really wanted to go to Stanford. Since we begged him to be closer to us, he has set very strict rules for me and my husband. I guess he learned from the best."

Harit chuckled—and was conscious that he was "chuckling." It was a word he attributed to Teddy, to Mr. Harriman, to other people, but not to himself. He hadn't enjoyed too much wine, either, so the chuckle was coming from something true. He had never been so happy to be the opposite of serious.

"What sort of rules did your son set?" Teddy asked.

"We can call him only once a day, and we can go visit only once a semester."

"Wow—that sounds harsh, given that you've spent every day of his life with him."

"It is a bit harsh, yes. But he will be home for fall break. And he made a good case for himself. He is majoring in chemistry, and his schedule is very grueling. He did very well on his AP exams and tested out of many early classes, so he is in very advanced classes already."

"And your husband does not mind this?" Harit asked. He felt the difficulty with which he pronounced the word *husband*. It felt indelicate to be questioning Ranjana about her family. Still, he was genuinely curious.

"My husband is a professor of chemistry," she said. "He, more so than anyone, understands the importance of one's studies." Harit recognized in this statement a tone of memorization. It was the type of tone he used when he explained his work at Harriman's to other Indian people: *It is a very helpful look at American culture.*

"How did you and your husband meet?" Teddy asked.

Harit and Ranjana exchanged another knowing glance, the wrinkles around their eyes agreeing in amusement. It was a question that Americans loved to ask, but it went directly against the decorum of Indians, who knew that meeting for them did not often have the serendipity that Americans expected.

"We were promised to each other." Again, a tone of memorization.

It was always surprising to see Teddy's interpretation of being sorry, and this was one of those moments. He set his wineglass down and dabbed at his mouth with his napkin. "My apologies. I always forget about . . . the . . . arrangements."

Harit and Ranjana shared another moment, another glance. "Americans are always finding different ways of saying 'arranged,'" Ranjana said. "What I think they forget is that many American marriages are arranged, too. Not as obviously as many Indian marriages are, but people are certainly encouraged here, especially among the richer families. I am sure that Prashant—that's my son—will encounter a certain number of them at Princeton." Ranjana was holding her own wineglass by her mouth now, and there was a new confidence in her posture.

The feeling of loneliness kept returning to Harit like a cap placed back on his head. He had to remind himself not to forge too much of a kinship with Ranjana. It was so easy to find a sisterhood in her, to share their culture as they did dessert, in similar bites of sugary crisp. But though the food was the same, the mouths it entered were not twins. Ranjana's mouth, as this latest exchange had shown, was capable of issuing eloquent, knowing sentences, whereas Harit's mouth knew more of stutters. They were both Indian, but they had different types of wisdom.

The end of dinner was refreshing, much less shaky than its beginning. They had, against expectation, enjoyed an enlightening time overall. Ranjana was surprised to see that Harit had a personality. She knew many Indians who existed merely as auxiliary characters. They reacted to others passively and held their beliefs like canned goods that they might consume later, perhaps years later. There was survival but not life. Harit, for all his reticence predinner, for all the nervousness that he exuded, had become someone to like. He had asked questions. He had stepped outside of himself. He had been bold enough to ask after her husband—Ranjana realized as she slung her purse over her shoulder that neither he nor Teddy knew what her husband's name was—and Ranjana had found, in those knowing glances, a true connection with him.

Whether or not this was because they were both Indian was uncertain. After her disorienting night at FB, Ranjana knew that her connection to Achyut was tenuous, and she knew instinctively that Teddy saw her as a means to an end more than a friend. Harit, however—he had the honesty that both Achyut and Teddy were missing.

This was not, she believed, a homophobic reaction. She had not absented Achyut and Teddy because they were gay; in fact, Harit himself could even be construed as effeminate in his movements. It was the intent of Harit's behavior that she preferred. He wanted to do the right thing. At any given moment this evening, he had wanted to do the thing that would most please his companions. It was commendable.

They were in the lobby of the restaurant. "What do you say, kids? A nightcap?" Teddy asked, pulling his jacket as closed as it would go. Though already rotund, his stomach showed the addition of their meal.

They had met at eight to accommodate Harit and Teddy's work schedule, and it was nearing ten now. Ranjana could not stay out. "I must get home. My husband will be home from tennis soon." She deliberately withheld his name. There was something to be said about mystery for mystery's sake. It was one of the few truly notable things that Roberta had said when leading their writing group.

"Well, it was a great pleasure, my dear," Teddy said, presenting his hands so that Ranjana could place one of hers in them.

Ranjana, just to see that look of unrest on Teddy's face again, dove a handshake forward and watched him flicker to receive her movement. "A great pleasure to meet you, too," she said.

"Are you on Facebook?" Teddy asked while she was already turning to Harit.

Ranjana puffed out a laugh. "I have an Internet-savvy son, Teddy. So, no." (A lie.) She turned to Harit and switched to Hindi. "*Ji*, wonderful to meet you."

"Do you have an e-mail address where we might reach you?" Teddy continued. Ranjana realized that if she had given her e-mail to Teddy the other night instead of her phone number, he would have already located her Facebook profile. He was a voracious social animal whose age would not prevent him from having a firm footing online. In fact, it would spur him on. She did not really want to give him her email address, but Teddy was nothing if not persistent.

Ranjana opened her purse to pull out a small notebook and pen, but Teddy plucked one of La Ronde's cards from the nearby hospitality stand and gave it to her. She wrote, "Mrs. Chaudhury, hecate868@gmail.com," and handed it over to Teddy.

"Thank you, Teddy. *Shukriya*, Haritji," she said. Then she swerved out of the restaurant and to her car.

Teddy asked Harit if he wanted a nightcap, but Harit cut him off with a pointed *Teddy*. Teddy nodded, the type of nod that went up and down and sideways in quick alternation.

"I gotcha, dear," Teddy said.

"But I had a lovely time, Teddy. Thank you."

"You two really seemed to hit it off." They were at Teddy's car now, flanking it and speaking over the roof.

"I cannot remember the last time that I met an Indian like that."

Teddy opened his door and unfettered the locks. They both slid into the car.

"Like what, exactly?"

Harit thought. "She seems very . . . American."

"But she's not even on Facebook."

"I don't mean like that. I mean that she really lives here. She belongs here."

As he spoke these words, Harit heard how American they sounded in and of themselves. The rhythm of them, what they conveyed, was American. The sense of belonging itself—it was something that preoccupied so many people in this country. It was why every immigrant he knew felt a social obligation not only to belong but also to know, to the exact emotional fiber, where he belonged. That had been the basis of his anxiety during dinner—determining where he'd belonged at the table and at the restaurant. Now he just had to figure out where he belonged everywhere else—at home, at the store, and beyond.

When they pulled up in front of Harit's home a few minutes later, Teddy said, "We will have to do this again soon."

"If Ranjanaji wishes to see us again, she will be in touch with us."

"No, dear, that's why I got her e-mail. I'm going to send her a message when I get home."

Harit wanted to challenge this. He wanted to explain to Teddy that it wasn't proper. He was already trying to imagine what the interaction would be between Ranjana and her husband, the professor. A man accustomed to problems and solving them, finding weaknesses and correcting them. It would be so easy for him to detect the slightly suspect behavior of his wife. Indeed, Harit was now assuming that Ranjana had detected in the evening the same kind of comfort that he had experienced. And he was assuming that she carried in her body the same tingling that he felt as he bid Teddy good night and walked up to his house in the dark. Interactions like this evening's, which made you feel appreciated and listened to, had no other result but to change your life for the better.

But as Harit turned the key in the back door, he found his comfort overtaken by the oppression of his home.

Mohan was not yet back from tennis. The silence was all the more pronounced following the rattle and hum of the evening. Ranjana wanted to call him on his cell and find out just how long he would be; she felt a great urge to write, if only about the evening and not about the supernatural, but she also didn't want to begin if Mohan was due in the door five minutes from now. Then again, it had been so long since she had phoned him like that. They had not shared a sense of urgency—apart from being parents to Prashant—in years. To call Mohan would be to disrupt this long-standing state.

She picked up the phone and called him anyway.

"Hello?" Mohan asked, as if their home number hadn't popped up on his phone. Was he even really at the club? Or was he with *her*?

"*Ji*, your food is getting cold." It was the shoddiest lie. Normally, she heated up his food when she heard his car pull up; or, if she had made it fresh that evening, she knew to keep it on the burner. No wonder he met this comment with confusion:

"Heh?"

"Will you be home soon?"

"I am in the locker room, *yaar*. I'll be home in the next half hour, forty-five minutes."

"OK." Good.

"What did you make?"

Oh, dear. What was she planning on serving him? She took a second to remember what was in the refrigerator but panicked. "*Rajma*," she said, even though she hadn't made any.

"Perfect, *ji*. I'll pick up some yogurt." Then he hung up.

Ranjana slapped the counter and harrumphed. Now she couldn't write at all. There was no *rajma* prepared, but her husband was bringing yogurt for it.

Somehow tipsy on the few sips of wine that she'd taken at dinner, she spent the next half hour rushing around to make the dish. Later, as Mohan was sitting at the kitchen table, spooning the red beans into his mouth and chatting about the match, Ranjana wondered which might taste saltier—this quick dinner or the tears of joy she would shed when she finally finished writing a book.

THEY DID NOT SEE EACH OTHER for a few weeks. Teddy e-mailed Ranjana that first night, of course—already suggesting dates in the next "fortnight" when they might meet again—but she deflected his invitation by saying that she had to go out of town unexpectedly. She didn't give a reason, thinking that the ball would stay in her court and she could reach out when her curiosity about Harit's well-being grew great enough. But the following week, Teddy found her on Facebook. A little note was embedded in his invite: "If you made it from Delhi to Ohio, Facebook is a piece of cake!" Ranjana had to laugh in spite of his persistence. She e-mailed him back and wrote, as charmingly as she could, that she had been admonished by her son not to engage with Facebook for fear that their social circles would intersect online. She thanked Teddy for the sentiment and wrote, "Hope all is well on your end."

He disappeared for a while after that. She returned to her routine—the office, Mohan, and, with less frequency, her writing.

Achyut had inspired her to write, but now he had retreated from the forefront of her mind.

Actually, he had brushed her off. A few days after the night at FB, he had called her and begun berating her without even saying hello.

"Why were you so weird to my friends?"

Sputters issued forth as if her lips had taken on a life of their own. "I—I'm sorry, Achyut. I wasn't prepared for everything that happened."

"What do you mean 'everything that happened'? Nothing was supposed to *happen* except for you meeting my friends and being nice to them."

"I'm sorry."

"Yeah, so am I. Look—maybe this wasn't such a great idea. I need to be surrounded with people that are supportive."

"I thought I was being supportive. I was trying to be, at least. Achyut, please—I was just out of my element. Please give me another chance."

"I'll think about it." He paused. "Also, I have something to tell you."

"What?"

"I kind of have a boyfriend."

"You do? That's wonderful."

"He's great. Older. More responsible. I'm probably going to be staying at his place."

"That's—I'm glad to hear that."

"Anyway . . . I'll . . . let me see how I feel about things and then I'll get back to you." Then he hung up.

He was still mulling things over, apparently, because she hadn't heard a peep from him. His next appointment was several months away, so it wasn't as if she was going to see him around the office.

The incident with him seemed all at once to have been a fever dream.

If she was being honest with herself, Achyut did not loom as largely in her estimation as he once had. Something about that night had changed her perspective. She had seen, in the neon carnival of his job, that she was one in a mere throng of admirers. She didn't exactly feel duped, but there was something off-putting about his socializing, to say nothing of his mercurial personality, which seemed more and more volatile. She did not feel enmity toward his sexual orientation—in fact, she congratulated herself for the even logic with which she thought of it—but she did have to admit that she felt some resentment for being a person in which Achyut could have no romantic interest. She did not wish to be his keepsake. Surely this was a natural reaction to have.

But at the same time, if she was being honest with herself, she couldn't help but feel that Achyut's new boyfriend would not only occupy the space that she had filled but also would be able to offer Achyut emotional and physical solace that she never could offer. And this stung.

So she regressed to the nights before she had met Achyut and the doldrums she had inhabited soon after Prashant's departure. Sometimes, when Cheryl unwrapped a candy and said something about the latest episode of *The Bachelor*, Ranjana would remember Achyut crumpled in her passenger seat as they watched the in-progress remains of Paradise Island, and she would feel physical pain. It was almost funereal—which was ridiculous. Achyut was very much alive, and she could break the détente and reach out to him. As with Harit and Teddy, the ball could be in her court, provided she wanted to put it there. But: routine.

Then, one day, she had an occasion to socialize. Preeti Verma, a casual friend, had lost her father to cancer, and there was to be a small gathering at the temple to do a *puja* in his memory. Would Ranjana and Mohanji please come, perhaps with some *prasad* for afterward?

"Of course, *ji*," Ranjana said, her body bending in assent even though they were speaking over the phone.

For some reason, even though Ranjana and Harit had discussed the temple at La Ronde, it did not occur to her that he might be there. There were so many different Indian circles, and Preeti seemed outside Harit's limited orbit. So when Ranjana and Mohan stepped into the temple with a stainless steel bowl of honeydew and grapes, and some store-bought *barfi*, Ranjana was surprised to see him seated, cross-legged, with the other men on the right side of the room. His back was toward her, but that hair was unmistakable, the beginning of a bald spot like a moon behind clouds.

It was uncanny how authentic their temple was, as if it had come out of a travel book. It was built on a gigantic plot of land, and this removed any noticeably American sight, so that the Indians in attendance could pretend that they were back in their home country. Even the trees that surrounded the place seemed Indian. The creek that ran behind it, the airborne dirt, the birds that flew overhead—you could swear that you were in Uttar Pradesh. And then there was the building itself. Funded with millions of dollars from the many affluent attendees, it was gilded in stone the way that a mirror could be gilded in gold. The various pieces had been carved in India, then transported on ships. Assembled, they rivaled the temples of Mahabalipuram in their ostentation, a forest of ornate stone thorns jutting every which way, here and there circling a tenderly carved deity. Wide steps flanked by humongous stone banisters jutted up into a grand threshold. The interior had a vaulted ceiling through which ten windows, like angry angels, shot sunlight onto the sprawling marble floor during the daytime. A series of six-foot-tall deities, posed as if in a godly fashion show, ran across the back of the altar. Red rugs ran askew like plush rivers. Gold exploded wherever possible. Then there were the bright swishes of the women's georgette, the white and beige tangle of the men's business casual.

As she had with Achyut, Ranjana felt an indefinite tension creep into her at the sight of Harit. Having Mohan by her side made the moment all the more bizarre. Mohan had no cause for concern, she reassured herself, but she hadn't even mentioned her dinner with Harit and Teddy to him. How could she have possibly explained it? In a way, it had been even more dangerous than the night at FB. The gay bar had been so outside her own understanding of life that it would have been hieroglyphs to Mohan. But the dinner with Harit and Teddy could at least find a footing in his mind. Two men accompanying a woman to dinner, her husband out of sight, eating at a fancy restaurant and speaking of her family unpoliced, one of them roughly her age, unmarried, probably seeking out a wife, however late in life. Then Teddy, truly different from Mohan in most ways but still his elder, capable of dispensing advice to Ranjana that she might, God forbid, take. She was kicking herself now as Mohan strode forward to shake hands with some of the other men. She made her way to the pantry, which pealed with the chickadee voices of the other women.

She set her various parcels on a countertop and said her *Namastes* to the room. However mournful they were all supposed to be, there was a jollity to the union of Indian women that could never be fully dispelled. Their whispers—the hushing of their mouths using the back of one hand—came across as gossip instead of reverent intonations of pity. Sonya Mehta, the woman who had gone night-riding naked through her dreamscape, was there in full force. Instead of wearing a demure outfit—a few of the women were wearing slacks instead of saris or *salwars*—she was wearing a gleaming sari with so many beads on it that it looked like someone had rolled her in glue and then pushed her down a hill of rubies. Ranjana sometimes wished that she could be this selfish yet clueless at the same time; Sonya did what she did, in life as in the presence of death, and perhaps that was why her beauty remained undiminished. It was self-consciousness that aged you, worrying about chance social encounters and your place in them that brought wrinkles as if they had been called to prayer.

When Ranjana got back to the main room, Mohan was already seated in the middle of the men, in front of Harit. Ranjana decided to seat herself and deal with Harit later. If she stayed just behind him on the left side of the room, he would not note her presence, and she could pay attention to her real reason for being here—the *puja*. Preeti and her husband, Anu, were seated in front, facing the pandit, and their heads were bowed. The people at the temple had been through countless ceremonies like this, but what pleased Ranjana was how the sense of reverence, at least before the altar, was relatively consistent. Whereas the babbling in the kitchen, however low voiced, went against the solemn purpose of the evening, the sentiment in here was respectful.

Their pandit was young, in his late thirties, a replacement for his predecessor, a beloved old man who had passed away last year, his resonant Punjabi accent still ringing in their ears. The injection of this new pandit's youth into their ceremonies gave them all a renewed sense of faith. So many of them worried that their children were not carrying on the Hindu tradition, and seeing a younger pandit offered some reassurance. Of course, Ranjana was one of the culpable crowd. As she had half-confessed to Harit, temple had not been a huge part of Prashant's life, even though she was somewhat exonerated due to the fact that his Hindi was not *that* bad.

She and Mohan had been stuck in their mother tongue for many years after their arrival, her English slang coming mostly from soap operas and trips to the grocery store and telemarketing tussles over the phone, so Prashant had grown up surrounded by both languages. Sanskrit often played a greater role in temple, however, so Prashant's Hindi failed him within these walls. That sense of ineffectiveness, for someone as smart as Prashant, was why he disliked going to temple. Ranjana could bet that, aside from the pandit himself, there was likely no one in this room right now who knew Sanskrit. She thought again of Seema's yoga companions and, for a moment, marveled at the shattering of the tongue, language repurposed and rethought and reorganized.

Her mind was wandering. This is what happened when she came to temple. Most of the time, she would conjure up characters and scenes; if she could have gotten away with it, she would have kept a small notebook with her and jotted down these ideas. Ranjana had not brought a *dupatta* but had a maroon wool scarf that she wore over her head. She wondered if describing blood as a maroon scarf might work. No—a maroon *dupatta*. That was culturally appropriate for the story.

She was so lost in her thoughts that she didn't notice at first that Harit was glancing her way. She had thought herself out of his line of sight, but he had shifted his legs so that he was tilted in her direction. He nodded his head slightly, in a way that indicated it was the last in a series of nods that he had tried to direct toward her. She nodded her head back in turn, felt the nervousness rise in her again. She looked at Mohan. Harit saw her look and then looked at Mohan, too. He faced forward for the rest of the *puja*.

Harit had probably gotten to know Preeti at the temple. Now that Ranjana saw him here, even though he was merely sitting and watching a *puja*, she realized that he seemed almost as out of place here as he had at the restaurant. She would have thought a place like temple would be a natural fit for him, but the unease of his posture made his reticence more evident than ever. She was overcome with sympathy for Harit. She had made her way through this country with the help of various Indians around her, and she wondered to what extent Harit had that kind of support system. Maybe Preeti had extended some kindness to him, and here he was, supporting her, his tenuous acquaintance, doing the only thing he knew how to do—to pray among others.

What if she had come to the States by herself, with no one to guide her? True, Harit had come with his mother, but Ranjana was thinking of people her own age, people who could share her experience. If you didn't have a family member to steer you through this mess of a country—and it *was* a mess—then what would happen to you? You would become the quiet, confused dining companion that Harit had been.

She had mistaken her budding friendship with Achyut as the logical replacement for Prashant's absence. But she saw now that maybe she could contribute to the greater good of her little world if she directed her kindness at Harit, a fellow lost soul.

The *puja* ended, and Harit was not quite sure how best to proceed. He had come here with hopes of seeing Ranjana, and upon seeing her, he felt an instant sense of communion. Nothing like this had happened since Swati's passing. Despite his interactions with Teddy, he didn't feel himself understood by anyone, but his dinner with Ranjana had assured him that he was a viable person. That was the word that kept coming back to him—*viable*. He was living as if incidental to the world around him instead of having an active part in it. Ranjana could help him change that.

He was overthinking this evening. Yes, he needed to figure out whether or not Ranjana's husband knew about their dinner, but it was no big deal. Indians met other Indians all the time. Meeting other people was not something that he did with any great frequency, but he could interact with Ranjana and her husband if he simply pretended that he was like everyone else.

The few moments after a *puja* ended were always fleeting, and he did not want to end up in some situation where all they did was say hello. He approached her, and her greeting betrayed no trace of deeper understanding. Her husband was in conversation with another man, a heart surgeon whose name Harit had forgotten, so he and Ranjana had a moment to themselves.

"How are you, *ji*?" he asked.

"Very well," she said. "I apologize for disappearing. It has been rather hectic at home."

This was a compassionate response because it directed blame at her instead of allowing any to come his way.

"How have you been?" she asked. It was a question he always found comical. As if there were any particularly intriguing answer anyone could give.

"Busy at the store," he said. "And you?"

"A doctor's office is always busy," she said. "People always getting sick."

"Cold season?" he said, proud to have used this phrase.

"Yes," she said.

"Is this your husband?" he asked, sensing that the conversation between her husband and his companion was making terminal overtures.

"Yes, it is. He comes home so late from tennis that I'm not sure I told him about our dinner!"

Perfect. She had helped him.

Her husband approached. He seemed gruff. Perhaps Harit was projecting a common stereotype onto Ranjana's husband—that Indian professors, more than any other type, had a haughty manner. The broad-chested stance that her husband took, even though he was very slight, even though he was clearly trying to emphasize his defiance, reinforced this idea.

"*Ji*, this is Harit Sinha," she said. "He is a friend of Preeti's."

Harit did not exactly love the fact that this was the introduction she gave him, but he understood why she phrased it this way.

Her husband inclined his head and pulled his pants up, his thumbs and forefingers pinching at the back of his waistband, which meant *Let's hit the road.*

"*Namaste*," Mohan said. "Are you new to the area?" He clearly felt obligated to ask this, given the flat tone of his voice.

"No, I have been here for a few years," Harit said, shrinking the tenure he'd had in the area so as to appear more agreeable. "I work at Harriman's." He appended this fact randomly, courtesy of his nerves. Her husband reacted accordingly, his brows raising, his head nodding to indicate that he knew the place but had no cause to value it.

"We would love to have you and your mother over for dinner sometime," Ranjana interjected.

He knew why Ranjana had said this—compassion, again, as well as an effort to ease the conversation along—but it stopped him cold. It was something he had not even considered as a possibility, the idea of taking his mother somewhere to meet potential friends. Of course, he thought often of his own home and how bizarre it would seem to visitors, which is why he did not bring others into it. But with this offer of dinner, he foresaw the challenge of making a friend of Ranjana: the little string of conversations like this one, the folded paper plates and tousled napkins, the head nods and kowtows, the clink of bangles and the pulling of waistbands, the subtle jokes and confusions, the mystery of his mother and her blankness, the secrets of his rum and Cokes and tangled saris.

He could see that Ranjana understood his discomfort, in the way that she said her good-bye and then bustled away with her husband. It was as careful yet respectful an exit as she could have made.

As they disappeared down the wide temple steps, he realized that he still didn't know her husband's name.

STEFANIE HAD WRITTEN A SECTION containing as many adverbs as it did mermaid scales, and Ranjana wanted to scream. Sometimes she wondered why she even came to this writing group, why she endured these strange people week after week. But she knew why: she needed a reliable tether, something to guide her. To lose herself at her computer and not have any outlet other than that was dangerous. She knew that people went to therapy to talk through their struggles, since worry led to off-putting behavior if left unchecked, so it was necessary for her to vent her literary frustrations here. Yet at times like these, when Stefanie was tugging at her daggered necklace, her neck practically painted in hives, her long nails scraping against the paper in her hands—it was times like these when Ranjana thought of turning to crime novels, of writing her own *Dexter*-like serial killer just so that he could prey on such people.

She wished that she could bring Seema to this workshop. Oh, the laughs they would have. There was practically no intersection between a woman like Seema and Stefanie apart from outspoken-ness and kohl, but Seema could have seen Stefanie as a scientific study, a fun organism to observe. Instead, Seema constantly chided Ranjana for continuing to go to the class. "If you're better than the people around you, it's time to go to a different class," she would say, and then Ranjana would call Seema out on her own yoga class, and then they would keen at the cyclical routine of their complaints, the fact that they simply continued to find new ways to malign the same old things.

Meanwhile, here were these classmates, writing about the same old things. How many times had Stefanie written about mermaids? At least a dozen. Cassie, her face especially sallow today, as if the sarcasm had sucked the blood from her cheeks, was massaging her temple with one hand, the other clutching her stomach. Wendy was staring at the ceiling. Colin was cleaning his glasses with the bottom of his *Return of the Jedi* T-shirt. The crumpled pages in Ranjana's own hands were an accordion of exasperation.

Then Stefanie stopped. The silence resounded with the sharp-ness of a halved sentence, and Ranjana had no idea what that sentence had been. Stefanie was staring right at her.

"You got a problem?" Stefanie said. She was still pulling on her necklace.

"Pardon?" was all Ranjana could think to say.

"If you were any less interested in my book, you'd be dead," Stefanie said.

"Now, now," Roberta said, her voice scooping with surprise. "Stefanie. Ranjana was paying attention."

"No, she wasn't," Stefanie said. "What just happened? What part did I just read?"

"Don't blame her for the fact that your book is boring," Cassie said. Ranjana had never loved her more.

"Cassie," Roberta said, rising in her seat and putting her hands out, as if calming an angry group of animals. "Ladies, please. Where is this coming from?"

Oddly, Stefanie started laughing. "I don't even know why I bother coming here. I'm clearly the only one who takes this seriously." Cassie made the beginning of a retort, her mouth popping open, but Stefanie was at the ready. "And don't even try to pretend like you take this seriously, Cassie. All you do is sit there and act like a sourpuss. I *like* writing erotic thrillers. It's what I do. Leave it alone."

"Stefanie, I really do think that you are mistaken," said Roberta. "Ranjana, you were paying attention, weren't you, dear?"

Never had Ranjana wanted to be a bitch more than she did right now, but she shuddered to think how much longer this outburst would last if she engaged with such pettiness. So she said as evenly as she could, "No, I wasn't paying attention. And I am sorry, Stefanie. It is not you. I have a family member who has been very ill, and it's put me in a bad mood."

An easy fib, and it had the desired effect: Stefanie held her tongue, and there a few seconds of silence as Roberta reemphasized her hands, as if patting the anger to the ground. Stefanie started reading again.

Afterward, Ranjana called Seema from her cell phone and asked to see her right away.

Seema was at her dining room table reorganizing one of her many cosmetics cases. She bought lipstick like it was Chapstick—frequently and almost medically—and the table had become a shiny arsenal of tubes and wayward pink splotches.

"Can you believe this woman?" Ranjana asked, blowing on her tea and remembering her awkward spill from weeks before.

"Yes, I can believe it," Seema said. "I have finally decided that nothing can surprise me about women in this country. Nothing. Yesterday, I was standing in line behind a girl at the grocery store, and one whole cheek of her bottom was sticking out from her shorts, they were so short." The way Seema said "cheek of her bottom" in Hindi, while caressing the imaginary protrusion in the air, made Ranjana's tea squirt back up her throat. "Laugh all you want, *ji*! It's not funny! No wonder this country has so few successful women politicians. They've gone mad! At least Indiraji kept her saris wrapped tight."

They'd read *Midnight's Children* in a two-person book club a year ago, and as a result, Indira Gandhi had become Seema's go-to political reference for any manner of occasion, even and especially when the reference didn't make any sense.

Like in some sitcom, Satish walked into the house just as she said this, shaking his head and sighing. "Always with Indiraji. Let her rest in peace, *yaar*."

"But look at Hillary Clinton," Ranjana said, nodding at Satish, who held a plastic grocery bag in one hand. "She dressed demurely."

"What a horrible example, Ranjana!" Seema yelled. "I'd rather wear one of Indiraji's saris from years ago than one of those pantsuits. And don't compare them to *salwars* because you know they aren't the same."

"Then what about Michelle Obama?" Satish said, turning toward the kitchen. "She's always been very stylish."

"Oh, God. Let's make a deal, *ji*—I'll stop mentioning Indiraji if you stop mentioning Michelle Obama." Seema leaned over to Ranjana, exaggerating a whisper so that Satish could hear. "He loves that Michelle Obama. I think they all do." Ranjana had not considered this before, but she did know that she found Barack attractive. Perhaps the other women did. She abstained from mentioning this to Seema in the presence of Satish.

"What are you really discussing?" Satish called out as he emptied whatever contents were in the bag into a variety of cabinets and drawers.

"What do you mean?" Seema said. She fixated on a lipstick that she had clearly not seen in ages. An intricate pattern of flowers was carved into its golden surface. She popped the tube open, a touch of dark pink.

"I mean, what are you talking about? American women?"

"We are talking about how American women are crazy." Seema slid the lipstick around her mouth.

"Not just that." Ranjana sighed. "They don't want to expand their minds and learn anything new. Or accept anyone new. Instead of supporting other women—in a world dominated by men— they're mean. And petty."

Seema snickered, almost smudging herself. "*Yaar*, what do you think you're being?"

"*Et tu*, Brute?" Ranjana said, sighing and picking up her teacup.

"What?" Seema asked.

"I thought you were on my side!" Ranjana clarified as Satish sighed in the kitchen.

"I am on your side, believe me." Seema turned back toward Satish. "*Ji*, all I mean is that we Indian women are so much more . . . civil and . . . well, smarter than these American women."

"But you *are* American women!" he called out.

It was odd that Satish was the one saying this. Mohan would never have called Ranjana American. He forever saw her as a transplant from India. In fact, he took pride in retaining his Indian nationality as much as he could.

"Are you really trying to tell me that there is no difference between us and the other women you see in this country?" Seema asked. "Weren't you just complaining yesterday about some woman who cut you off on the highway?"

"Well, she couldn't drive because she was a woman, not because she was an *American* woman." Satish cackled while Ranjana and Seema rolled their eyes.

"There is no such thing as an 'American woman,'" Satish continued, finished with his chore and returning to the doorway. He leaned against its frame with his stomach as a cushion. He had a common Indian male physique: second trimester with a possible sail into the third. Ranjana remembered Dr. Butt telling her that the reason why so many Indian men looked like this was because their ancestors had spent centuries farming in the fields and doing other hard manual labor, whereas now, in this modern world, their heirs were much more stationary and, well, lazy. "So all of the fat gets pushed to the front," Dr. Butt had said, pushing his hands together in front of his own flat stomach and pantomiming a potbelly.

Satish continued: "America has become full of so many different types of people that we can't define it anymore. It's true!" he was saying to Seema's scoff. "Just look at you, *yaar.* Look at this mess on the table. You and Hillary Clinton and Michelle Obama are all 'American women,' but I'll bet their dining room tables don't ever look like this."

"But that isn't really the point," Seema said. "Fine, there are different *types* of American women. But what we are talking about is whether we Indian women in America are more open to change, more accepting, and I think the answer is a resounding yes."

Ranjana found herself agreeing with this blunt statement. Not just because of someone like Stefanie or someone like Cheryl. It was because, if she stepped back and considered her life in relation to those of the American women around her, she had a firm sense of having always been criticized, at once exoticized because she was Eastern and resented because she was different. If American women had been more accepting of adaptation, then she and all of the Indian women she knew would have felt validated. But they constantly felt self-conscious—indeed, this entire conversation with Seema was predicated on feeling self-conscious—and so the only possible explanation was that Indian women hadn't been made to feel comfortable. Wasn't "diversity" the word that everyone used about creative industries now? So why was her writing group, her creative outlet, not providing a safe space for her? Because she was seen as inferior due to her ethnicity.

She wasn't a particularly political person. Whenever an argument broke out in their temple about the controversial organization Vishva Hindu Parishad and how its increasingly nationalist followers were forming a small but dedicated group within their community, she shrugged and complimented herself on having a drama-free family in this regard. At the same time, she also couldn't slough off politics entirely. She had always found inspiration in the ascent of Sonia Gandhi, whose own political career seemed to have embodied the confused nationality of Ranjana and her contemporaries. The Italian woman who had married Indiraji's son, Rajiv—not just married but fallen in love with him, leaping over the chasm between their two cultures—seemed like a rare branch of India's political tree, and Ranjana loved this idea of an interloper, an oddball. More than this, though, she loved how Sonia Gandhi had defied the defeatists around her, the people that had predicted that she would die a quick political death after Rajiv's assassination. Everyone had expected her to bury her Italian face in her Indian shawl, grab her children, and become a shut-in, but she had seen the opportunity to wrest every last bit of power her husband had left her, and soon she had become a nationalist heroine. She argued and debated and showed up to rallies where her face was enlarged on billboards and placards; she had inhaled whatever political fervor had blown into the wind with her husband's ashes.

Sonia Gandhi was not American, of course, but Ranjana did find some solace in the idea that a nonconforming woman could enter and fully master a culture while respecting it all along—and be embraced by it! It was possible to move to a new country, to absorb it and to be encouraged. Ranjana wanted this kind of encouragement from the non-Indian women that she knew—especially from ones who had the secret, fragile material of her writing in their hands.

"I just wish that these women—at the very least—would see me as equal to themselves," Ranjana said, plainly.

Satish sucked in his cheeks and went back into the kitchen. Seema just batted her hand in the air.

A few minutes later, Ranjana was back in her car, driving home, and her forehead tingled from all of her confusion. She had driven to Seema's house with the aim of commiserating about her treatment at the hands of American women, but something flashed into her head now: she wasn't sure whose side Seema was on. She felt scrutinized, beaten down by the constant anxiety of dealing with her writing class (not to mention her writing itself), but she didn't exactly feel comforted when she was with Seema and Satish. Not only had their conversation become something more of a comedy act—something they performed for her rather than a true translation of their feelings—but now that she had her own problems with Mohan to deal with, she felt every one of their "jokes" as small, burning reminders of her own problems at home. And they would engage with her only to a certain extent: Seema was more focused on organizing her lipsticks than listening to Ranjana's concerns.

As she pulled into her driveway and saw the pale lights on in her living room, Ranjana thought of Harit—someone neutral, someone also caught between social circles, someone equally confused. She had always hoped that there would be some friendship with an American woman that would zap her out of her status as an Indian immigrant and legitimize her connection to America, that she would find a sidekick who truly understood her and introduced her to the complex social structure of this country. But what she hadn't considered was that another Indian immigrant, one who was stuck between India and America, could play this same role, and perhaps more effectively. This man, this prisoner between worlds, might be the confidant that she had been searching for all this time.

HARIT DID NOT HAVE RANJANA'S luck: he had to see Teddy at the store, so he had to face Teddy's entreaties to hang out in person. Harit's response was to propose more trips to TGI Friday's.

He and Teddy were sitting at their usual table and having martinis. Harit had come around on martinis; they were like alcoholic bombs, targeted and potent. Accompanying the drinks was a large plate of mozzarella sticks, which Harit found irresistible. The tang of the cheese resembled the taste of really firm *paneer*, and the crunch of the breading felt like an achievement when your teeth clamped down. Harit had taken to asking for crushed red pepper to mix into his side of marinara sauce. Teddy recoiled from such a taste and said that his head would pop off and land in the kitchen's deep fryer if he ate it. Harit imagined the sight of Teddy's head dipped in batter. He chuckled into his glass.

They had gotten down to one stick, and Harit reached for it, feeling no bit of remorse whatsoever. If Teddy wanted more, he could order more, and he would likely eat all of them. But as

Harit was lifting the stick off the plate, Teddy slapped his hand playfully and said, "Naughty girl!" Teddy was giggling, an act that made him seem even older. Harit offered a smile back, though he felt strange about the moment in a way that he couldn't quite place.

They felt it before they heard it; you can feel spite.

"Look at these fucking fags."

A trio of college-aged guys was standing near the table, their faces cracked in two—grin on the bottom, glare on the top. All three young men wore heavy coats and baseball caps, and a gold chain gleamed from the neck of the one on the right. Harit had endured his share of racist experiences, but he understood in this instant how different a gay comment felt. It felt alive, like he could pull the slur off of him and feel it pulsing in his hands.

Both Teddy and Harit were silent. Then, to Harit's surprise, Teddy spoke softly, "Please leave us alone, guys," and leaned forward to take another sip of his martini. Harit almost started to stop him, because he could see, in this action, Teddy's effeminacy at its full impact, the pursed lips, the grand lift of his arm as the glass neared his mouth.

"Oh, we should probably leave you fags alone so you can drink your faggoty martinis," the one on the left said. His voice was deeper, though goofier.

Teddy set his drink down, betraying his efforts at composure by spilling a bit. To Harit, he said, "Don't listen to them, hon—" and then caught himself. Here, in this riveting, crushing moment, he finally seemed to truly hear the tone that he affected when addressing Harit.

"Don't listen to them, *what*, faggot?" the one on the left coughed out, coming closer to the table. The three were all laughing now. It was the funniest bloody thing that they'd ever heard in their lives.

Just then, Harit and Teddy's butch waiter walked past the table, and one look from him sucked out some of the menace in the air. A guy like him could tell when guys were trying to act like him.

"Everything fine here, fellas?" he said. Harit and Teddy had recently discovered that his name was Brian. Harit held on to that fact now as if it were some precious gem.

"Just enjoying this little show," the middle one said, pointing unabashedly at the table.

Brian sighed and said, "OK, come on, now, guys. Let's move it along."

"Come on," the one on the left said. "We're just having a little faggoty fun."

"Heyyy," Brian said, like they'd just spilled wine on his shirt. "OK, let's not do that, guys."

All three laughed and shrugged. "Whatever," the middle one said. "What-ever. Let's go. No one wants to be at homo hour." Brian was gesturing around them to the manager, who was acknowledging the issue from across the room.

They steered the men out, and both Teddy and Harit could see the group crossing the mall floor outside. The man with the chain turned around. Harit and Teddy ducked down quickly, as if someone were about to shoot a gun. Harit looked over at Teddy, crouched amidst the mess of dirt and gum on the ground.

They lifted themselves up. Teddy started laughing nervously. Harit stared into his martini glass. He felt a combination of drunk and ashamed, then realized that the two things often went hand in hand.

"I'm so sorry—" Teddy said, leaving a breath where a "honey" would've once lived. "It's . . . it's nothing. That sort of stuff happens all the time. They're just stupid kids."

"What if they're waiting for us outside?" Harit asked. He wanted to be in bed.

"They won't. They won't. They're stupid kids. They have a frat party to go to or something." Teddy started giggling again. It was awful.

They asked for their check. "Thank you," Teddy said to Brian, who said back quickly, "Don't worry about it. Sorry for that, guys." Brian: their unlikely savior.

As they left, Harit felt a desire to cling to Teddy and a will to never see him again. In the parking lot, he could feel both of them trying not to look around. A burst of laughter came from somewhere, and they both cringed. They got into Teddy's car and took off. Neither spoke, and when they got to his house, Harit left the car wordlessly, running to the back door.

He dreamed that night of the guy on the right, who had never said a word at the restaurant but who, in the dream, seemed full of them. Yet Harit couldn't make out his words, only a sensation of them. The sensation crept its fingers into his chest and opened it slowly; a sliver of pink smoke curled up from it. It took Harit what seemed like hours to register that this thread of smoke was some version of his heart, which was no longer solid but which could blow away if the air caught it. He understood that he had been foolish about sex, or what he thought about sex. Those men, despite their boorishness, had hit upon some fundamental element of his urges. He was a middle-aged man who put on woman's clothes (for something necessary, but he still did it), and who was he to deny the harsh name-calling of those men when he had never explored another person's body—woman or man—to see what would give him comfort? The real danger of an insult, even in sleep, was that it put into slurs what you put into poetry in order to protect yourself.

THE CALLS BEGAN INNOCENTLY ENOUGH. Ranjana would be coming in the door from work, hear the cordless phone warbling in the kitchen, and rush to pick it up. "Hello?" she would say, and then there would be a few short puffs—not frenzied or sexual, thank God, but still serious—and then a quick hang-up. Immediately, she thought of Achyut, his pretty face twisting into anxiety under its scruff. At one point, a call came in the night while she and Mohan were both asleep. As she awoke, she heard Mohan grumbling. He slammed the phone back into its position beside their bed.

"Who was it?" she felt obliged to ask, though she knew the caller's identity was as unknown to him as it was to her. Mohan let out an unintelligible swear and then rolled back into sleep. Now Ranjana really began to worry. She could not sleep the rest of the night.

The next day at work, she was useless. She was more tired than she had been in a long while, perhaps since Prashant's early high school days, when he would come home, his backpack containing so many books that it looked like a giant sea turtle, and she would stay up with him as he sorted through his myriad assignments. Today, she tried to yawn inconspicuously, afraid more of Cheryl's attention than of Dr. Butt's surely taciturn reaction. Her fears were confirmed when Cheryl bothered her an hour before lunchtime.

"Babe, if you yawn one more time, I'm gonna think you have mono." Cheryl crossed her index fingers over each other in an exorcist-like staving-off.

"I don't have mono, Cheryl," Ranjana said. "Someone called while we were sleeping last night, and I couldn't get back to sleep."

"Who?"

"I don't know."

"You don't know? Ohmigod, are you being stalked?"

"Don't be ridiculous," Ranjana admonished, but as soon as she heard the word *stalked* come out of Cheryl's mouth, she realized how scared it made her. Could it be true? Why? Who? How?

Cheryl picked up on her fear. "Ohmigod, maybe you should file a police report."

"Cheryl, it happened just this once. You're running away with this. Haven't you ever had a wrong number in the middle of the night?"

"Oh, honey, I've had *many* a wrong number in the middle of the night." From somewhere, she pulled out a small packet of sugared pecans and started to munch on them. She had a habit of producing snacks as if they grew on her. "All I'm saying is that you wouldn't look so tired and worried right now if it didn't have you scared."

"It's nothing Wendy's can't cure," Ranjana replied, knowing that the mere mention of fast food would save them from exploring the topic any further.

As they ate their lunch—Cheryl alternating between dipping her sandwich in hot mustard sauce and barbecue sauce—it dawned on Ranjana that Teddy may be her secret caller. She recalled his general fidgety nature, his eagerness to know her and befriend her, and this thought made her even more frightened than the idea of Achyut or a stranger. It was silly, to be afraid of such a goofy man, but it still unsettled her. She reassured herself that it had nothing to do with his being gay, but at the same time, she felt guilty about the idea of assuming him harmless simply because he preferred men sexually. Was it bigoted to assume that gay men didn't have the fortitude to be stalkers?

About an hour after lunch, she realized: Harit. It was clearly Harit. The tone of the breaths—it was the first time she had ever thought of breath as having a tone—something in it mimicked the overall carriage of Harit's body, the weightiness mixed with a dispersion of energy. It was Harit. All sense of fear left her and was replaced with compassion. Harit. Friendless except for Teddy— alone and meek and with that swaying shyness from the temple.

She thought back to a tense memory from many years ago, soon after her arrival in the U.S.: a picnic table, its bright checkered surface crowded with an assortment of large bowls, each one filled with a colorful fruit or vegetable salad, the sickening but increasingly reliable smell of cooking meat, a lawn fragrant and strewn with freshly cut shards of itself, the laughter of children, her own newly pregnant belly under her hands. It was a faculty picnic, a gathering of white women with tapered hair and freckled noses, and their spouses, long-locked at the temples and wearing wide ties and long shoes. She had been standing, holding her stomach, not saying a word to anyone for a good twenty minutes, just taking the scene in, trying to find some connection between the world she had known and this one. She settled on the table itself as the only comforting sight. It reminded her of the one that had been behind her house in Delhi and on which she'd made mud pies with her next-door neighbors. Their voices were lighter and more joyous than the cries of American children, who always seemed to be doing something to each other instead of simply being with each other. The palpable sense that she would likely never know what it felt like to live simply, now that every moment was overwhelming. Her reverie was broken by an older woman who had spilled punch on her cream blouse, a blood rose of fruitiness. The woman approached Ranjana in a panic with some club soda and salt—because Ranjana's skin had turned her into a servant—and Ranjana used them properly, something she couldn't remember having learned explicitly, which meant she had learned it from the endless depths of her TV watching. She vividly remembered that sense of connection as she helped this woman, then the distance returned as the woman thanked her tersely and resumed a conversation at the other end of the table.

Ranjana had not thought of this moment in a long time. She had thrown out the dress she had worn for that occasion, her body having shifted after Prashant's birth. But something about how she had felt at that party was echoed in the breaths that she had heard on the phone, and Ranjana knew that she would confront Harit the next time it rang.

It happened, luckily, when she was home alone. Before a second breath was even huffed out, she said, "Haritji?"

She expected him to hang up, but then she heard him say, "...*Ji?*"

"Haritji, *kya haal hai?*" She wanted to sound nonchalant, not wanting to frighten him off.

"*Theek hai,*" he managed to get out. He sounded like he was in an airtight chamber. Perhaps he was calling from the bathroom.

"All is good?" she continued in Hindi, not sure what else to ask. She should let him lead the conversation. He obviously had something important to tell her.

"Fine," he repeated. "Just fine."

Ranjana wasn't sure what to ask next. "Can I help you with something, *ji*?"

The breaths came again, and she realized that he was crying. Not a full-on sob, but it sounded as if his whole body was trembling. The muscles in her upper back tightened. All this time, she had seen him as some shy creature, but in this instant, she sensed something much darker and more significant.

She wasn't sure how to respond, but she tried. "Would you like to meet for some tea?" She began to give him directions to the coffee shop where she'd met Achyut, but when Harit stuttered on the other end, she remembered: he had no car. She volunteered to pick him up, and when another series of stutters came through, she cut him off and said, "It's no problem." Like that, he burst out with the address, and she jotted it down so quickly that she feared that she may not be able to read her own handwriting later. She was more intent when writing a note to put on the fridge for Mohan: *Went out to get a couple of things from the store.* Then she was on her way.

Harit had heard people use the term "nervous breakdown" before, and because of his tendency to translate word-by-word instead of seeing a phrase whole, he had seen this term as particularly full of meaning. He felt, indeed, that his very nerves were breaking. It wasn't until now, when he felt himself falling apart, that he realized how much tension had crept into his body over time, how he had long ago given up full control over his movements and thoughts and actions. As with his Swati routine, he felt that someone else had taken over his behavior. It was done to him instead of something he did. This kind of passive behavior could be comforting: if he didn't have to insert himself into the proceedings, he was free of responsibility. But now, he understood just what he had given up by resigning himself to such a thing. He had let his life be dictated by others and had shut down his own desires in doing so. He had lost not just his sister but his center.

It surprised him that he had not yet had this breakdown in front of his mother. Certainly, she would have been an ideal audience for such a thing, present and therefore witness to his unraveling but unable to process it adequately and resent his insanity. Yet some part of the reverent relationship remained with his mother, and even in the midst of this agitated state, he could not let her see him like this. Plus, she could offer no care for him, as he was *her* caretaker. He needed the comfort of a woman, but he needed a woman who was comforting, and now with Swati gone and his mother a statue and the women at temple strangers in their giggles and gilded saris, he thought of Ranjana. He knew that she would understand.

But understand what, exactly? What was he planning on telling her? *My sister died and it's my fault and my mother has gone insane and I am wearing saris to keep her stable?* How could he begin to explain this to anyone? Every night, he cataloged these problems in his head and thought how much easier it would have been if one or more of them could be erased. Each one was devastating, but taken together, they created a broken man.

Compassion was being able to put yourself in the place of another, to draw from whatever experience you had to relate to someone else's trauma and therefore strengthen the both of you. But how could anyone understand what he had gone through? To live in this body, shackled in its self-doubt, to wander these meager rooms and understand how tiny a human life could feel, to see the strong will and bearing of your mother reduced to a joke of itself, to see Swati's body, crumpled, at the foot of the stairs . . . Each night, he would think of his body as an assemblage of conditions, things gone wrong—his diminishing hairline and spot-mottled hands and hairy gut and unsavory private parts, the corns on his feet and tiny hairs in his ears and in his nose, clustered together as if sharing secrets or telling rumors about the person on whom they grew. How could this be desirable to someone, and if it happened to be desirable to someone, how could that person be expected to move past purely physical concerns into the much more dangerous world of emotion and friendship and, hardest of all, love? He felt detached not just from himself but from anyone who could attach value to him. For, clearly, anyone who found him attractive—emotionally, physically, romantically—had to be a complete disaster.

Nevertheless, regardless of the fears that had struck him the night of the confrontation at TGI Friday's, he believed a woman's presence, the softness of her body and the roundness of her hips and emotions, was welcome to him. Ranjana carried with her a combination of the motherly, the sisterly, and the wifely that he wanted so desperately. She had to be the one to take the mess of his feelings and, from them, make him into the functioning man that he wanted to be.

Hovering in the doorway to the kitchen and seeing that his mother had fallen asleep, he was prepared when he heard the tires of Ranjana's car crackle over the street. For a second, he feared that the headlights would pierce the darkness of the room and give his escape away, but they made nothing more than a soft glow, and soon Harit was slipping out the back door, around the house, and over his lawn. He could see Ranjana's hunched form and already knew that she was tense, too. This did not deter him but compelled him forward. He did not wish to see her agitated, but he wanted someone who could understand the direness of his situation. If she were already showing signs of worry, then she was all the more suited to what he had to tell her.

As he opened the door and slid into the car, he had the vague memory of seeing something like this in an American movie, a high school comedy in which a girl and a boy slipped away into the night and wound up talking until morning. He felt his posture straighten: to imagine himself in such a casual social situation gave him a sense of belonging and progress, a small confidence.

"*Namaste, ji,*" she said, pulling away from the curb and already, he could tell, more nervous than he had imagined. He adopted this feeling in turn, wishing for just a moment that he had never called her, that she had never answered the phone. As they drove farther and the silence between them continued, he started to feel comfortable again. The fact that she did not break the silence, did not try to fill it with unimpressive facts of her day or unnecessary questions into his, expressed to him that she knew that their eventual conversation would be serious.

For the past few weeks, Ranjana had asked herself what Achyut's presence in her life had meant. Surely, she had not endured such a bizarre occurrence for nothing; her instincts had been motherly, and she deserved some kind of reward for trying to help out a young person in need. Now, as she drove, a similar air seizing her car, she saw that her nurturing of Achyut had prepared her for this: the nurturing of Harit.

Harit had not sounded suicidal on the phone, but his voice had sounded resolutely irresolute; he needed her. She could not leave someone in a position like that, and Harit was not just someone. She was too involved to let him keep struggling.

She had intended to take him to Buzzed (even though the thought of running into Achyut was nightmarish), but as she neared the place, she realized that it was later in the evening than she had thought. By the time she and Harit bought their tea and sat down, they would have very little time to converse, let alone process the surely upsetting news that Harit had to share. Her next thought was Paradise Island, but knowing how dark and isolated it could be in that spot, she could not bring herself to take him there; he would find it just as reckless as she did. Then she had a genius idea: she had told Mohan that she was going to the grocery store, and since it was a superstore, it was no mere collection of produce, canned goods, and paper products but, rather, a veritable shopping mall with a café at its center.

She broke the silence, merely saying the word "groceries" as she turned into the massive parking lot, and Harit seemed to relax. She imagined that he saw the same series of reliable things that she had in mind: the cool grip of the shopping cart, a serene village of greenery and colorful packages arrayed in its netted-metal bottom; the strangely satisfying image of your face glimmering back at you on the glass of large refrigerators and freezers. And then, of course, there was the café, nestled between the produce and dairy sections, where you could get a cheap cup of tea or coffee amidst the frenzy of shopping. This is where she led him, after stopping to place a small tub of Dannon yogurt and a block of Land O'Lakes butter in her cart.

Ranjana would hear the story about Swati as a short story, and she would write it down later.

ON HER EIGHTH BIRTHDAY, Swati received a Barbie doll from her aunt Manisha, her father's sister. Swati had seen the dolls, usually tucked away in display cases behind store counters and shimmering in their gowns. To actually hold one in her hands, to see the butter-colored tug of its hair and the high arches of its small feet, felt like stealing. The doll stayed in her possession at all times, except when her family went to their temple in Delhi and she kept it under her pillow at home. Had her brother been remotely mischievous, he would have seen it as an opportunity to torment Swati, hiding it in unexpected places or even disfiguring it. Instead, he was a quiet, respectful child who clearly adored his sister, and if Barbie was the most important thing in her life, he would pay the doll dutiful attention.

Barbie was dressed in a demure blue dress with a checkered pattern on its front. An apron, tied with a neat blue bow in the back, hugged her waist and curved over her ample bosom. The blood-drop of her lips and her arched, dark eyebrows seemed to come equally from India and another planet, and Harit dreamed of these things whenever he had the chance. (Later, he would realize that the attention he paid to the doll had less to do with whatever feminine prowess it exhibited and more to do with how much his sister adored it.)

In a household with very little in the way of decoration, a doll as beautiful as this was able to hold sway over everyone. Because Barbie had been given as a gift from a family member, she was not banished from the dinner table but, rather, sat next to Swati's plate, as if she were judging every dish placed on the table and every bite of food that each person took. Swati would begin to tell the family what had happened during her day by speaking directly to the doll. "Barbie, today we learned about Nehruji and how he studied a man called John Maynard Keynes, and now we have to write three pages in our copybooks about economics." Harit's mother and father would smile between themselves and occasionally roll their eyes, and Harit himself began to see how important it was to be as creative as this, to find life as imaginative and decidedly odd as Swati made it to be.

Children have the tendency to pick up and then quickly discard their toys in favor of other ones, but Barbie maintained a powerful spell over Swati. As the years passed and Swati became a more self-possessed young woman, Barbie began to assume a symbolic role in her life. Even as Swati grew up and the doll was in her possession less and less, it seemed to leave an impression of its presence, charmed and strange. As one might associate Harit with the clip-on maroon tie that he often wore as a child, one would imagine Swati as she had been with the Barbie in one hand or positioned next to her plate or keeping watch from the windowsill near her bed as she slept.

Although Swati was not vain, she began to resemble the doll

more and more. She exaggerated the kohl around her eyes, flicking up two streaks toward her temples, and her lipstick became redder. As she developed breasts, the white cotton shirt that she had to wear as part of her school uniform began to expand, completing the mimicry. She looked at that doll and said, "That's what I want to be." And, more or less, she was.

To Harit, it was fascinating that aging could make you a more defined version of what you already were. Swati seemed to grow in confidence because she practically willed it so. She seemed to be asserting herself as a strong-minded, smart, and worthy woman—not just something to be looked at but someone to respect and admire.

Then, eight years after she had received it, Swati lost the doll. It was on the windowsill next to her bed, and then, the next morning, it was gone. She berated Kamila, their housekeeper, because she was convinced that Kamila had taken it to give to her own daughter. This accusation seemed not only rash but unfathomable, as Kamila and her daughter would never have dared to commit such an indiscretion.

Swati searched the house. She checked under the couch and among its cushions. She got on top of a chair and scanned the surroundings of her bedroom, then accidentally toppled off and bruised her elbow. She explored their foul-smelling toilet, thinking that it may have been thrown in there (by God-knew-whom and for God-knew-why). With no one else in the house but her parents, Harit, and Kamila, she began to suspect that a burglar had taken it. But what kind of heartless, juvenile, and deranged burglar would break into a house just to steal a doll?

Like something out of a dark fairy tale, the doll began to assume, in its absence, an even stronger and decidedly destructive hold on Swati. She was a charming and pretty girl with lots of friends and the clear adoration of her family, yet this one little thing seemed to affect her extraordinarily. She was a teenager, a young woman with more important things that she should be focusing on, yet she seemed to be acknowledging a sad fact of life: she had come to that moment that a growing child fears but never suspects will actually happen, that at some point the symbolic accessories of youth will have to be discarded in order to acknowledge the serious responsibilities of adulthood. Begrudgingly accepting this fact, Swati began to pay less heed to her looks. Gone were the exaggerated lashes, the confidence in her appearance, the graceful but excited gait of her walk.

Her mother finally said something. Harit was making roti with Kamila, the kitchen alive with floating flour particles that caught the light. He heard his mother call Swati to the sitting room, and he knew that Barbie was going to be the focus of her speech. Kamila clucked her annoyance (she couldn't believe that this ordeal was still happening), and Harit craned to hear the conversation.

"*Beti*, you must stop worrying over this. It is gone, and it is not coming back."

"*She* is gone, and *she* is not coming back," Swati corrected her.

"Whatever, *beti*. The point is that you cannot worry about something—*someone*—who is gone. You can carry a memory of that thing—that *person*—in your heart, but you cannot let everything else in your life fall to the side."

"I am not letting everything fall to the side," Swati said. She had a habit of wringing her hands when she was being criticized, and from his position in the kitchen, Harit could hear the jingle of her bangles. "I am doing well in school. I am helping Harit with his schoolwork, too."

"It is not just those things. This is a time of your life when you must be thinking of your future. No man is going to want a woman who complains about losing her favorite toy. This is not normal."

Harit was surprised at this comment. One thing that their parents were not was normal. They were some of the most self-possessed people in their circle of friends, known for their fine looks and their calm surety when it came to socializing. Their father, Jaideep, was a respected accountant, and even though Kamila handled many of the cooking duties, their mother was nevertheless famous for her *mattar paneer* and *kadhi*. "Unfair!" Swati said. "This is so unfair. You've always encouraged us to be unique and successful. I don't think anyone would accuse me of not being successful."

"Ah, yes, but it is a question of in *what* you are successful," her mother said. "Being charming will get you only so far. You must be likeable and approachable, too."

"So you're saying I'm not likeable?"

"I am not saying that at all. I am saying that you may want to think about how you use your likeability. That is important, especially for a girl as special as you are."

Even at this young age, Harit was aware of what his mother was doing. She was using the doll as a springboard to another topic entirely, a topic that girls dreaded: image. This was, in a word, cruel. It was cruel to take a boisterous young woman like Swati and make her question herself. Yet Harit also felt—and was sure that Swati felt—an unavoidable desire to heed his mother's words.

And so, gradually, the doll was forgotten. Swati set herself even more fervently to her studies, and she learned how to re-create, in a poof of spice and milk, flour and greenery, the *mattar paneer* and *kadhi* of her mother's renown.

But despite this change, despite the efforts that Swati made, there were the vestiges of her personality that could not be swept away. She was and would always be a headstrong woman, and men continued to sense this and back away. There was a close call, a young doctor—well, podiatrist—who took a liking to Swati immediately, but Harit's mother caught him looking too lustily at the tender flesh of Swati's ankles, and suddenly, the reason for his choice of vocation became all too clear. As Swati's mother hurried him out the door, he scoffed, "No need to tire those pretty little feet searching for a husband—because you'll never find one!" Men were prone to grand, harsh statements like this in Swati's presence, but her tough demeanor refused to surrender to them. This was to their parents' chagrin, but for Harit, it was one of the things that he revered most about her.

Harit and Swati grew up and went to school and became young adults, and then their father suffered a heart attack and was swept away as quickly as that doll. His spirit was repurposed to his family in varying degrees—Harit's mother became more imperious, Swati more compassionate, Harit more afraid of being the man of the house—and then they came to America and found themselves irrelevant outside the confines of their household. Harit found a janitor job at a medical supplies company, and Swati found work as a part-time nanny, not just for Indian families but also for American ones. The Americans loved her energy, her smile, and they loved how expertly she played with little girls—the voices she could do for any stuffed animal and or for a variety of dolls. She began to get more work, more hours, and her mother did not mind simply because the money kept them afloat.

Then, years after their arrival in America, Harit, opening a box of cups and saucers that had escaped their notice, was astounded to see the Barbie—the very same doll—placed atop them, as if someone had meant for him to find it. The doll was bent so that it was curved into a cup, its arms and legs stretching upward like those of a baby calling for its mother. Harit let out a gasp. It looked no different from the way it had all those years ago, the dress as crisp and colorful as ever.

He was not a natural prankster. He had once tried to throw a surprise birthday party for Swati when they were back in India, but he had not told people to stagger their arrivals; he had also failed to have someone tail Swati to make sure she didn't come home too soon. So there she was, falling in step with at least four guests and so unsurprised that she went over to the cake and presented it to the guests as if she herself had baked it that afternoon. Therefore, Harit worried about how to present this long-lost possession to his sister. Should he reseal this box of dishes and send Swati to open it later, so that she might experience the kind of excitement that he had experienced? Should he wrap it up as a separate gift and give it to her on a special occasion? Should he let his mother in on the secret?

No, he decided firmly—especially when it came to this last question. He remembered his mother's conversation with Swati in that sitting room years before, and he knew that his mother would not share his elation at having rediscovered the doll, especially since Swati was as single as ever. Moreover, he wanted Swati to credit him with the doll's reappearance.

Swati woke at five in the morning every day, before any of them, and the first thing she always did was scurry downstairs to take a shower in the first-floor bathroom. She preferred it to the upstairs bathroom because it had a slanted window that allowed the bather to look up at the sky without being viewed by passersby. Harit decided that he would pose the doll on a window opposite the bottom of the stairs. The oblong window, with its floating lace curtains, looked out on the street and would act as a frame for Barbie. Nothing could be more impressive than for her to see this childhood ghost, backlit by the breaking dawn and framed in soft white cloth. Meanwhile, Harit would conceal himself in the sitting room so he could see Swati's reaction.

He didn't want to waste any time. He had discovered the doll on a Saturday afternoon, and so Sunday morning would be the time for his surprise. Swati did work on Sunday afternoons, babysitting for a nearby trio of kids while their parents attended church.

Their mother normally went to bed early, at around nine o'clock, but Swati usually stayed up late, fascinated by late-night television. She loved to make fun of Conan O'Brien, his long, red-topped form, and many nights found her enjoying a plateful of *chaat* while giggling at his non sequiturs and flimsy tosses of hair. Harit didn't have the stamina to remain awake as long as Swati—he marveled at how she could go to bed after one thirty and wake as early she did—but he could usually manage to stay awake until just after midnight. So, to prevent his sister from being suspicious, he went to bed at his usual hour, kissing Swati on the cheek and padding up the stairs. He spent the next few hours listening to her, her giggles and chomps, the rustling of her *salwar* as she fidgeted comfortably on the couch. Then, the TV clicking off, her wistful ascent of the stairs, the creak as she curled into bed, deciding not to change out of a garment that doubled as sleepwear.

At quarter till five, Harit plucked Barbie from under his bed, then spent an excruciating ten minutes slowly descending the stairs so as not to wake anyone up. Finally, he reached the bottom and placed Barbie on the sill. He had little to do besides this, the light outside striking the window just as he had envisioned and the curtains framing the doll perfectly. Harit tiptoed over to the couch, in the same spot where his sister had been just a few hours ago, and waited.

He would hear people's compassion as anger, feel their pats on the back as if they were slaps on the face, see their drooping gazes as upside-down mockeries of the doll's eyes.

If his mother's madness had one upside, it was that it prevented her from looking at him as if he were responsible for Swati's death. Harit may never know what his mother's true judgment of the situation was, but his mother would also not know what it felt like to see Swati scurry down the steps—then catch herself midway, shocked by what greeted her below, only to trip and get caught in her own *salwar*. His mother would not know what this looked like, although perhaps the cause of her hysteria was that she could envision a million ways in which the fall might have occurred. (The medical term for what had actually killed Swati—"an epidural hematoma due to blunt impact to the head"—would forever repeat in Harit's head like a demonic mantra.)

It was just so vicious—that a life woven of such charm and oddity could be ended in such a ridiculous manner. And of the three of them to go, why Swati? His mother had lived at least six decades; Harit was the quiet standby to Swati's star. He had needed her. They had needed her.

The family for whom Swati normally babysat called later that afternoon, angry that she hadn't shown up. Theirs were the first voices that cracked in whimpers as Harit informed them of the accident. He wasn't sure what slapped him across the face most: the fact that a doll, of all things, had led to her death, or the fact that the first people to hear of his sister's passing had nothing at all to do with where she had begun her life. It was only then that Harit understood that all of these Indians who had come to the States would end their stories here. For some reason, he had always envisioned their deaths as occurring on Indian soil, their bodies cremated amidst the rustic-commercial swirl of their upbringing. But there was no guarantee that they would make it back to their homeland before they died. Life wasn't a circle but a line. The blurry opening of the film may have taken place on the subcontinent, but its counterpart, the fading into darkness, was decidedly American.

AFTER HARIT'S STORY, he and Ranjana remained quiet—a space filled by the sonic knickknacks of the café. It seemed odd to hear an assortment of canisters clicking shut and mugs being stacked and coffee beans being packed away, but Ranjana was grateful for these noises. She knew that she could not let this moment hang in the balance for too much longer. She had to offer something to assuage his fear.

"*Ji*, I am very honored that you have told me about this. I know this could not have been an easy thing for you to do." This was not as noble-sounding a response as she had hoped to make, but she was distracted by how despondent Harit looked.

He made one simple nod of the head downward—no upward movement to complete it, so that he looked like he was slouching instead of acknowledging her comment. Clearly, recounting the events of his sister's death had thrust him back into its trauma, but she had to do her best to draw him out of that period and into the present moment.

"I cannot imagine going through what you have gone through." Equally unimpressive a response, but she had to keep his attention. "This was not your fault, *ji*. It was an accident. And to think that you've been keeping all of this inside you . . . To me, what you have done is heroic."

This word changed him immediately. He seemed to be mulling over the magnanimousness of it, its weight and nobility. It *was* astounding, what he had endured, and he deserved to be exalted. The achievement being, of course, simply being able to put one foot in front of the other, given the circumstances.

Struck by some Edith Whartonian inspiration, the first thing that came to Ranjana's mind was throwing him a dinner party. Well, a dinner party in the Indian sense, which meant that she and Mohan would throw a regular party but that Harit would be in attendance—a small but still noticeable addition to their social circle. His attendance at temple had already started this process rolling, so it would not be totally out of the ordinary for him to make his way into their home.

She and Mohan were not known for their entertaining; in fact, she knew that compared to the sprawling, buttressed palaces of their friends, their house was rather modest. But Prashant's recent departure gave them a reason to have a party. They were newly freed parents—their own bosses now—and it was time to be "Ranjanaji and Mohanji" instead of "The Chaudhurys."

She was already thinking of the menu as she drove Harit back to his house. Harit seemed relieved to have told someone his troubles. Ranjana assumed that he had not gone into nearly as much detail when recounting the situation to other people; perhaps he hadn't told anyone. She had gotten the real story, and as a writer herself, she understood the preciousness of this. Perhaps he had sensed this ability in her: he could see that she would appreciate the drama that he had endured.

Here was a man stunted by tragedy, not by the made-up troubles of a woman who was, frankly, dabbling in self-absorption. While Ranjana was crumpling up pages in her hands, amidst the petty grievances of her fellow writers, this poor man was grieving without being consoled. She had not been in his house, but since Harit had said that his mother was basically paralyzed by her grief, Ranjana could envision what it would be like inside, the usual disarray of an immigrant household: dishes washed and rewashed and leaving watermarks on shelves; bedsheets repurposed into curtains or throw rugs; the general smell of bodies recently slept and food recently eaten. No wonder Harit seemed so lost. He was basically an outsider in his own home.

She realized, again and more fully this time, that it was her responsibility to give Harit a sense of belonging. She saw now that friends were not simply presences that came into your life; you had to inject personality into the relationship so that you could both become more than yourselves. In short, she wanted to give Harit the gift of her own recent realization: she wanted him to discover his own personality, his own sense of humor, a way forward through his grief to a place of resilience and acceptance. But even more than that, she wanted to provide him with a sense of community, the security that he need not suffer his troubles alone, even if others had not endured the kind of trauma that he had. It was possible and necessary to protect him like this.

She believed this firmly, yet she knew that trying to comfort a man who had endured its complete opposite was dauntingly naïve. It reminded her of fashionable American women who would come up to her when she was newly arrived from India, still swaddled in saris that she had owned from her teenage days. These

Americans would approach her and marvel at the fabric, not understanding that even more intricate and impressive garments existed in her own closet, let alone the closets of other Indian women. These girls assumed that she cared about fashion and style as much as they did, not seeing that simply trying to have a mundane conversation was a much more pressing issue for her.

She worried that she might not be able to help Harit through this period of his life when her own experience had been drastically different. But she had to try. She knew that she had to play some integral role in his rehabilitation, even though "rehabilitation" didn't seem like the right word. He didn't need to be rehabilitated; he had to be habilitated in the first place.

HARIT MADE THE MISTAKE of telling Teddy about Ranjana's party.

He hadn't intended to do it. Teddy came upon him while he was tallying a figure in his head, and he was so lost in his calculations that when Teddy asked him if he wanted to go to an art opening that weekend, Harit simply blurted out that he had an event to attend. The last thing that Harit wanted was for Teddy to think that he was invited to the party. Teddy was already such an anomaly amidst Americans that Harit could only imagine the impression he would make on a group of Indians. They would find nothing savory about him.

If there was one thing that Teddy couldn't understand, it was a hint. Naturally, if Harit brought up the party, Teddy would assume an invitation was implied.

Harit thought of a quick solution: he would say that the event was for Hindus only. He would deem it a *puja*, like the one that he had just attended for Preetiji. He would tell Teddy that there had been a death in the host's family and that the Indian families were gathering to pay respects and pray. Harit couldn't believe that he was using this as an excuse, given his family's tragedy, but this only underscored his fear of Teddy's attendance.

Teddy seemed as shocked by the prospect of Harit's socializing as Harit himself was. "You're going out?"

"Yes," Harit said. "We Hindu families have these every so often. They cleanse the house of any bad spirits or feelings."

"'We families'? Not to be rude, honey, but I don't recall you ever going to anybody's house for . . . well, anything."

"I—I have. I just haven't mentioned them before." Then, with more force: "You know, I don't have to tell you *everything*, Teddy."

Teddy chuckled, either not noticing—or willfully deflecting— the steel in Harit's voice. "There, there, sweetheart. I'm going to the art opening that night anyway. I'm happy for you. It's good for you to get out and about."

"Thank you."

"Will Ranjana be there?" Teddy continued to pronounce her name correctly, which irritated Harit. He was used to Americans garbling Indian names, but he somehow felt more unsettled by Teddy's correct pronunciation. To hear Teddy speak her name made it seem as if he were equally worthy of it, that he had as much of a claim to Ranjana's friendship as Harit did.

"I believe that she will be there, yes." Harit neglected to mention that Ranjana herself was the hostess.

Harit noticed the difference in his behavior since his confession to Ranjana. It wasn't as if his stress had left him entirely; there was little chance that such a thing would ever happen. Rather, he understood why people sought therapy: it was true that simply talking about something made it at least slightly more manageable. A few days after their secret meeting, Ranjana had called to invite him to the party, and Harit's first instinct had been to begin another emotional outpouring. Instead, he caught himself: he couldn't approach every situation with the same level of drama. After all, being involved in a regular event like a get-together was already a big step in the right direction.

What was more, although he had told Ranjana about Swati's accident, he had not told her about his mother or his dressing up. These still felt like impossible topics to talk about, and he didn't want to scare her away. A possible friendship with her seemed as fragile as his emotional state, and he would take this party as the next step and then see if it brought him any closer to sharing more of his personal issues with her.

Although Harit had successfully prevented Teddy's invitation, that didn't prevent Teddy from bothering him about the upcoming party. Tuesday, in the break room, Teddy said, "So, tell me what actually happens at this *puja*." He got that word right, too, and Harit thought of Teddy before a home computer, typing in the word to do research before bringing it up casually like this. This was something Harit himself had done. *LOL, bee tee dubs, tweet, obvi*—these were words and phrases that he had heard from younger customers, constantly clicking gum into their cell phones, never understanding how much harder it would be to learn their made-up slang than to learn Harit's native language, and he had searched them online at the local library in order to educate himself.

"A pandit comes to the house," Harit said, "and performs rituals."

"What kind of rituals?" Teddy asked. Harit imagined what might have popped up during Teddy's online research. Perhaps he had found pictures of a stooped pandit, legs crossed, hands pecking at uncooked rice or crushed flowers or ghee, garlanded portraits of deities flanking him while a couple dozen families surrounded him, their legs also crossed, backs straight, bedsheets carpeting the carpet underneath them. This is what Harit described to Teddy, who took it all in and seemed to understand the image that Harit was creating (possibly because Teddy had, indeed, looked up images online already).

"You know, I might be able to skip my art opening that night and come with you . . . ," Teddy began, but Harit immediately said no.

"Ugh, fine. I would have been *so* good as your wingman," Teddy said, but even though Harit didn't know what that meant, he was sure it was the last thing in the world that he wanted Teddy to be.

Things with Harit's mother started to shift. She had become a nonentity in the house, a responsibility that ebbed and flowed depending on the ebbing and flowing of Harit's drinking. Harit had gotten used to her stillness, and as awful as it seemed, he had begun to think of her as something that needed to be polished instead of cared for. His guilt would have been stronger if she had given him anything, but by maintaining her stillness, she indicated to him that she didn't want to be moved, didn't want to be handled, didn't want to be part of his life. Swati was who she wanted, not Harit.

But two mornings ago, he had come downstairs to find her standing in the middle of the room, the sari fallen from her head and trailing behind her like a wedding gown. Her eyes were still unseeing, but there seemed to be a sense of purpose in her posture. For her to be standing, in the daytime, was a breach of their unspoken rules. To move around during the day was a Harit thing to do; Swati was a nighttime creature. Had his mother begun to sense that something was amiss?

He approached her carefully, asking her if she wanted more chai. She barely moved, her chin dipping slightly, and then he moved her back to her chair, as if repositioning a mannequin in the store. Once she was seated again, he instinctively reached for her throat, as if there were a tie there that he needed to tighten, then stopped himself.

A few minutes later, he heard Gital Didi shuffle her key into the front door and scurry in. She stopped short when she saw him hovering over his mother.

"*Ji*," she said. She was holding her usual family of grocery bags. Her expression was mysteriously unreadable, and Harit challenged it with an equally taciturn expression of his own. "*Kya hua?*" she asked defiantly. *What's the matter?*

"Nothing," he said dismissively. "Ma was out of her chair."

Gital Didi tsked, then headed into the kitchen. "She likes to get her exercise."

Harit broke his stance and followed her into the kitchen. Under his breath: "No, she doesn't. You know she doesn't."

Gital Didi was ducking into the cold shelves of the refrigerator and placing coriander into the crisper. "She likes to exercise lately. You just didn't know because you've been occupied." Although her back was turned to him, he saw the sneer that framed the word "occupied," as if it had ricocheted off the refrigerator's walls and into his eyes.

Harit didn't know what rejoinder to give, so he strode out of the kitchen and upstairs to his room. Fine. If Gital Didi wanted this *badmash*, she could have her.

Her mother wouldn't pay attention to him, but she cared about Gital Didi. Her vision was blocked by white fissures, but she apparently liked exercise. Did she understand where he was headed this evening? Perhaps Gital Didi was helping her piece together his social engagements. No, his mother had been incubated for so long that she probably didn't even remember the staid dowagers who sat guard at every Indian get-together—white-bunned, cardigan-clad women with hands like gathered rope, nodding their approval or assent when necessary, reminders that every adult in the room was nothing more than an aged child. His mother could have been one of these women—had, in fact, been one before Swati's passing. What if he could take her with him, steer her into an armchair and lend his presence a bit more importance?

If he were thinking of logistics alone, this would not work. Harit, of course, had no car in which he could drive his mother—and he was *not* going to ask Gital Didi to be their escort. In any case, Ranjana had arranged for her son, now on "fall break," to pick him up and bring him to the party. This struck him as particularly awkward, but Ranjana had insisted, saying that it was "no problem." If Harit had learned one thing, it was that "no problem" never meant no problem, especially when teenagers were involved.

He didn't know much about Prashant, but he could imagine a pimple-faced, slouching youth sighing with every turn of the steering wheel. What would they possibly talk about? Harit knew that he should play the inquisitive adult, finding out all he could about Prashant's time at university and his studies, yet he knew that Prashant would have to draw conversation out of him like water out of a shoddy well. As Harit tightened his own tie and smoothed his bramble of hair back in front of his bedroom mirror, he thought of possible topics besides academics and the weather—*new Bollywood films, the holidays, did Prashant want a discount on some suspenders?*

He couldn't remember the last time that he had gotten dressed up (that is, when a sari wasn't involved), and he had forgotten how nice it felt. He spent his days helping other men buy accoutrements to make themselves look handsome, and he had become so used to other people grooming themselves that he typically set aside such concerns when it came to his own appearance. It was here in front of this mirror that he decided to dive into his small savings and buy some new dress clothes in the store. If he wanted to change the course of his day-to-day existence, he was going to have to prolong this sense of being "suited and booted," as Swati used to say.

He closed his eyes and tried to envision himself in some of the clothes that he saw in the store. It was shocking that he had never thought to do this; he had somehow never picked up a Geoffrey Beene shirt and considered how it may look against his chest. How could he extol the benefits of a French cuff to a prospective buyer without thinking how it would fit against his brown neck? He wondered these things, yet he knew the answers. He didn't picture himself in stiff, colorful fabric because it seemed like a joke to think of his appearance as important. When he saw a new white collar, he immediately thought of the scrubbing it would take to undo the eventual ring-around-the-collar, an inevitable result of his sweaty skin rubbing against the threads all day. When other men put shirts on, did they think about this?

The hardest part of these thoughts was knowing that he was in the dark but not knowing what he didn't know. If he couldn't think of something as simple as his neck without imagining the grime it would impart to a starched collar, how could he imagine someone kissing that neck? Worse: if the first thing that he associated with his neck was its potential for grime, he would never know what it felt like to think of *only* what it felt like to have someone kissing his neck. For the rest of his life, regardless of how he tried to rethink it, he would always have experienced the potential of grime first. Meanwhile, people who had never had this thought would never understand that a whole other level below their worry existed. It was as if they thought they were on the last rung of a ladder, completely unaware that the ladder pierced through the earth beneath, where, underground, Harit was clawing his way through the dirt and roots. Harit—and Harit alone—knew that he was looking up from his ignorance and seeing a ladderful of people fretting over their deepest despairs.

RANJANA WAS SHAPING HER LIFE into a plot from her romance novels. In all of those books, a simple-seeming but truly remarkable woman found herself saddled with a slob of a husband who paid her little attention—especially sexual—and sought out what was missing from her life in the arms of a quiet but romantically robust man. Or if the husband wasn't a messy pig, then he was a milquetoast, a stick in oversize shirts and pants who put the "oaf" in "loafers." In fact, if she removed herself from the world of potboilers and down-market romances, if she examined a book like, say, *Madame Bovary*, she still found the same conceit—the boring husband whose wife looked for excitement outside marriage. She felt doubly guilty—for trying to fit Mohan into this idea and for betraying her love of the genre itself by lamenting a situation in which her life mimicked it. The women in her writing group, whatever their faults, still thought of their writing as vital, and they would never laugh openly at its contrivances.

The reason why so many people—women, in particular—read romances of all kinds was because they found them legitimately compelling. They also bought fully into the idea of Romance with a capital *R*—and all its attendant glamour. Irony, sarcasm, haughty literary criticism—these were not things they cared about.

Still, Ranjana couldn't let it go. She couldn't help but notice, for instance, that she could guess almost to the exact minute when Mohan would take to his armchair every night, like the lights they had on a timer for the front porch. No matter how much she didn't want to, she noticed how, when he burped, he always did so in three distinct humps of liquid and air. The constant utterances that came from him during a cricket match on TV; the way he would mutter *Ar-RE* when leaning over to pick up something; the blanched crud of his shaving cream remnants in the sink; the monochromatic forest of his dress shirts hanging in the closet; his ever-pervasive smell of Aramis cologne and armpit activity. These all seemed like staples of a literary cuckold. If Mohan wanted to be more dynamic, then he would have to shun these things.

Here is where she was truly wrong, though: Mohan wasn't choosing anything. It wasn't like he behaved this way to seem off-putting or uncaring. It was simply who he was. What she wanted was more *wanting* on his part. She wished that he could show his hand more often. If he could get legitimately worked up about something besides finances and sports, he might be more interesting.

She could feel an arrogance rising in her, the sense that she was Working on Herself and it bothered her that a similar sizing-up was not occurring on her husband's part.

It reminded her of something that Prashant had said under his breath last New Year's Eve. His scheduled plans with the other boys had fallen through due to a freak outbreak of pink eye, and as he sat on the couch watching TV with his parents, he muttered, "If only you guys drank . . ." At first, Ranjana was baffled by this comment—what kid admitted to his parents that he craved alcohol, and what kid wanted to drink *with* his parents?—but she held her tongue to keep the evening lighthearted. A few days later, as she was pulling laundry out of the dryer and the fabric softener's soapy dryness hit her nostrils, she realized what Prashant meant. He didn't want them to be drinking with him; he wanted them to be drinking for themselves, to lighten up their moods. He wanted his parents to be a bit more unpredictable, cooler, more capable of having a good time. He wanted them to be as surprising as the act of doing laundry was mundane. Ranjana was wishing a kind of tipsiness on Mohan: she wanted him to be a bit more spontaneous. She wanted him to surprise her in ways she hadn't seen since the early days of their marriage. All the same, she wondered if his actions back then had been surprising simply because everything was surprising back then.

When they first arrived in America, they didn't have a telephone. They didn't know all that many people, and they hadn't been in the habit of talking on the telephone that much back in India. They soon realized, however, that not having one was a huge problem here, where people seemed to take pride in how tangled the cords on their phones were.

They would go to the department store together, arm in arm, as if they were Americans visiting the grave of a deceased beloved, and while Mohan tried, in vain, to bargain on a clock, an end table, or a bookcase, Ranjana would wander through the store and marvel at the high prices. It was during one of these strolls that she encountered the glassy, flashy collection of TVs in the electronics department. Mohan found her standing in front of one of them. He had apparently called her name several times, but she was so engrossed in a football game—of all things—that she hadn't heard him. They couldn't afford a TV, *of course*, he said. They didn't even have a telephone! Yet Ranjana couldn't stop thinking of how marvelous it would be to have one in their home. Seeing a fancy TV up close made her recognize how much she loved to witness good storytelling and how it could be the very thing to make her new life here engaging. So she had marched up to the salesperson and implored him to give them a discount. "We know all of the Indian families, and they'll see this beautiful TV and want one of their own. I can guarantee you at least a dozen more sales." The salesperson looked astonished and impressed, and soon, Ranjana and Mohan were watching as their TV was carried into their living room by two able-bodied men. Mohan could not stop talking about how beautifully Ranjana had negotiated the TV's way into their house. It was easily the most impressive thing that she had ever done. Although this thought troubled her, she also felt great pride in having pulled it off.

This was the kind of surprise that Ranjana wanted from Mohan. She wanted him to do something charming, something unprecedented and unpredictable, much as she was doing with Harit. She wanted him to drop whatever romantic conquest he was pursuing and direct some love toward her. She deserved it. She deserved to be a sought-after heroine.

But how could she forget? There very possibly *was* a sought-after heroine, just not her. Ranjana had noticed that Mohan was home less often. She had even checked the odometer on his car, the way that Mohan used to check the odometer on the Camry that they shared years ago, so obsessed was he with conserving as much gas as they could. He was driving somewhere now, in small increments. Driving to *her*. So, perhaps Ranjana couldn't predict his every move, after all. Perhaps Mohan really had done something out of the ordinary and become a brazen hero—*Monsieur Bovary*—to someone else.

OVER FALL BREAK, when Prashant entered his house for the first time since leaving for school, he detected a difference in its smell. It wasn't just the pungent film of masala and onions that covered every surface—something you could smell only after having been away from the house for more than a few days. The scent was stale; the ground floor had the air of a basement. It was as if his departure had sapped all sense of youth or energy from the house.

What surprised him most was that his mother's behavior had prepared him for something livelier. The depression of the house seemed directly at odds with her disposition, which was noticeably elevated. This created a tense but still dreary atmosphere. No matter how many bowls of *chaat* or plates of samosas his mother set out, no matter how thoroughly his father scrubbed the bathrooms and puffed flowery air freshener through each room in atomized garlands, his parents nevertheless seemed out of sorts.

Ten minutes into his return—he had taken a Greyhound bus, of all things—his mother asked that he pick up Harit Uncle. This is how she referred to him—*Harit Uncle*—with no preamble or further explanation. Prashant had to ask her to explain, and she said that Harit Uncle was a new member of their circle. Prashant should have been used to hasty additions like this. His mother took pride in cultivating a catchall social world; the odd Indian had a tendency to creep into their crowd as she assumed the role of guide and adviser. There was Sita Kumar, a bumbling woman in her midfifties whose husband, Tipu, constantly licked his black lips; it was silently decided by their circle of friends that Sita Auntie was far too loud, and the strategy was to let her talk herself tired until another woman swooped in and changed the subject. There was the interloping Mahajan family, transplants from Kenya whose two young sons, Shawn and Ritesh, weirded everyone out with their inexhaustible, preternatural knowledge of physics and who clearly—at least to Prashant—suffered from an undiagnosed form of Asperger's. Despite this, his mother gathered the Mahajans into the house like found treasure, and it was silently decided by their circle of friends that the Mahajan matriarch, Mina, was beautiful enough and fluent enough in Punjabi to socialize with them. (In time, Shawn and Ritesh, wise beyond their years, learned that they were going to be each other's best bet for conversation, so they sequestered themselves in whichever corner was closest and discussed their equations in private.)

And now this Harit Uncle. Prashant found it odd that a man would come to visit them by himself, but he figured that Harit Uncle would be some old widower with burlappy jowls and hair like milkweed. Consider Prashant's surprise, then, when the GPS led him to a mustachioed, middle-aged man in a blazer and tie waiting outside a small house. He wasn't wearing a coat or a scarf, which was odd, given that there was a sharp fall chill in the air. Harit Uncle couldn't have been older than fifty, and he seemed petrified to approach the car. He looked like someone checking to see if an animal were alive or dead. The whole awkwardness of the situation propelled Prashant out of his seat, and he found himself opening the door for Harit Uncle, marveling at the sheer volume of the man's obviously thinning hair.

Prashant hoped that their ride together, albeit brief, would not be nearly as strange as he feared. He regretted driving his father's Acura; its quiet maneuvering was usually enticing, but it rendered their situation eerily silent. (One of his snobby thoughts hit him: he realized that his parents were the only ones in their group not to have a Lexus or a Mercedes.)

To his surprise, Harit Uncle was the first one to speak.

"*Beta*, thank you very much for picking me up. I do not have a car."

Harit Uncle had not said that he couldn't drive. He had said that he didn't have a car. Prashant wasn't sure why he found this observation notable, but he did.

"It's no problem."

"So, are you enjoying school?"

"Yup. Yes."

"And what are you studying?"

"Chemistry."

"Chemistry. That is very interesting."

Which was more than Prashant could say for this so-called conversation.

"I was never very good at chemistry in school," Harit said. "I guess that's why I never became a doctor." He chuckled sadly, and Prashant felt instant sympathy for him. That's all it took, evidently: self-deprecation. Prashant had become so agile with his own self-deprecation that he respected those who shared his tendencies. "Are you studying to become a doctor?"

The simple fact that Harit Uncle thought to frame this as a question indicated a larger understanding. Most Indians assumed outright that anyone who was studying chemistry was doing so for medical purposes, even when the person was the son of a chemistry professor. "I actually want to be a chemist," Prashant said. "I'm fascinated by research."

And then it just came out of him: "But lately, I've been thinking of switching my major to literature."

He made this confession because Harit Uncle was like a blank slate. He knew virtually nothing about Prashant—aside from whatever pleasantries Prashant's mother might have offered—and what did he care about some kid's college concentration? It was a win-win: Prashant had confided something in him, and Harit Uncle's raised eyebrows (even behind those ridiculous glasses) showed that he appreciated the confidence.

"Literature? That is something." He pronounced the word *literature* with a grand lilt.

"We'll see, though. I don't really have to declare a major until sophomore year. What did you study in college?"

"I didn't go to college."

"Oh."

Harit Uncle sighed. "Don't worry, *beta*. It is not a big deal. I am much more concerned that you Indian kids here get a good education."

Prashant had to stop himself from asking what Harit Uncle's kids were studying. Obviously, he didn't have any: he was unmarried. Harit couldn't remember the last time he had met an Indian man this age who didn't have a wife.

Wait a second.

Holy shit, this dude was gay.

Of course—he was wearing way too many accessories. Uncles

were supposed to wear dress shirts—open at the collar—the skeletal silhouette of a T-shirt underneath them, and some gigantic wristwatch. *Maybe* a gold chain, though this seemed to be an accessory indigenous only to those who smoked. Yet Harit Uncle was wearing not only a blazer but a tie and a cardigan, as well as tinted eyeglasses, a slender watch, and actual loafers with tassels on them. There was also some kind of cologne in the air, as well as—what was that? Something sweet, like flowers.

Oh—it wasn't just cologne. It was whiskey. Prashant was playing chauffeur to a gay alcoholic.

"Why didn't you tell me you had a problem with this earlier?" Ranjana said as she was peeling a marigold-shaped *bindi* from its sticky backing and affixing it to her forehead. The first time she had ever noticed a worry line was when she was performing this action, and over the past few years, a single, small bindi had gone from covering one line to two.

"You said you were having a get-together! Not a welcome party."

"It isn't a 'welcome party' at all. It's a get-together. Haritji is simply getting together, as well."

"It's not right. You know it's not right." Mohan was standing in his V-neck undershirt and briefs, both off-white with use, both marked here and there with faint spots of indeterminate origin.

"It's only a big deal if we make it a big deal. He's lonely, *ji*. You remember what it was like."

"Heh? What *what* was like?"

She sighed, focused on digging the right earrings out of her jewelry drawer. She had to remind herself that Mohan hadn't gone through her experience. He had never felt the kind of despair she had upon arriving in the States, what with his job and the quick assimilation it required of him. (She had this thought almost weekly, even though they had been in this country for years. It was astounding how many times you could discover anew the same revelation.) As much as she wanted to remain in this argument, she knew that her approach was inherently faulty. There was so little in common between Harit and Mohan, and she was trying to plan this party according to *her* logic, forgetting that she was an outlier and that Mohan, who had always viewed their community as solace, was unlikely to understand, let alone share, her empathy.

They were having yet another get-together in an ocean of get-togethers, and Mohan, in his half-dun undergarments and matted chest hair, was echoing his usual worries. How many years would it take for Indian people here to realize that they had to leave at least a bit of their Indian decorum behind? All of the women had smartphones, for God's sake; surely, this was evidence enough that they had moved beyond the past. To have a stranger in their midst—even an Indian stranger—seemed enough to put Mohan over the edge, and Ranjana found this ridiculous.

She was both sad and glad that Seema and Satish couldn't make it tonight. They were out of town, visiting relatives in Pittsburgh, and Ranjana could have used Seema's moral support. At the same time, though, she felt protective of Harit and didn't exactly need Seema's gossip and scrutiny right now, especially after how Ranjana had felt at their own house.

It wasn't that she didn't love Mohan. She did, indeed, love him very much, or at least cared for him so much that the idea of love entered the picture—even if he could be so cold. The fact was, though, that she was interested now only in surprises. Once she saw that she was capable of not only changing but of discovering new things about herself—things long since abandoned, or perhaps never even considered—she was no longer interested in people who wanted only stability, who did not want to discover who they were but who wanted to live comfortably by firm principles.

There was nothing for it but for her to seize upon the first full set of earrings she could find, a tawdry pair of faux pearls that looked like pieces of a candy necklace. As Mohan moved on to grumbling about something involving Avnish Doshi's "money-making house-flipping plan," Ranjana tugged on the earrings. Over time and age, the hole of each earlobe's piercing had come to resemble the mouth of the man in Edvard Munch's *The Scream*. When a party was beginning with fierce antagonism toward her earlobes, there was little hope for a smooth evening ahead.

Harit had never been in a confined space with a younger person like this—not since he had been young himself—so he held on to the revelation about Prashant's switch in major as if it were a source of oxygen. It was clear that Prashant hadn't meant to divulge this fact, but it was also clear that both of them were enjoying some relief from its admission. Contrary to what Harit often thought, he wasn't totally out of it: he knew very well that literature was not a common course of study for Indian kids, and he could only wonder what Ranjanaji would make of Prashant's confession. She seemed like a supportive woman, and perhaps she would delight in her son's unique choice. But even before arriving at the gathering tonight, he knew that the other Indians there would frown upon it, and he felt sorry for the boy.

He felt a bit calmer by the time they pulled in front of the house. He understood, however, as he got out of the car—feeling as if his body were moving of its own accord while his mind exercised above it—that the car ride was to be the least uncomfortable part of the evening. Here was the real challenge: an entire houseful of new people. It was enough to send him screaming back into his sari. He soon saw, though, the benefit of having been sent for by the hostess's son, which was that he was the first guest to arrive.

The Chaudhurys lived in a modest two-level home that was still much wider and taller than Harit's house. It was much newer, too. His own house often felt like it was performing a miracle simply by not collapsing. Every *desi* house had its own version of Indian cooking smell, and the one here—heavier on onion than was typical—had been undercut by air freshener. The Chaudhurys' living room wasn't garnished solely with embroidered Indian art or gold plates or plants. Instead, Ranjanaji had brought her own touches, like Western paintings in pastel swirls and odd little dishes in sharp colors and, even, a black statue of some non-Hindu goddess dancing while a row of birds paused in flight above her delicate hands.

Harit saw all of this eventually. First, he followed Prashant through the side door, through a laundry room still shining from cleaning fluid, into the kitchen, which was the biggest room in the house. There was Ranjanaji, wearing an apron that Harit knew they sold at Harriman's—red apples on its front. It made a peculiar sight given her maroon *salwar*, which boasted several sequins and an intricate trim along its hem. She looked noticeably better in Indian clothing. Not just because she was Indian but because she didn't seem to be pretending.

They exchanged *Namastes*, though hers was rushed, given the number of things she had going on. To look at all the food, a hundred guests were expected. She had a series of pots on the stove and an even more impressive number of covered dishes on the island. She had made samosas, of course, then *pakoras, aloo gobi, mattar paneer, chole,* some eggplant concoction that looked highly experimental, *raita,* and a jolly-looking mass of dough for roti that had yet to be parceled, rolled, and cooked.

"Hope you brought your appetite," Prashant said as he strode out of the kitchen. Harit would have taken offense at how quickly the boy discarded the intimacy they had constructed during their car ride, but he was too busy noticing that Prashant hadn't said a word to his mother. Ranjanaji took note of this:

"Please pardon Prashant. Ah, how alliterative!" she said, tittering, not noticing or caring that Harit didn't understand what that word meant. "I've just gotten used to how he disappears for stretches at a time. I tell you, kids these days see their phones as faces. They carry on more conversations with those things than you and I do with each other."

Harit wasn't really listening to her because he was remembering his biggest fear about the evening: how to deal with her husband.

Harit tried, in these moments before Mohanji appeared, to imagine what an Indian man like Mohan would think of him. Even though Harit had few male friends besides the Indian boys that he saw sometimes in the stockroom, he knew that Indian men had little room for emotional engagement when it came to each other. (Teddy had shown him an article in *The New York Times* on the custom of men holding hands in India, but Harit chose every day to forget that this had ever happened.) They measured in material things—a fact that Indians tried to conceal from Americans. Americans, according to Indians, focused on making everything bigger—houses, cars, bank accounts. The only things they focused on making smaller were their bodies, which revealed the excesses of their gluttonous eating. Although Indian men tried to act as if they were different, they were very much the same. Their responsibilities were to provide for their families an Americanized sense of material wealth while still sticking to the Indian courtesies—in essence, to justify a well-turned sitting room, a spacious kitchen, and a fancy car by pointing to a child's mathematical prowess, a rigorous schedule of temple-going piety, and carefully planned marriages.

None of this seemed surprising to Harit. These were the same old things that people said about immigrants of all stripes. What was continually surprising was that these Indian men didn't seem to realize that they were falling into the stereotype. Each carried himself with a combination of poise and slovenliness that he thought was unique, but since Indian men never discussed these things with one another, they could never fully understand what they had in common.

Although it was clear from this home that Mohanji wasn't stupendously wealthy, Harit was sure that Mohanji would look at him as inferior in every way. Unmarried and living with his mother—without the promise that a family represented, Harit was hardly worthy of much. He prepared himself accordingly, crossing his arms behind his back and rocking gently to calm himself down.

"*Ji*, I'm so glad that you came," Ranjana said. She was jumping from task to task, pulling a stack of napkins out of its plastic skin, liberating plastic forks, knives, and spoons and placing them in a trio of foam cups, producing a fully stocked tray of spices and garnishes out of thin air. Harit couldn't help but feel that the bond that had brought him here was broken, that the party as an entity mattered more to Ranjanaji now than he did. He tried to dispel these thoughts. She was a hostess, and naturally, it was her job to attend to her guests. The more successful the party was, the more successfully he had joined them. The less attention paid to him, the better.

The party had been scheduled to start at 7:00 P.M., and although Harit knew it was customary for the guests to be delayed in arriving, he didn't think it was customary for the man of the house to remain out of sight. At last, Mohanji appeared ten minutes later. Harit watched him through the arched doorway between the kitchen and sitting room. Mohanji was busy sweeping imaginary dust off shelves, tabletops, and the TV. His hair was still dripping from the shower, and there seemed to be remnants of shampoo still mixed in with his streaks of gray. He was the kind of man who grunted at the littlest thing. Finally, after running a hand through his slick hair and pulling a last cushion into place, he darted into the kitchen, ready to say something to Ranjanaji. He stopped when he saw Harit.

"*Namaste, ji,*" he said, barely putting his hands together. Harit had hoped that there would be an understanding between the two of them that the night was awkward enough without making their interactions even more strained, but that wasn't going to be the case. Mohanji clearly had a problem with his being here, and Harit couldn't fault him for that. Everything involving Ranjanaji, it seemed, was required to be strange.

An hour into the allotted start time, there were only six people in the house besides the Chaudhurys and Harit. Then, as if the other guests had conspired, they arrived all at once in their luxury cars, transforming the curb into a de facto showroom that you could view from the front window. These people smelled like money—but money mixed with something else, something musty and sweet at the same time, the smell of an antiques store.

Harit sat in the corner in a comfortable armchair. The divot in the middle of its seat indicated that Mohanji spent a significant amount of time planted there. Ranjanaji made a grand show of introducing him to the others, but perhaps sensing his discomfort at being presented this way—always with a flourish of her hand and a reassuring nod of her head—she soon transitioned into merely saying his name and letting him do the rest. He bowed, mumbled a few words about being happy to be in attendance, and then returned to the armchair and watched as the women began to clump together in the kitchen and as the men trundled into the den with their tumblers of whiskey. He had rarely observed this ritual up close, and he soon realized that it would be his duty to join the men and leave the haven of his corner behind. He felt entirely unprepared for this maneuver yet knew that the longer he avoided it, the worse it would be. If only he could have a moment in which one of the women pulled him aside and started chatting him up in front of the men, just so that he could stay behind without being judged. Instead, he was left alone to make his way into the den. Then he remembered his empty hands, his drinkless state, and pondered what to do.

He had already consumed a quick drink back at the house to alleviate his preparty stress. That effect had worn off already, and he wanted another. He couldn't get drunk in front of these people, yet he also knew, without having to be told, that he couldn't join those men without seeming like he could hold his liquor. Thankfully, the whiskey bottle was on the kitchen counter instead of in some fancy decanter in the den, so Harit swerved around the chattering women and poured himself a neat glass.

He nodded at Ranjanaji and she at him, and he knew that she understood how uncomfortable he felt and what he was about to do, and it made him able to do it.

The fears of childhood never went away. He might as well have been trying to join a gathering of bullying classmates on a dirty pitch of land outside his primary school. He might as well have been entering the staid setting of his father's weekly card game back in India, its huffy men and sparse cigarette smoke.

There was only the slightest break in the men's conversation as he came upon them, a momentary silence before Mohanji, with every bit of stress that Harit could have expected, motioned to an open spot on the couch next to two more slender men who were already halfway through their tumblers. Harit gave them *Namastes*, wondering if they had expected him to shake hands, though they hadn't offered theirs.

The conversation was about a Pakistani car salesman who had just set up a gigantic lot on the outskirts of town. Harit had not seen it, but Avnish Doshi gave a long, detailed, practically enraged description of its grounds, its teal-colored light posts and newly poured blacktop and rows and rows of shiny cars. The whole group agreed that the place was a foolish, foolish undertaking, the work of a madman, and there seemed an implicit understanding that the man's folly was a result of his nationality.

Harit was so busy keeping track of his own movements—well-planned head nods, slight but effective grunts of agreement—that he had not noticed who the man was seated to his right, on the perimeter of the conversation. It wasn't a man at all: it was Prashant. Harit realized that there was no one else in attendance who was Prashant's age, so the teenager had nowhere better to be but here. If Harit had been Prashant, he would have used this as a convenient excuse, shutting himself away in his room and relishing his solitude. Then Harit saw the expression on Prashant's face when Avnish Uncle went to refill his glass of whiskey, and Harit understood the intrigue: Prashant was sitting in wait for a chance to drink, as a dog may wait for leftovers.

Avnish Uncle noticed this soon enough. "Prashant, *beta*," he said, reaching out as if to pat Prashant, even though he was seated once again on the other side of the room, "perhaps you should join us in a whiskey. You look just like me as an eager young man." The room chuckled in unison, and Prashant clearly considered the possibility of this actually happening, his eyebrows rising and his spine straightening. A brief shake of the head from his father set the chuckles aside and reminded everyone that such depravity would never be condoned in polite company like this.

In hearing Avnish's comment about being an "eager young boy," Harit realized that he didn't share this point of view at all. He didn't see Prashant as a younger version of himself. There was Young Harit, whom Harit had a difficult time picturing as anything but a younger version of his current self, so Young Harit didn't look like a young man but like a less-stooped, less-disheveled, less-sallow, less-troubled man. Harit no longer saw life as a forward-moving thing but as a carefully maneuvered looking-back. Alongside his day-to-day life, there had been a constant assumption that he could go back and take up the life that he had always wanted. In other words, he was in the habit of living a version of his life, all the while forgetting that there were no other versions but the one life itself. Trying to go back and correct what he saw as the mistakes of his life was not merely implausible; it was impossible. Not only was Prashant far from what Harit had been as a young man; he was something Harit never would have been. You either did something, were something—or you didn't, weren't.

Prashant wondered if his mother had witnessed one of these conversations before. Did she know the ridiculous things that were coming out of the mouths of these so-called men? They were lambasting Obama, blaming his presidency for all of the turmoil in the Middle East and the rest of Asia. Prashant knew that many Indian men were Republicans due to their frugality—they appreciated a tight-handed fiscal policy—yet this type of blatant delusion truly mystified him. Just now, Avnish Uncle said, without a trace of humor, "Not all Muslims are terrorists, but all terrorists are Muslim!" Prashant had half a mind to invoke the name of Ted Kaczynski.

Forcefully and acutely, as if it were being pushed into his limbs, he could feel the insanity of this moment breeding with another problematic thought, one completely disassociated from political matters:

It came upon him like someone putting a coat over his shoulders: a powerful feeling of spite. He felt a dart of metal flick up his throat. He was sizing up Avnish Uncle, his blocky torso, face encased in thick glasses and topped by a shiny, perfectly symmetrical swath of black hair. Here was a man who had never worried about his appearance in his life. Sure, he had to be mindful of hygiene—he had likely learned, via his mother, how to chew aniseed to keep his teeth clean and how to put baby oil into his hair to keep it soft. But these concerns were dictated by routine, not by the motive of wanting to seem attractive. If he had a sense of his appearance, it was cultivated by tradition, not vanity. Diploma and engineering expertise in his hands, he had been married off to Manjeet Auntie and had continued his life methodically. Here he was, exactly where he wished to be, successful by every measure he valued.

And yet, what use did he have for that hair? None. He had never really had any use for it. Sure, not being bald had perhaps made him a more sensible suitor, but Prashant was pretty damn sure that during their courtship, Manjeet Auntie had never pined for the thick strands of Avnish Uncle's hair, never imagined her painted fingernails running through it. If she thought of it, it was in miniature, how it would give rise to children with equally black strands of hair. It made Prashant furious that he, now in the throes of love for someone as polished, classy, and beautiful as Kavita—who not only deserved but needed someone handsome—was saddled with this horrible puffball of hair while someone like Avnish Uncle got the hair that Prashant deserved.

Whether God was one or several entities, he was cruel. Prashant pictured the numerous portraits of Ram, Krishna, Vishnu, Shiva that he had seen over his lifetime, and in every one, God had an enviable cascade of hair that could be styled and cut and primped into any number of impressive styles. Prashant, meanwhile, a mere mortal, had this mess on his head to deal with. And Avnish Uncle—far from a hero but, rather, an extra in a film—got the prized looks. Avnish Uncle had not only been given everything that he desired; but he also had been given things that Prashant desired, both a certainty and nonchalance about the pleasures of life that Prashant didn't know if he could ever experience. The fact that he continued to second-guess every move he made with Kavita confirmed this. Even if, by some miracle, Prashant cleared that hurdle, he would still know that, deep down, he was fragile and vulnerable.

He wanted to start from scratch. He wanted to be born again and restart his entire history with women. He would be more assertive, focus less on masturbating and more on sex, do away with his high schools friends' "bros before hos" mentality and instead focus solely on hos, the way true players did. For all of his pretension, for all of his newly groomed snobbery, for all of his collegiate airs, what he wanted was to be a straight-up cad. But a smart cad—a hardworking, bright, smart cad with legitimately phrased political opinions. Was that so much to ask?

Hearing these men talk about the president in such a demeaning way—this was unbearable. He needed to get up, leave the room, and blow off some steam. Maybe he'd take a drive; maybe he'd find Gori's number and see if there still remained a spark—or at least a joint—from his long-ago fling with her.

As soon as he made a motion to rise, Avnish Uncle gave him an odd crick of the neck and asked what was wrong.

"Nothing," Prashant said dismissively, but Avnish Uncle laughed and nudged him ever-so-slightly down.

"*Beta* . . ."

Avnish Uncle had chosen the wrong time to touch him. What may have been intended in that moment as a friendly jibe was, to Prashant, no less than a shove.

"Fine," he said. "You want to know what the matter is? It's the fact that you're all fucking bigots."

His father would have leapt up and started scolding him if he hadn't been as dumbstruck as the other men. Prashant, exhilarated by how he had disarmed them with one expletive, felt his anger transform into bliss.

"Are you fucking kidding? Obama was a Muslim and a terrorist? Are you hearing yourselves?" He saw his father stir slightly, in the beginning stages of a reprimand, but the steel in Prashant's voice stopped him. "What kind of *community* is this if we start criticizing the first minority president? Did you guys ever think you'd see the day a person of color was the leader of the free world? It's like you've taken thirty years of progress—that *you* started, mind you—and thrown it out the window! Can't you see that Modi is just riling up nationalist sentiment, making puppets of you all? Shouldn't you be focusing on *that*?"

He felt like a hero, a sterling product of his college. This was exactly what he should have been doing with his education. He wasn't even sure if he'd ever said Modi's name out loud before, but here he was, proselytizing like a revolutionary.

(He knew as he was delivering his tirade that he was doing it because it was the type of passion that Kavita would find sexy.)

However, once the initial rush of this speech faded and he surveyed the room, he saw that all of his father's friends wore bemused, condescending grins on their faces. He had seen this face before, a look that simultaneously laughed at youth and reiterated the superiority that these men had demonstrated in traveling halfway around the globe. They didn't appreciate Obama's struggle— his ascent from a mixed-race, gangly teenager to a highly educated senator to the commander in chief—because they already saw their own journeys as vastly more impressive. They were not looking for a sense of communion with other people. They were looking to lord their accomplishments over others, as they lorded their accomplishments over each other—*who had bought which car and who had won whichever game of cards and whose kids had gotten into which college.*

Prashant's father finally, hilariously shouted, "Prashant! Go to your room!" If Prashant were still in high school, he might have replied with an equally melodramatic "I'm eighteen; you can't tell me what to do!" Instead, he snickered. He was better than this, better than these petty men. It was upsetting that they suffered from such myopia—he thought of this word specifically, savored it—but he didn't need to save them. They couldn't be saved.

Harit had never seen a child behave this way, and he greeted the moment with a surprising feeling: relief. The outburst made Prashant the oddity of the room, not Harit. If anything, Mohanji was more polite to Harit after Prashant's spectacle. Mohanji seemed too proud to let a new guest in his house feel uncomfortable or inconvenienced. He offered Harit another drink, then made sure that everyone made it to the kitchen in an orderly fashion so that dinner could be doled out. He waited until everyone—the men, the women, the few grandparents tucked into corners like gifts, the two random young children—had served themselves food before picking up one of the sectioned foam plates and scooping dinner onto it.

After a few minutes, the party appeared undisturbed. Prashant was, presumably, in his room. The women were chatting animatedly in the living room, the men had moved from political matters to money matters to school matters to family matters—who was sponsoring which family member to emigrate to the States—and Harit responded to all of this by tipping his head to the side in agreement or crinkling his head back in soft disapproval. He had worried that he would be the center of attention, but this was just another routine party for them; they did not fear such gatherings as Harit did.

Just as he began to worry that he may not get a chance to converse with Ranjanaji, she tapped him on the shoulder and asked if he might help serve the chai. He didn't need to be an expert at parties to know that this was rather unorthodox—a man helping a woman prepare chai? He knew that to object would make the situation even worse, so he followed her into the kitchen.

She had taken down a large assortment of cups and saucers, and a shiny silver serving pot presided over them like a proud parent. Fancy, loose tea leaves, and containers of cardamom and ginger were at the ready. The kitchen was made beautiful with their smell. She was going to make true Punjabi tea.

"So, *ji*, have you had a good time?" she asked, pretending to ignore the outburst in the other room that she had overheard. Then her face cracked into a playful smile.

Harit laughed uncomfortably.

"It's OK, *ji*," Ranjana said. "It's Prashant's first time home. I know that he misses school already. We're not the easiest people to deal with, especially at a party. As they always say, you shouldn't talk politics at a party."

"I didn't know that," Harit said, "but I do now."

They both laughed, Ranjana more so. The water was boiling. She sprinkled the tea leaves into its pitching heat, their smell instantly more fragrant. "*Ji*, can you get the milk from the fridge?" she asked. The word "fridge" struck him like a coin tossed in his face. As Harit extracted the cool carton from its shelves, he wanted, as always, to be as well-versed in such turns of phrase as Ranjana was.

"What did you think of President Obama?" Ranjanaji asked. Harit had not expected this question. The truth was that he didn't follow political matters very much. It wasn't like Obama's health care initiative had affected how many tea bags Harit bought or how many nonmeals his mother ate. He had never visited a doctor in the U.S., and neither had his mother. The only thing he had thought about Obama was that it was peculiar to see a black man as president of the United States. Compared to the complex political makeup of India—Modi's constant struggle with Musharraf, the old days of the Gandhis, the constant upheaval in Kashmir—this American landscape wasn't particularly new.

"I don't know, *ji*," he replied, honestly.

"Between you and me," Ranjana said, "I thought he was wonderful. Not perfect, but I certainly didn't think he was a Muslim or a terrorist. I wouldn't want you to think that I thought those things."

Harit nodded. He was queasy discussing this with anyone, but especially with a woman while preparing tea. Nevertheless, he found himself strangely compelled. He had been in several unexpected situations in recent weeks—the dinner with Ranjanaji and Teddy, his confession about Swati's death. But this, being in this cluttered kitchen, so much brighter and alive than the one in his gloomy, dark house, with the chitchat of men in one ear and women in the other, and speaking to this woman, this progressive, Americanized, compassionate woman—this was the most significant oddity of all.

And now, a revelation. He felt something along the lines of real affection for this woman. She was at once plain and fascinating, her hands preparing tea as every other woman did, her bangles clinking innocently, her face scrunched up in mild concentration, her hair doing its usual free-form billow, her motions mundane but her intentions unlike those of anyone else. It had taken him too long to make the obvious connection: there was something of Swati in her. The same spontaneity, the same joy, even if it was conditioned with some sort of disappoint or boredom. Harit understood the root of such boredom—being surrounded by others who didn't stimulate you.

Ranjanaji paused in the middle of her tea preparation. She was staring at the tea, watching the steam rise from it. Her face was bent so far over it that the steam seemed to be breaking against her face. It must have been scorchingly hot, yet she seemed unfazed by it. Harit was leaning in to ask her if she was all right when she pulled back. "I'm so sorry, *ji*," she said. "I've been feeling under the weather these days."

He had already been leaning forward to say "Ranjanaji," and in this moment, as she pulled back, his hand met her forearm. She looked at him, and he could see in her eyes that she also understood that their friendship was strengthening, bringing them closer and providing a sense of security.

They separated from each other and finished preparing the tea. As Harit helped Ranjana to distribute the teacups to everyone, he found his mouth incapable of not shooting into a grin.

EVENTUALLY, PRASHANT WAS SUMMONED from his room by Ranjana and charged with driving Harit home. Given the events of the evening, the ride was even more stilted than the one that had preceded it. Harit tried to pay no mind to this. He was still basking in the moment that he and Ranjana had shared in her kitchen, and he wasn't going to let this car-confined awkwardness, nor the thought of his mother at home, diminish its joy.

When they reached his house, he let himself out of the car and gave Prashant a short head nod. Prashant did the same, clearly ready for Harit to shut the door and be gone. Harit obliged, then strode across the lawn and made his way into the house.

He hoped that Gital Didi had already taken her leave for the night. And she had. Perhaps it was the relief of her absence that propelled him forward, that made him drop to his knees in front of his mother and begin sobbing, the sounds caught in his throat, as if a creature were trapped there.

"Ma, I have made a real friend. A real Indian friend. And it is a woman. And she is not like anyone I've ever met. She . . . listens to me and respects me and wants to make others listen to me and respect me. And just being around her—it makes me wish that we still spoke to each other. That I could tell you everything that I want to tell you."

He paused for a moment to let the creature in his throat struggle a bit more, and then he let several strong breaths in and out, trying hard to calm himself down as much as he could. Then the words poured out of him, as he began to tell her about how, exactly, he had met Ranjana, about the party she gave, about her kindness to him. He wasn't sure why he was speaking or why he was telling her all this. He felt the recklessness of it all, how it would only injure his mother further, to know that he had found some kind of version of—no, *replacement for*—Swati. But he could not have foreseen what happened next.

His mother moved, decisively. She pulled off her purple sunglasses, and she stood. Not the stark position in which he had found her earlier, right before Gital Didi had come in and interrupted, but a position of resolve, of meaningfulness.

"Harit, *beta*," she said, her voice tough and smooth, like a healed wound. "You've finally saved us."

She spoke to the point of being long-winded: she told him that she had been waiting for him to finish his mourning and find his own way before engaging with him. She explained to him that she could see, that Gital Didi had taken her to the doctor, that her cataracts were manageable—and that, because of this, she knew full well that he had been dressing up. Harit froze at this, this information almost too much for him, but she touched his face, ran a finger over his mustache, then pulled him close, and they wept against each other. There was something about the way that she both received his weight and pushed against it that acknowledged that Swati's passing was not his fault. Even given the pleasure of having a conversation with his mother after all this time, Harit saw this physical language as perhaps the most wonderful revelation of all.

Then Harit told his mother the kinds of thoughts that he never believed that he'd be able to tell anyone, let alone her. How, in India, it had been very easy for him to plan his future: his family would find him a girl when he was the right age—midtwenties, perhaps—and there would be a lovely but brief ceremony, an exchange of gifts, and he would continue living his life, giving his wife a child or two and feeling terror over being a father. In the end, bolstered by his wife's responsibility and goodwill, he would settle into the role and assert his fatherhood by way of routine tirades. This is what he saw other men doing, so he assumed it was what he would be expected to do. Knowing his own shyness, he feared this entire process, but at least he knew what the process would be.

All of this was the plan until his father clutched his chest, until the sweat collected in the grooves above his collarbone and his eyes became protrusions in his head, the whites expanding, and Harit knew, even as he saw the violent knocking of that body on the kitchen floor, that everything he had assumed about his life was going to change. The family flew across the world, as far away as his mother could get from the tragedy, not knowing that she would trade tragedies just as she would hemispheres. As Harit watched the world unspooling under the plane, he couldn't tell what was stronger—his terror at having to decipher America or his relief at having dodged married life, at least for the time being. He had been in India just long enough to see his marriage prospects pale in comparison to other men's, to see how undesirable he was. As the world changed, as American culture inserted itself into Indian life more than he could have predicted, women were starting to introduce rules and standards where few had been before. It was possible now for the girl down the street, so convinced until recently that she deserved nothing more extravagant than a market owner, to expect an attractive husband where an industrious one may once have sufficed. The same woman would make it understood that Harit was not handsome, that his hair and his rumpled clothing and his rumble of a voice were not so valuable, after all, not when the Internet was making layers of romance more visible than ever. There were no longer categories as simple as "handsome" or "ugly"; there were subcategories of "marriageably handsome" or "unmarriageably ugly." As Harit explained all this, standing in his living room, his mother wiped more tears from her eyes, then hugged him once more, her physical gesture telling him that he was being too harsh on himself.

Ironically, he told her, he had always had Swati to protect him from women. Dazzling—so dazzling, in fact, that she dazzled herself out of the marriage game—she had been such a large part of his life that he had no reason to seek the charms of women outside his home. Sex was something discussed in vulgar terms by other boys in passing, and Harit, so accustomed to turning away from the other daunting things in life, turned away from it, too. He turned to Swati, to the only embrace that truly mattered. And how he missed Swati! How he knew his mother missed Swati! *Swati*—a word that they now passed back and forth like a prayer.

"Swati taught you more than I could," his mother said. Harit shook his head no, but she stopped him. "I have been wrong about many things. Swati was the better teacher. But what I did get right was hope itself. I hoped that you would come to discuss these things with me, in all the ways that I have not been able to discuss them with you. I've failed—but my hope did not."

This admission, that hope had never left them, allowed Harit to consider a question, a question that was in itself an answer, yet he had to ask it instead of state it, so afraid was he of telling her too much before he even understood it himself:

"What if who I want—*in that way*—is not a woman at all?"

At that, Harit's mother told him one last story: the truth about her and Gital Didi.

Harit fainted.

PRASHANT RETURNED TO CAMPUS from fall break not know-ing what his mood was. It shifted quickly from moment to mo-ment, to the extent that he wondered about his mental health. He had seen a commercial for an antidepressant that featured a suc-cession of people sitting on couches one moment, riding a bike the next, and he considered going to the school's medical center to dis-cuss whether he should go on medication. He found himself so swept up in his schoolwork that it was as if academics had made the decision for him: he didn't need a prescription. He needed to study.

For reasons he couldn't quite process, he actively avoided Kavita. There were no more desultory trips patrolling the student center, no unnecessary coffees in cafés simply for the sake of crossing her path. Instead he kept mainly to his room; it was oddly suited to getting work done even when the inviting berth of his bed lay mere feet away. He learned to deliver the line "I can't—too much work" with a credible inflection that deterred people from asking him to hang out at all.

His efforts paid off: another A on a quiz or problem set, another shout-out from the professor, another passive-aggressive exchange with a classmate who envied his success. He came to see himself as two separate people: the Prashant who second-guessed his every move, who constantly lamented the late start he had when it came to social interactions, and the Prashant who was beyond social acceptance, who needed only to sharpen his mind. He came to see this second self as not only more desirable but practically Einsteinian.

All the while, he was conscious of why he had desired Kavita so desperately: she was these two selves concurrently. She didn't need to make a choice. She simply had to be.

Thanksgiving came soon after fall break, but he decided to stay on campus. It would have been melodramatic to say that he was avoiding his parents' house due to his outburst at their party, but regardless, he was relieved that he was not spending the holiday with them. He could detect the lack of concern in his father's voice when he told them his plans. His mother, for her part, seemed genuinely sad, but he also sensed the same air of detachment that had clouded her presence during the past several weeks.

He spent Thanksgiving dinner at the house of one of his chemistry professors, Gary Dominick, a man who had lived several lives. On his faculty page, the professor listed the numerous professions that he had attempted before his current career: dishwasher, guitar player in a café, hotel concierge, fire inspection specialist, the now-ubiquitous yet amorphous term "social worker." His wife, Gina, was equally versatile; she was a former high school biology teacher who now had some moderate success as a songwriter for P!nk. Although they were both in their late forties, they had a one-year-old baby who seemed, magically, theirs and not the result of adoption or surrogacy. To celebrate the miracle of conception and the joining of their genes, they spent a great part of the evening hoisting her like a rocket above their heads, at one point narrowly missing an unkempt bookshelf when the professor's wife tripped on their Oriental rug.

The Dominicks lived in one of the stately, stunning mansions that stood on flat, unobstructed lawns outside of town. Their place was a series of high-ceilinged rooms with thick, dusty curtains and pale green paint flaking along the walls. Dilettante debris lurked in corners like pets—a dulcimer; a fanned-out collection of tarot cards, midprediction; an old rocking horse; decorative plates from Africa and South America; a fragile-looking cabinet with Japanese characters in red paint on its front.

They had put up flyers that any Thanksgiving strays were welcome at their place, so the other attendees made a motley assortment—three undergrads and one taciturn grad student. The undergrads were all freshmen, all young women, all as clueless as Prashant. The taciturn grad student, Oleg, was from Warsaw. He was very thin and his hair was insane, a copse of curls set so thickly that they all looked tangled with one another. He was an unabashed flirt with all three of the young women, who politely rejected his attempts until Oleg silenced himself with a pair of pumpkin pie slices.

The entire evening felt slapdash, and Prashant welcomed it. It was nice to be in a neutral space on campus, surrounded by academics yet not at risk of running into Kavita. She had e-mailed him a few days ago, but his response? "I can't—homework." She had probably decamped to Chicago for the weekend, and Prashant, between bites of butternut squash gratin, let himself envision what her Thanksgiving looked like. He imagined a look of satisfaction crossing her face while she savored a creamy spoonful of buttery mashed potatoes.

"So, Mr. Chowdery," Professor Dominick said, "has our fair campus been to your liking thus far?" Even though he had worked several blue-collar jobs, he spoke with a stilted air.

"I feel very at home," Prashant said. He didn't know that this was how he felt until he said it. The consciousness that his rightful place was here, the academic promise that he exhibited with every meticulously composed problem set, gave him a sense of belonging that he had never had before.

"That's so lovely to hear," Gina said, looking up just briefly from her daughter, who lay cradled in her arms like a scepter. "Destiny brought you here, then."

"Indeed," Professor Dominick said, cutting through his adobo-rubbed turkey. "But don't get too comfortable. That's when you let your guard down and your grades start slipping. You're here for only four years."

Oleg made an intentionally loud clearing of his throat, revealing to them that he had spent not just grad school but his undergrad years on campus.

"Well, true," Professor Dominick replied to this, swiping another forkful of turkey into his mouth. "You could be like my dear protégé Oleg here and parlay your avid facility with thermodynamics into the hell of being my TA."

"I'll take your hell over a literary heaven any day," Oleg said, clearly brightening at the chance to be engaged in conversation once more.

Clara, one of the young women at the table, piped up: "I happen to be an English major, and I'm very proud of it." Her voice contained an air of indignation that was at odds with her otherwise reserved appearance. Prashant realized that her schoolmarmish outfit was the result of hipster posturing, not a poor sense of style.

"Let's see what you think when you graduate and can't get a job," Oleg said.

"Now, now," Professor Dominick said sternly, though laughing. "There's no need to be rude, Oleg."

"Yeah, especially when you're just a TA," Clara said. She swept her fingers through the air to form a Stop sign, the universal gesture for "Talk to the hand."

Oleg pressed on. "Do me a favor and try to learn some computer languages if you're going to be an English major," he said. "At least some basic HTML, if not Python and Joomla."

"Oleg," Gina said, looking up from the baby again, but with fire in her eyes. "Please have some respect. This is a Thanksgiving dinner to which you have been invited."

"I'm just trying to be helpful," he said.

Prashant noticed, around the lip of the table, the flask jutting out of Oleg's pocket. Given that the dinner was mainly composed of underage students, there was no wine or liquor offered, but Oleg had clearly seen this as a surmountable obstacle. Oddly, Prashant found himself sympathetic. After all, he himself had been the fraught center of attention at a party mere weeks ago.

"I think they're both right," Prashant interjected. "I admire Clara for pursuing literature, since it's probably her passion." He tilted his gaze toward Clara, who met the gesture with a guarded acknowledgment, as if she thought he was joking. "But—and I don't say this just because I'm studying chemistry—I do worry that, as Professor Dominick says, if I don't acknowledge a real world that will want actual 'marketable' skills from me"—he found himself about to make the air quotes before he did so—"my time here, however enjoyable, will be for nothing."

"Well said, young man," Professor Dominick responded. "Now, it's time for some jazz."

They were all escorted from the dining room to a parlor that lay beyond two large oak doors. From one corner, an old record player scratched out 1920s music. A glittering assortment of tchotchkes covered every surface, a collection of fake jewels and mirrored boxes and pewter figurines. Half a dozen large-faced clocks stared from various corners. No two couches in the room matched. Professor Dominick started doing a loose-limbed dance, his arms swooping, Gina following with their rocket-baby. Professor Dominick switched out the record, and John Coltrane's *A Love Supreme* bounced off the walls.

Prashant was dancing stupidly, but he felt more relaxed than he had in quite some time. Even the girls seemed to warm to Oleg when they saw his embarrassing attempts at playing an air saxophone. Soon, they were all bouncing around, leaving the cliché of the too-cool-for-school college student behind. It wasn't until Gina made a swift exit to deposit the baby into her upstairs crib that things came to an end, and they were all soon filing out of the massive front door laden with foiled leftovers that caught the glint of the moonlight.

Prashant didn't notice until they were halfway back to campus, wending their way past more looming mansions, that he and Clara had separated slightly from the others. Her double-breasted blazer and roomy skirt caught the wind, as did her asymmetrical, curly hair, and he felt a small shock run through his crotch.

"Thanks for sticking up for me back there," she said, dipping her head into the wind and avoiding his gaze as if she were wearing a lorgnette.

"No problem," he said, flatly. He felt his outspokenness from earlier dissipate like their breath in the cold. Clenching his fists, he tried not to let the moment slip. "To be honest, I've been thinking of switching to English myself. It's just that, well, I'm Indian, and I'd be killed by firing squad if I don't study science."

"You shouldn't subscribe to such horrible cultural stereotypes," she said, a smile still peeling her lips back.

"In that case, wanna make out?"

It popped right out of him, completely unbidden, and he felt himself grow hot in the middle again, this time with embarrassment. Within seconds, she was teasing his tongue into hers with the alacrity of a seasoned professional.

Clara's last name was Windsor, and she was one of a long line of extraordinarily wealthy patrons of the university who had funded the construction of several buildings on campus—including one of the buildings that housed Prashant's statistics class. He didn't have to hunt for this information; she told him outright once he saw her dorm room, a laughably large haven high atop one of the oldest Gothic buildings on campus. They kicked off their shoes as they stumbled through the doorway, something he'd seen in romantic comedies but that he didn't think actually happened in real life. Another thing he didn't think happened in real life was the ease with which he kissed her. He wasn't 100 percent sure, but he was pretty sure that he was doing well.

He started to slide his fingers under her bra, hoping to see if her nipples were hard, then realized that this was a total porn star move and pulled back. He knew many guys who had botched their chances with girls on campus simply because their porn education had been received with utter disgust. Clara felt his hesitation and brought his hand back to her chest. Soon, they were on her bed in nothing but their socks (her comforter oddly smelled like Lucky

Charms). Hers were white and frilly, a hipster's delicates. Whatever her privileged background, she had the lighting favored by students on college campuses everywhere—white Christmas lights—and their bodies glowed under dozens of pixie-like pinpoints tacked around her bay window.

Clara seemed perfectly in her element, and she showed absolutely no shame about being naked in front of him. Prashant reproached himself for having thought her plain before. Underneath her affected schoolmarm chic, she was beautiful. He had always convinced himself that he liked slender girls with full chests—porn caricatures—but now that he saw the soft roundness of Clara's curves, the slightly gangly but appealing spill of her chest, the fullness in her tummy above her pubic hair, he realized that he had avoided an entire realm of sexual fantasy simply because he had deemed it too ordinary. In reality, it was extraordinary. And it was extraordinary that this—being here, with her—was reality at all.

III

AS YOUR BODY AGES it acquires new sensations, very few of which are actually pleasant. Frederick's body worsened from year to year, to the point that at least once a day when he noticed a pain, almost a burning, along the line where his belly sagged over his belt. When he was younger, he had no belly to speak of, his stomach's tautness barely touching a shirt's fabric back then. These days, he was conscious of how every part of his stomach ached, from belly button to love handles to coarse happy trail. Meanwhile, all of the other parts could ache, too. Every knuckle contained a universe of hurt. He could feel every bone of his foot when he climbed steps. His lower back felt like someone was pushing it all the time. The older he got, the more flesh he had, and that flesh was full of nerves, and those nerves were conspiring to tell him this: *Just because there is more of you doesn't mean that there is more of you to love.*

Most of the time, he wasn't as gloomy as all that. Even during his darkest moments, when he sat on the couch with a book sliding from his fingers and his eyes fixed on the ceiling, he knew that there was some part of him—a part that true depressives didn't have—that felt hopeful and resilient. Honestly, if it weren't for that inexorable optimism, he probably would have killed himself years ago. He'd lost three—four?—friends to suicide, but he couldn't bring himself to feel such despair in any legitimate way.

He spent most of his life convincing himself that he was young, and for many years, certain aspects of his appearance allowed this delusion to persist. As a blond, he skirted the presence of gray hairs because they played hide-and-seek so furtively among their flaxen peers. He had oddly healthy skin, so smooth that people always asked him what moisturizer he used. For a long time, he looked younger than his age; at forty, he still looked as if he were thirty.

Something changed during his late forties. Because he had always been blessed with natural youth, he didn't know what to do to create the illusion of it. He refused to get plastic surgery. He had seen his share of men whose faces were pulled into masks; the only thing he detested more than a woman who penciled in her eyebrows was a man who did the same thing. He had always assumed that his body would continue to be spry if he kept the right attitude. But in recent years, no matter how happy a demeanor he effected, his body charged ahead, finally accepting its deterioration even though he would never have agreed to such a thing. And so, in short stabs to his underbelly, in the pregnant flicker of a vein in his arm, in the heat of indigestion that felt increasingly like heart trouble, he came to see that he was getting permanently, irreversibly older—even though he had accomplished very little of what, in his youth, he thought he would accomplish.

He had grown up in Youngstown, Ohio, which his own father referred to as a "shithole" even though both his father and mother had been born and raised in the city. At least his father had refused to join the hordes of people working in the steel industry and opted to become a car salesman. He worked at a Ford dealership where he had a facility for selling vehicles but also for spending his earnings on copious amounts of booze. Frederick's mother had taken a job at a jewelry store but seemed to have no great sense of style, always choosing the gaudy beaded necklace over the carefully appointed brooch. The great irony was that she, who spent her time among women who couldn't afford Hollywood luxury but tried to evoke it, had no real understanding of that world herself. Frederick, on the contrary, had a firmer sense of style; he was the one who snuck out to catch screenings of old movies, Marlene Dietrich and Barbara Stanwyck and Katharine Hepburn.

Frederick had the innate sense that he was going to get away from this place and go to New York City. This was why he took the other boys' insults and punches and the teachers who gave him lower grades when he wrote too passionately about Lady Macbeth or Daisy Buchanan: because he knew that this was all a means to an end.

His parents never expected him to go to college. His older brother, Simon, on whom they had used up all of their energy, had graduated high school and become the manager of the local Big Boy, which he ran amiably and proudly, white apron tight over his chest and his hair closely cropped. Frederick's whole family knew that he was different—their eyes followed his elaborate hand gestures when he spoke like they were watching a pilot do a loop-de-loop in the sky—but they didn't address it, nor did he say anything. He was handsome, better-looking than any of them, but there was a grace in his movements that prevented people from commenting on it, afraid that merely acknowledging beauty would make them queer, too. Many years later, he would be reminded of this when supermodels talked about their gangly period, those clumsy days before a scout happened upon their otherworldly beauty in a mall and told them that their bony ankles, sunken cheeks, crooked teeth, and frightening height were, in fact, assets. There was no such scout in Youngstown. Frederick was never approached about his supple skin, the patches on his cheeks like liquid rouge, the mount of his thick hair, or the grace of his gait. Instead, Frederick, ever aware that he deserved something besides his hometown, was his own scout.

His parents did not object when he told them that he was going to New York, as if they had always assumed that he would leave them after high school and that the city would be his only destination. In 1980, he packed two duffel bags and took three trains, each filled with more and more people of color, something that he had experienced only tangentially, however racially charged Youngstown had been. It was on the last of these trains that he saw a lanky black man, no older than twenty-five, board the train and plop himself onto a nearby seat, his tight clothes highlighting the bulges in his chest and crotch. Frederick had never allowed himself to think of a black man as attractive. He had known, even then, that his idea of black men was as fetishistic as his parents' was narrow-minded. So when he saw this man, undoubtedly beautiful but not a disco boy or a model, he realized that he could make his desires concrete.

This was the first confirmation that, unlike the bleach-blond, lithe things that he saw on porn tapes—their groins crossed by tan lines—he had a predilection for men of color. He knew that this would be the most upsetting thing to his parents—that if they knew that he was leaving not just to be gay but also to be a gay man sleeping with these men, they would seize him by the collar and throw him back in his room until he assumed his role as assistant manager at Big Boy or toiled in the spitballed silence of being a substitute teacher.

They hadn't known this because *he* hadn't known it. It had taken a random man on Amtrak to reveal to him his own inclinations.

In fact, it would be months before he would even kiss a man. First, he had to sort out the terrifying steps of settling into city life. He found a dingy studio in the West Village almost by accident: he was helping an old woman who had fallen over on Seventh Avenue, so laden was she with a grocery bag of potatoes and medications, and when he was on her doorstep on Charles Street, she revealed herself as the landlady of the residence and offered him a unit, which was one floor underground and which dispensed roaches like a pinball machine. Yet it was a godsend: New York at that time was a war zone, leering men cascading by his window every night, their voices riding up the sides of buildings and into the thick night air. He would perch on his rickety couch like a Catholic kneeling at confession, gazing upward through his windows and observing people from below, their wingtip shoes and chains and the moonlit feathers of their hair. He felt his lust as if it were a stash of money in his pocket, something valuable but daunting to transact. If he gave it away and got something in return, he wasn't sure how valuable that something might be to him.

He busied himself during the day looking for a job, which he found in a deli. The irony of making sandwiches, given his brother's line of work, was not lost on him. He loved it, though. As demanding as his customers could be, he had a fondness for them, their quirks building his impression of the city face by face and gripe by gripe. They were a varied bunch: grandmothers and addicts, effete painters wearing berets, rabbis clutching worn copies of the Talmud. His bosses were a husband-and-wife team from Malta, and they both seemed grateful for him because he came across like their

son. He would take himself out for a drink—just one—at a bar
adjacent to the gay ones, steeling himself to venture Out but stopping short. One time, he wavered outside Stonewall after a strong
martini, but after getting an arch glance from a gray-haired older
gentleman, he retreated to a bar where women's hips rubbed against
his back.

In the meantime, he auditioned. He knew how completely naïve
he was in thinking that he would land a gig, but he thought that
acknowledging his naïveté would put him one step ahead of most
people and lead to success. (Nothing envisioned a future more in-
accurately than naïveté.) As if it were a talisman, he treasured the
fable of Betty Buckley, who had stumbled off a bus from Texas
in 1969, walked by an open call for *1776*, and booked the role of
Martha Jefferson immediately; she had been a famous Broadway star
ever since. Every time he saw an audition in the paper and showed
up, his hair parted and his black clothes laundered with his last
batch of laundry quarters, he assumed that his perfect pitch and his
handsomely ruddy face would pave his path to the stage.

The auditions were always in some ill-lit and downright dingy
room with uncomfortable plastic chairs and a gaggle of peak-eyed
people who all seemed to be hiding a murder from one another.
They were all, undoubtedly, attractive—the women with eyes like
ceramics and their limbs thin and lovely; the men—well, the men
as tall and noticeable as he was. They looked him up and down
unabashedly, and once, one approached him and let a finger trail
along the back of his neck, startling him so much that he simply
froze.

He'd be pushed into another ill-lit yet larger room, with a long
tableful of people wearing black sweaters, or turtlenecks. He expected a gregarious bunch of free spirits, charming cultural pur-
veyors of the Big Apple. Instead he found group after group of

casting agents, directors, and choreographers who resembled college professors—stoic, unsmiling. He pared his audition songs down to two—"On the Street Where You Live" from *My Fair Lady* and "We've Got It" from *Seesaw*. He soon learned that the former was a total no-no, its melody aped by scrawny queens all over the city. At least the latter made people pay more attention to him—*when* they paid attention to him. He would get through four of his sixteen measures before one of the people behind the table, as if asking for a bill at a restaurant, would flick a dismissive hand in the air. The first time that it happened—indeed, the first few times that it happened—he was confused, standing dumbly in place. The creative teams were used to this. They laughed and said, "Oh, honey, don't call us. We'll call you."

Still, he clung to that Betty Buckley story as if it had been passed around solely for his benefit, a message by carrier pigeon that had found its way magically from Manhattan to Youngstown. He knew that perseverance was the name of the game; he knew to expect rejection after rejection. In the meantime, he continued working at the deli, happy to be doing something that he genuinely enjoyed, despite the meager setting.

Soon, in the evenings, when he went out, he'd find himself ordering more than one drink. One summer evening, he got cruised so aggressively by a handsome guy in a straight bar that he followed him to a gay bar. He wasn't even sure which bar it was because they proceeded to get royally drunk. Ken confessed that he was a performer, too, and he promised to share his wisdom on auditioning in exchange for more and more drinks. Later that night, in the doorway of Ken's apartment, Frederick found himself close to being sick. Surrendering, he stumbled into Ken's dark apartment and blindly groped his way toward the toilet, into which he ejected their countless Long Island Iced Teas. Ken unleashed a torrent of anger so strong and focused that it made Frederick sick all over again. He kept yelling, "'Frederick'? 'Frederick'? Classy name for a fucking disgusting guy who can't hold his liquor!" Then he practically pushed Frederick into the street, from where, at 6:00 A.M., Frederick managed to make it home—not before tripping and falling painfully on his steps. It was when he was hoisting himself up, his knees bleeding through his pants and his forehead scraped, that he heard Ken's voice ringing again and again in his head: "'Frederick'? 'Frederick'?" He decided to change it immediately.

It took him over a year to make a friend, then another year before she became his best friend. Séverine—a painter whom he met on New Year's Eve in the West Village. They were crammed next to each other at Stonewall, which he now visited regularly, no longer afraid to declare himself. What the other swanning, laughing gays there didn't know—regardless of his handsomeness, regardless of his gazes, regardless of the confidence he exuded when ordering drinks and carrying them like a glass bouquet back to his and Séverine's table—was that he was still a virgin. He had only kissed men, but he still found himself hesitant to go home with them, because of that failed night with Ken several months ago and because he had begun to hear more and more about the disease striking young men down across the city.

It was so easy to take refuge in Séverine. She had emigrated to the States from France right out of "art school," though Teddy could never quite get out of her which school that had been. She shared his height and thin frame, her shoulders and elbows pointy, her knees like fists through cloth, but she had the undeniable fashion sense of a Frenchwoman, a penchant for dark clothing, black hair dye, and abundant eyeliner that was in stark contrast to her paintings (which even she admitted were ersatz Chagalls). Her eyes were black, too, their irises and pupils indistinguishable from each other, giving her the look of someone perpetually enthralled even when she was three sheets to the wind.

Speaking of three sheets to the wind, they both were, often. They spent that first New Year's Day sprawled on the Oriental rug in her loft apartment, a harem's quarters of palm fronds, patterned silk, half-empty perfume bottles in varying shades of amber, and discarded underthings. Her easels formed a painted hall of mirrors, their truncated animals and disembodied eyes reflecting each other across the gigantic space.

"*Ça va?*" she asked Teddy.

"What?" he replied, kneading his forehead, which had lain flat against the carpet all night.

"That is the reason why you do not feel like a New Yorker yet," she said, crawling over to a little bookshelf, from which she produced a packet of cigarettes and a rusty lighter. "Everyone in New York should be able to speak French."

"People barely know anything about French where I grew up," he said. "Except if it's dressing."

"*Pardon?*" she said, and at first, he thought that she was trying to pronounce the English word, hindered by her accent.

"French dressing. Have you never had French dressing?"

She had never heard of it. Then Teddy realized that he had absolutely no idea what was in it, either. It became their catchphrase. From then on, when they didn't understand something—when they couldn't hear a subway announcement clearly, when a person at a bar gave them a lame line, when they couldn't agree on a time over the phone when they should meet at Caffè Reggio—they'd just mutter "French dressing" but with an exaggerated accent— "Frawnsh dressink."

By the time that they became good friends—drinking bottles of port by the Hudson; getting mugged in Herald Square and, by divine fortune, finding Teddy's wallet ten minutes later in a nearby trash can; spending another New Year's Eve at the Stonewall while a couple not-so-discreetly exchanged handjobs at a nearby booth—Teddy had more or less given up his auditions and his sandwich-making. Instead he took a job at a small but popular department store in Chelsea.

The job had come through one of Séverine's expat friends who worked "in fashion"—all of Séverine's expat friends worked "in fashion" or "in art." He had mentioned it to Teddy and written down the owner's number on the back of a matchbook. Teddy had called, spoken to a Piaf-voiced Frenchwoman named Michelle, and forty-eight hours later, he had quit the sandwich business and found himself behind a glass counter.

It was at the store that he tended his budding sense of fashion. The seed had been planted by Séverine, who gave him scarves and sweaters as if he were a sibling who needed hand-me-downs. Michelle—in her fifties, wide-hipped, emphysemic from smoking—had a habit of taking his hips from behind and burying her tiny head in his back whenever business was slow, and she gave him perk after perk, from free winter coats to theater tickets that she "couldn't use."

It was also at the store that he began to piece together French. He had gleaned words and phrases from spending so much time with Séverine, but they took on new meaning under Michelle's tart tongue. She had the thickest French accent that Teddy had heard—it truly seemed that New York was teeming with more French people than Paris—and soon it was easier for Teddy to interpret her French, punctuated purposefully by her lively hand gestures, than it was for him to understand her English. He didn't overlook the real reason why he had dived so intently into his new job and this lingua franca. He had still not dated anyone seriously, and he took solace in Séverine because she represented so much of what he wanted to be: stylish, cool, and beautiful. But also earnest, romantic, and easily romanced by life itself. She encouraged him to seek someone out, even volunteered to set him up with one of her few gay friends—most of them French. There was one, in particular, Edouard, whom she introduced to Teddy with an eyebrow arched and lips pursed meaningfully, but Teddy found him somewhat boring, his Frenchness concealing the fact that he didn't have all that much to contribute to the conversation. Teddy's dismissal of him finally led to a revelatory conversation with Séverine.

"You confound me," Séverine said, sitting on the couch and cutting hungrily into a leftover piece of chicken that she had slid onto a plate with some cold salad and canned chickpeas. "You don't have to be looking for love. Have sex. That's what this city is for. That's what any city is for."

"I don't want to just have sex, especially with people getting sick," Teddy said, lying flat on the rug and lifting his legs languidly in the air in a mock-effort of exercising. "I'm looking for something *bouleversant.*"

"My friend, if everyone in this city waited for something like that, no one would ever get laid. And then everyone would be as miserable as you."

"I'm not miserable," Teddy said. He wasn't, not truly. He was just lonely. (Although perhaps loneliness was inherently miserable.) It wasn't just something extraordinary that he wanted. He knew, in fact, what that specific thing was, but never having verbalized it, he kept catching himself. In this moment, with Séverine looking somewhat drab for a change with her meager dinner, Teddy felt compelled to share it with her. "I'm not miserable. I just have a specific fantasy."

She threw her plate across the couch and crawled onto the floor next to him. "A fantasy? Oh, do tell." She propped herself up on an elbow, and he mirrored the pose. He then proceeded to tell her about that first train ride, the heft and beauty of the man, and when he finished, he let himself fall back flat onto the floor, melodramatically emphasizing his sense of relief.

"Oh, Teddy," Séverine said, disappointed. She returned to the couch and picked up her plate, resuming her dinner as if he hadn't told her anything.

"What?" he said, taken aback by her indifference. "I'm not joking."

"I know you're not joking. That's the worst part."

An uneasy feeling crept over Teddy, like a lemon squeezed into milky tea until curd formed. "What's the matter?"

"You're not really going to take a black lover," Séverine said, not a question but a dismissive observation.

"I'm not?"

"No. You have more imagination than that."

Teddy couldn't tell if she was joking, but her body language, normally open and friendly, had turned stiff and uncaring. "*More imagination*? What are you saying?"

"Oh, come off it. I'm not racist. I've dated black men before. I had a black boyfriend at university," she said.

"'Some of your best friends are black'?"

"I said come off it! It's just so *cliché*, my friend. The white boy arrives in New York to be fucked by a big black man? I thought that you had grander aspirations than that."

They had been crass with each other before, but not like this. Normally, they spoke in deliberate innuendo, the kind easily established and maintained by bar buddies that painted everyone as the generally promiscuous type, but this bore an air of archness more pointed than their typical talk. "Séverine, this isn't just some fetish. At least I don't think it is. It's just what I find attractive. What I think I find attractive."

"What you think you find attractive? Stop thinking so much. Go out and actually do something."

Though Séverine's treatment of him had been harsh—downright cold, even—there was truth in it: if he held this idea inside himself and didn't act on it, he was turning his fantasy into a fetish.

Despite realizing, in light of Séverine's remarks, how earnest his intentions were, he could not decide how to go about acting on them. That encounter with Ken, however insubstantial it may have been, still smarted. For him, every encounter felt insubstantial and crushing at the same time. If the topic of race, now soured by Séverine's reaction, also entered into the picture, Teddy feared that he would commit some horrible faux pas and ruin everything.

He continued, working at the store and accompanying Séverine on her adventures but, now more than ever, willfully resisting any thoughts of further encounters. He felt old and washed-up. Worse, he felt that he had missed the narrow window in which sexual exploration was acceptable. All this time, he should have been seeing his early time in New York as if it were college—a time for intent study of the sexual landscape, when he would learn the skills necessary to find men, date them confidently, pleasure them, and, when necessary, exchange one for another until he had landed the right man, as a professor landed tenure. Instead, he had squandered whatever sentimental education had been offered to him, so the only real choice was to embrace his ignorance. Denying himself sexually felt like denying any further development of his personality, as if he were trapping his mind in the foolish pen of youth while the rest of his body moved forward and announced a level of wisdom and experience that he simply did not have.

It was so terrifying at the time that it puzzles him how people forget about it now. Since he was so solitary during those days, he experienced it as if he were watching a horror movie. The constant fights between sensationalist headlines and angry protestors, the thinning but passionate-voiced ACT-UP members thronging his neighborhood, Reagan's maddening evasion. His trips to gay bars of any kind had diminished more and more over time, but that didn't stop him from imagining, at the beginning of things, that he, too, had somehow been infected. When he thought of his aborted tryst with Ken, he thought not only of the virus but also of how pathetic it was that this was the sole sexual encounter that could have put him at risk. When he was able to calm himself down, he felt horrible in knowing that he was healthy. He could feel a second closet being built around him: he knew that, however strong his lust could be, his fear would always be stronger. There were only so many lesions, only so many men ghostly in their premature age that he could take before he saw his celibacy as a dear treasure.

Jance, the kind-eyed, able-fingered hairdresser from the corner barbershop: gone. Nico, the waiter at the Waverly Restaurant who had served him countless plates of runny-on-purpose eggs and snappable bacon: gone. Mike, the sinewy, crew-cut ex-army guy who always dipped a five into the tip jar after getting his BLT: gone, but in stages, walking down the street weaker and weaker until he no longer appeared.

Then it hit closer to Teddy than he had anticipated. He had been seeing less of Séverine since her upsetting critique of him, but they hung out sometimes, though not at her place. They met at Caffè Reggio or for a movie at the Film Forum, went for cocktails at the Chelsea Hotel or a wine dinner at The River Café. One night, she showed up at the Waverly. Her eyes were glassy with tears.

"Are you OK?" Teddy asked, suddenly as caring and affectionate with her as he had been in the past. He had never seen her distressed.

"You were the wise one! You knew! How did you know?" She huffed into a handkerchief, something that she never carried and had once called disgusting.

Teddy knew immediately what the subject was but didn't know whom she was mourning. Then it hit him: it was Séverine herself. It was the oft-overlooked group, the straight people who were ignored so that his kind could be demonized instead.

"Séverine! No—not you?"

She flicked her head up and, unexpectedly, rolled her eyes. "Oh, come on, Teddy—don't be insane. I don't have it. It's Edouard! He has it." Her face crumbled again, as if someone had drawn a tragedy mask over it, and she hunched over again.

At first, he didn't even remember, but then he realized: Edouard was the quiet/boring Frenchman with whom Séverine had tried to set him up. Teddy felt especially sympathetic because he had become boring, too: he worked his job in the store and spent his days in delis or cafés, went on occasional theater outings—during which he sat in his seat and pouted about his bad luck with love— while someone like Edouard probably had fulfilling sexual and romantic conquests and was repaid unjustly.

"I'm so sorry, Sev," Teddy said, leaning over the table and stroking her hair. He had seen many pairs of people in similar positions these past several months.

"It's just not fair," she said, raising her head again. "Why can't this just be a city of love?"

For all of her flightiness, Séverine would say things like this, and they would lodge right into Teddy. It *could* have been a city of love for him, but then he might have ended up among the afflicted. Instead it wouldn't be a city of love for him. His time with Séverine, the glories and splendors of downtown life, their adventurous loft dinners, his days doling out gently used foulards and minks to the fashionable, his strolls along the Hudson, dodging shady people but enjoying the view—it was all going to end sooner than he had planned, and he was going to have to begin extricating himself from the city before it ended his time with it first. He would break ties and his heart.

It all happened, then: Edouard died among the masses, and Teddy accompanied Séverine to the somber memorial. Séverine took her leave of New York the following year, returning to Paris and becoming somewhat well known as an artist. Her letters to Teddy lasted a whole seven months before she was gone entirely. She had lumped everything in New York into one disillusionment; to engage with Teddy would mean showing mercy to a place that had dumped her quest for romance in the mud.

A year after her departure, Teddy finally moved away, all the way to Cleveland, an hour and a half from where he had grown up. He hated the idea of returning, but it was cheap, and at least it wasn't Youngstown. He found a small but clean one-bedroom apartment on the third floor of a brand-new building. Because he had spent so much time belowground, he luxuriated in the place's light as if it came from a thousand gilt candelabras. He found the job at Harriman's soon enough.

He eventually engaged in the type of meaningless, hurtful flings that he had avoided for so long—lust won out, in the end—but any dalliance that he had always felt like a one-time miracle, a condescension on the part of a guy who might take him to bed, and their activity was always fueled by alcohol. When the world of "dating" apps arrived, Teddy felt as if he were seeing a concrete depiction of the many ways in which he had failed to enter the hallowed, privileged world of romantic success. Indeed, he had still never experienced true romance. It, too, had been interred.

"**OPHELIA HELD IN HER HANDS** the dead turkey, its bloody feathers matching her own headdress. Suddenly, she bit into its gizzard and drank its blood down. It was total nourishment. She would never be Hamlet's slave again. She would never be anyone's slave again. That is . . . unless she wanted to be."

This was Stefanie's interpretation of Thanksgiving, and these gruesome words ended her half-hour reading. Ranjana felt herself recoil. How on earth could someone take a seemingly peaceful holiday and transform it into this agonizing, overwritten bloodbath? The other writers seemed to share her reaction: Roberta attempted a brief clap; Wendy was biting her lip and pretending to look over her own pages; Colin pretended to be taking notes; and Cassie, of course, looked like she wished that Stefanie were as dead as the turkey.

"It's, um, *spirited*, Stefanie," Roberta offered, "but where does this fit into your novel? I don't remember there being a character named Ophelia before."

Stefanie—who had chosen to stand in the front of their circle, turning as she read in some sort of occult-themed incantation— let out an exasperated whisper. "I told you—this is a story within Esmeralda's story. She's having a daydream. It's the same one from chapter three, but it's continued here."

Stefanie had never read chapter three to them, mainly because she had been writing this manuscript—which Ranjana had taken to thinking of as "her messterpiece"—for so many years. Looking across the circle, Ranjana saw Cassie unfold her arms and slide herself up by gripping the sides of her seat. This was a sign that Cassie was about to launch into one of her diatribes, so Ranjana piped up.

"I like the way that you're playing with the *Hamlet* theme and retelling it from the woman's point of view," she said. It had been years since she'd read *Hamlet* (Wait—had she ever read *Hamlet*?), but she knew this: any time that you could say something complimentary about Stefanie's work, you made her feel rationalized. The entire group, sensing the efficacy of Ranjana's comment, nodded enthusiastically and looked at Stefanie's seat, willing her back into it. She complied, too wistful in her self-love to see how excruciating the past half hour had been.

"*Ran-ja-na*, did you have something that you wanted to share today?" Roberta asked, jutting her head toward the fresh roll of pages that Ranjana had, once again, choked in her hands.

"Oh, it's really nothing," Ranjana said, feeling at once determined to read what she'd written and afraid at the prospect of doing so. She had written the pages out longhand, lest any electronic record of them ever be accessible to anyone else.

"My inner goddess is looking to have someone else's inner goddess released alongside her," Stefanie said, sparks in her eyes. She normally didn't afford people this kind of enthusiasm, but she was still aglow from Ranjana's fabricated praise. She motioned to Ranjana to move to the center of the circle.

This was too much to ask, but Ranjana stood.

Shakuntala met Kalpan three weeks ago—the same time that almost the entire village had. Her parents had been searching for a husband for the past year, trying every last family in the area that they could possibly find. At one point, they had even considered the idea of marrying her to a distant cousin with a missing arm, but when the man had come over for dinner with his family and ate a paratha *in their presence, the sight of his one remaining arm whipping slivers of food into his mouth—like he was eating moths—had been so unsavory to Shakuntala's mother that she had practically turned the visitors onto the street once the last bite of food was out of sight.*

Then the rumors about a new man in town began. At first, Shakuntala's family merely ignored the talk, since any new man in town who was a bachelor was surely to be wed off to one of the prettier, more desirable, richer girls. Then the rumors turned dark. The man went from "wealthy and handsome" to "reclusive and troubled." Only a handful of people had beheld him with their own two eyes. One of them was the owner of the general store, Mr. Seth, who said that the man had approached him as he was closing the shop one night and asked if they could set up a weekly delivery of goods in the dead of night instead of during the daytime. The only reason that Mr. Seth agreed to this was because the man had compensated him handsomely. But soon enough, Mr. Seth seemed to regret his decision.

"It is such a weird arrangement," Shakuntala overheard him telling a woman at the store one afternoon. "I make my way to him at midnight on Wednesday. He lives in that old house in the middle of the wood, you know, and he does not seem to have any mode of transportation. The day I first met him, he walked to my shop from his

place. So my assistant and I have to take the cart to his house at midnight and drive up to the back of the house. He has a lady-servant greet me. She is almost as odd as he is, with skin that is just as pale and eyes with the smallest whites I have ever seen. She helps us unload the goods—oh, and here is the strangest part! He does not order food! No, it is only inedible materials—rope, chain, wood, candles, bed linens. I gave his servant a gift of mangoes once, and she flinched. I insisted that she take them, which she finally did, but Atul says he is certain he saw her toss them into the trees just as we were pulling away."

Soon after this conversation in the general store, the animals started disappearing. At first, it was a goat here or there. They would be found with their limbs missing and their bodies startlingly tiny, the blood practically evaporated and the little hub of their bones and flesh barely anything. But then cows started to be mauled—and then to disappear. This was, of course, not only terrifying but sacrilegious. People would gasp as they saw the limp, soiled hides in the road, but a more gradual, more terrifying fear would set in when they took count of their livestock and realized that a cow or two had gone missing entirely. What sort of person could steal a cow without leaving a single trace of its kidnapping?

Several weeks after the disappearances had begun, a very bizarre invitation was nailed to the front post of Mr. Seth's shop. Written on gold-plated paper in a script much pointier than normal Hindi, it invited everyone in town to a gathering at the old estate:

To the new neighbors,

Please come for an evening of dance and song at the home of Mr. M. H. Singh. November 4, at ten o'clock in the evening. Potluck. Please, no children.

Cordially,

Radha Mehta for Mr. M. H. Singh

The invitation was odd for a number of reasons. First, it indicated no address, although the town was so close-knit that the only house left as a possibility was, indeed, the old estate that had become newly inhabited. Second, it was a strange time for a party to begin, and it seemed redundant that children were forbidden, considering that ten o'clock would be too late to take children to a party in the first place. But the strangest issue was one of food; what self-respecting host would make his first event a potluck dinner? Why invite people out for dance and song but no prepared food? It seemed a particularly selfish—and lazy—thing to do.

And yet, everyone went. It was whispered around town that people would meet at Mr. Seth's store and then make their way through the woods to the estate, their various dishes cupped in earthenware pots still hot from the heat of their respective ovens. Mr. Seth stood in his doorway dressed in his best kurta, of brown raw silk and with matching shoes.

"Welcome, welcome, yaar," he said to each person that joined the group, and he seemed at once excited, scared, and anxious. Every time he put his hands together in greeting, he made sure to show off the big ruby ring on his right index finger—clearly a fake, but nevertheless showy. He had done an amazing lot of business in the past week, as everyone had bought groceries for the potluck dinner from his store. He must have taken great pride in seeing the vegetables, spices, and meats from his shelves reconstituted in these pots, but still, it seemed to unsettle him that Mr. M. H. Singh had never used any of those products himself. Why hire a storekeeper with such a vast array of foods to deliver inedible goods these past few weeks, only to have everyone bring food from that store in one fell swoop, to be tried in one sitting?

By the time all of the guests were assembled, it was ten minutes until ten o'clock. About forty people had shown up. The hubbub was deafening. They set out in a crowd, laughing nervously and stepping lightly, with kerosene lamps held in front of them. Had they pickaxes and knives instead of lamps, they would have been a mob ready to take on a dastardly foe. Indeed, any foe would have been truly disarmed by the delicious smells emanating from their dishes. By the time they got to the estate, they were ten minutes late, and the heat of their food had dropped to a comfortable warmth.

At first, they thought they might have gotten the house wrong. All of the lights were out, and if they hadn't brought their own, they would have been standing in complete darkness, as tall trees swayed ominously over their heads and twigs cracked underneath their feet. But then they saw the front door of the house open—a darkness opening among the darkness—and two figures emerge from it. It was hard to make them out.

"Mr. Seth," a man's voice said, calmly but so coldly that there was a collective stiffening of the crowd. One woman, Mrs. Jindal, dropped her rice; the clay pot landed with a tough crunch.

"Yes?" Mr. Seth said, in a voice that was as timid as his usual voice was assured.

"Mr. Seth, please come forth," the voice said again, and it was so commanding that Mr. Seth found himself running to the front steps of the house, his lamp threatening to spill its oil onto the ground. As he approached, the light illuminated the two figures bit by bit until the lamp was snatched by the figure on the left, a woman, and threw the two people entirely into view.

The crowd gasped. The man and woman were dressed in elegant robes unlike anything anyone in the crowd had ever seen. The robes were red; the light of the lamp sank into their folds and lit the edges. The man wore his hair in two long braids, the woman in the same manner, except she wore a peculiar hat with feathers coming out of its top. They looked out at the crowd, ignoring Mr. Seth as he shrieked and covered his mouth.

"Welcome, my new neighbors," said the man. "I am M. H. Singh,

and this is my maid, Radha Mehta. We would like to invite you all inside for a beautiful evening of revelry." At this, he clapped his hands, and—the people of the town would all remember this for the rest of their lives but would never utter a word of it to each other—Mr. Singh's house lit up like a carnival. The front doors swung open to a brightly lit hall full of candles and flowers and furniture so elegant that it could have come from the queen's parlors at Buckingham Palace. The top floors beamed light into the night sky; even the lights in the basement cast bright carpets on the dirt below.

Nobody moved at first, and the terrifying duo in front of them did not budge. Everyone knew that danger lurked here. There was simply too much that was unfamiliar in this situation, and this was a town where everyone could map the events of any given day before it happened, so engrained were they in their day-to-day business.

Perhaps it was this that made Shakuntala detach from the crowd and finally make her way through. She had a dish of mattar paneer *in her hands; although the* paneer *had come out a bit tougher than she had hoped, she felt confident that the tang of the curry, mixed so gently with goat milk and cashews, would be enough to impress this strange pair. As Shakuntala took her first few steps, her father lunged forward, then caught himself with a hiccup of fear. Shakuntala knew he was struggling between keeping her safe and saving himself, and it came as no surprise to her that his own safety was the bigger consideration. After all, she was an aging, unmarried woman whom all the town's men had dismissed. This was as good a situation as any in which she could find herself.*

She walked up and presented her offering to Mr. M. H. Singh, closing her eyes, bowing her head, and holding the dish up as if it were a sword being presented to a knight. She heard Mr. M. H. Singh and his maid chuckle—their laughs could have been encased in glass— and then her chin went cold. It took her a moment to realize that her host was lifting it up with his hand. Shakuntala froze in fear. She looked into Mr. M. H. Singh's eyes, and she could have sworn that their irises were made of silver.

"Thank you for your bravery," Mr. M. H. Singh said, and— dare she think it?—Shakuntala thought that there was a tone of love in his voice. "Will you join me for a dance?"

Soon, she was being led to the middle of a giant room with tall curtains stretching from the bright floor to the ceiling. From somewhere came a strange, plunking sound like the extended chirping of crickets, an attempt at music. Mr. M. H. Singh moved her body across the floor, one arm raised in hers, the other around her back, the way that English people danced. She had no time to think of being scandalized—this strange man's arm on her back, her body so close to his, the folds of her sari dangerously close to coming undone entirely. And soon enough, she looked around to see all of the villagers dancing in a similar manner. Her own parents moved with a grace that she could never have expected. Her mother looked serene, lovely, and her father, always so stern, had a smile on his face, rapture in his eyes.

Then they were all eating off copper plates, their various dishes piled high, the food hungrily shoved into their mouths as their host and his silent maid stood in the middle of the floor, watching them intently. Shakuntala felt at once invincible and ravenous for the food. Anytime that she made eye contact with Mr. M. H. Singh, she felt an odd flutter deep in her body, a feeling she thought at first to be a stomachache. But then she realized that it was coming from below her stomach, and she shivered.

There was more dancing, and even though so many of the people in attendance were old—in their fifties, sixties, even seventies—they never tired. Mr. Seth was more energetic than he had ever been. He detached himself from the group and danced by himself, a blend of kathak *and an Irish jig. At one point, he climbed halfway up one of the curtains; a gaggle of women surrounded him and ordered him down, laughing all the same. Shakuntala looked at her host, thinking that he would find this amusing. After all, he had assembled them all and given rise to this madness. However, he gazed at Mr. Seth with a look of hardness, even disgust. Shakuntala, in spite of herself, found this alluring.*

Shakuntala noticed that neither Mr. M. H. Singh nor Radha Mehta had partaken of the feast. Shakuntala peered over the rim of her glass at her host, her mouth half-sipping more wine, the other half grinning stupidly. She had never had wine before, had never thought she would enjoy it, but its oily sweetness appealed to her and made her feel warm and comfortable. She closed her eyes and felt in this moment that she had finally reached adulthood. Here, of all places, where the aunties and uncles with whom she'd grown up were darting about like little children. Here, where, for the first time in her almost thirty years on earth, her mother and father kissed in her presence.

"Have you ever been in love?"

It was her host. He was terrifying. Yes, his eyes really were silver, and his smile, like his laugh, seemed encased in glass. Shakuntala had never been so frightened, but she laughed. The whole situation was so peculiar.

"Why are you laughing?"

"Please pardon me, Singh Saheb, but do you not find this situation rather odd?"

His face looked the same as when Mr. Seth had climbed the curtain. "Odd? I do not find that word pleasing."

She wanted to apologize but kept laughing. "Oh, Singh Saheb, surely you must know how odd this all is to us. This is a small town. We do not do such things." She pointed to a corner where two women and two men were drinking bhang, increasingly intoxicated on the elixir.

"But clearly you do do such things, if you are doing them now. Just because you have not yet done them does not mean you do not do them. You have not had the chance to do them before. And yet——" And he gestured in the same manner to the same foursome of bhang drinkers.

Mr. M. H. Singh had a point—we could not know what we were capable of doing unless the opportunity to do such things was presented to us. So here she was, in an old, wooden mansion in which her family and friends became something other than themselves and where she, Shakuntala, could be something besides an unwanted daughter and sister. As much as this man scared her, she now saw in him salvation.

She continued to see salvation in him even as his true nature revealed itself, even when he kissed her behind one of those curtains, his mouth tasting of chilled water. Even when, the next day, Mr. Seth was said to be missing; and even when she attended another potluck dinner at Mr. M. H. Singh's a week later and saw the faux-ruby of Mr. Seth's ring gleaming from her companion's pale pinky finger.

Ranjana looked up and saw that the room was silent, markedly different from when Stefanie had read. They looked confused, almost offended, but also gleeful. Ranjana, conditioned to look at Cassie for approval whenever anyone read, saw that she was perched on the edge of her seat, leaning far forward, squinting at the floor, as if trying to figure out an unusually difficult piece of trivia. Roberta had crossed her arms and was frowning, but this was something she did when a piece of writing moved her; it indicated that it was something beyond her own efforts or interests as a writer. Stefanie, oddly enough, appeared relaxed. She must have still been thinking of how her pages had been "well received."

"That was your best writing yet," Cassie said, still looking at the floor.

"Yes. It certainly was . . . intriguing," Roberta said.

"The Force is with you," Colin said.

Stefanie made a short humming noise.

"What's it part of?" Roberta asked.

Ranjana didn't know what to say. "I don't even know, really. I haven't quite figured out if it really is part of a novel or if it's just a story."

Their looks of approval shaded into looks of consternation. They were not in the habit of writing as an exercise and an exercise alone. Cassie, however, nodded her head.

Ranjana backed up and bent down, groping for her seat with one hand behind her. Once she found it, she felt some stress slip out of her body. She hadn't realized how tense her body had become.

"How can you not know if you're writing a novel or not?" Stefanie asked. Ranjana saw a desperation behind her eyes, as if Stefanie herself were just coming to the realization that not every wayward thought that came into her mind had to be committed to the depths of her phantasmagoric opus.

"She's perfecting her technique," Cassie said. The exhaustion in her voice made Ranjana wonder, as she often did, why Cassie deigned to participate in this class at all. Ranjana knew why, though: there was a satisfaction in being the star of the class when you felt that you were surrounded by fools.

"Maybe I don't feel like something's real unless I write about it," Ranjana said. This was helpful to vocalize. She felt herself shed a further layer of stress simply upon saying it.

"Well, I think that's a lovely idea," Roberta said, clasping her hands together as if she had organized a tea party and they'd just finished their finger sandwiches. "Who else has something to share?"

Cassie started to say something, sitting up in her chair, but Wendy piped up and unfolded her stash of papers, which were light green today. Ranjana and Cassie exchanged a look, an understanding that the past few minutes had been edifying for the two of them.

It occurred to Ranjana as they all got up to leave that what she had just felt with Cassie was the kind of warm moment that she and Prashant used to share when he was young, when she would teach him something helpful or, more often, when they would commiserate about Mohan's idiosyncrasies. This is why she found it all the more comforting when, just as she was getting in her car, she heard Cassie call out, "*Ran-ja-na?*"

"Yes?" Ranjana said. As Cassie ran to her, her hair bouncing up and down and her legs thin and agile, Ranjana could see how young and energetic she really was. Ranjana suspected that she was a completely different person outside of class—gregarious, funny, perhaps mischievous.

"I was hoping that you may be able to come to this with me," Cassie said, handing her a pamphlet. In large white lettering, against a red background, were written the words *The Writer's Journey*.

"What is it?"

"It's a writers' conference," Cassie said.

"What's a writers' conference?" Ranjana asked.

"It's a lot of readings by authors and workshops to improve your writing, but the best part is that they have all of these professional editors and agents read your work and tell you if you have what it takes to get published. I went last year and learned a ton, and although I got a lot of passes from the people I saw, they told me to come back this year. I really think that you'd enjoy it. I don't think you need me to tell you this, but you and I are the only people in this class who belong there."

Ranjana didn't know what to say.

"Please say you'll come," Cassie said. "It'd be a great experience for both of us."

"I'll think about it," Ranjana said, with a flatter voice than she intended. Cassie met her tone with a slight frown, but her face still seemed hopeful. She said good-bye and hurried over to her own car.

On the drive home, Ranjana realized that she would be a hypocrite to judge her classmates and then demur when an event like this came along. She had a distant cousin who lived not far from Chicago, where the conference was taking place, and she could use visiting her as a pretense to placate Mohan. As she pulled into the driveway and saw her husband's slight silhouette cutting through one window, she knew that she would have to go.

She had just acknowledged publicly that writing made her feelings real. Attending this kind of event would make her appreciate herself infinitely better than she did now—which, as she entered the house and saw the expectant look of hunger on Mohan's face, was very little, indeed.

It was her own fault that Cheryl found out about the conference. Typically, Dr. Butt frowned upon the use of their work computers for anything other than official business during operating hours (though he must have known that forbidding Cheryl from such a thing was a fool's wish). Ranjana rarely broke this rule, but there was a lull in the office that afternoon, so Ranjana typed in the Web site from Cassie's pamphlet. A bright, busy page greeted her with the faces of some authors she recognized, some she did not. The biggest image was of Pushpa Sondhi, the megabestselling writer, who was the keynote speaker. Ranjana felt scared just seeing this image. This conference was the big leagues.

Just as she was looking at a page about a workshop on "International Culture and Fiction," Ranjana smelled Cheryl's mint-scented breath over her shoulder.

"What's this all about? You changing jobs and not telling me?"

"Shhh!" Ranjana snapped, whipping around and making sure that Dr. Butt hadn't heard. "No, I am not changing jobs. It's a conference."

"A conference for what?" Cheryl asked, shifting to get another look at the screen while Ranjana shielded it.

"For writing," Ranjana said quietly. She had never mentioned this to anyone besides her classmates, Seema, and, sadly, Achyut.

"Writing what? Like *Fifty Shades of Grey*? Who knew you were such a deviant!"

Ranjana looked over the desk to see if the three patients in the waiting room had overheard. They were all pretending to read magazines but were clearly holding back snickers. "No," Ranjana said, even though she had read the entire *Fifty Shades* series and kept it tucked away discreetly on a shelf in her "study."

"It's nothing," Ranjana continued. "Just something I thought might be interesting."

"I love to write," Cheryl said as she sat down. She was wearing large earrings that looked like golden tortellini, and they jiggled every time she moved. "You may not know this about me, but I love to write poetry."

"I see," Ranjana said, closing the writers' conference window on her screen. Then, as if it were a burp that Cheryl had been trying to suppress:

"Maybe I should come to this conference with you."

"Oh, I don't know about that."

"Why not? It's a writers' conference, isn't it?"

"Yes, but, well, I wasn't even sure if I was going myself."

"Now you have a good reason to go! Two sassy girls on the road! It'll be like *Thelma and Louise*. Or more like *Thelma and* . . . Sorry, I don't know any Indian names that start with *L*."

"You don't know any Indian names at all."

"Oh, snap!" Cheryl said, smiling all the same. "I know yours. And I know Dr. Butt's name. Don't I, Butt?" she shouted, craning backward and lifting a hand to her mouth as a mock-megaphone.

"I have to check with my friend Cassie," Ranjana said, feeling the word *friend* sour in her mouth. "She's the one who invited me."

Dr. Butt soon emerged, mercifully ending their conversation, but Ranjana knew that the damage had been done. She knew that there was absolutely nothing that she could do to deter Cheryl from coming. The more excuses she invented, the more defiant and assertive Cheryl would become in her responses. It was like struggling in quicksand. Ranjana did come up with one potential deterrent—the conference did not actually encourage poets to attend, since it dealt exclusively with prose—but Cheryl cheerily informed Ranjana that her writerly gifts were not confined to poetry and that she had several short stories somewhere. Ranjana e-mailed Cassie to float out the idea of Cheryl's joining them, but the response was both pleasantly surprising and somewhat hurtful: Cassie hadn't planned on traveling to the conference together; she had merely encouraged Ranjana to attend for her own edification.

Next, Ranjana tried to suggest that taking the train would be the best option. If anything, it would spare her from tussling with Mohan about taking the car, but more important, it would spare her being in such a confined space with Cheryl (the office was bad enough already). No luck: Cheryl insisted on driving because she had always wanted to take a "girls' road trip." Already, the journey had become much more frightening than anything in Ranjana's novel.

A solution to this two-person confinement occurred to her while she was stirring *daal*. She loved hovering over the pot longer than was normal, letting the steam float up and heat her face until it came close to burning. It was her version of a face mask. It reminded her of when she had been sick as a child: her mother would scoop the crystal goo of Vicks VapoRub out of its sapphire jar and drop it into a pan filled with just-boiled water. She would then tip Ranjana over the searing mixture, covering Ranjana's head and the bowl with a damp towel as one might cover a parakeet's cage. Unlike her siblings, Ranjana never once complained about this or pulled her face away from the heat. Instead, she would pretend that she was a princess in a goblin's lair, like one of the heroines in a George MacDonald Fraser tale.

Something about the imagination that it took to retrieve this memory triggered a response: she thought of being in a cave, and then she thought of Harit's house.

She had been looking for ways to entertain him after the party, which had been too tense for her taste. Not just because of Prashant's outburst—though that had certainly been the most cringeworthy part—but also because Mohan's enmity toward Harit had been so palpable. She had to make it up to him somehow, and a small journey, though in the presence of Cheryl, would provide a unique opportunity. Who knew—maybe he was even a fledgling writer himself? He may very well find it cathartic to put into writing the story that he had told her about Swati. If the act of writing was proving so helpful to her, perhaps it could have a similar, welcome effect on him.

The phone rang, pulling her out of her daze and making her

294 • RAKESH SATYAL

see that the *daal* was starting to burn at the bottom. Reaching for the cordless with her left hand, Ranjana jabbed at the burned bits on the bottom of the pan with the spatula in her right hand, pressed the phone's ON button, and said, "Hello?"

"Hello, stranger." It was Seema. Ranjana felt instantly guilty. She had been so lax at keeping in touch with Seema recently.

"*Ji*. Hello. I'm so sorry. Things have been so crazy around here."

"Oh, I'm sure. But we have to keep in touch, Ranjana. If we don't get to the gossip first, others will beat us to the punch."

"True." Ranjana was only half-listening, since the burnt *daal* was drifting around in the pan like debris in a flood.

"Can we hang out soon? Why don't you come over for lunch tomorrow?"

"I can't. I'm working." A thought zapped into Ranjana's brain. She was suggesting something before she knew it: "Hey, do you know where Paradise Island is?"

"That weird . . . thing they're building? What about it?"

"Meet me there after work tomorrow—I mean, after I leave the office."

"What? Did you join the CIA or something?"

"Just do it. We'll chat."

Seema was silent on the other end of the phone.

"*Ji?*"

"What's this I heard about a new friend that was at your party when we were in Pittsburgh? You're acting very strange, Ranjana."

Ranjana tried to flip this comment into a joke. She didn't feel that she had the energy or patience to succumb to a serious conversation. "Don't we always act strange? That's our thing."

Seema sighed, annoyed. "I'm not meeting you at some hidden place like we're planning an assassination, Ranjana. Call me when you have time to have lunch like a normal person."

Seema hung up, and Ranjana took out her surprise on the *daal* by sloshing it around the pan until the nicely cooked and badly burnt pieces collided. "A normal person"? Seema was one to talk. In fact, Seema really was *one to talk*; she was probably calling someone else right now to relay the odd conversation that they'd just had. In one phone conversation, Seema had managed to solidify Ranjana's thought that Harit—peaceful, earnest, nongossiping Harit—was just the person she needed right now.

SEVERAL DAYS HAD PASSED after Ranjana's party, and Harit worried that he'd never hear from her again. Perhaps she had found their moment in the kitchen strange instead of special. But soon enough, she called him. He could hear the frustration in her voice immediately.

She went on to describe her upcoming trip, which sounded odder than most things he had encountered. Harit couldn't quite understand what she meant by her "writing," but she sounded so desperate for his attendance that he found himself assenting. When he told his mother about it—*When he told his mother*; he could still not believe that he could do such a thing now—she encouraged him to go.

The next day at the store, Teddy approached Harit, who was, shockingly, completing a very successful sale: five pairs of cuff links, a belt, and an expensive Kenneth Cole bag that he managed to suggest subtly to the customer, an amiable guy in his twenties.

Perhaps it was the momentary gush of excitement about this rare achievement that led Harit to say "I'm going on a trip!" when Teddy asked him if he had any plans for the weekend.

"With whom?" Teddy asked. Harit struggled for one second to provide a lie, but Teddy was too fast: "Ranjana?"

Harit knew better than to lie now; there was no way that he could pull it off convincingly.

"Yes."

"And what merry event awaits you?"

"I'm not sure," Harit said, relieved to be able to deliver this response in absolute honesty. "Some kind of conference."

"A conference?"

"Yes," Harit said.

"How fascinating. And you're just going as friends?"

"Um, yes," Harit said, but the slight pause before his response lifted Teddy's eyebrows.

"This is all such a coincidence," Teddy said, his eyes ablaze. "I was going to ask you to go to a conference this weekend."

"What?"

"Let me guess: you're going to a writers' conference."

The first thing that occurred to Harit, in spite of his Internet ignorance, was that Teddy had hacked into Ranjana's computer. "Well, yes."

"I'm going to the same one! Pushpa Sondhi is speaking, as you probably know. Ever since I met Ranjana, I've tried to read everything of consequence when it comes to Indian literature, and I've already read all of her books. What's the matter with you?"

Harit was half-laughing, half-guffawing. Of course something like this would happen. Of course. God forbid that anything in life be easy, especially an outing between him and Ranjana. There was no way that he and Ranjana and her friend would escape Teddy's detection now, so Harit revealed that they would all be attending the very same event. Teddy clapped his hands rigorously.

"This is the most exciting thing that has happened in forever! Do you guys need a ride?"

"Actually, Ranjana's friend is going to be driving us, so I'm not sure if it would be polite to add another."

"Oh, forget 'polite.' This is a once-in-a-lifetime trip. I'll ask Ranjana myself."

Harit didn't understand how, exactly, this managed to make things less awkward, since Ranjana would then have to arbitrate between Teddy and her friend, but he decided to let it be. Ranjana was better equipped to handle social situations like this, and Harit had already seen how a passing conversation could reveal too much too quickly.

Teddy called Ranjana, of course. Teddy chimed on and on about how he had seen a pop-up ad for the conference ("You order one Pushpa Sondhi book and you're in the NSA's system"). He had immediately thought of her and Harit and what a great adventure it would be for all of them. Somehow, Ranjana found herself sympathetic toward him. Whereas in the past she had been annoyed by his overeager approach and his lack of social delicacy, she could hear, as she did in Prashant's voice, a combination of hope stirred with disillusion—the sense that Teddy was one disappointment away from becoming depressed. She couldn't allow herself to find him annoying.

Teddy and Cheryl would either adore or loathe one another. Now that Ranjana thought about it, they seemed almost like siblings.

Yes, Teddy was over a decade older than Cheryl, and no, Ranjana had no idea how Cheryl would react to a gay man, but there was some undeniable overlap. Whatever the case, they were all in for a very long ride.

Cheryl picked Ranjana up in her Taurus, the one that they often used for their Wendy's excursions. It had thankfully been cleared of its usual trash (fast-food wrappers, countless rubber bands, stacks of gossip magazines), and Cheryl had installed a peppermint air freshener. Ranjana had never seen Cheryl out of her office scrubs. Her outfit was actually more tasteful than Ranjana could have imagined—sleek black blouse under a leather jacket, tight blue jeans, brown boots. Ranjana was just about to compliment her when Cheryl spoke:

"Why, don't you look wonderful! Did you get a haircut?"

"Yes," Ranjana said. The hairdresser had chopped and shaped her hair into a subtle bob.

"Nice. And your outfit—did you buy that in India?"

"Actually, I bought it here, but it is from India," Ranjana said. "And thank you. You look wonderful, too, Cheryl."

"Oh, it's not often that this girl gets out, sister."

Ranjana placed her purse at her feet and straightened the *salwar kameez* that Cheryl had just complimented. It was teal blue with gold embroidery, and she had worn it with a strategic purpose in mind. If this was a writers' conference and she needed to impress publishers, then she needed to present herself as a beguiling Indian woman. After all, Pushpa Sondhi was one of the most beautiful women in the world. Ranjana had to aim for some kind of elegance.

"Teddy is, you know—he is gay," Ranjana said. She tried to say the word *gay* nonchalantly but ended up prolonging the long *a* sound.

Cheryl widened her eyes. "You made friends with a gay man? Aren't you something."

Ranjana took this as a signal that everything was fine.

Her chest tightened as they drove the few miles to Harit's house. After Teddy had called her, she had called Harit, reassuring him that telling Teddy wasn't such an imposition. As they pulled up to his house, he looked—could it be?—excited. He was holding a dish of some sort, and he had also dressed nicely—crisp brown slacks, tan jacket, shiny black shoes, a thick wool coat. He had combed his long hair. It didn't matter how dated the clothes were or how forced the hairstyle seemed; there was something charming about his having made an effort.

Ranjana got out of the car to greet him.

"*Namaste, ji,*" she said, and he repeated her greeting. "Did you make something?"

"I brought some *pakoras,*" he said, offering them to her as if they weren't both getting in the car. She took them anyway, then motioned for him to get in the backseat. She knew that he would feel weird if she opened the door for him, and she would have felt weird, too. So they opened their respective doors as Cheryl's voice spilled out.

"Why, hello, there! I can't believe that I'm finally meeting one of Ranjana's friends! I'm Cheryl, but you probably already know that."

"Of course." Through the visor mirror, Ranjana could see Harit nod kindly.

Ranjana had printed Google directions to both Harit's and Teddy's houses, but Cheryl had a GPS device clipped to her dashboard that she insisted on using, so she typed in Teddy's address while Ranjana recited it. Harit interjected, saying that he knew the way, but Cheryl insisted, saying that she had a way of getting lost even when people were giving her directions. Ranjana and Harit caught each other's eyes in the mirror at the exact same time.

"So, how long have you been in America?" Cheryl asked, shouting over the robotic GPS voice as if it were a football game.

"Over fifteen years," Harit said.

"And you live in that house all by yourself?"

"No. I live with my mother."

"Oh, I see. God, I would die if I had to live with my mother. I mean, she's dead already, but I mean if she were still alive."

"How is your mother?" Ranjana asked Harit quickly. In her haste, she had asked the question in Hindi and was aware that this would make things harder for all of them. "I asked him how his mother is doing," she said to Cheryl, who nodded.

"She is fine," Harit said shortly, the statement thudding.

"Great," Ranjana said. She was actually looking forward to picking up Teddy now.

"What's your mom's name?" Cheryl asked.

"Um, Parvati," Harit said.

"*Um-par-vutty*. What a pretty name," Cheryl said, of course. "How do you spell that?"

Harit spelled it.

"Oh! Like in *Harry Potter*!"

"What?"

Ranjana clarified. "There's a character in the Harry Potter books named Parvati."

"Oh," Harit said.

"She has a twin sister," said Cheryl. "What's the other one's name?"

"Padma," Ranjana said. "Actually, Parvati and Padma are the names of twin sisters in *Midnight's Children*."

"Oh—is that a TV show?"

Ranjana pushed ahead. "Harit works at Harriman's."

"Oh?" Cheryl said. "Do you get a big discount?"

"No," said Harit.

It was something out of one of those indie movies that she and Mohan would see with Prashant—stories about white families who wore solid colors and moved in worlds of carefully plucked ukuleles. These characters always found some common bond, and it usually resulted from being in a car together. Here she was, surrounded by a mint-chewing coworker, a gay stalker, and an Indian man who thought it normal to bring *pakoras* on a road trip with strangers. Wes Anderson would have had a field day.

Naturally, Cheryl talked the entire time. She thought she had sciatica. She needed a new recipe for Rice Krispie Treats. She could never remember which one was Sasha and which one was Malia. She loved cashews more than walnuts. She could eat a Spicy Chicken Sandwich from Wendy's every day for the rest of her life and be happy. ("You should buy stock in Imodium," Teddy responded.) She wanted to go to Bermuda because she was "fascinated by the Caribbean." She had psoriasis. She had once done cocaine at a friend's intervention. She loved eating popcorn with peanut butter on it. She had buried her dead cat in her backyard.

Etc. Etc. Etc.

What made this bearable for Ranjana was watching Harit's reaction to everything. Cheryl might as well have been speaking Japanese backward. At one point, Harit rested his head against the frosty window and closed his eyes, though it would have been impossible to sleep while listening to this barrage of commentary. Nevertheless, Ranjana had to admire Cheryl, someone so unabashedly unaware of tact or discomfort. Even Teddy, for all of his similar inclinations, seemed to throw in the towel when Cheryl began her disquisition on using lemon juice to clean furniture. Finally, they found a rest stop outside Fort Wayne that had a Wendy's. Ranjana stayed in the car, joining Harit and Teddy for ten blissful moments of silence while Cheryl went inside to enjoy her sandwich.

IN THE BEGINNING, Ranjana was wary of reading Pushpa Sondhi's work. She first learned about the author in a praiseworthy *New York Times* story. In the glamorous photo that accompanied the piece, Sondhi was almost in profile, the light catching the right side of her face, her hair pulled behind her. She wore a ribbed turtleneck, the kind that a stylish professor or art curator would have worn, and her mouth fell into a calm half-smile. Because the photo was in black and white and the lighting was so bright, she didn't look Indian. She looked like a South American aristocrat, maybe a wealthy Middle Easterner. The more that Ranjana ran her eyes over the photograph, the more she felt herself being effaced in two ways: by seeing a writer deemed important yet culturally neutered; and by thinking that a foreign, female author could not succeed on merit alone.

In protest, Ranjana avoided reading Sondhi's first book, *Wisdom of Ages*. Only a couple of years later when she came across a paperback copy at a bookstore selling used books did her curiosity finally get the best of her. Mohan was working late at the university, so she took the book with her to a diner, where she sat with a piece of apple pie and a hot tea and read it cover to cover. She wasn't one to cry when reading—and she didn't cry then—but she felt the book in her gut as if she had eaten it along with the pie. The lyricism of the writing. Its stark depictions of immigrant life. Its even starker depictions of married life, which involved so many nuanced characters. *The New York Times*'s fixation on the author's attractiveness had been no more than a brown herring.

Proud of herself for having judged the work instead of appearances, Ranjana felt justified in judging the attractiveness of Sondhi's ensuing author photographs. The next one was even more arresting, another black-and-white photo shot in some kind of high resolution that made it seem like a portrait drawn in pencil. Not only had that first photo deprived Sondhi of her true ethnicity, but it had repurposed the lines of her face so that you couldn't see its beautiful width, the round eyes that drew the light straight into them. Not so with the second photo, which seized upon those eyes to momentous effect, revealing more of her heritage. The sprawling silk shawl covering Sondhi's shoulders gave off the air of otherworldly aristocracy.

Eventually, the photograph for *The Forsaken*, the author's third book, got everything right: there she was, in color, her Indianness complete, her face earnestly tilted forward while a caftan-like blouse, zebra-striped, floated around her. It was the first photo that captured the integrity of the author's background and the integrity of her beauty.

Ranjana had become a dedicated fan. She felt a bit predictable, since everyone who engaged her in any discussion about books always brought up Sondhi. Ranjana would usually slough off the conversation and move to another topic; she wanted to insulate her legitimate enjoyment of the author's writing from any possibly racist observations that would have debased it. She felt a deep connection to the work—a connection that she viewed as unique, hallowed. The greatest skill that an author could possess, she thought, was the ability to make a reader see a book as his or her child, someone only the reader in question could truly appreciate, love, and protect.

Ranjana wanted to be able to take her robust knowledge of Sondhi's work, shift it from the container of her brain to the tips of her fingertips, and pour some garbled but nevertheless potent version of it into her own writing. She wanted to believe that if you worked passionately enough, you could create the appearance of something truly great.

They all realized quite quickly that there was nothing more terrifying than a group of amateur writers.

All the attendees were jittery—clutching their folders and messenger bags and dog-eared books and rubber-banded manuscripts. Even though each writer was allowed only a twenty-page sample to share with the visiting editors and agents, many seemed to have printed out their lifework. They held the manuscripts to their chests as if they had to be fiercely guarded, lest someone steal their ideas through the pages.

Ranjana, Harit, Teddy, and Cheryl checked in at the front desk, then were signed into the conference by a perky young woman who looked as if she could have imagined no greater gift than passing out name tags on lanyards. Both of Ranjana's names were misspelled, which would normally have been unsurprising, but this was a writers' conference, so it seemed particularly egregious.

Harit's first name was fine, but his last name had two letters switched.

"Maybe we should just switch name tags. No one will notice," Harit said, and Ranjana laughed out loud. Despite the ordeal that it had taken for them to get here, Ranjana knew: she was glad that they were doing this, pleased to discover that you could feel a friendship's construction if you took the time and care to notice it.

"Should we drop our stuff off and then head to the panel?" Cheryl asked. She had signed all of them up for one of the first panels: "Who Should an Author Be?"

"Sounds like a plan," Teddy said. Having been steamrolled by Cheryl during the road trip, he seemed newly energized.

They headed up in the elevator. It was a bit tense, given that Harit and Teddy were taking separate rooms while Ranjana and Cheryl were inhabiting the same one. Ranjana and Cheryl got off on the ninth floor, and Teddy and Harit headed to the tenth floor—of course, they had ended up mere doors apart from each other.

Despite the reinvigorating change back at his house, Harit felt the emptiness of his hotel room as if it were a long-coveted gift. There was poetry in the smooth comforter, the stiff curtains, the tasseled pillows, the sheen of the dresser and end tables. When he sat on the bed and caught his reflection in the mirror, he saw it as a portrait that had taken decades to paint. He felt a catch in his throat. He had worried that he might cry as soon as he got into this room, and he bent over and let it happen. His voice snagged on his sobs before laughter overtook them, and soon he was lying flat on the floor and feeling the rise of his stomach under his hands. It seemed so simple, but perhaps what he had needed was to be in a different city—to be somewhere away from the small square mileage of sidewalk, bedroom, bus, and aisle that had been his life for so long. He had never seen this ceiling, would probably never study its cake-smooth whiteness again, and he loved it for that. He loved it for its newness and its unimportance and its fleetingness. For a weekend, this room was his and no one else's. Hotels let you be as selfish as you wanted, and he was going to be selfish, selfish, selfish.

Harit was the last to rejoin them back in the lobby. He seemed to have splashed some water on his face and combed his hair. They headed to where the panel was being held, a compact space made all the more compact due to the partition that had been dragged across the room to separate it from another event. About forty chairs were arranged in neat rows, and very few of them were empty. Ranjana asked if a few people might shift to accommodate her group, and they rearranged themselves quickly, mostly because no one wanted to be the last person standing up and complaining when the event began.

The room fell silent as a group of three professionals, two women and a man, was led in. The women had the easy fashion of New York City diehards, but the man was unkempt, with long, curly hair and an outfit of half-unbuttoned shirt, chinos, and loafers.

A woman in a bright yellow blouse greeted the room and asked everyone to turn off their cell phones, which was met with a titter of laughter and no activity on anyone's part.

"I'm Sandy Gearhardt, one of the founders of the conference and a writer myself." She tossed her head to one side and licked her lips as the audience produced a small burst of claps. "I want to welcome you to today's panel, 'Who Should an Author Be?' Our guests are Suzie Hart, owner of her own boutique literary agency; Cathryn Calyer, senior editor at Spectacle; and Ezra Mann, publisher and editor in chief of Green Umbrella Press. All of them are successful and accomplished publishing folk who count Pulitzer Prize winners, *New York Times* bestsellers, and yes, superstar YA authors among their lists. Please join me in welcoming them."

A labored round of applause echoed around the room.

"We'll start with an easy question," Sandy said, settling into a seat and pulling out a series of salmon-colored index cards. "How much does an author's personality have to do with whether or not you decide to publish his or her work?"

The publishing trio sighed, its members looking at each other as if they'd never seen each other before and would never speak to each other again. "I guess I'll start," Suzie said, freeing a strand of chocolate-dyed hair from her cheek by flicking her head. "If I'm being prim and proper and 'literary'"—at this word, she rolled her eyes and jutted out her jaw—"I'll say that it doesn't matter at all. It's all about the writing. It's all about what I see on the page. It's all about that lightning moment of finding a writer with a fresh, surprising point of view. It's about the truth and power of the written word. But the truth is that I've definitely turned down books after speaking with the author and finding out she's a total basket case."

A few gasping laughs popped up.

"You see, I'm an agent," Suzie said. She flipped her hair again. "It's not just about the writing. It's about forging a longtime collaboration with someone you're going to do book after book with. And if the person writes like a dream, that's what you want; that's fantastic. But if the person can't carry on a conversation like a normal human being, then who wants to work with that for years? I had an author once who was like Rumpelstiltskin. She would take the English language and spin it into beautiful sentences and stories. And I loved her; I really did. But she was always having some crisis that I couldn't even try to deal with. She was one of these people who always sounded like she was collapsing under the weight of her own genius. And when that constant collapse gets in the way of being able to sign a contract or deliver a manuscript on time, it's just not worth my fucking time."

Then she added, "Sorry—time. Not 'fucking time.'"

"Well, that's *one way* to put it," Ezra began, leaning on the table and holding his head up with one hand. "As a publisher, I must respectfully disagree. Our job is to publish great writing. It's to nurture great writers. It's to show that, in this tiny, oft-forgotten forum of the literary arts, that we are capable of putting aside psychological trauma and its victims and getting wonderful stories in front of readers. That's what we do. That's the job. At least it is for me."

The laughter in the room was becoming more strained.

"And you, Cathryn?" Sandy asked.

Cathryn didn't look as if she wanted to enter into this discussion.

"Um, I just like to publish fun stuff!" she said, eliciting more genuine laughter amidst the tension. "I don't really think it's rocket science. Writers are inherently kind of loony. I mean, it's the truth! You have to be a little bit insane to want to write anything down and have people read it. It's sheer madness. With all of the things that people have in the world to divert their attention, with media and texting and whatever people are doing—"

"With social media," Ezra muttered.

"With social media! It's so hard to know what the writing life *is* that we have to be a little off-kilter to even enter into this world.

So I always take authors with a grain of salt. Honestly, though, I feel like we've veered somewhat off topic."

"Well, sorry," Suzie said, coughing out a bitter laugh.

"Let's move on to the next question," Sandy said. She flipped to the next card, frowned, then flipped to another, then another. "How about we talk about who your favorite authors are. Ezra, how about you?"

"You mean which of my Pulitzer winners do I love the most?"

Afterward, there was a buffet lunch in one of the ballrooms. Although they had been encouraged to socialize with other people and keep their literary conversations going, Ranjana, Harit, Teddy, and Cheryl huddled at their own table. There was surprisingly a lot for Harit and Ranjana to eat; they piled steamed vegetables and rolls and fruit onto their plates while Teddy and Cheryl assembled towers of thick cheese and cold cuts.

Everyone seemed energized, but Ranjana felt alienated. There seemed to be so much stacked against writers, and the publishing bigwigs had seemed so jaded. She began to understand how special and heartbreaking her nights in front of the computer were—the comforting glow of the screen and the silence except for her tapping fingers or sips of tea. All of that crumpled under the continuous tut-tutting that assailed everyone's hopes in a setting like this.

"Did you enjoy the talk, *ji*?" Harit asked her in Hindi. Ranjana took comfort in being able to converse with him without worrying that people nearby would understand. You could pull a foreign language over yourself like a cloak and retreat into a private world, she thought. Given the weekend's keynote speaker, there were, of course, handfuls of Indian people lurking about, but they were clustered in their own enclaves at other tables. As for Teddy and Cheryl, they had finally found their ideal icebreaker—their mutual affection for *Fifty Shades of Grey*—and were busy revealing their favorite scenes.

"I'm just glad you're here," Ranjana said. She didn't want to reveal her unease, for fear that her discomfort would heighten his.

Harit could sense that something wasn't right, but he knew what Ranjana was thinking—that he should staunch his discomfort for her sake. He found this refreshing, being able to know someone your own age well enough to react in kind. Teddy was the only other middle-aged person with whom he conversed regularly, and that was, of course, a very different type of interaction, like an awning pelted by the rain.

Cheryl turned to Ranjana. "Is that what you're writing, sweetie? Are you off on your own, writing little erotica stories?"

"Oh, Cheryl. No. I am not writing 'erotica stories.'"

"But that's where the money is at. Don't you want to make money?"

"People don't just write for money, Cheryl."

"Be honest: if you could make the type of money that these women are making, you wouldn't give a damn what you wrote. I heard that Danielle Steel has twenty cars."

"Danielle Steel writes romance, not erotica," Ranjana said, quoting a line that Stefanie loved to blurt out.

Cheryl: "What's the difference between romance and erotica?"

Teddy: "Where did you hear that she had twenty cars?"

Harit: "Who is Danielle Steel?"

Soon the room stirred as the masses departed for their next events, leaving the debris of crumpled napkins and shiny pieces of plasticware. Their day progressed with more panels and snack breaks. Ranjana finally ran into Cassie, who chatted briefly before saying she was late for a panel; this was their sole interaction. Ranjana felt increasingly ill-informed about the literary figures in attendance. On more than one occasion, there was that movement, that wind of recognition, when a writer of some note appeared on a panel or moved down a hallway. Most of the authors looked amiable enough, but many of them seemed resentful of the people stuffed into these compact, too-bright rooms. At one panel, a big-faced man—bushy eyebrows, wide jawline—was introduced as Aidan Nolan; he was an Irish author of three novels who was just now seeing his first novel being published stateside. Despite his being a novice on this side of the pond, he refused to answer most questions during his Q&A and scoffed through the answers he did provide. By the time the last panel of the afternoon started—"From Self-Publishing to Self-Actualization," where a fight almost broke out due to overcrowding—everyone looked closer to Self-Mutilation.

The keynote dinner arrived, along with scores of faces that had not been seen during the rest of the conference. It seemed as if many attendees had signed up for the weekend simply to attend this one event. Everyone tried to ignore this and focus instead on the excitement of being in such proximity to a superstar. She was nowhere in sight, at first, but everyone knew that somewhere within the hotel, the eminence for whom they had shelled out a couple of hundred bucks was ready to appear, to educate, to enlighten, to pass along the warmth and impact of her words like God engaging the finger of Adam.

The catering was more careful for this event. Food appeared on the tables by way of a more fastidious waitstaff. Bleu cheese nestled among glistening greens and sugarcoated walnuts. Two baskets of crust-cracking breads and pastel butters were distributed to each table. There was an elaborate eggplant lasagna for the vegetarian-inclined, and Cheryl and Teddy were treated to large cubes of filet mignon with pert green beans and baked potatoes that looked like fashionable prawns. There was wine—red, white, and rosé carafes—and Ranjana was surprised to see how tipsy people were willing to get. She wasn't shocked to see Teddy and Cheryl drink, but she was somewhat startled to see Harit dispose of three glasses by the time the entrées arrived.

"I used to be able to cook like this," Cheryl said. "Long before I was married. I dated a chef, and he was always teaching me to make things."

"Get out of town," Teddy said. "Or, um, more out of town."

"Not joking. His name was Bobby, and he made it a point to teach me one new thing a week. I could make filet mignon as good as this. I could make lamb. I could make the perfect roast chicken. I could make cock-oh-ven."

Ranjana spoke as Teddy's mouth was opening to correct her: "That's *coq au vin*."

"Oh, whatever," Cheryl said. "It's not like I make it anymore."

"Why not?" Harit asked. He was pouring himself another glass of white wine, and the too-deliberate way in which he did so revealed his tipsiness.

"Dear, when you get married and have kids, you don't have time for that kind of crap anymore. Plus, if your kids grow up eating filet mignon, they'll probably turn out to be assholes."

"You should write that down," Teddy said.

As Ranjana enjoyed the last bite of her lasagna, she thought of her countless Wendy's lunches with Cheryl, of how Cheryl had gone from cooking fancy meats to eating electric fries. Ranjana couldn't find any trace of sadness in Cheryl. As usual, she couldn't tell if Cheryl's happiness was authentic or the by-product of an overwhelming mental dimness.

Sandy, the conference organizer, approached the lectern in the middle of the long dais, which was decorated with bouquets of water lilies and framed by royal blue curtains. The room achieved another one of those complete silences—somewhere in the vaulted ceiling, you could hear the gargle of a radiator—and everyone could see the flutter in Sandy's movements. No one was listening all that well to her introduction; necks were craning ever-so-slowly to see where the author was standing in wait. Sandy ended by saying, "The extraordinary Pushpa Sondhi," and everyone saw that she had been waiting in the hallway.

She was even more beautiful in person. There is a quality that beautiful people have that causes their features to take on different meanings, depending on the angle of their heads. That wide, eye-hooded face was arresting even from far away, but there was also an unassuming matter-of-factness to her mien. She was not dressed extravagantly; she wore a blue silk blouse and black slacks. Her hair was short, not even shoulder length. The outfit made Sondhi look more maternal and younger at the same time—like a protagonist in one of her short stories.

Ranjana felt it: jealousy, the top of her mouth turning to metal. All the goodwill that she had built up—the warmth that she had felt upon ingesting the stories and their beauty—was effaced upon the author's entrance. Ranjana felt sick to her stomach, not because of the jealousy itself but by its speed and thoroughness. There was no emotion as swift and complete. Happiness spread through you and tingled. Sadness hooked your limbs and pulled them down slowly. But jealousy yelled hello from within you.

The topic of Sondhi's speech was the ability to step outside of one's native culture and view that culture anew, from a remove. In her case, it was Portugal; she had moved there with her journalist husband (a Chilean) and their two young children. Ranjana remembered reading that they had a brownstone in Brooklyn; on a particularly low evening, she had even clicked on Google Street View to see if she could espy a smudge of Sondhi's form somewhere in a tall window. These days, in Lisbon, the family was surrounded by buildings of yellow stone, cypress trees instead of leafy maples. Sondhi had taken to reading in Portuguese, and it had given her a new perspective on English, on the turns and twists of its borrowed words. She was reading poetry in Portuguese, novels in Portuguese, grocery store circulars and traffic signs in Portuguese. It was evolving for her into a language of real substance and utility. She was an English-born, American-raised, Portuguese-immigrant Punjabi woman whose own sons would speak fluent English, Punjabi, Hindi, and Portuguese. She was her own fantasy novel.

This should have been evident to Ranjana all along: Sondhi wasn't some frozen entity contained in the pressed pages of a paperback or the gray static of a Kindle. She was a human who created elegant sentences and fully formed characters, characters whose lives resonated more than Ranjana's all-too-real but ineffectual life. Hundreds of people had gathered with their breaths caught in their throats to see this woman speak; they craned forward for even the slightest chance to hear something that revealed the inner lives of her characters. Meanwhile, nobody but the people at this table would care about the events of Ranjana's day.

As a beautiful dance was set to gorgeous music, Ranjana set the eloquence of Sondhi's speech in this banquet hall to the eloquence of Sondhi's stories. This led her to a gut-punch conclusion:

She might never be good enough to give her characters the writing that they deserved. If she were a visionary artist like

Sondhi—a beautiful thinker, with Portuguese-fluent sons and a glamorous husband—she could give her characters lives full of careful rumination, well-worded wit, boisterous parties populated with smartly observed acquaintances, delightful bedroom escapades. But she was not exceptional, so her characters would never have exceptional lives. An untrained painter couldn't depict Cézanne's *The Card Players*; a pitchy singer couldn't produce an affecting "Nessun Dorma." There was that extra dimension, one step below the surface, where the emotions of the best characters roiled. Ranjana could not access that layer, so her characters would be doomed to live without those charms. Sondhi's version of failure was making the Pulitzer short list and not winning the prize; Ranjana's version of failure was actual failure.

Ranjana knew this kind of Indian woman, someone born into privilege but without an exaggerated sense of it. Ranjana knew that Sondhi's father had been an English professor—thank you, Wikipedia—so she knew that Sondhi had grown up with the base-level studiousness that Indians typically possessed. Ranjana could envision what Sondhi had been like in her American classrooms. She could see the jiggle of Sondhi's hand as it rose to answer a question; she could see the respectful family dinners and the stern, beautiful mother. She could see the good grades, wished for and then zapped onto report cards and college transcripts. She could see the boys, both Indian and American, who snuck lustful looks at her light eyes.

There was no room for anything flippant. Composure had always been key because composure came with the territory. Children like this came from evolved lines that had perfected their efficiency and their comfort with success. Everything about Sondhi corroborated this: the evenness with which she spoke about her education, especially her grad school education in literature, and then the charming matter-of-factness with which she discussed her constant and steady success. Just as beautiful Indian girls earned the adoration of their fathers, the approval of their mothers, and the fawning dedication of Indian boys, so they attracted the expected achievements—from the academic to the romantic. And because these channels of merit were so engrained at this point, there was no element of legitimate surprise. With no surprise, there was no unexpected event—no serendipity—so there was nothing particularly funny. And when there was nothing particularly funny, there was only time to reflect on the things that might disrupt one's success. And the disruption of success was always sad, never funny.

Upon looking across the table at Harit, Ranjana understood where she was in the literary hierarchy: in terms of writing, she was to Sondhi what Harit was to her in terms of cultural intelligence. She would never approach Sondhi's level of discourse just as Harit would never approach her own understanding of American ways. It was an unsavory thought to have, but Ranjana was old enough to know that when something felt sticky like this, it was true.

The more she considered her tablemates, the more she felt that they were making a mockery of her writing. Yet the reason for her anger was her own ineptitude. She had invited them here so that she wouldn't have to reckon with her own weaknesses. Their entire presence was an excuse for her to ignore this keynote speech and focus instead on the half-drunk coffee in Cheryl's cup, the pilling on Teddy's beige sweater, the descent of Harit's eyelids, heavy with wine. She would collect these small scraps, these ministories, in lieu of being able to craft grand musings.

She couldn't tell if it was defeating or liberating to realize that she wasn't destined for greatness. It wasn't like she was declaring herself a literary genius. She was simply trying to create stories that people would enjoy. Or was she? Whatever her weaknesses, she was not Stefanie; she had some level of talent. At some point, she had bitten into the forbidden fruit of seeing what good writing could be, and now she couldn't shut herself back in the bliss of ignorance.

But then Sondhi poured herself a quick glass of water and said, "Many of you in the audience here are not going to believe me when I say this, but I have periods of great frustration and failure, when I fear that I will never write another sentence that matters to anyone, let alone to the critics who seem to cluster with their knives raised. Still, if you take one thing away from this speech today, I hope that it will be that the fear is not only valid but necessary. Fear is as common as blood. It courses through us and is, in its way, a vital source. It is the requisite formula for our continued work as writers. Without it, we would weaken and wither away. We feel it constantly, which means we can harness it and use it as a driving force. That's what I'm encouraging you to do today—take that fear and put it to work for you. Turn it into the apparatus by which you get work done instead of making excuses. It is a rite of passage to acknowledge your challenges and then overcome them."

This speech immediately reenergized Ranjana. So she had weaknesses and challenges. What woman didn't? And especially, what *immigrant* woman didn't? That didn't mean that she had to give up altogether. It wouldn't be easy to push forward; to be sure, she had lofty goals for herself: she didn't want to be incidentally or circumstantially funny. She didn't want to make other people laugh by making her stumbles seem charming. She wanted to be pointed in her humor, capable of meeting someone and pinpointing exactly what might make the person laugh—or at least cause the person's eyebrows to rise in appreciation. That could be a point of differentiation in her work. It could be hard to infuse this kind of humor into her writing, but it might be possible. It was a delicate balance, trying to cater to the strictures of the genre while bending them just enough to allow an appreciative laugh. Perhaps this form of writing had no Literary-with-a-Capital-*L* equivalent, and perhaps she couldn't match the sophisticated tone of Sondhi's wry cultural observations. But she could at least strive to do so.

There was a signing after the talk. A stylish young publicist, her hair pulled into a tight chignon and her body slinky in a navy suit, hovered over Sondhi with a clipboard. Her function was to move the long line of fans along as quickly as possible. The audience had been instructed to bring only one item to be signed, and photographs were permissible only if the phone was already in camera mode. One click was allowed, and there were many instances when the delight of having a photo with Sondhi was immediately overshadowed by the result of a bad shot, discovered only once the fan had been shepherded away and deposited at one of the hall's doors.

The room was unnervingly quiet; everyone in line seemed to be craning forward to hear what the current person in line was saying. All of them were trying to find a way to twist their compliments into something more expertly worded and impressive. There was a moment of collective jealousy, cut with pity, when one woman was heard confessing that she had lost her baby at childbirth, a horrible event recounted in one of Sondhi's most famous short stories.

For her part, Sondhi was gracious, signing swiftly but engaging directly. For someone who had performed this task countless times, she never flagged, industrious yet approachable. A chief benefit of signing books, Ranjana thought as she shambled forward, was that Sondhi could find a crop of new characters by interacting with readers as varied as these. As one woman approached the table, her hair so long that it fell onto the table and near Sondhi's signing hand—the publicist broke her martial pose momentarily to flick it away—Ranjana imagined her as an art teacher in a future short story.

Once they were about ten people from the front of the line, Cheryl turned around and popped up on her heels. "Oh, I don't even know what I'm going to say. What should I say?"

"Just tell her how much you love her work," Teddy said. To Cheryl, this advice may have sounded genuine, but they all knew: Cheryl had never read a word of this woman's work.

"Yes, but everyone's saying that," Cheryl said. "I want to make an impression."

"Honey, I don't think making an impression is ever a problem for you." The steel in Teddy's voice was turning molten.

"Ranjana, what should I say?"

"I agree with Teddy," Ranjana said. "That's what every author loves to hear. I'm sure it means something to her every time someone says it."

The man ahead of them, a wiry guy wearing thick glasses, looked back at them and blinked, then turned around.

"You guys are no fun," Cheryl said.

Ranjana had a feeling that Cheryl's interaction with Sondhi was going to be even more dramatic than the interaction with the woman who had lost her child.

Cheryl handed a conference volunteer the copy of *The Forsaken* that she had bought in the lobby. People had been instructed to write whatever they wanted on a tiny slip of paper, which was vetted by the volunteer and passed onto Sondhi. Ranjana scanned Cheryl's paper, which read, "To Cheryl: Love your work!" Why couldn't Cheryl demonstrate this kind of wit more regularly?

The volunteer laughed as Cheryl handed her the paper. "Good one."

"I try," Cheryl said.

The volunteer handed the paper over. "That's funny," Sondhi said, looking up at Cheryl and then bending over to inscribe the title page.

"I lost a child, too," Cheryl said.

Ranjana almost dropped her book.

"I'm so sorry to hear that," Sondhi said. She stopped writing and looked up at Cheryl attentively.

"Cancer," Cheryl said.

"That's awful. I'm so sorry."

"It's the reason why I've always appreciated when people are totally honest. When my son was sick, the doctors would tiptoe around his problems because they were so afraid to hurt him—or to hurt me and my husband. But I told them, 'Just give it to me straight. I'm a big girl.' So what I'm going to tell you is that I've never read a lick of your work. But I will. I will. Thanks for signing my book."

"Take care. I'm sorry for your loss. I appreciate your candor."

In light of this conversation, Ranjana could hardly focus during her own interaction with Sondhi and ended up just asking for an autograph. She managed to say "I love your work very much" before shuffling away. Harit looked as if he were in pain as he had his book signed; he didn't say a word. Even Teddy was so taken aback that all he could muster was "You're even more beautiful in person" before he joined the rest of them.

"I had no idea that you lost your son," Teddy said, gently taking Cheryl's elbow in his hand.

"Ha-ha. Oh, that? I was just kidding."

"What?" Ranjana swung violently around.

"You were *kidding*?" Teddy said. Harit looked as if he were going to collapse.

Cheryl's face went still. She pursed her lips. "No, I wasn't kidding. It's true."

"I . . . don't understand," Ranjana said.

Cheryl sighed. "It's true, OK? I'm just playing with you. It was just nice to be taken seriously by someone. Too bad it had to be a stranger." She turned around and walked into the lobby.

"THIS IS ALL I NEED TONIGHT," Teddy said, holding up a martini so dirty that you couldn't even see through it. "I've had enough of these people. It's like they want to be writers without any of the alcoholism."

Harit had sobered up after a nap in his room, and here, in the hotel bar, despite Teddy's complaints, he ordered a Diet Coke with no booze in it. Although they had eaten at the banquet earlier, they were both pulling cheesy shingles from a tall hut of nachos. At nearby tables, other attendees were huddled over signed Pushpa Sondhi books and similarly slimy snacks.

"You're awful quiet tonight," Teddy said. "Even for you." The large olives in his glass huddled, freezing in the cold.

Harit wanted to be with Ranjanaji, but Cheryl, who had reverted after the signing to her usual, laid-back self, insisted that she and Ranjana have a "girls' night out." Ranjanaji looked less than pleased with this suggestion, which made Harit's evening with Teddy at least somewhat tolerable. If she had seemed happy, Harit would have just assumed that she had no desire to spend time with him.

He was ashamed of his drunken behavior at the banquet. He had sensed Ranjana's judgment of him as if she were his mother. There was a restraint in her watchfulness that wasn't outright disapproval but that was cutting, regardless. Her sweetness made you feel as if you were missing a chance to honor it. More important, he still had not found the opportunity to tell Ranjana about his recent breakthrough with his mother, how he had even confessed to a possible lifestyle that left women behind romantically altogether. So now he felt the extra weight of having to tell his new friend about everything all at once, and this sunk him back down into a pit of worry from which he had hoped to emerge.

"Hello? You OK?"

Harit thought for a second before responding, chewing a nacho and waiting for it to slide down. "I'm not sure why I came here," he said. "I should have known that I wouldn't have a nice time."

Harit expected to see Teddy curl his lips, that habit he had of gathering his anxiety in one place lest it affect the rest of his body, but Teddy lifted his martini and took a slow sip. He set his drink down and leaned forward on the table, his upper arms straining against the striped sheen of his dress shirt.

"What would it take for you to have a nice time?"

Teddy's face reminded Harit of how Cheryl had been right after the signing—serious and angry. Harit looked into his Diet Coke and thought of how nice it would be to lie on one of the smooth, cool cubes, bubbles popping around him like determined jellyfish.

"I worry that you don't even know how to be happy," Teddy said. "You don't even let yourself have a good time. Ever. I always have to drag it out of you."

"You're the one having a martini, Teddy. That's what you do when you're feeling unhappy." Harit didn't know how he was finding the strength to be combative without the aid of alcohol.

"I'm not feeling unhappy right now, actually. But you're like this even when we're at the store. You're always wallowing in your grief."

People always used this word *wallow*. For a long time, Harit thought they were saying "swallowing in your grief," which was, in fact, a fitting way to describe a martini.

"Why shouldn't I?" Harit could feel his neck heating up.

Teddy leaned even closer. "Come on. Look at all of the things that you have to be happy about these days."

The heat rose into Harit's face and came out of his mouth in a puff. "You're crazy. 'All of the things'? I have *many* things to be happy about? You're so insensitive."

"Insensitive is the last thing I am. I'm trying to help you. That's all I ever do. I'm your friend, Harit. Whether you like it or not, that is what we are now—friends. That's something to be happy about. If I weren't with you right now, you'd be home with Mommy."

"At least my mother knows when to leave me alone," Harit said, again surprised that he was capable of fighting fire with fire, especially when his words were unfounded: his mother was *not* leaving him alone anymore. "You're the type of bad friend that I deserve."

"Oh, burn!" Teddy said, leaning back melodramatically and putting a palm to his chest. "You're a regular Kathy Griffin. Keep 'em coming, smart-ass!"

"You're fat."

"That's original. Keep going."

"That shirt is ugly."

"Really? Your shirt makes you look homeless."

"I hate it when you sing in the store. You are never in step with the music. Even Mr. Harriman talks about it. Everyone does."

"I know they do. That's why I keep doing it. They also talk about how your hair looks like pubic hair. Because it does."

"You wear too much cologne."

"*I* wear too much cologne? You smell like a French prostitute."

"At least French prostitutes know how to speak actual French."

"Oh, ho!" Teddy said, pushing his chin out and lifting his eyes to the ceiling in a gesture that signaled both being impressed and being wounded.

They went silent for a few seconds.

"Haven't we gotten eloquent," Teddy said.

Harit *had* gotten eloquent. He had begun to cultivate a different language. Not a vocabulary of household objects and restaurant foods and asking directions and making small talk and greeting customers with courteous phrases in passing. The heat had moved back into his body and into his back, his feet, into the hardness of his teeth and the tip of his nose. He had learned how to be constructively mean to a friend—which was a different vocabulary and a rare type of happiness.

"Can I get you anything else?" the waitress asked, taking Teddy's empty glass off the table.

"Two gin martinis, dirty," Harit said.

"You sound like James Bond," Teddy said.

Indeed, he felt like James Bond.

"I really threw you guys for a loop back there, didn't I?" Cheryl hoisted the bottle of red wine and poured herself another glass, the brim seeming to quiver.

"I was so sorry to hear about your son. Why didn't you ever tell me?"

Cheryl had ordered a plate of ravioli even though she had eaten a fair bit at the banquet. She halved one of the ravioli with her fork and stuck the meaty grin into her mouth. "It doesn't exactly come up in regular conversation."

"Yes, but . . . I don't know. We work in a doctor's office. How do you work in a doctor's office all day after that?"

"It's the reason *why* I work in a doctor's office." Cheryl maintained the same even tone, as calm now as if she had never snubbed them after the banquet. "I want to help people. Even if it's with their asses."

Ranjana was enormously impressed with this reveal of Cheryl's troubled history. Only someone of true fortitude had the ability to hide such a tragic event, not to have it seep into every movement and cause hard-edged resentment toward the littlest things. Take Harit: he had been felled by his loss. It outlined his every action.

Ranjana took a sip of wine. She didn't want to drink, and this wine tasted like eating the rind of some fruit, but she didn't want to do anything contrary to Cheryl's wishes. "I have to ask you something," she said.

"Shoot," Cheryl said, looking Ranjana right in the eye. Cheryl must have been very pretty once. No exotic beauty, but Ranjana could see that the soft wrinkles of her face were not etchings but arrows, pointing to where her youthful girliness had been at its strongest: her eyes had been the bright centers where her enthusiasm had pooled, and her mouth had been a stage for smiles and retorts. Her kooky personality—the false naïveté had fooled Ranjana. If they had grown up together, Cheryl would have been the more popular of the two.

"Do you think that I've been horribly rude to you?" Ranjana asked. "All this time? The whole time we've worked together?"

Cheryl pushed her hand through the air, as if to send the words back into Ranjana's mouth. "Ranjana. No. We're friends! Unless, well—have you *meant* to be rude to me this whole time?" Cheryl folded her hands one over the other and rested her chin on them, her eyes eager at the idea of finding out some great trespass.

Cheryl could have been friends with Seema, Ranjana thought, whatever Seema's hang-ups may have been. Or no—not friends. They would have made great nemeses. They were both protected by their eccentricity; in the company of comparable eccentricity, they would have felt threatened.

Ranjana felt the need to be honest. "I must admit that I've never thought of you as a real friend until today. Or perhaps 'friend' isn't what I mean. I mean that I have never given you the benefit of the doubt until now." Ranjana paused, processing her next sentence and understanding how true it was just before it left her lips: "I think that I have a habit of thinking I know exactly who people are as soon as I meet them." She had done this to Achyut. She had judged him immediately. He had been surprising and abnormal in so many ways, yet her opinion itself had not really wavered. She had worried that he'd be problematic, and she had made him problematic. Then he was gone from her life. Such things didn't happen in books. If he were a character in one of her stories, he would have had a nice throughline, a satisfying plot. But life wasn't one of her stories. Achyut could vanish, and he had.

"As I said earlier, I appreciate honesty," Cheryl said. Having finished her ravioli, she touched her napkin to the red-tinted corners of her mouth. "So let me say this: I grew up in our town. I've lived there my whole life. I've seen my childhood friends grow up, get married, push out kids, get fat, not learn anything. They drink and smoke and stay the same. They're not going anywhere. I'm not going anywhere. But what people forget sometimes—people who haven't grown up in our town, people who turn their noses up at us from far away or even close by—is that some of us choose to stay there. It's not because we're too dumb to move away. It's because we've found something comfortable. Comfort is a really underrated thing, Ranjana. My son didn't know much about it. And I wish he had. I'm not stupid. I know I'm not the smartest person in the world, but I do know one big thing: being cheery, even when you're not feeling cheery, even when you actually feel like walking into traffic from being so sad, brings cheer into your life somehow. I'm smart because I know that. Don't you forget it."

Forcing yourself to be cheery. Happiness begetting happiness. Ranjana wanted to think it ridiculous, yet that is why she had come here: to tell stories. To fabricate things. This was its own kind of forced emotion. If you had the capacity to install fear in a fictional person's heart, if you had the capacity to shove love into a princess or fury into a winged monster, you had the capacity to generate passion or mirth or humility or patience in yourself. It wasn't just pen to paper or fingers on a keyboard. It was through your own generosity of imagination that you made yourself good.

SCRIBBLED CHECK AND LIFTING up from the table and the carpet's paisley and weaving out of the doorway and the weight of Teddy even heavier than you thought and there are people in the lobby in some bright T-shirts must be some other conference and the woman behind the front desk in her sailor-like outfit and her face is looking concerned but detached she doesn't want to deal with it tonight and this is what happens at hotels anyway and they're at the elevator and it takes a long time to come the numbers are lighting upward as one elevator ascends away from them and the numbers are lighting downward closer to them but someone must be getting out at the seventh floor and saying bye because it continues to take a long time and Teddy suggests that maybe they should take the stairs and they make a few steps in that direction but it's too hard so they turn around and there's the elevator, at last, so they get onto it and can't remember which floor they're on and Teddy starts to hit every floor in a row but Harit remembers that they're on the tenth floor and so they go into the elevator and then they're stumbling out of the elevator and down the hall and Harit accidentally swipes a plant off of a decorative table and hears it hit the ground with a thump and they're staggering down the hallway and there's no sound except for their feet plodding on the carpet and their breath, which is rhythmic and heavy, and then they're in front of a door—is it Harit's or Teddy's?—and it must be Teddy's because Harit is magically in the room without having used a key and then he stumbles into the room as the light is coming on and feels himself give way to the ground and he's on the floor and his cheek is against the carpet and it feels so, so comfortable and it's actually the most comfortable he's ever been.

Harit wakes up in a small lake of his own saliva. Directly in front of him is the large mahogany dresser, gold knobs up its front like a soldier's buttons. Harit feels like a being contained within his clothes. He shifts and finds that he is less light-headed than he expected. He hoists himself up and checks the clock on the nightstand. It is 2:28 A.M.

Teddy isn't in bed. Harit hears something from the bathroom. The door isn't closed, so he walks forward and peers into it. Teddy is just rising from his hands and knees. Harit pulls away slightly, fearing that Teddy has been sick, then sees that Teddy holds a dirty towel in his hand: he's been cleaning.

"Don't worry about it," Teddy says. Harit feels his stomach and mind flip at the same time. It's his vomit that Teddy has been cleaning up.

A flickering recollection of pushing himself up and retching his drinks into the toilet and missing, then retreating back into the room and onto the ground.

"Teddy, I'm so sorry. Let me help."

"There's no need to help now," Teddy says, chuckling—but not bitterly. He knows to disarm Harit's self-punishment by offering a bit of laughter. Teddy is walking out of the bathroom. Harit has to step aside to let him pass. Harit has no idea what time he fell asleep. How long has Teddy been cleaning the bathroom?

"How are you feeling?" Teddy asks. He opens the closet and pulls out pajamas that hang blithely on a hanger. They are silken and night blue, like an expensive kurta.

Harit actually feels fine, so he says so.

"Good," Teddy says. "I'm going to change." Harit steps aside again, to let him pass, and then the bathroom door closes.

Harit doesn't know if he should go back to his room or not. He feels indebted to Teddy because Teddy has just taken care of his mess—a mess from his body, horrible to clean up even if it were your own—but Harit also feels that he is hovering for a reason. Upon hearing Teddy's movements, the clothes being taken off and jettisoned for his pajamas, Harit feels a lift of his body. It feels like a lift of Harit's whole body, not just the lift of one part. He is eavesdropping on his friend and taking pleasure from what he hears.

Harit ventures back into the room and sits on the end of the bed. The place where he lay on the beige carpet looks like a rough patch of sand. He thinks again of Teddy bent over the toilet, the gentle care in his posture. He thinks of the countless times that he's wanted to smack Teddy across the face but then can't think of anything but the funny curve of that face and the cartoonish expressions in which it often contorts itself. He has convinced himself all along that he has no friends and that no one truly understands him; he's been trying to build his first true friend with Ranjana. He now realizes that Teddy has been the steadfast one—the one who has tried to smooth out his tragedy until it is no longer a barrier in his life but simply a thing that happened, a thing to be dealt with and then discarded.

He has studied the art of restraining his sexual self so fully that he never knew what lay beyond the restraint. He has thought of ballet dancers whose legs stretch farther than he could ever stretch his; this is because they are used to years of bending and stretching and scurrying. He has thought that he couldn't attempt a leap where he has only ever attempted a walk.

But now he sees that he has to. He has to learn these things now or he will simply stay in the same spot, trapped while people like Ranjanaji try to show him that a leap is possible. She has come into his life so that he can open himself up and begin to answer some of the questions about his life that he has been afraid to answer for so long.

Teddy comes into the room and seems about to say something until he sees the wonder in Harit's eyes. He sits down next to Harit and sighs. The sigh carries with it an air of understanding mixed with exhaustion. He does not move. In fact, he does not move for so long that Harit sees that he will not move. It is not Teddy's movement to make. So Harit puts his hand on Teddy's, and Harit nestles into Teddy's chest. In a short but thorough monologue, Harit tells Teddy everything about Swati and his mother—everything, that is, but his many times wrapped in a sari. He has just now decided that he will keep this between his mother and himself. He will not even tell Ranjana about the sari. This confidence makes him finish his monologue gracefully and strongly. Only then does Teddy lean his head on Harit's head and wrap his arm around him.

ATTENDEES WHO WANTED to do so could sign up for a one-on-one consultation with a publishing professional. Ranjana had signed up for this, not thinking about how daunting it would be; the head shot–like pictures of the agents and editors had looked benign on the Web site. This morning, however, after the tension of the past couple days and after having seen many of these people in the flesh, Ranjana was terrified of what this meeting would be like. She had been inspired by Pushpa Sondhi's talk, but now she panicked again, worried that her writing was as insignificant as ever—flimsy, aimless, uninspired. And since the consultation was over a sample and not a full manuscript, the writing would seem even more insignificant.

Her meeting was with Curtis Strong, an editor at Crumley. Curtis's photo on the Web site showed an intense young man with a sea foam scarf swooped around his neck and shoulders. He edited "literary fiction and narrative nonfiction," a phrase that almost made Ranjana's teeth fall out. One of Curtis's books, about a schoolteacher who had taught a school of Ghanaian children how to salsa dance, had spent months at the top of the *New York Times* bestseller list. Another was a memoir by a cop-turned-chef whose pen name was Miranda Rice.

The consultations were being held in another nondescript multipurpose room: a dozen small, round tables were spread at even intervals on its hibiscus-printed carpet. Each table had a tablecloth with a sunflower pattern, giving the entire experience the aura of being trapped in Alice's Wonderland. On each table was a white placard bearing the name of the agent or editor, and there was (thankfully) a volunteer who directed people to their tables.

As Ranjana approached Curtis Strong's table, she was surprised to find that she felt calm. Her lack of confidence in her writing made her feel practically invincible.

Curtis Strong was wearing a gray jacket and thick black glasses. Ranjana knew right away that he was hungover. The gray jacket seemed like an attempt to hide this. Ranjana's confidence deflated. He couldn't be receptive to her work if he was hungover.

The first thing that he said was "How do you say your name?"

Ranjana sat down, letting her purse fall unceremoniously to the carpet. "RUN-juh-nuh."

"Ha-ha, OK. Well, we've got twenty minutes, so I want to make sure we spend it the way you want."

"OK," Ranjana said, straightening herself and getting ready to deliver her prepared sound bite. "The most important thing to me was—"

"Tell me what you want the story to be doing."

"Pardon?"

"What do you want the story to be doing?"

Ranjana had never heard this type of sentence before.

"'To be doing'?"

Curtis laughed and looked askance, as if his eyes couldn't be bothered to watch such stupidity.

"What is your book about?"

Ranjana had the distinct feeling that this man hadn't read her work at all. After everything that she had endured with Cheryl last night, she didn't have the patience for this.

"Did you read my sample?"

Curtis took his hands off the table and crossed them over his chest. Ranjana was aware of the pair seated near them, a woman and a man who were discussing a crime thriller.

"There's no need to be rude. I read your sample. I was just trying to get a sense of your book. What happens after she notices the ring on the vampire's finger?"

Damn. He *had* read it.

"Um . . ."

"I like you," Curtis said, reaching for his glass of water and taking a big sip. "I have to say that I'm very charmed by your whole shtick."

What to say to this? What did this—

"How are you on social media?" he asked.

Possible meanings of this:

(A) How did you come to be on social media?

(B) What is your demeanor on social media (which you use rarely)?

Ranjana couldn't answer either of these questions easily, so she remained silent.

"I like your writing. I mean, this isn't the type of thing that I normally see," Curtis said.

"I know. I wasn't sure why they paired us," Ranjana said. Curtis's face fell at this comment. "But I'm glad that they did!"

This was a disaster.

It continued to be. Curtis segued into a discussion of his experience with Indian people, which involved a childhood friend named Priya, who had gone on to be a professional model, and an editor in his office who had just given birth to twins. ("Her husband's white, so they're obviously adorable.") How could the world put people like this in positions of creative power while Ranjana sat at their beckoning? This man had published *New York Times* bestsellers and had once been at a book party with George Plimpton and Francine Prose (thanks, Google Images), yet Ranjana hoped that Prashant had never read a word that Curtis Strong had edited.

Twenty minutes passed. Ranjana's work was virtually untouched. Curtis was gray with hangover.

"You know the vampire thing is over, right?" Curtis asked.

"Pardon?"

"I mean, it's kind of over. *Twilight* was years ago at this point. You might want to rethink that angle."

"Um, thank you," Ranjana said, thinking of the long ride home.

"Good luck," Curtis said, getting up and shuffling past. He approached the volunteer and said, "Quickest way to Union Station?" Then he was gone.

His printout of Ranjana's pages was still on the table. It was unmarked.

"Excuse me," said a woman nearby. It was the "professional" half of the duo that had been seated next to them. Ranjana pushed away the sleeve of her *salwar kameez* and looked at her watch.

"It's nine thirty-four," she said.

The woman sloughed this off with a laugh. She was African-American and very pretty, with red lipstick so bright that it looked orange. "No—sorry. I couldn't help but overhear your conversation. Don't pay attention to Curtis. He's an asshole. Did I hear that you write paranormal fiction?"

"You made brownies to bring for a weekend away?" Ranjana asked. She was holding a smushed brown wedge that Cheryl had pulled out of a Ziploc bag. Harit and Teddy were nowhere to be found; there was no answer when Ranjana called their rooms, and Teddy's cell phone was apparently dead. In the meantime, she and Cheryl were sitting at the round wooden table between their maroon-curtained windows.

"This is my special recipe," Cheryl said. "I make it for special occasions."

"You didn't know today was going to be a special occasion."

"Some part of me did. I have a sixth sense, obviously."

"Obviously."

The unmarked pages that Curtis had left on the table were now in the hands of Christina Sherman, the agent who had been sitting right next to Ranjana. Ranjana already had Christina's card in her pocket and a text on her phone: *Love love love these pages!! Drop me a line this week. xx Christina*

This had all happened in the past hour.

Cheryl was right: Ranjana deserved a treat. She took the brownie and bit off half of it. Cheryl's eyes widened, and she half-rose out of her seat while a smile flickered on her face.

"What?" asked Ranjana after swallowing. There was a strange taste in her mouth—dense and plantlike.

"Bottoms up!" Cheryl said as she took the other half of the brownie and popped it into her mouth.

"Are these mint brownies?" Ranjana asked, though the flavor was clearly too rough to be mint.

"No—not mint." Cheryl got out of her chair and flopped onto her bed. She lay on it as if she were about to make a snow angel.

Something slithered up Ranjana—a scent memory. Prashant ducking into the house on a Friday night in high school and hugging her briefly, then swerving upstairs to his room and shutting the door. "Cheryl. What was that?"

"Come and lie down on your bed. This is your celebration."

"Cheryl. You didn't."

Ten minutes later, Ranjana felt as if her own mouth were telling her a story.

"It's just that—I'm—he's my husband, but even I don't understand how he could do this to me. I do everything for him. I raised his son! I've done—I've—I deserve good things. And who knows what things he's up to while I'm here?"

"You do deserve good things!" Cheryl said, several seconds or several minutes later. "You deserve all the good things in the world! You're going to be a famous author."

Even in her hazy state, Ranjana found these words unlucky. She rolled over, turning her back toward Cheryl, and shook her head. "No. No. I don't want to curse myself. Just because she said she liked the pages doesn't mean she'll represent me."

"*Loved* the pages—not liked them. She loved them. You're as good as gold. You're as good as gold!"

Suddenly, Cheryl was flailing around, almost dancing. "You're as good as gold, good as gold!" Cheryl kept saying. Ranjana writhed with chuckles.

Obviously, she had never tried pot, but even in this state, she could see the appeal of being high. Her limbs were loose, her head expansive, and she allowed herself to be legitimately, unobtrusively excited about the prospect of being represented by Christina Sherman. She had worked hard and endured so much. She deserved to be successful! She deserved to be seen as an important and unique writer! All the other people at this conference were slow-moving farm animals compared to her, a literary steed, and she would charge ahead, hair billowing in the wind, and claim the success that she deserved.

"Fuck Mohan," her mouth was telling her. "Fuck him."

"Yes—fuck him!" Cheryl screamed. "Fuck him! Wait a second—what did your husband even do?" Cheryl asked.

Ranjana realized that she had begun her tirade against Mohan without having divulged the details of his transgression. The pot was making her jump forward in her thoughts. This is what pot did, apparently: it made you race toward a lofty conclusion, leaving all nuance behind.

Ranjana found this luxurious. She was glad that she hadn't stated outright what Mohan had done because, truthfully, she didn't want Cheryl to know the truth. Ranjana was hot off a great success—Christina's interest in her writing—and to reveal the cracks in her marriage was to relinquish this crown and open herself to Cheryl's criticism. Instead of letting the pot push the truth out of her, she would harness its comforting messiness and roll on this bed, rub the tough fabric of the comforter against her cheek and move her legs as if riding a unicycle. She ran her fingers through her hair, pushing through the knots until some of the strands came free.

THERE WERE OVER TWENTY GAS STATIONS within five miles of Mohan's house, and they were all owned by bastards.

The stations in his area collaborated to plot against everyone. They knew how to control prices so that no customer could ever feel satisfied. Constant innovations in wireless technology made it all the easier for them to communicate with each other. Mohan lay awake some nights and imagined the cellular signals flying like silver bats through the air, all of them working to mask which station had the lowest gas price at any given point in time.

Perhaps this was true of establishments everywhere. When Mohan visited other parts of America, he looked at the crooked black letters or red digital clicks of their gas station billboards and wondered if the men who controlled them were equally odious.

Today, the first four stations he visited were all on the same intersection. He glided among their entrances. The Sunoco and the Marathon were both down five cents, whereas the Shell was down seven and the Mobil down eight. Although they were all lower, they were still too high. Then he drove to the BP, which he always assumed, ever since that catastrophic oil spill years ago, to have the lowest price. Nope. So then he drove another mile to the Speedway, which, down ten cents, was not a blessing from God but at least tolerable.

During the first year of their marriage, Ranjana would join him in this pursuit. In fact, she had been more enthusiastic than he. They would pass a billboard, their necks craning in sync, and she would chuckle with exasperation or delight as the price revealed itself to be too high or acceptable. Mohan would think of how valuable pennies could be: they could lead to a joyful game shared by spouses.

It wasn't this fact alone that propelled him to love the game so dearly. It was that Ranjana was participating in a game that *he* had created.

When Prashant was a baby, he would tap his toy car against the window and cry out at the billboards. When he was a teenager, he began to voice his disapproval. By this time, Ranjana had grown tired of the game, too, and although mother and son didn't always see eye to eye, Mohan could tell that their shared annoyance with the game was one of their most enduring bonds.

Mohan thought that his wife and son were very, very wrong to ignore his obsession with gas stations. After all, one of the main things that anyone discussed in polite conversation was gas prices. The local news, the national news, people in line at the grocery store—they talked about this subject as often as they did the weather.

When he spoke on the subject with his friends, he did so moderately so as not to reveal his secrets. Delighted and jealous, his audience would shout out the names of specific stations and ask what their latest prices were. Mohan had all of the numbers memorized. Seeing his friends grin into their tumblers of whiskey, he treasured this knowledge. He was proud that he had put in the effort to earn it.

The owners of the stations all knew him. Many of them shouted at him for parking on their blacktop, standing in front of his car, and scratching his pencil into his notebook, but he would just shout back, "Saving money is not a crime!" before slouching back into the front seat and driving to the next station. A part of him felt remorse for antagonizing the fellow South Asians who ran the stations, but he also felt a sense of injustice about their practices: if he had played fair and square and made his way honestly in American, then they should be expected to do so, too.

His madness was informed by math. After many years of simply recording the figures for his own knowledge, he began to have his students take the data and interpret patterns in the numbers. And they did, even though they were chemistry students and not statisticians. They were able to see that the stations worked in a specific pattern, the numbers dropping at every other store to keep people guessing. It wasn't just something from Mohan's imagination, a theoretical system that he kept trapped in his brain. It was a legitimate trap of checks and balances, a group of men feeding each other's coffers and families. This was unacceptable.

For many, many years, Mohan had been wary of using the Internet to solve his problems. He associated the Internet with that one-time Hollywood actress whose name was like his—Lohan, which people pronounced either "Low-HAN" or "LOW-en," the latter closer to the pronunciation of his name—and he thought it to be a foolish, dangerous place. Although he was a scientist, and although he had seen men of his generation amass their fortunes by bending the Internet to their will, he saw his status as a chemist as hallowed, loftier in its bonds and formulas than the nutty code of computer engineers. Recently, though, upon noticing his wife's behavior, he had relented. It was useless to resist the knowledge that could be uncovered by typing a few words into a thin, clear box and hitting ENTER. Not using the Internet was the same as pretending that he didn't notice his wife's actions: she was driving around, traveling to places that were eating up their gas. (Of course Mohan kept track of how much gas they both used, not least because he was guilty, too. Every mile that he spent driving among the gas stations, keeping track of their prices, was a lost mile of gas, even if it was in service of eventual savings.)

He would use the Internet now—Lord, would he. Mohan went to the university library, and in forty-five minutes of research, he was able to see that the gas stations were owned by subsidiaries. In five more minutes of research, he was able to see that these subsidiaries were linked by a holding company owned by one family. In one more minute, he wrote their names down and placed an anonymous call to the police about their price-fixing.

He parked at a Dunkin' Donuts near the intersection where those four stations faced off—the Sunoco and Marathon, the Shell and Mobil. He went inside the store to get two glazed doughnuts and a hot tea. The owner, Kailash, served him quickly but with a smile; he knew Mohan's usual order and didn't miss a beat. Mohan went back to his car and watched.

He had used the Internet as if he were a detective. He wanted to use it again to figure out what was going on with Ranjana. He loved her dearly. Couldn't she see that? No, she couldn't. She was sick of him—he knew this. He always prepared himself to be kind, but he found himself reacting with defiance instead of kindness every time he spoke to her. It was too difficult for him to tell her the truth:

Now that Prashant is gone, I need you. I want us to do things together. I want to sit on the couch with you and drink some tea and watch the original version of Lagaan. *I want to drive to one of those glassy new restaurants and perhaps have a bottle of wine. I want you to forget that we were married to each other by our families and appreciate me for who I am.*

I want to go to the bedroom with you and undress and not feel ashamed, look at each other's bodies and see that no, we're not what we used to be— maybe we were never what we thought we were—but we're here now, and we can try. I've done my research. I've looked up things that I never thought I'd look up. And I've even forced myself to consider doing those things, trying them without disgusting you entirely.

I've studied how to be good to you there, in that room, with nothing but our nakedness and our determination.

Half an hour later, Mohan watched as a police car approached. Which station would it choose? It was the Shell. A fitting symbol— the conch-like announcement of a fallen dynasty. Mohan let himself snicker for a few moments, then drove home. He didn't want to miss the nightly news, when he'd see one owner, then another, then another, then another in handcuffs, all of their heads bowed, the gold watches on their wrists glinting in the winter sun.

THEIR BAGS WERE PACKED, and they were facing each other, clones of themselves reflected in the dresser's mirror. In Teddy's stillness, Harit could see the handsomeness that was normally masked by layers of moving, jesting flesh. Teddy's eyes moved from Harit's glasses to the tufts at his hairline, then to the lightly wrinkled folds of his neck. Outside, a fast winter wind made its way among the tall buildings.

Their reflections moved toward each other and hugged. Harit's nose was nestled in the soft crisscrosses of Teddy's houndstooth jacket. It smelled of sharp cologne and something soap-like.

"You know I adore you, but you don't know what you're doing," Teddy said. He had said this several times already. He had said it last night when Harit pulled away from that first embrace on the bed and touched his lips to Teddy's. Teddy had gently pushed Harit's head back onto his shoulder and demurred. It wasn't right to take advantage, he said.

"You're right," Harit said now. "I don't know what I'm doing. But that doesn't mean that I don't want to be doing it."

He kissed Teddy again.

He was surprised when the tip of Teddy's tongue emerged and found its way onto his. Harit felt the tension rush back into his body, but Teddy had his arms around him, always gentle, and Harit leaned into the roundness of Teddy's stomach and let his head tip back. He had never known how complex the movement of tongues could be; he had never had anything move his tongue for him. It tasted unlike anything—it was as if he were tasting himself—but he enjoyed it. So much, in fact, that he enjoyed it for an hour more.

"I insist. You drive. Ranjana and I will take the backseat." They were all standing outside Cheryl's car.

"I don't really feel comfortable driving your car," Teddy said.

"Honestly, I'm not really in the state to drive right now." Cheryl leaned forward, the balls of her feet rising off the ground, and she gave Teddy a knowing look—or, as knowing a look as her bloodshot eyes could give. Teddy took the keys from her and headed to the driver's seat. Harit, at a loss, got into the passenger seat, then looked in the visor mirror at Ranjana. Her forehead was against the window, and she was blowing circular mists against its cold surface. Her hair looked insane; she couldn't stop smiling. Harit didn't know what was making her so giddy, but he was happy if she was happy.

Teddy produced a CD from his blazer pocket and popped it into the car's player. It was Taylor Swift. Harit was pleased with himself for knowing this; they played her music all the time at Harriman's. Cheryl sang along to every word. At first, Teddy appeared annoyed, but the unrelenting brio with which Cheryl seconded these stories of heartbreak and resolve, these fairy tales and nascent adulthood, won him over. Soon, he was belting his head off.

In the backseat, Ranjana kept giggling. Harit looked over at Teddy, who was obviously singing to ignore what had happened earlier. Everyone around him was smiling, and he found that he was, too. The rest stops and fast-food signs and check-cashing shops and fat motels and odd churches that they had passed on the trip to the conference took on new appearances now, becoming a succession of cheerful places where people did their best to live lives of contentment and purpose. He could absorb this energy and fill his house with it. Taylor Swift's voice—moving from coquettish to wizened—urged Harit on, told him that he was capable of being something other than doleful.

They didn't hit traffic, and they pulled back into town right as the sun was settling down for the evening. Ranjana had fallen asleep, and Cheryl woke her with a tickle, which didn't make Ranjana laugh but made her pop up and look horribly paranoid. Where were they? What time was it? She was babbling about how she and Mohanji needed to pick up their son from the airport, that she had entirely forgotten that he was coming into town. Teddy decided to drop her off first, and the car was soon empty of her, the silence settling as Cheryl joked about the clumsy way in which Ranjana approached her porch. Ranjana rang her doorbell and waited for a few moments. Then, snapping out of her daze, she popped up, realizing that she was at her own house and not a friend's. She set her bag down, pulled out her keys, and let herself in.

"Exactly how much weed did you guys smoke?" Teddy asked, changing gears and squeaking the car forward.

"We didn't smoke," Cheryl said. "It was a pot brownie."

Harit was so surprised that he started sneezing.

PRASHANT INSISTED ON FLYING HOME this time. No more bus rides full of quasi-homeless people, he thought. But when he got to the airport, people were lying around the terminal as if in some grown-up pajama party, pillows and blankets more plentiful than baggage. Somehow, though, Prashant proceeded without obstruction, right through security, ticket taken, the seat next to him left unoccupied even though the flight was otherwise full. Once they were in the air, he peered out of the window and saw the fiery stitches of the cities below. Down there were thousands of guys who were struggling just as he had struggled before Thanksgiving. He let his gaze fall back against the window, studied his reflection to see if he could detect the bloom of happiness that he felt inside. He was probably imagining this, but he liked to think that he saw a certain confidence, a firm jut of his chin and a face made narrower with calm. He was a straight-A student at one of the most prestigious universities in the world, and he had a smart, beautiful, and—though he would never say this outright to her—rich girlfriend.

Not that he planned to tell his parents about Clara just yet. She wasn't Indian, for starters—though he had considered saying that she was and changing her name to Chitra.

Someone in the row behind him was speaking French, and as if a tall stack of books had just been set on his lap, he became instantly weighted with the idea of Kavita. He had not had this feeling in weeks—had, in fact, been so thorough in his scraping-off of her charm that he hadn't replied to her last three e-mails, had managed to avoid seeing her at all in December. He knew why he was doing this, of course: beyond not wanting to see her and therefore compromise his ardor for Clara, he wanted his new relationship to reach her by word of mouth. Ideally, she would find out during some innocuous conversation and crumple, however slightly. She would understand that you couldn't do this to someone; you couldn't come along all brilliant and beautiful and gracious and funny and expect not to experience pain of your own. You couldn't be impervious to knowing that other people had found love, nosiree.

Yet she probably wouldn't care. She had scores of people who found her attractive and beguiling, and she didn't need Prashant's attention. If she found out about his relationship, she'd smile genuinely and feel happy for him, certain that she would find the man of her dreams just as easily. Then they could all double-date and be friends!

By the time the plane landed, he was glum. Aircraft in a holding pattern, stopgap at the cabin door, luggage delayed twenty minutes, Dad calling him every five minutes to see when he was coming out, bag arriving fifth from last, he stalked out of the airport and threw his bag into the trunk. He got into the backseat and muttered "Hey" to the backs of their heads.

"Hello, *beta*," his dad said. They had spoken very little since his outburst, but he could tell from his father's tone of voice that he was trying to be sweet. This softened Prashant a little. He turned to his mother and said, "It's good to see you guys."

"It's great to see you, too, *beta*," she said, reaching one hand behind her and toward him. "Want an orange?"

It was actually a trio of orange slices, and he took them even though he wasn't particularly in the mood to eat them. He wanted pizza.

"How was the flight?" his father asked.

"Ugh. Sorry I was so late. We got caught on the runway."

"See—I told you," his mom said through a half-mouthful of orange.

"*Arré*, eat your orange, *ji*," his dad said. Prashant couldn't tell if his dad's tone was mock-reproachful or legit-reproachful.

His mom pressed on. "Are you hungry, *beta*? I have *rajma chawal* at home."

His dad snorted. "Oh, he doesn't want *rajma chawal*. He wants McDonald's. Right?"

"Pizza."

"*Pizza*." His father always said this word as if it referred to a made-up food that appeared only in fairy tales.

"Please tell me that you're not just eating pizza the entire time you're on campus," his mom said. "What about all of that food that we brought you?"

"No offense, but I went through that in, like, two weeks. I'm a growing boy."

"You're not giving it to your friends, are you?" his dad asked.

"No, Dad."

"At least charge them if you do. Don't give it away for free."

"I didn't give anything away."

"Do you know how much it cost to buy all of that food?" his father continued. "I can't believe that you would give it away."

"*Ji*, didn't you hear him? He didn't give anything away."

They were speaking as if they were in their eighties, not their forties. Again, he couldn't take the temperature in the car. Were they willfully playing at being mad, or had something terrible happened? *Repartee* was not a word that he attributed to his parents. Prashant was pretty sure that his dad didn't even know what it meant.

They pulled into a Domino's. His father hated the idea of delivery because he hated the idea of tipping, so when he could actually be convinced to eat pizza, he insisted that they carry it out. He went into the store to order and then stayed inside. He always did this to make sure that the order was prepared properly.

"So, tell me all of the stuff that you can't tell your dad." His mom was disposing of the orange peel in a plastic grocery bag.

"Oh, Mom. What kind of stuff would that even be?"

"Girls. You're with girls now, aren't you?"

There was that stack of books on his lap again—Kavita. "Mom."

"What—you are, aren't you?" she said.

Something was definitely up. His mother never engaged him in talk about dating—a holy, holy blessing that he had never fully appreciated until this moment.

"Mom."

"Oh, *beta*, I'm just joking, but you know you can talk to me if you need to discuss it."

"Did you just watch an after-school special? What is this?"

His mom turned around in her seat. He hadn't noticed until

now, but her hair was different. It was cut to shoulder length and was inexplicably straighter. It looked nice.

"Wow. I can't even remember the last time you changed your hairstyle. Have you *ever* changed your hairstyle?"

His mom simply shook her head no. She had this weird smile on her face. She looked high.

"Mom . . . are you high?"

"*Beta!*"

"If you're going to ask me if I'm not a virgin anymore, I can ask you if you're smoking something."

She gave him a stern look, then turned back around and was quiet for a moment. Then she said, "I cannot *wait* for that pizza."

"*Mom!*"

CHERYL LOOKED PUZZLED when Harit insisted that she take the wheel. She did so anyway, her eyes less wild but still roving. Now, Harit stood outside the door to his house, Teddy beside him, both of them teetering.

They entered, Harit moving slowly but confidently. He could hear Teddy's timid footsteps behind him—the first person he had ever invited over the threshold. Without having to turn around, Harit could see his house through Teddy's eyes—the careful emptiness of the counters and tabletops, the tapestry of browns and dusty greens, the silence and the torpor. He could sense the shift in Teddy's body as they crested the doorway to the sitting room. Harit was reminded of fairy tales, the feeling of impending fire when a knight neared the nexus of a dragon's cave, the telltale refuse of dismantled skeletons and purposeful splatters of blood.

There she was, steady and silent and thrown into relief by strategic shadows. Equally quiet and still was Gital Didi, kneeling beside her and clasping her hands. When Teddy assumed a position beside Harit, his mother turned her head toward him.

Her face brightened as if a plate of candles had been placed before it. Instead of freeing her hand from Gital Didi, she tightened her grasp and sat up, flicking her eyes upward for a brief moment before settling them upon Harit, upon Teddy, upon Harit, upon Teddy.

Harit still was not accustomed to seeing her look at things with firm resolve, but that's what she was doing, ingesting the sights of the room through her eyes. He understood that there was a fundamental shift in behavior happening, an allowance of sorts, and he moved to her feet, knelt at them and kissed them, felt their cracks against his lips as if they were coconut flakes. Teddy remained behind, but his mother kept looking at him.

"Ma, I'd like you to meet my friend Teddy," Harit said.

"Harit, I'd like you to meet my friend Gital," his mother replied.

WHATEVER MIGHT HAVE HAPPENED recently in their friendship, Ranjana decided to tell Seema about Mohan. After her pot incident, she woke feeling that her bones were flimsy, that her skin was sagging. She was losing control of herself as if she were a car on an icy road.

She knew what was causing this: the anxiety of thinking about Mohan and his indiscretion was coming to define who she was, and the only way to stop it dead was to tell someone. Someone who had one foot in Ranjana's past and the other foot in her cultural reality.

They met at the mall food court. For all of her gestures at holistic healing, Seema could not shake a crippling addiction to frozen yogurt, and the mall's installment, Freeze 'n' Cold, provided mounds of soft serve and toppings at prices so low that it was as if the store had low self-esteem.

Ranjana and Seema wiped down a flat white table and set their full bowls on top—Seema's bustling with blackberries and kiwi while Ranjana's was Oreo-encrusted.

"You're having an affair, aren't you?" Seema said.

Ranjana coughed as a fleck of cookie flew down her throat. "What?"

"With Haritji? That man from your party?"

"No!"

"Yes, you are. *That's* why you brought up that Paradise Island place. It's where you two go."

"Seema. I am not. We are just friends."

"Well, everyone's talking about it."

Ranjana stabbed her spoon into her yogurt and leaned back. Around them, people were shoving cheesy pizza slices into their mouths and little children were crawling on the ground.

If Seema knew that people were saying these things about her, then Seema had been part of those conversations. Ranjana cringed internally, sad to second-guess Seema's loyalty yet again.

"I am not having an affair with Harit. We are friends."

"Then why did you want to come here? Something's obviously bothering you."

"Mohan's having an affair."

It was Seema's turn to choke. She raised a hand to her mouth, her bangles pealing like a group of gossips. "Mohan? Wow. I wouldn't have imagined it. How did you find out? Who is it?"

"I don't know. But he's been researching . . . things on the Internet."

"What kind of research?" Seema pushed her unfinished yogurt to the side and leaned over the table.

"Online. Learning how to do certain things." Ranjana felt the words tugging themselves out of her mouth even though she worried about saying such things to Seema. "Sex things."

"What kind of sex things?"

Ranjana set her cup aside, too. "Doesn't matter. The point is—"

"Pussy licking? Anal?"

Ranjana almost vomited up her yogurt.

"Well, which is it?"

"Seema, you go too far."

"*You go too far.* That's what you always say. Now Mohan is going far into someone else."

Ranjana started to get up.

"*Ji*, sit down. I'm sorry. Just because he looked those things up doesn't mean that he's sleeping with someone."

"Seema. Come on. If you're going to be blunt, at least be honest with me."

"Well, true. Unless he's tried those techniques on you . . ."

"Seema."

"Fine, fine. The point is, you need to find out who this woman is and—wait. Do we know that it's a woman?"

"Seema!"

"He did love *Dostana*. Didn't he buy it on DVD?"

"Mohan is not gay."

"Maybe *he's* into Haritji!"

Ranjana started laughing in spite of herself. Seema was a certified lunatic, but at least she was entertaining.

"What am I going to do?"

"I'll tell you what you're going to do: you're going to buy lingerie."

"*Ji.*"

"Let's go."

"You're not serious."

"I am totally serious."

"Please don't tell me you've bought lingerie before," Ranjana said. "Please don't tell me you have a 'place' where you buy lingerie."

"I have, and I do. Let's go."

Seema pulled Ranjana into a store called Le Grand Finale. Lace glared at them from every angle; there were so many blond mannequins that it looked like a Hooters. Ranjana and Seema were the only ones in the store besides the saleswoman, who was wearing a suit but had her cleavage, lace-cupped, hanging out of the V of her jacket. "Can I help you?"

"We're looking for a negligee for her. Something that will match her skin tone."

The woman moved silently to a florid red number that had so many intricate bows and ruffles that it looked like three negligees sewn together. "This is the Parisian Fire."

"I have the same in orange," Seema said, as plainly as if they were picking out a cardigan.

"I can't do this," Ranjana said. She disagreed with this sentence as she said it. She could do this—indeed, she wanted to do this—but the store, the possibility of what Seema may tell their friends, the worry that Ranjana might look absolutely insane trying to pull this off installed indecision in her voice.

A switch flicked in the saleswoman, and her face glowed synthetically. "Of course you can, dear! We all have a vixen in us waiting to get out."

Even Seema cringed at this statement. "She doesn't want to be a vixen," Seema said. "She wants to be *sexual*."

The woman's face fell, the switch flicking off. "Honestly, that's a line that my manager wants me to use on people. I'd never say that in real life, I promise." She was probably in her midtwenties. Along the curves of her ears, a series of piercings looked like additional confidantes watching this interaction. "You just need to find something that makes you comfortable."

Seema clicked her tongue. "Don't tell her that. She'll end up picking a pair of sweatpants."

"*Arré*," Ranjana said, turning to Seema and clicking her tongue, too. "No need to be rude—to me or to her. She's just trying to help."

"Of course I am," the woman said. She looked at Seema. "I appreciate you bringing your friend here and getting her to try something new. Let's see if we can find her something good."

They went through negligee after negligee—billowy silks and busy teddies, wrought bodices and garters that dangled seductively. There were pink ribbons and red buttons, black ropes and white frills. The garments all looked downright elegant on the manne-quins, but when Ranjana imagined them on her own body, she wanted to rip them into tatters and go have another cup of frozen yogurt. How could she wrap these soft pieces over the striated dough of her thighs, the jiggly wideness of her breasts? How could she even entertain the sharp diagonals of these panty lines when she hadn't trimmed for years? Worse yet, what was she to make of the quivering rope of flesh at her waist, which would have caused the silk to strain and fray like some alien baby trying to escape from her womb? *Negligee* was not the right word for these things; they weren't for the negligent but for the willfully fit.

The phone rang, and the saleswoman went to answer it. Ran-jana turned to Seema.

"I'm going to say something to you, Seema, and I want a help-ful answer, not sarcasm."

Seema was already formulating a giggle, but Ranjana gave her a grave look.

"I'm being serious, *ji*."

"All right, all right. You're the one who's always sarcastic," Seema said.

Ranjana decided to ignore this comment. She was too preoccupied with the shambles of her body to parse out who was more sarcastic between the two of them. (It was Seema by a long shot.)

"I would feel like a fool wearing any of these things," Ranjana said. "I'm not fishing for compliments, but I do not have the body for any of this."

"That may be true, but here's what you do—"

Seema continued, giving some kind of pep talk, but Ranjana was already seizing upon these initial words—*That may be true, but*—and how unsupportive they were. Whether it was a lack of empathy or just general nonchalance that motivated Seema, she wasn't a very good friend. She should have had the tact to treat this situation with the proper understanding, but she took Ranjana's homeliness as a fact instead of trying to show Ranjana what could be beautiful about herself, what might actually cause Mohan to see her as someone worthy of being desired. Seema was picking up a cream-colored pile of silk that looked like a bakery cake, then holding it against her torso. Ranjana picked up a boxy but night-silken number and headed to the register, leaving Seema midsentence.

"Great choice. I have the same one," the saleswoman said. She pulled back the frills at each of her cuffs, the navy tips of tattoos poking out, and she set to wrapping the garment in crispy papers in shades of black and pink.

As Ranjana thought of what it would take to have someone carve images into your flesh, she wanted to match this woman's resolve with her own determination. Everything that she had experienced in the past few months—Prashant's absence, whatever was going on with Mohan, Achyut's proximity and his slinking-away, the harangues of her writing group and Harit's devastating existence and Teddy's nosiness and now the revelation, right here in this store, that her friendship with Seema was once again a flimsy thing—it had all seeped into her and forced itself into her bones. She could choose to be in control of her reactions and her decisions. She could create a sense of self as a writer and a wife and a woman to be desired. She could be what she wanted to be in this thin slip of sinuous stitches and threads. Just watch.

MIDWAY THROUGH HIS WINTER BREAK, Prashant got up late, at around noon, and went downstairs for a bowl of cereal.

It was a Saturday, the doctor's office was closed, but his mother was out of the house anyway. His father was in his study, which was attached to their living room and which lay behind two white French doors that signaled a firm KEEP OUT when closed. Prashant chewed his cereal and thought about the house's stillness, perforated by an occasional groan or clearing of the throat from the study. It was strange to think how few plans his parents had, how their weekends were not defined by unpredictable outings or raucous conversations. Instead, they would usually get a phone call at around 4:00 P.M. on Saturdays from an auntie telling them that a get-together was happening, and they would throw on some clothes and head out with a hastily assembled dish in hand. As Prashant tipped out some more cereal, he thought of how he, in fact, had been the one anomalous component of their parties in a long time.

As he was finishing up his second bowl, his father came shuffling into the kitchen, his sandals clapping against his feet and his breath wheezing out of his nostrils. Prashant didn't often find himself at home alone with his father, but in the past when this had happened, it seemed as if both of them were waiting for his mother to return, biding their time until she came in and started asking about their days. Now, Prashant noticed that his father seemed to have more of a claim to the house. Prashant felt like exactly what he was—a visitor, someone who didn't technically live here anymore.

His father strode toward the refrigerator and took out a bottle of water and a small package of dried nectarines. He then pulled up a chair and sat down at the table with Prashant, not having said a word.

"How's it going in there?" Prashant asked. It sounded like a strange question, which it was, but he wasn't sure what else to say, especially since his father hadn't started any conversation.

"Kids don't study anymore, *beta*," his father said. "Only half of the students passed this quiz." His father pulled a small tag of plastic from under the rim of the package of nectarines. The lid popped up.

"I study," Prashant said, encouragingly.

"That's because you are a good student. You're like your dad." He took the lid off the package, dove his fingers in, and put a nectarine into his mouth.

"You've never called me a good student before," Prashant said. He wasn't usually so blunt with his father. "I appreciate it."

His father paused, midchew, and looked right at him. It was a rare thing for him to do this. His eyes softened, and he swallowed. "I am very proud of you, *beta*." He looked down and placed his hands flat on the table. "I don't ever tell you that."

Prashant knew that he should have seen this moment as

incredibly touching, but he actually found it comical. They made such a strange duo: he, still in his boxers and high school community service T-shirt, the box of cereal before him as loudly colorful as a calliope; his father, in old slacks and an undershirt, eating dried fruit like some kind of lemur. Prashant had never given it that much thought, but his father was mildly attractive—or had been. He had obviously let himself go a bit, but he must have once been relatively hardy, with a firm swing in his step and some kind of glint in his eye.

"I don't tell your mom that, either," his father continued. "But I should."

"You should," Prashant replied—less because he felt like fighting for his mother and more because it seemed like the only logical response to such a comment.

His father shrugged, picked up his bottle of water, and downed it. He picked up the nectarines and patted Prashant on the head. "Very proud," he said, almost mournfully. Then he went back to the study.

Prashant went back up to his room and threw on some clothes. He checked his phone and saw a text from Clara: *My familys gonna be out of the apartment 2nite. Do u wanna call me for some . . . fun?* Prashant went to the bathroom attached to his bedroom, shut the door, locked it, and started jerking off. It was Clara's words that had started this, but his thoughts went immediately to Kavita.

He had performed this act so many times in this bathroom, but when he finished, he realized that he felt like a sociopath. He had barely thought of Clara; he had replaced her all too easily with Kavita, altogether negating his existing relationship. He wasn't someone to be proud of. He was pretending at having a real relationship while, just now, he had reverted to his primal interpretation of romance.

He sat on his bed and, without stopping to second-guess, composed a quick but earnest e-mail in which he told Clara that he wanted to have a conversation with her about their relationship when they were back on campus. He wasn't sure if he was in the right place to be in a relationship and didn't think that he was treating her with the utmost respect. He hit SEND, then headed downstairs and told his dad that he was going to go for a drive. His dad, as usual, didn't see the purpose of such a thing, but he seemed OK with it, probably because he was still feeling emotional after their brief interaction in the kitchen.

Prashant drove to the parking lot of his high school, where he used to meet the guys after school. He felt like calling Vipul up and seeing if he wanted to hang, but he wasn't sure that he wanted to go through the boring details of his college life instead of delving into these large existential issues. So, he stayed in his car and listened to a Beatles playlist on his phone, not worrying that the car was getting colder and colder as the winter settled into it.

At a certain point, you had to make a decision about what kind of man you wanted to be. He was far from being a man, he knew that, but he wanted to lay the foundation. He wanted to be the kind of person who would have an honest, adult conversation with Clara about what he was thinking and feeling, and he wanted her to see that he was making an effort to be better—even if she hated the idea of a breakup at this point in time. He had sat there observing his father's middle age, the fractured nature of his parents' interactions, and he didn't want to fall into that trap. He felt extremely lucky to be learning this lesson now, before college was fully under way: he still had so much time to be an upstanding guy. There was poetry to realizing how much work it required for a person to be respectable.

As he studied the red bricks of his school and the sun-catching metal of the large flagpole that rose in front of it, he knew for certain that he was going to change his major once he got back to school. He wouldn't tell his parents now. He would wait until sophomore year, when he had to officially declare it, and by then, he'd have so many credits toward a literature degree that there would be no turning back. He wasn't going to throw everything away—he would still minor in chemistry—but he wanted to honor his love of books and stories. He hoped to do this without tipping into self-indulgence or being absolutely insufferable, but he was going to trust his instincts and try it anyway. Not for Kavita. Not for his parents. Not even for himself. For something larger and grander, something that rebuffed a life of narrow-minded safety.

RANJANA LOOKED GOOD. She performed a series of half-turns in her mirror, smoothing the silk against her thighs and trying to see them as roundly alluring. No—she didn't even have to *try*. They looked good, without any effort necessary on her part. Self-esteem was like a pyramid: once you had a solid base, you could keep sliding more blocks onto it and make something sturdily impressive.

Here was a series of blocks that had been hoisted onto that foundation in recent days: Ranjana received an enthusiastic e-mail from Christina Sherman telling her that she was "delightfully mad to represent" Ranjana's writing. Two short but meaningful phone calls later, Ranjana received a contract by e-mail that she filled out online and shot right back. She didn't share this news with anyone, afraid that she would reverse the spell and jinx herself, but she relished it. On New Year's Eve, Prashant, in an endearing burst of selflessness, decided to cook his parents an elaborate dinner of *mattar paneer*, rice, and homemade naan, all of which he created by consulting a Madhur Jaffrey cookbook. (Ranjana and Mohan flicked a pinch of extra masala onto their plates when Prashant ducked out to take a quick call from Vipul.) Seema called to apologize for her bluntness in the lingerie store, though she followed this up with a question about when Ranjana was thinking of "springing the surprise" on Mohan. Ranjana ended the conversation soon after. Then, perhaps least likely of all, Ranjana received an e-mail from Achyut, who apologized for his treatment of her and for having dropped off the face of the earth. He finally wanted her to meet his boyfriend. Despite whatever might have happened between her and Achyut, she was both surprised and glad that his relationship had lasted all this time.

With the exception of her contract with Christina, these were all relatively small successes, yet taken together, they gave her the confidence to slide this garment onto her body. Prashant was back at school now, and it was a Saturday night. Mohan had gone into the office at the university to finish a few things, and he would come home and find the first floor singing with a chorus of long-tapered candles, bowls of rose petals with floating candles in them, and an ascending pilgrimage of paper-bagged candles up the stairway.

She knew the irony of greeting her adulterous husband this way, but she comforted herself by not jumping to conclusions. As much as she didn't want to admit it, there was a possibility that Seema was right: maybe Mohan hadn't been trying those moves on someone else. Maybe he was just watching porn like so many other men did. She couldn't blame him for this, could she?

She could. She wanted to. Instead she chose to straighten herself in front of the mirror. She saw the silk stretch over her skin, and she felt like someone that she would have written about. She would try controlling the story of her marriage, finding whatever allure she could in herself and seeing where it took her.

She mounted her bed, relaxing her limbs and feeling this simple act to be part of a choreography. She felt conscious of her brain, shifting gears to move the complex machinery of her body. In turn, she wanted her husband to appreciate the complex communication that it took for her to translate her body into sex.

Downstairs, the garage door retracted with a snarl, and she heard Mohan's car roll forward, another snarl announcing its enclosure. He entered, his papers and briefcase swishing as he went into his study, calling out *"Ji!"* Unsurprisingly, he didn't seem to notice the vigil in the house until he was out of his study and in the kitchen. She could hear his puzzlement all the way from here. *"Ji . . ."* he said more softly. She heard the cordless phone beep as it was switched on, the long *ahhhhhh* of the ringtone, and she realized that he was about to call 911.

She rose up on her elbows, then heard him hanging up the phone. Finally: he understood that a seduction and not a burglary was taking place.

He emerged out of the shadows like a creature in a trance. By now, she was flat along the bed, her head bent on the pillow and her eyes doing their best to keep his engaged. He went to speak, then closed his mouth.

All along, her plan had been to seduce him in silence, merely to look at him suggestively and have him embrace her, but she found herself speaking. "Show me what you've learned," she said, and his mouth fell open again.

"Ji . . ."

"Show me all of the tricks that you know," she continued.

"Tricks? What tricks?" He still seemed to be in some kind of trance, his arms limp at his sides. His beige jacket was still on and zipped. Then, his face moved knowingly. It was unclear whether he knew that she had discovered his antics online, but it was obvious that he knew what she meant by *tricks*.

She could tell that he was about to start back, flip on the light switch, and hustle this moment away, so she did the unthinkable: she reached down and lifted the hem of her negligee up, revealing herself. Earlier, she had used a pair of orange-handled kitchen shears to sculpt herself, and she felt the full effect of this now.

His eyes went to hers again, his mouth still open. "I was studying those . . . tricks . . . for you."

If she weren't so determined to see this delicate dance through to its finish, she would have crumpled and begun crying, eternally grateful that he hadn't strayed. Rather, she tightened her gaze and slid the hem higher, and Mohan advanced.

She had been writing herself forward these past few months, trying to guide the narrative of her life toward something exciting and meaningful and frightening and enlightening; she had seen the great benefit in having a firm hand in your own attitude. However, as she felt his alternately tender and ardent touch, she could not have foreseen the cataclysm of real attention paired with real affection. The fluctuations of his mouth were uncharted territory that she had never thought to seek because it wasn't even part of her imagining. In waves, in an important amassing of energy, her body became more than itself: it left her mouth in a prayer-like moan.

She had made this happen. She had set out to find this and had succeeded. Feelings of satisfaction, flying, and boiling coursed through her, and as she began yelling, she felt it mixing with something else:

Laughter.

She pressed her hands to her face, huffed through them, pleasured and giddy, and Mohan brought himself up to her, fell onto his back, and panted beside her. She turned her head to his and pressed her laughing mouth to his agog one. She kissed the man who had brought her to this country, to this house, who had watched with wonder as she saw that TV hoisted into their living room by two delivery men.

As if she had passed some illness along to him, he started laughing, too. Ranjana and Mohan laughed together. The Chaudhurys laughed. They laughed and laughed and laughed.

THE BOOKSTORE WAS ALIVE, with at least a hundred people clustered around half as many chairs. A large posterboard with the cover of the book stood before a lectern. On it was an image of an Indian woman, cunning in a sari, with a man, pique-eyed and pale, leaning over her seductively. Over them, the title: *Deranged Marriage.* Under them, the author's name: R. J. Cherish. Miniature slabs of this image filled the room, tucked under people's arms, held in their laps, or halved by pens that would be used to solicit the author's inscription. The crowd was varied, with some teenagers giggling in loud pockets, and even a healthy contingent of men, too.

Harit looked at his copy of Ranjanaji's book, ran his hand over the smooth cover. He had never read a book during his time in America, but he had read this one three times. The book in Harit's hands felt as if someone had manifested it there via some black magic. That was what the ink of books was, he guessed—some kind of black magic.

"They're going to sell out of copies," Teddy said. The copy in his hands was dog-eared; this was his reading copy; he kept a pristine copy on display in his apartment. "Can you believe our girl is a bestselling novelist?"

Harit could believe it. Ranjana had revealed her news to everyone several months ago during a get-together at her house. She had received a sizable contract—for three books—and she was quitting her job to write full-time. (It turned out that there was a big demand for paranormal Indian fiction, after all.) At the party, Mohanji and Prashant *beta*—the latter on spring break from his sophomore year at school—stood beside her with big grins on their faces. Contrary to what Harit might have expected of Mohanji, he seemed genuinely happy for his wife, not at all threatened by her success. After the announcement, Ranjana was seized upon by Seemaji, who smiled next to her as if she had written the book herself. Prashant told Harit later, as people bit into their *barfi*, that he was glad for his mother because she was finally "living for herself." This caused Harit's body to flutter. He was trying to do the same thing.

Ranjana appeared next to the lectern, and the crowd clapped loudly. The manager of the store gave her a quick introduction— "Ladies and gentlemen, I give you R. J. Cherish"—and then Ranjana took her place.

"I'm really just so touched that so many of you have come here today," she said. Although she was addressing these words to the many strangers in attendance, she was looking at Mohan, who was filming the event from the sidelines. She had her hair pinned back with a clasp in the shape of a butterfly, and her face was painted brightly but simply. "I'd like to thank my husband and son, both of whom are here." People craned to see: Mohan waved with one hand but kept filming; Prashant turned around from his seat in the front row and nodded his head. Seated next to him was a beautiful young Indian woman—a close friend of his from school. "Many of you who are writers will know that nothing is harder than fighting off all of your self-doubt to finish a story, and I could never have finished this book without the help of my writers' group—all of whom are here. Fellow classmates, would you stand?"

A group of people in the first row stood and faced the audience, who acknowledged them in even louder clapping. A couple of them looked uncomfortable; one of them, the youngest, smiled earnestly with her eyes; one of them, a man, saluted the crowd; and one of them, with very bright orange hair and a large pile of pages in her hands, curtsied.

Once they were seated, Ranjana continued. "I'd also like to thank a very wonderful friend who has come into my life, the person who spurred me to finish this thing and transform it from a pile of thoughts into a pile of pages. And that's my dear friend Harit Sinha. Haritji, would you stand?"

Harit would have been embarrassed if he hadn't been so touched. He stood, Teddy patting his lower back, and bent slightly to acknowledge the crowd, who clapped less loudly but looked at him appreciatively. Ranjanaji had her hands fully outstretched and beating against each other, her bangles jingling. Mohan swung his camera at Harit, then moved it slowly back to Ranjana. Seemaji, close to the front, had something between a smile and a frown on her face. It had become quite clear that she didn't like Harit, that she felt threatened by his friendship with Ranjana. Ah, well.

Harit still thrilled to see his name in the dedication at the front; the fact that Ranjana had thought to thank him publicly like this when it was already in there seemed like an unnecessary, if welcome, treasure. She had told him that she was going to dedicate the book to him as soon as he had finally, after many months into their friendship, told her about what had happened with his mother, how she had once been confined silently to her chair. Harit still had not told Ranjana—or Teddy—about the sari. It was still a secret that he wanted to keep to himself, something that he now cherished instead of regretted. And somehow his mother had understood this, never bringing it up when Ranjana had finally started visiting their house. They would all have a cup of chai while playing Parcheesi or watching *Jeopardy!* or listening as Teddy recited poetry by Arthur Rimbaud.

The crowd in the bookstore followed along as Ranjana began to read from her book. They giggled at her clever turns of phrases and hummed appreciatively at the flourishes of menace that moved the plot along. The book was already number five on the *New York Times* bestseller list. Ranjana's agent had told her that she should not define the monsters in the book as vampires because she worried that vampires had already had their cultural moment, so Ranjana had treated them as undefined yet undead beings that still bore the staple characteristics of vampires. This seemed to delight and engage her readers, appealing to their established sensibilities while still seeming fresh and unexpected. The Indian people in the crowd—about a third of the people—appeared to glow with the knowledge that the movie version starring Priyanka Chopra and Jake Gyllenhaal was to begin filming soon.

When Ranjana was finished, the crowd ignored the manager's directions to form a straight line to have their books signed and rushed toward the signing table like prisoners after a hunger strike. Cheryl acted as an intermediary, sculpting people into an orderly row by yelling at them and pointing.

The signing went on for almost two hours. People snapped photos, some of them even getting Ranjana to strike the pose that the woman was striking on the cover. (Teddy was among this camp.)

"You must be so proud of her," Achyut said as he neared Harit. His boyfriend, Luis, shook Harit's hand. Luis was close to Harit's own age, handsome and broad-chested with two straight rows of off-white teeth and carefully brushed black hair with evenly spaced streaks of white through it. Harit couldn't help but be jealous. They made a beautiful couple, and everyone in the crowd gave them low-lidded looks as they passed.

Harit had met Achyut at FB, when Teddy and Ranjana had taken him many months ago. Achyut had hugged him, Harit marveling at the smoothness of his skin, brightened by the jukebox—alight, screeching in a corner—and the mace-like fixture on the ceiling that cast rainbow colors all over the bar. Harit felt the beginnings of a depressive spiral, but as Teddy had taught him, he scrunched up his body and thought of what he had gained: Teddy's friendship, and with it the introduction to the alternately painful and wonderful world of sex.

Now, Achyut and Luis showed Harit and Teddy their signed copies, all of them feeling Ranjana's influence, as if her success were their own incredible story.

After the signing, Teddy drove Harit back to his house, the two of them silent in the way that had become common in their romance. Harit sighed as they passed the sign for Paradise Island, which was still not completed, though there were rumors that a Chinese entrepreneur had bought it and was going to turn it into a hotel.

They were not a couple, per se. Everything at work remained mostly the same. They still did the occasional evening at TGI Friday's, but they relented somewhat, stopping after a couple of drinks and making sure that Teddy wasn't tipsy before getting behind the wheel. Then, depending on how vocal they were about wanting to have sex, they would spend the night at Harit's house or Teddy's apartment. They weren't sure where their relationship was going or if they even wanted it to go anywhere. Instead of being tormented by this fact, they felt comforted by it. There didn't seem to be any great rush, not even after all of these months, not even after the passing of Harit's mother three months ago.

She had passed happily, her and Harit's secrets unfurled fully and no palpable resentment left in the wake of this. A few days after that moment in the sitting room, with Teddy and Gital Didi standing there, everything between Harit and his mother had opened up. His mother had even joked to him about how lovely a figure he had made in their home during his sari era. At this comment, she presented him with a brand-new golden *dupatta*, and they laughed, gleeful but unsure that this was even really happening. Almost a year later, his mother took to her bed downstairs and repeated to him for a final time the details of her life before her children were born, her time at Allahabad University, the long blackness of his father's hair and the things that she had willingly surrendered for Harit and Swati. She was up front about her love of Swati, how she had originally favored her firstborn, but Harit believed her when she looked at him, the webs in her eyes now decoration instead of a barrier, and said that she had grown to love him more than she had ever loved anyone. She loved him especially, she said, because he made her certain that moving here had been the right decision, even in light of what had happened to their family.

"You used to come to me all of the time and say, 'It is Swati,'" she whispered. "And the truth, *beta*, is that you *are* Swati. You are everything good about her, everything sweet and good and loving. You get to carry the best parts of Swati through this world."

A few days later, she shut her eyes—two pearls in brown pouches—and took her leave.

"I'll have to get gas in the morning, so I'll probably be here closer to eight," Teddy said as they pulled in front of the house.

"Sounds good," Harit said. He leaned forward, as did Teddy, and they touched lips as friends might do, then harder, as non-friends might do. "See you then," Harit said.

He let himself into the house. Gital Didi had tidied up, as she did every Sunday. She said that she needed to do it to keep her sanity; she still wanted to make sure that Harit had a truly "Hindustani home." Harit took no issue with this. He, more than anyone, could understand such coping mechanisms.

He made a cup of tea and put three butter cookies on a plate. He did all of this in the dark, not bothering to turn on the light. He enjoyed it like this now, not having to worry about darkness and what level of sanity or insanity it indicated.

He went to the living room and set the food on his TV tray, then nestled into the armchair. He lifted the neatly folded sari from where it lay slightly hidden behind the chair and draped it over his shoulders. He had Ranjana's book in his lap. The sun descended as if the world outside were rising up against a gleaming curtain. As the light grew fainter, Harit bit into his cookies and savored them, how they married the sweetness of the tea's sugar and the thick milk. Soon, the sun was replaced by the bright lights of the baseball diamond.

Harit picked up his cell phone and called Ranjana. He had to try twice, since his fingers were still not used to this type of phone, particularly its round, make-believe buttons.

"I'm so glad you rang," Ranjana said. Somewhere near her, Mohanji and Prashant were having some kind of excited conversation.

"How many books did you end up signing?"

"Over five hundred. So many people bought more than one copy."

"I think Teddy has five now."

"Don't tell him, but Cheryl bought ten."

"Yes, but how many of them do you think she's read?" Harit asked.

They both giggled.

"Did you ever suspect," she asked, "all that time ago, when we met for dinner with Teddy, that you and I would be talking like schoolgirls on the phone all the time?"

"Never," Harit said. "But then again, did you think that your name would be in *The New York Times*?"

"That's not really my name, *ji*."

"Perhaps not, but it is *you*."

She sighed sweetly, her breath like the movement of a brush through long hair. "Thank you, *ji*."

After their call, Harit shut off his phone and turned on the stereo. Asha Bhosle's trilling chirp enlarged the room. He remembered his sister, her beautiful smile, how she would sing along to these songs while moving her feet in a made-up dance. He remembered his mother, watching them from the crook of the kitchen doorway, all the while with her hands clasped calmly against her stomach. Harit smiled as tears slipped out of his eyes and onto the sari. At nine, the lights of the baseball diamond shut off, leaving him to enjoy the music in the dark.

ACKNOWLEDGMENTS

First, I must thank my wonderful editor Anna deVries for her incredibly perceptive work, which made this book stronger and richer. She has been a tireless champion of this story and its characters; I wish that every writer had the opportunity to work with her.

Thanks to the entire team at Picador: Stephen Morrison, Jonathan Galassi, Steve Rubin, Elizabeth Bruce, Kolt Beringer, Jeremy Pink, Lisa Goris, Shelly Perron, Steven Seighman, Darin Keesler, James Meader, Declan Taintor, Shannon Donnelly, and Molly Fessenden. Thank you, Henry Sene Yee, for the gorgeous cover.

Thanks to my agent, Maria Massie, for finding this book a perfect home.

Thank you, Owen Pallett, for your music and for the permission to use your lyrics as an epigraph.

I must thank the New York Foundation for the Arts, for its generous support of this project. I must also thank the Norman Mailer Writers' Colony and my fellow residents, for their input as the novel originally took shape; thank you, Colum McCann, for leading those discussions.

Christine Pride acted as a personal and professional mentor throughout this process. The only thing that I value more than her editorial opinion is our friendship (and mutual worship of Shonda Rhimes).

Special thanks to Mala Bhattacharjee and Devi Pillai, for letting me interview them specifically about the character of Ranjana.

Thanks to other readers who gave me fantastic feedback along the way: Karyn Marcus, Ursula Cary, Jenny Jackson, Sarah Jenks-Daly, Adam Rathe, Karen Kosztolnyik, Kendra Harpster, Lea Beresford, and Helen Atsma. Thank you, Marissa Conrad, for letting me use your former Long Island City studio apartment as an occasional staycation writing retreat.

Thanks, as always, to the creative writing program at Princeton—the best damn place of all.

Thank you to all of my friends, for your support—especially Chris Henry and Ashwini Ramaswamy, for your endless passion and enthusiasm.

Thank you to my family: my mom, Lalita (who offered very useful comments on the penultimate draft); my father, Vinay; my brother Rajiv and his wife, Harsha; and my brother Vikas.

Most of all, much gratitude to John Maas, who has changed my life altogether. This book started in a sad place and ended in a hopeful one, and it is due to your kindness, humor, and generosity that such a thing was possible. I love you so much.